THE GRAVES

A Max Strong Thriller

MIKE DONOHUE

ALSO BY MIKE DONOHUE

MAX STRONG/MICHAEL SULLIVAN PREQUELS

Sleeping Dogs

The Devil's Angel

MAX STRONG THRILLERS

Shaking the Tree

Bottom of the World

Hollow City

Trouble Will Find Me

Burn the Night

Crooked Prayers

The Salt House

MARTI WELLS THRILLERS

Hidden Twists (novella)

Hidden Chains

Hidden Sins

SHORT STORIES

October Days

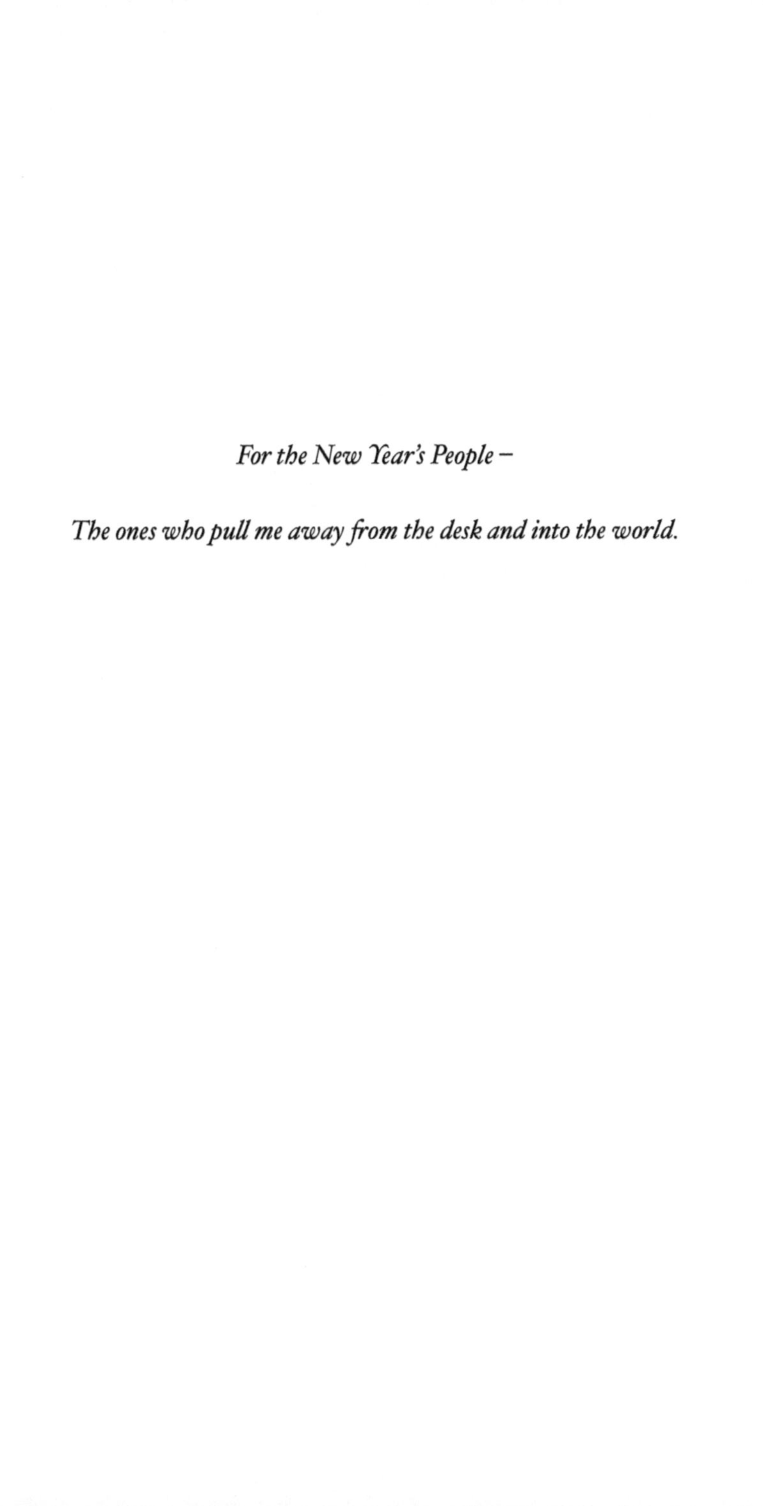

For the New Year's People –

The ones who pull me away from the desk and into the world.

I am haunted by humans.

— MARCUS ZUSAK, *THE BOOK THIEF*

THE GRAVES

CHAPTER ONE

The late-day sun filtered weakly through the dense canopy, casting long shadows across the rugged Appalachian terrain. The forest had an unsettling way of making Sarah Keller feel both watched and utterly alone, as if the shadows themselves held their breath in anticipation. She glanced around as she made the top of the rise. Sarah had stopped noticing the natural beauty sometime after lunch when they'd wandered through the strange upside-down gardens in the ravine. That had almost broken her brain in a beautiful way. Since then, it had been uphills, downhills, and mosquitoes with the occasional cluster fly for variety. Sarah's legs ached and her clothes clung to her sweaty skin. She was in good shape and an avid hiker, but Jake had been pushing hard all day, they must have covered seven or eight miles, and she was beat. They'd started at a trailhead and on marked, groomed trails, but Jake had quickly deviated and the terrain had become more rough and less traversed. After the ravine, her head was down and she was concentrating, putting one foot in front of another.

Now, she forced herself to take in the austere beauty of the Monongahela National Forest.

Towering oaks and hickories thrust upward, their tangled branches creating a dizzying fractal pattern overhead, an ever-shifting kaleidoscope of wood and sky that seemed to pulse with each gust of wind. The forest floor was a patchwork of moss-covered rocks and fallen logs, punctuated by the occasional burst of wild rhododendron, their pink blossoms a bright contrast to the muted greens and browns that dominated the landscape. In the distance, blue-tinged mountains rose like slumbering giants, their peaks shrouded in wispy low clouds.

Sarah wondered if there was another human within 20 square miles. They were not hiking in a popular area. Hell, they were barely hiking on a trail. The isolation was both exhilarating and unnerving. She felt a disquieting feeling creep along her neck. Just then, a twig snapped loudly behind her. She spun around, heart racing, only to see a curious white-tailed deer regarding her with liquid brown eyes.

She stuck out her tongue at the animal. "Geez, give a girl a heart attack, why don't you?" she said, forcing out a laugh that sounded fake even to her own ears. "What are you doing out here all alone, huh? Same as us, I guess." The deer bounded off. Shaking her head at her own jumpiness, Sarah grabbed her water bottle from the side of her pack, the cool metal a comforting anchor to reality in this wild, primeval landscape.

She paused, wiping sweat from her brow, then took a quick swig from the almost depleted bottle. Jake was a hundred yards ahead, already on the next uphill, his lean frame silhouetted against the verdant undergrowth. From this angle and this distance, he looked beautiful. Young and strong and unstoppable. Living in the same apartment for the past year, she knew Jake Cotter was all those things, but up close, she also knew those same attributes might destroy him. And her, if she let them.

She tucked the bottle back in its place and followed him. Her boots scuffed against exposed tree roots and loose shale as she carefully picked her way down the steep incline. Downhills were far worse than uphills. It felt as if little trolls were stabbing her quads with tiny knives. She made it to the bottom and the trolls dissipated, but she knew they'd be back.

"Jake," she called out. "We should start thinking about making camp. It'll be dark soon."

Jake turned, his face flushed with exertion, eyes bright with determination. He pulled out a crumpled map and studied it intently. "Just a little farther. I think we're close."

Sarah sighed, adjusting her heavy pack. "You said that an hour ago. This deer trail, or whatever it is, doesn't seem to be leading anywhere."

"Trust me," Jake insisted, tracing a line on the map with his finger. "Or trust the deer. If the coordinates and map are right, we should be approaching the area soon."

———

They pushed on, the faint trail weaving through a landscape that seemed increasingly untouched by human presence. Gnarled trees clung to steep hillsides, their roots forming natural staircases over moss-covered rocks. The air grew thick with the earthy scent of decaying leaves and damp soil.

She gave it another half hour before she tried again. "Jake, seriously," Sarah said, her tone more urgent as the light continued to fade. Dusk and then darkness came on fast this time of year. Out here, in the back of beyond, it would be pitch-black. The clouds would blot out any moonlight, and they were miles from any artificial light. "We need to find a spot to set up the tent. This terrain is getting dangerous."

Jake hesitated, glancing between the darkening sky and his map. "Okay, you're right. Let's just crest this next rise and see what's on the other side. If there's nothing suitable, we'll backtrack to that flat area we passed earlier."

Sarah nodded, relief washing over her. They'd been off the main trail for hours, following Jake's cryptic directions based on what he generously called a 'map.' In reality, it was little more than a set of coordinates and hastily scribbled notes on the back of a greasy diner placemat. Their destination was more myth than fact, a place whispered about in hushed tones on hiker forums but never definitively located.

Three days ago, they'd met up with Daniel, no last name, maybe a fake first name, a local Jake had somehow struck up a correspondence with online. He swore he knew the area better than anyone. For some reason, or reasons that Sarah wasn't privy to, Jake believed him. Sarah, however, remained skeptical.

Daniel looked every bit the Biblical prophet, with his wild beard and clothes that had seen better days. He seemed more comfortable communing with nature than people, rarely making eye contact and speaking in a voice barely above a whisper. Despite Jake's assurances, Sarah couldn't shake her unease about following directions deep into the West Virginia woods from a man who appeared more at home in a cave than civilization.

As they pushed through a dense thicket of hemlock saplings, Sarah's pack snagged on a branch. She tugged, hearing the fabric tear slightly. "Dammit," she muttered.

"You okay?" Jake called back. "Another casualty for the pink parade?"

"Fine," she replied, freeing herself. "And leave my pink pack alone. You know why I like pink."

"I know," Jake's voice softened. "Your mom would have loved it. Not sure how your dad would feel about that pink Red Sox bandana tied to the strap though." He smiled. It was a well-rehearsed back-and-forth. Her dad had strong feelings about the type of baseball fans who wore non-traditional team colors. The pink hatters, he called them

But after her mother's battle with breast cancer, pink had become more than just a color to Sarah. Some might call it a coping mechanism, but it made her feel connected, some-times hopeful to have her mother, even just the thought of her, close by.

"Just ready to be done for the day," she said, adjusting her pack and moving forward.

They emerged from the thicket to find two massive boul-ders leaning against each other, creating a narrow passage. Jake's face lit up. "This matches the description. Daniel told me about this. Come on!"

The rocks pressed in so tightly they had to slip off their packs and edge through sideways, the rough stone scraping against their clothes. Sarah hesitated, the claustrophobic passage almost daring them to turn back, but she knew Jake wouldn't. Gritting her teeth, she followed.

As they emerged on the other side, both hikers stopped short, momentarily stunned by what lay before them. They found themselves standing at the edge of a clearing, but unlike anything they'd encountered in their years of hiking.

The space was almost perfectly circular, a natural amphitheater nestled within the forest. Smooth, gray stone formed a shallow bowl, its gently sloping sides rising to meet a ring of weathered rock outcroppings that encircled the entire area. The floor of the clearing was carpeted with a thick layer of emerald moss, dotted here and there with clus-ters of tiny white flowers that seemed to glow in the fading light.

At the center of this otherworldly glade stood a single ancient tree. Its gnarled trunk twisted skyward, its bare branches reaching out over the clearing like protective arms. The tree seemed both part of the landscape and somehow separate from it, as if it had been placed there by some unseen hand.

A pair of crows swooped down from overhead, landed on a branch of the ancient tree, and started bickering. That broke the spell.

Sarah immediately shrugged off her pack and dropped to the ground. "This is it," she declared, massaging her sore muscles. "I'm not taking another step tonight."

Jake surveyed the area, his expression a mix of satisfaction and lingering restlessness. "Grave's End. I didn't..." His words trailing off, but Sarah knew what he was thinking. He'd had his doubts, too. After a moment, he regrouped. "It's as good a spot as any to make camp."

As Jake began to unpack the tent, Sarah couldn't shake a nagging feeling. Despite her earlier insistence on not taking another step, she now felt a powerful urge to get up and leave. The clearing felt almost too perfect, too convenient after their grueling day of bushwhacking through unforgiving terrain. Its pristine beauty seemed at odds with the wild, untamed forest they'd battled through, as if they'd stumbled upon an oasis that didn't quite belong. She stood up, ready to say something to Jake, when the trolls came back out. God, just standing up hurt, and exhaustion quickly overwhelmed her unease. Whatever mysteries this place held could wait until morning.

————

The miles had taken a toll. She felt a bone-deep weariness as she crawled into the tent after a light dinner. Sarah had always been a heavy sleeper but that night the mossy ground felt like a California King. She fell asleep almost instantly.

She floated in the darkness.

She didn't dream.

She never heard the keening wail.

Or the crashing in the trees.

Or Jake get up and leave.

CHAPTER TWO

Sarah stirred, her eyes still closed as she savored the last vestiges of sleep. The familiar sounds of the forest filtered through the thin nylon walls—chirping birds, rustling leaves, the soft whisper of wind through the pines. She breathed deeply, inhaling the crisp mountain air tinged with the faint scent of last night's campfire.

Then a new sound intruded on the tranquil morning chorus. Something that didn't quite fit. *Ting.* Sarah's eyes fluttered open, her brow furrowing as she tried to place the noise. Not unusual, it was familiar, but out of place. She turned to Jake, to see if it had awakened him as well and was surprised to find his sleeping bag empty. She reached out. It was cold to the touch. She sat up, not exactly concerned—Jake was usually the early riser—but a faint uneasiness began to creep in.

The tent flap was unzipped, morning light spilling onto the ground. Sarah slid out of her sleeping bag. It was the end of August, and while the days were still hot, the morning air was cool and raised goosebumps on her arms. Maybe Jake had just needed to use the bathroom. She poked her head out of the tent, surveying their campsite.

The morning dew clung to the tent's fabric, tiny droplets glistening in the pale light of dawn. Nestled at the edge of the circular clearing, the natural amphitheater stretched before her, the smooth gray stone forming a shallow bowl that seemed to cradle the morning mist. Gently sloping sides rose to meet the ring of weathered rocks that encircled the area, their jagged silhouettes like the broken spine of a fossilized beast against the brightening sky.

Everything was as they'd left it the night before. Their backpacks leaned against the lowest rocks. She could see the bear canister securely latched on the other side of the clearing, resting on the thick carpet of emerald-green moss that covered the clearing's floor. The small firepit, carefully constructed at the bowl's edge to leave no trace on the ancient stone, held only ashes. Their cooking gear was neatly stowed beside it, ready for the morning's use.

At the center of the glade, the lone ancient tree stood sentinel. In the soft morning light, the tree seemed more otherworldly, as if it held secrets from ages past.

Everything was here. Except Jake.

She stepped out of the tent, bare feet sinking into the soft earth. What was that sound that had woken her? Sarah stood still, waiting. There it was again. *Ting.* Faint, but distinct, drifting down from the jagged rocks like a whispered secret.

"Jake?" her voice wavered. She doubted he would have heard her, even if he'd been standing only ten feet away.

Ting.

She quickly pulled on her boots and grabbed a long-sleeved tee from her pack. She crossed the clearing to the base of the encircling rocks. The rocks and trees loomed above her, a wall of green and gray pierced by shadowy depths. She scrambled up the rocks. It wasn't difficult, most were flat, almost like the bleacher seats at any high school stadium. She stood at the top, peeking through the gaps in the rocks. The forest was a black wall. Just a few steps in and you might easily become disoriented in the dense undergrowth.

Ting.

Closer. Much closer now.

She moved to her right and climbed through a space in the rocks. There was a small ring of needles and ankle-high brush before the forest leapt up. It felt like a warning: This is your last chance to turn back. Taking a deep breath, she crossed it in three steps and entered the woods. The canopy overhead blotted out much of the morning light, leaving the forest floor in deep shadow. She pushed through a tangle of undergrowth, twigs scratching at her bare legs.

Ting.

Sarah's heart began to race as she pushed in. What was making that noise? Where was Jake? She tried to focus on the questions, pragmatic, logical questions and not the sound of her heartbeat in her ears.

She rounded a massive oak tree and froze, her breath catching in her throat.

She took a step closer. A pile of belongings—Jake's belongings—jacket, small camera, water bottle, the map— were strewn across the forest floor.

Ting.

Two crows were ripping and tearing at the items. One was trying to break through the metal of the water bottle with his beak. *Ting.* The dam broke then. What was going on? Where was he? Her heart pounded as she turned in a circle and scanned the area for any sign of Jake, feeling a chill at the thought of him disappearing without a trace.

Just like his brother.

Sarah's heart raced as she stared at Jake's scattered belongings. The crows, however, showed no signs of fleeing. They turned their beady eyes toward her, regarding her with an unsettling intelligence before casually returning to their inspection of Jake's possessions, their sharp beaks pecking and probing at the fabric of his jacket.

Determined to reclaim Jake's things, Sarah scanned the ground and spotted a nearby stick. She snatched it up and tossed it in the crows' direction. The birds hopped back a few feet, more out of curiosity than fear. They cocked their heads, watching her with what almost seemed like amusement. It was a tense standoff over Jake's scattered possessions.

Frustration mounting, Sarah's eyes landed on a fist-sized rock. She clawed it out of the dirt. She hefted it, feeling its weight, then threw it. The stone rumbled past the crows, missing them but rolling close enough to finally startle them into action. With indignant caws, they both took flight and landed on the lower branch of a nearby tree.

As she lifted the jacket, something caught her eye. Dark spots marred the fabric, standing out against the earthy tones of the well-worn canvas. Sarah's breath hitched as she brought the jacket closer, her heart pounding. With trembling fingers, she traced the outline of the largest stain. The spots were a deep crimson, tacky to the touch but not yet fully dry. Blood. Jake's blood.

Her nurse instincts kicked in as she examined the stains more closely. The largest was about the size of her palm, with several smaller spatters surrounding it. Not arterial spray, she noted, which would have been bright red and more widely dispersed. This seemed more consistent with a deep laceration or puncture wound. Sarah's mind raced, calculating roughly how much blood had been lost based on the stains' sizes and distribution. Enough to be concerning, but not necessarily life-threatening—at least not immediately.

She turned the jacket over, finding more smears on the back. Had Jake been dragged? Or had he stumbled through the underbrush, leaving traces of blood in his wake? Sarah pressed her nose to the fabric, detecting the metallic scent of blood mixed with the earthy smell of the forest floor. Pine needles and bits of leaf clung to the sticky patches, telling a story of recent movement through the woods.

The clinical part of Sarah's brain cataloged these details, but her emotions threatened to overwhelm her analytical thoughts. This was blood. His. He was out here somewhere, injured and alone.

Her mind raced with possibilities, each more terrifying than the last. Had he fallen? Been attacked by an animal? Or was there a more sinister explanation lurking in these woods?

"Jake!" she called out, her voice cracking with a mixture of fear and desperation. "Jake, where are you?"

The forest seemed to swallow her words, the dense canopy muffling any echo. Sarah clutched the jacket to her chest, fighting back the panic threatening to overwhelm her. She closed her eyes, took a deep breath, and forced herself to think rationally.

Lists. She needed to make a list. It was a habit ingrained in her since childhood, a coping mechanism taught by her father, a former Army Ranger. 'When the world's spinning out of control, Sarah,' he'd say, 'you make a list. It gives your mind something to latch onto.'

Sarah could almost hear his calm, steady voice now. She'd scoffed at his advice as a teenager, but it had saved her more than once in her time working at Boston Medical as a nurse right out of college. The lists had gotten her through chaotic nights in the hospital when multiple patients rolled in at once and everything threatened to spiral into chaos. She hadn't needed those list-making skills that much in recent years. She'd been a nurse in a suburban family practice office for the past eight years. The most chaos she'd seen recently was when Mrs. Belisle's twin toddlers both caught the stomach flu and redecorated the waiting room. Now, facing the unknown in this vast, indifferent forest, she returned to the familiar process.

She pulled out her phone with shaky fingers. There was no service, of course—there hadn't been any since five minutes after leaving the trailhead almost two days ago. Still, she opened the Notes app and began typing.

What I know:
 Jake's belongings scattered
 Blood on jacket - injured, extent unknown
 Not responding to calls
 Last seen at campsite

She paused and her mind raced back to the previous night. They had gone to bed early, after eating a small dinner. They didn't talk much; they were both tired, but Sarah could sense the live wire of energy in Jake still humming below the surface. She knew that he thought they were close. As close as he'd ever been. He was stopping for her. If he'd been alone, he'd push his body past rational limits. Darkness be damned. He'd keep searching for Riley.

Had he gotten up early to search the immediate area? That might explain why some of his belongings were here, but not his whole pack. Sarah glanced at her watch. It was just past 9:00 a.m. She'd woken up alone sometime around

7:00, assuming Jake had gone to relieve himself or fetch water. But that was... nearly two hours ago.

A cold knot formed in her stomach. Two hours. Jake had been missing for two hours, likely more if he'd left in the pre-dawn light. Sarah took a deep breath, forcing herself to focus. She returned to her list, updating it with this new realization:

Last seen:
    Asleep in tent around 10 PM
    Missing for at least 3 hours

Next steps:
    Search immediate area - 100-yard radius
    Look for trail - broken branches, disturbed leaves
    Check map for nearby landmarks/water sources
    Stay put. If no sign in 1 hour, return to car and call ranger station

Sarah's finger hovered over the screen, trembling slightly. The last item on her list loomed large, a decision she dreaded making. Not just the waiting, but the leaving. Should she really wait another full hour before calling for help? If Jake was injured, every minute would count. But if she left now to get help, she might miss a crucial clue, a faint call, a sign of his passage.

Her mind raced, calculating distances and times. It would take at least a day, maybe two, of grueling hiking to reach somewhere with a cell signal. Two days of Jake alone, hurt, possibly...

No. She couldn't think like that.

Sarah bit her lower lip hard enough to draw blood, the metallic taste grounding her in the moment. Stick to the plan, she told herself. One hour of searching, then she'd figure out how to get help.

Suddenly, a memory flashed through her mind. The beacon! Jake had an emergency personal locator beacon in his pack. How could she have forgotten? Hope surged through her veins as she spun around, nearly losing her footing on the uneven forest floor.

She hustled back out of the forest, branches whipping her face as she ran. Sarah scrambled down the rocky slope to their campsite, her boots sliding on loose gravel. She grabbed Jake's pack, her fingers fumbling with the zippers and clasps in her haste.

"Come on, come on," she muttered, upending the pack.

A cascade of items tumbled out: a first aid kit, a small folding knife, a water filter system. No beacon. Sarah's breath came in short gasps as she turned the pack inside out. More items fell out: a crumpled map, a headlamp, spare batteries, energy bars. Still no beacon.

With trembling hands, she unzipped the main compartment and dumped Jake's clothes onto the ground. T-shirts, socks, and underwear scattered across the dirt. Sarah pawed through them frantically.

Nothing.

The beacon was missing.

Sarah sat back on her heels, her mind reeling. Jake never went anywhere without that beacon. It was his failsafe, his insurance policy against the unpredictability of the wilderness. If he'd taken it out of his pack...

A chill ran down her spine as the implications sank in. Whatever Jake had gone to do this morning, he'd thought it might be dangerous enough to warrant taking the beacon. And now both he and the device were gone.

CHAPTER THREE

Sarah took a deep breath. She didn't have the beacon, but she still had a plan. She pulled her phone out of her pocket and re-read her list. It wasn't much, but it was a plan. Or, the sketch of plan. Or, random scribbles from someone losing her mind. She closed her eyes briefly, took a deep breath, held it. Let it out. No, she wouldn't go there. She wouldn't let the panic rise any further. She glanced at the list. *Search immediate area - 100-yard radius.* She could do that. She'd start at the top. Jake's last known location.

She pocketed the phone and climbed back up to the top of the rock bowl and into the forest. The crows were gone. She carefully folded Jake's jacket and placed the other items on top then placed the loose package on the edge of the woods. With a renewed focus, she began a methodical sweep of the area, her eyes scanning the forest floor for any clues, any disruption in the natural pattern of leaves and twigs that might indicate Jake's passage.

That's when she heard it.

A faint sound, barely audible, came from somewhere to her left. She froze and strained to listen. Had she imagined it?

It could have been a voice. She wanted it to be a voice. She really, really wanted that. But perhaps it was just the wind playing tricks on her ears.

Where had it come from? The left? Was she sure?

"Jake?" she called out tentatively, already moving in that direction. "Is that you?"

She pushed through a thicket of rhododendrons, their leaves slick with morning dew, soaking her arms and legs. Other thorny vines snagged at her clothes, but she barely noticed the sharp pricks as she pushed ahead.

Another sound, not from the left this time, but from behind her. A rustling, too deliberate to be the wind. She spun around. Nothing but trees and thickets. Keep going or go back? She hesitated a moment then reversed course, retracing her steps through the undergrowth. The forest floor was a tangle of snaking roots and loose rocks. Sarah's foot caught on a root. She stumbled, tripped a second time and went down, wincing as her palms scraped against bark, briars, and sharp pebbles.

As she pushed herself back up, leaves and dirt clinging to her dampened skin, she heard it again. A crack, like a branch breaking. This time the sound came from her right and farther away than before.

Sarah's head whipped around, her eyes darting between the trees.

"Jake!" she shouted, not tentative now, but loud, fear and frustration coloring her voice. "If that's you, please, say something! This isn't funny."

Still no response. Just the soft rustle of leaves and the distant call of a bird. Sarah stood still, one, two, five minutes, straining her ears for any further sounds or movement in the underbrush. Blood pounded in her ears but the silence surrounding her stretched out. Whatever had made those noises was gone. Doubt began to creep into her mind. If they'd ever been here in the first place. Was she really hearing something, or was her frazzled mind playing tricks on her? No, just like her list, she would hold onto this bit of reality. Those noises were real. She had definitely heard something. But if it wasn't Jake, what was it? An animal?

Sarah took a deep breath and forced herself to focus. She needed to find higher ground, to get her bearings and figure out what Jake might have been up to. Where he might have headed from here. She spotted a rocky outcropping nearby and made her way toward it. It wasn't yet noon, but she already felt exhausted.

As Sarah climbed, the terrain grew increasingly bleak. The dense forest thinned, giving way to a weathered landscape of boulders and thin, tenacious vegetation. Reaching the summit, she paused to catch her breath. Her eyes swept the horizon, desperate for any sign of Jake or a clue to guide her next move.

The land beyond Grave's End fell away sharply, swallowed by an unbroken canopy of green. She understood now why this place remained hidden; even knowing its location, one could easily lose their way in the vastness of the forest. If Jake had ventured in that direction, finding him on her own would require more than skill—it would take a miracle.

Turning back toward the bowl of Grave's End, Sarah's gaze snagged on an unexpected sight. There, in the face of a second nearby hill, to the west and above Grave's End, a dark opening yawned—a cave entrance, nearly obscured by a tangle of vines and stubborn shrubs. It would be difficult to spot unless you were standing above it like she was. She felt a jolt of adrenaline. If Jake had found this cave...

Sarah's mind raced. Had Jake known about the cave? Could he have gone inside alone? Gotten trapped or hurt? He was impetuous enough that Sarah thought he might go on ahead, not intending to leave her behind, but impatient to explore. She didn't want to repeat his potential mistake. She carefully scanned the horizon, turning in a full circle, the Monongahela stretched out before her, an ocean of green swaying gently in the breeze, but she didn't see anything else as promising. She had to check it out. She fixed the spot in her mind and then carefully made her way down the slope and worked her way around and then back up the second hill.

As she got closer, Sarah noticed something unusual about the entrance. The vines covering it appeared disturbed, as if someone had pushed through them. She picked up a piece of brush and examined it, finding fresh breaks in the woody stems. The leaves were still green and hadn't yet wilted. Someone had been here, and not long ago.

"Jake?" she called out, her voice echoing slightly in the cave's opening. No response.

She couldn't see beyond a few feet. She pulled out her phone and turned on the flashlight. The beam revealed a narrow passageway that sloped gently downward before quickly curving out of sight. She wasn't claustrophobic but something made her hesitate. Just a cave, she told herself. She took a deep breath and stepped inside.

The temperature plummeted 20 degrees. She felt goosebumps prickle her arms. The sudden temperature shift was disorienting, like plunging off a dock into icy water. She took a few tentative steps, the phone held out in front of her. Water dripped somewhere in the darkness, each small splash marking time like a sinister metronome. The cave walls felt rough and cold against her fingertips as she reached out to steady herself. After ten steps, the passage narrowed until her shoulders nearly brushed both walls. She looked back. She could no longer see the cave's opening. The gentle curve had been almost imperceptible. She felt her breath quicken involuntarily and she forced herself to take three slow inhales and exhales.

She checked the battery on her phone. Still plenty of charge, but she turned down the flashlight's intensity slightly. Her eyes were adjusting. She could save a little battery...just in case, but she didn't want to think about filling in that blank. She moved deeper into the cave.

The cave felt almost alive, watching, waiting. And Sarah couldn't shake the feeling that she was descending into the very bowels of the earth itself. The air grew thicker, a mix of mineral-rich dampness and the musty odor of long-undisturbed dirt. She focused on her breathing and the reason she was there. Find Jake. But with each step deeper into the cave's depths, the primal part of her brain loudly screamed: Go back! Find the light!

Doubt was creeping in, along with a sense of her depleting battery, and she was considering turning back, when her light glinted off something that made her pause. There, on the dirt floor, was a discarded energy bar wrapper. She poked at it with her foot, feeling its crinkly texture against her boot. It wasn't weathered or dirty—it looked shiny and new. Sarah's pulse quickened. Someone had been here recently. But was it Jake? Or someone else? She tried to remember what Jake had packed. He was always picking up different gels and bars, never finding one that he liked.

"Jake?" she called out. Her voice bounced and echoed. She waited, holding still, listening, but there was no response. No noise at all, save the slowly dripping metronome and the occasional low moan of shifting slabs of rock deep beneath her feet, a sound she felt more than heard. She kept going, all senses turned up to 11 now, ready to pounce on the slightest sound or movement.

The passage began to slope more steeply downward. A trickle of water had begun to run along the edge of the passage. Suddenly, her foot slipped on a wet patch of rock. Her arms windmilled as she tried to regain her balance, but it was too late. She fell backwards, her head striking the cave wall with a sickening thud.

A starburst of pain exploded behind her eyes as she began to slide down the sloping passage. Her body tumbled and rolled. She tried to grab onto something, anything, to stop her descent, but there was nothing to grab. She tried to dig her heels into the floor or walls to slow herself down. Then her left foot snagged in a crevice, wrenching her ankle with a sharp, painful twist, but also bringing her to a stop.

The unexpected halt jolted her body, leaving her gasping and disoriented. The cave walls tilted and whirled around her. She fought to keep her eyes open, blinking rapidly as dark spots danced across her vision. No, no, no. She couldn't pass out here. Her ankle throbbed, each beat sending a wave of nausea through her body. She tried to focus on that, to use the pain like a cattle prod to keep herself awake, but the darkness at the edges of her vision grew like an incoming tide. She was helpless. She felt herself get pulled under and then she was gone.

———

When Sarah came to, she wasn't sure how much time had passed. Minutes? Hours? She turned her head slowly, fighting back the bile that rose in her throat, and spotted her phone a few feet away. The flashlight was still on and threw off a muted glow. She blinked, trying to clear the spots in her vision. The spots didn't budge, but they faded a bit. She looked around. Her backpack had been jarred loose during her sliding fall but lay nearby. She was lying on her back in a much larger cavern. It was brighter in here than it had been in the passage. Partly due to the flashlight, but partly due to something else. Cracks, or something, letting in light and if light got in, so did air. One less thing to worry about.

Her head throbbed, and a dull ache radiated from her left ankle. She gently tried to flex it and hissed at the lance of pain. It already felt stiff. Sarah lay there, staring at the ceiling, trying to gather her wits and assess the extent of any other injuries. Her whole body felt like one giant bruise, but her ankle and her head appeared to be the worst.

Then, as her eyes adjusted to the light, something else caught her attention.

There, nestled in a small natural depression about 10 or 12 feet up the cavern wall, was a small, blinking red light. Sarah squinted, trying to make sense of what she was seeing. It took her scrambled brain a moment to understand what she was seeing.

A camera. Someone had mounted a camera in this cave.

CHAPTER FOUR

The wipers squeaked across the windshield, fighting a losing battle against the relentless sheets of rain. Max Strong squinted through the gray haze, barely able to make out the flashing lights of the police cruiser up ahead. He eased off the gas and pulled over to the shoulder, gravel crunching under the tires.

Max took a final sip of coffee from his travel mug. The gas station brew was far from gourmet, but the familiar ritual of caffeine and winding roads had kept him alert and content for the past six hours. He'd deliberately chosen these back roads, eschewing the faster but chaotic interstate. Route 95 would have been quicker, taking him east and then up the coast, but that meant passing through Washington, D.C.—a place he'd rather avoid after his last unpleasant experience there.

Instead, Max had opted to stay inland, roughly paralleling I-81 as he wound his way through Tennessee, Kentucky, and now into West Virginia. These quieter roads suited him, allowing him to drive at his own pace without the stress of constant lane changes and impatient drivers. It also meant fewer encounters with highway patrols, which was always a plus in Max's book.

He'd hoped to push farther north before stopping for the night. While he had a destination in mind, he wasn't in a rush. But now, faced with this roadblock, it seemed Mother Nature had other plans. And ironically, here he was, face to face with the very law enforcement he'd been trying to avoid.

Max squinted through the rain-lashed windshield. Ahead, a police officer was helping a mud-splattered Ford F-150 with a gun rack and a 'Salt Life' sticker execute a careful K-turn on the narrow road. The truck's tires squelched in the sodden grass as it maneuvered, headlights cutting through the gloom as it finally straightened out to head back the way it came.

As the pickup's taillights faded into the stormy night, the officer turned his attention to Max's car, gesturing for him roll forward. Max pulled up to the roadblock and rolled down his window, immediately letting in a gust of wind and rain.

"Evening, Officer," Max called out, raising his voice to be heard over the storm. "What's the situation?"

The cop leaned down, water dripping from the brim of his hat as he peered into Max's car. A thin, white scar ran from his left temple to his jaw, pulling slightly at the corner of his eye. "Road's washed out about a mile north. Tropical Storm Debby's done a number on us. You'll have to head back to Grimswood and wait it out."

Max frowned, gripping the steering wheel tighter as another gust of wind rocked his car. "Is there no way through? It's urgent I get to—"

"Sorry, sir," the officer cut him off, shaking his head. "It's not safe in this direction. You can try going south, maybe get back on 487, head west, get around the mountains. It's a long way around though and you might run into other washouts or mudslides before you get clear. My advice? Turn around and wait it out in town. It's likely going to get worse before it gets better."

Max hesitated, glancing at the ominous sky. The name Grimswood did little to ease his apprehension about seeking refuge there.

Max sighed. "That's the problem. Bridge is out to the south, too. Logging truck overturned. Bridge crew's working on it, but it could be a couple days at least. They said they'd have to get some engineers in to check on structural integrity."

"Well, shit," the officer muttered. He scrubbed a hand over his stubbled chin. "Hadn't heard that. Guess we're all stuck for the time being. Guess that makes your decision easier."

"And up there? How long you think? Once the storm passes?"

The cop barked out a humorless laugh. "Don't hold your breath on that one. We're talking major washout. Could be a week, maybe more."

Max nodded, resignation settling in his gut. He glanced back over his shoulder. "Thanks," he said. "Any recommendations on a room?"

The officer's scar twitched as he gave a wry smile. "If you're coming this way you must have passed through town. The good news is Grimswood's got one of everything. What you see is what you get. There's the Crossroads Inn right as you come into town—it's not the Ritz, but it's clean enough. Across the street, you've got the Sunrise Cafe. Food's decent, and Patty keeps it open late for truckers. There's also the Crooked Nail if you need a stronger drink to weather the storm. Gas station's on the corner, doubles as our general store. We've got a small clinic next to the post office if you need it, but Doc Peterson's probably battened down the hatches by now."

The officer paused, rainwater streaming down his face. "That's also the bad news. It doesn't leave you with a lot of options. But it'll keep you dry for the night."

"Appreciate the rundown," Max said, already planning his next move.

"Stay safe out there," the officer replied, tapping the roof and stepping back from the car. "And welcome to Grimswood, I suppose."

Max ran the window back up, water dripping from the armrest onto the floorboard. He sat for a moment, hands resting on the wheel, and let out a long breath. The universe, it seemed, had other plans for his journey back to Vermont and Vic.

He put the car in gear, carefully turned, and slowly rolled back toward town. The diner's windows glowed warmly in the greasy twilight, and his stomach gave an involuntary rumble. One more cup of mediocre coffee and maybe a slice of pie suddenly didn't sound so bad.

Max pulled into the Sunrise Cafe's lot, his gaze drifting to the Crossroads Inn across the street. The motel's generic sign loomed above the glowing 'Vacancy' light. The parking lot was mostly empty, save for a long 18-wheeler with a red cab and unmarked trailer and a silver Toyota Camry tucked in at the far end.

Over the years, Max had developed a strange affinity for roadside motels, with their scratchy sheets and flat pillows. The ubiquitous motel art, however, was another story. He made a mental bet with himself: his room would feature a mountain landscape print, probably depicting a sunset.

Cutting the engine, Max sat listening to the rain drumming on the roof. Grimswood, West Virginia. Population: who knows. His current residence for the foreseeable future. He retrieved his phone from the cupholder, thumb hovering over Vic's number. Better to call now and let her know he'd be delayed. As he waited, watching raindrops chase each other down the windshield, the call failed to connect. A glance at the screen confirmed his suspicion: Grimswood's list of services apparently didn't include a cell tower.

CHAPTER FIVE

The bell above the door jangled as Max stepped into the Sunrise Cafe, bringing with him a gust of wind and the patter of rain. The aroma of coffee and fried food enveloped him, its pleasant warmth fogging the cafe's front windows. Overhead, fluorescent lights buzzed, casting a pale-yellow glow on the scuffed linoleum floor.

The cafe was a simple square box. The entrance occupied one wall, with the counter and kitchen along another. Blue vinyl booths lined the remaining two walls, their seats creased and cracked in a patchwork of age and use. Max mused that if a place lasted long enough to break in the vinyl, it couldn't be all bad. Then again, in a town like this, he didn't imagine there was much competition.

A corkboard hung on the wall just inside the door, its surface a collage of faded flyers for local events long in the past. Beside it, an old payphone was anchored to the wall, its receiver dangling from a metal cord that had seen better days. Out of habit, Max dipped a finger in the coin return slot, an old forgotten childhood ritual. It came up empty.

As he stepped farther in, he noticed a series of black-and-white photographs lining the wall behind the counter. They depicted the town's central junction and its history—old storefronts, stern-faced settlers, and a landscape that hadn't changed much in the intervening years. It was as if Grimswood had found a moment in time it liked and decided to stay there.

Behind the counter, a woman Max assumed must be the Patty the deputy had mentioned was wiping down the surface with practiced efficiency. She looked up as he entered, her lined face breaking into a welcoming smile. Patty's gray hair was pulled back in a loose bun, wisps escaping to frame her face. She wore well-worn jeans and a light, short-sleeved polo shirt in a faded blue that had seen better days. Sweat glistened on her brow in the warm diner air. A slightly askew nametag was pinned to her shirt. Max wondered how many people needed the nametag in a town this size. Maybe she wore it out of habit, or perhaps for the occasional lost traveler like himself.

"Well, hello there, stranger," Patty called out, her voice warm and slightly raspy. "Pick any seat you like. We're not exactly in the lunch rush anymore."

Max picked the last booth, farthest from the door, and put his back to the wall. The dying light, muted by the storm clouds, cast long shadows across the diner. From here, he could see a man working the grill in the back, his white apron spattered with grease. The sizzle of meat on the hot surface and the clank of a spatula against metal provided a rhythmic backdrop to the quiet diner.

As Max settled in, he took stock of the other patrons. An elderly couple occupied a booth near the door, sharing a piece of pie and speaking in low, comfortable murmurs. At the counter, a man wearing a worn trucker cap nursed a cup of coffee, his eyes fixed on the small, muted TV mounted in the corner. Maybe he was also stranded between the bridge and the washouts. Two booths from the elderly couple, on the opposite wall from Max, a woman with short blonde hair sat across from a bearded man, papers spread out between them. Their hushed voices carried the tone of a heated discussion, though Max couldn't make out the words. The woman was doing most of the talking, punctuating her statements with short chops of her hands.

A moment later, Patty approached, notepad in hand, tucking a strand of gray behind her ear. "What brings you to our little slice of paradise on a day like this?" she asked, arching an eyebrow.

Max ran a hand through his damp hair. "Roadblock about a mile north of town," he explained. "Officer said the road's washed out."

Patty clucked her tongue sympathetically. "Ah, that's a shame. But you're in luck—storm's supposed to blow through overnight."

"That's good," Max nodded, "but the roads might not be clear for a few more days."

"We've had so much rain this summer. Bound to happen." A knowing smile played on Patty's lips. "Good for me though. Good for business," she said. "Now, what can I get you?"

Max's eyes flicked to the small, laminated menu tucked next to the napkin dispenser. A quick glance confirmed his suspicion: the Sunrise Cafe was like every other small-town diner he'd frequented in his travels. Comfort food classics, all-day breakfast, and daily specials that probably hadn't changed in years.

"I'll have the chicken fried steak with mashed potatoes and green beans. And a coffee, black."

"Good choice on a dreary day," Patty said with a nod. "That'll stick to your ribs. Anything else?"

"That should do it, thanks," Max replied.

Patty jotted down the order and walked back behind the

counter. With practiced efficiency, she slipped the order slip onto the rotating rack, spinning it so the cook could see it. The man at the grill grunted in acknowledgment as Patty picked up a clean mug and poured his coffee, and Max found himself wondering how many thousands of times she'd performed this exact sequence of actions over the years.

Patty returned and slid the mug and a set of silverware onto the table without a word, then walked over to the older couple's table. Max sipped his coffee, hot but slightly burnt, and looked over to the booth with the man and woman, dishes from their meal now pushed to the side.

The woman, probably in her late 20s or early 30s, continued to punctuate her statements with animated hand gestures as she spoke, her brow furrowed in concentration. A distinctive streak of silver ran through her hair at the temple, standing out against the golden blonde. It seemed too striking to be natural for someone her age, yet too precise to be accidental. Her companion, about the same age with long, brown hair that covered his ears and sporting a neatly trimmed beard, leaned back in his seat, arms crossed, a look of skepticism etched on his face.

If this was an argument it was largely one-sided. The woman jabbed her finger at one of the papers, then looked up at her companion expectantly. The man shook his head, leaning forward to point at something else on the table, but not saying a word. That set the woman off again. Max could sense her frustration from across the room.

The bell above the door chimed again. A tall man in a dark overcoat entered, shaking raindrops from his hat. Without hesitation, he made his way to the corner booth and slid in next to the younger man. The newcomer's presence seemed to intensify the discussion. He picked up one of the papers, studied it briefly, then set it down with a shake of his head.

Max found himself straining to hear their conversation, curiosity piqued by the mysterious meeting. But the clatter of plates interrupted his eavesdropping attempt. He looked up to see Patty approaching with his order.

"Here you go, hon," she said, setting down a steaming plate. "Anything else I can get you?"

Max shook his head, thanking her as the aroma of his meal wafted up. As Patty walked away, he cast one more glance toward the corner booth. The trio was now huddled even closer, their heads almost touching, their voices low murmurs beneath the ambient sounds of the diner.

Turning his attention to his food, Max picked up his fork. Whatever was happening in that booth, it wasn't his business. He had his own problems to worry about. For now, he was content to be a silent observer in this small-town tableau.

Max pushed his empty plate away. The meal wasn't destined for any culinary hall of fame, but it had hit the spot. The chicken fried steak's exterior had been perfectly crisp, giving way to a tender interior. Clearly, the grill man knew his trade.

As he debated between a slice of pie and another cup of coffee, Patty approached to clear away his dishes.

"How was everything, hon?" she asked, picking up his plate and stacking the silverware on top.

"Just what I needed," Max replied. He hesitated for a moment, then added, "I was wondering...since I'll be here at least a day, why is this town called Grimswood?"

A smile played at the corners of her mouth. "Well now, that's a question with more than one answer. Or maybe answer's too strong a word." Patty glanced over her shoulder, checking that the other tables were okay, then she placed the plate back down and settled into the booth across from him.

"First off," she began, "there's old Jeremiah Grim. Town founder, way back in the 1800s. Tough as nails, that one.

Story goes he came out here with nothing but an axe and a dream."

Max nodded, took a sip of coffee. Patty continued.

"Now, Jeremiah, he picked this spot for a reason." She leaned in. "There's a natural spring here, pure as can be. Still is, almost 200 years later. And the valley's protected, good for farming. But the woods..." She gestured vaguely toward the window. "They're different. Dense. Dark. Even on the brightest day, you step in there and it's like twilight. The trees were perfect for lumber, hard wood, but they gave folks the creeps."

Patty lowered her voice, as if sharing a secret. "Legend has it that when the settlers first started chopping down the trees, the woods...well, they fought back. Axes would bounce off trunks like they were made of iron. And the sounds..." She shuddered slightly. "Folks swore they heard wailing on the wind every time a tree fell. Some even said they saw faces in the bark. The settlers started calling it the Grim Wood long before the town proper had a name," Patty finished. "They say that's why so many of the original buildings here are made of stone instead of timber."

Max raised an eyebrow. "Not a bad tale for tourism. You could do a good business in Halloween tours."

Patty chuckled. "Not a bad idea, but it gets better. See, there's an old legend tied to these parts. They say the woods are home to...something. Something that's been here long before us and will be here long after. On quiet nights, folks say you can hear it moving through the trees."

"Grimswood is home to Bigfoot?" Max said.

Patty dropped the smile, suddenly serious. She leaned in closer, her voice dropping to a conspiratorial whisper. "Some say Jeremiah Grimwood made a deal with whatever's out there. That's how the town survived when so many others around here failed."

"And what do you think?"

Patty straightened up, shrugging. "Me? Like you said, I think it's a good story, worth its weight in gold, especially in a small town. But I will say this—there's something about Grimswood. Once it gets its hooks in you, it doesn't let go easy." As if to punctuate her point, a gust of wind rattled the cafe's windows, drawing their attention to the forest on the town's edge.

As she got up and walked away, Max found himself wondering just what kind of town he'd stumbled into, and how long the storm would keep him here to find out.

CHAPTER SIX

Max pushed open the door of the Crossroads Inn, a blast of stale air greeting him as he stepped inside. The lobby, if it could be called that, was little more than a cramped space that seemed to have been frozen in time since the 1970s. Dingy yellow wallpaper, peeling at the corners, covered the walls, while a threadbare carpet in a faded floral pattern absorbed the sound of his footsteps.

To his right, a worn counter of scratched Formica stretched along one wall, its surface littered with coffee stains and old receipts. Behind it, a pegboard hung askew, its hooks bearing a haphazard collection of room keys, each attached to a plastic fob so large it could double as a weapon. A rack of faded tourist brochures stood nearby, its metal frame rusted and contents curled with age and humidity.

Behind the scarred counter, a man in his 60s looked up from a thick, well-worn book, its cover depicting a sepia-toned battlefield strewn with cannons and fallen soldiers. The spine read *The Civil War: A Narrative* in faded gold lettering. The man's face was a roadmap of wrinkles, with deep furrows etched around his mouth and eyes, a topographical map of a hard-lived life. His balding head gleamed under the harsh, buzzing lights.

"Need a room?" The question tumbled from his mouth like gravel from a cement mixer, each syllable rough and weathered. As he spoke, he carefully placed a tasseled bookmark between the pages and set the book aside, revealing nicotine-stained fingers and nails bitten to the quick.

"Yeah, just for tonight. Hopefully," Max replied.

The clerk grunted, reaching for a key. "Fifty-five a night. Cash only. Checkout's at eleven."

"Any chance the storm will clear by morning?" Max asked, fishing out his wallet.

The clerk snorted. "Weather around here's about as predictable as my ex-wife. Wouldn't count on it."

The clerk took the money, and it disappeared under the counter with a practiced motion. No mention of change. He shifted to the right and pulled out a thick, leather ledger book. The spine was cracked and mended with electrical tape. It fell open to a well-worn page.

"Name." He nodded toward a chipped coffee mug stuffed with stubby pencils and dried-out pens. Max selected one that looked like it might still work.

"You got a car?"

"Sure."

The clerk tapped a yellow fingernail on the ruled line below Max's signature. "Put it down."

Max wondered how else people arrived in Grimswood—horseback? covered wagon?—but kept the thought to himself and wrote down the plate number.

"Listen, if the roads or the bridge aren't passable in the morning, would it be a problem if I need to stay a few more days?"

The clerk's eyebrows raised a fraction. "Suppose that

wouldn't be an issue," he drawled, sand and rocks scraping together. "Three other rooms are taken currently but I've got no other advance reservations on the books." What passed for a smile cracked his face, exposing jagged teeth—yellowed parchment scraps haphazardly jammed into his gums. The smile didn't reach his eyes, which remained as dull and lifeless as tarnished coins. He reached behind him, took a key off the pegboard and slid it across the counter. "Then again, I wasn't expecting you, so who can say? Folks don't usually plan on sticking around. You expecting trouble?"

"No, no trouble. I just like to have a plan," Max said, taking the key.

The clerk shrugged. "Your business is your business, long as you pay upfront and don't make a mess. I ain't seen nothing, I ain't heard nothing." He reached for his book. "Room nine, third from the end. Vending machine's busted, so don't bother. And the TV only gets three channels on a good day."

———

Max pocketed the key and nodded a wordless thanks to the clerk, who was already lost back in the battlefields of his book. He pushed open the lobby door and stepped back out into the rain. He grabbed his duffel bag from the car and made his way down the line toward room nine.

His shoes crunched over loose gravel as he made his way along the covered walkway that fronted the rooms. The building was a long, low-slung affair, its once-white paint now a dingy gray, peeling in large flakes to reveal the weathered wood beneath. Each door was painted a faded green, the numbers barely legible, some hanging askew. He passed the vending machine, its light out, a handwritten 'OUT OF ORDER' sign taped haphazardly to its front.

The room was exactly as Max had imagined: faded wallpaper, a sagging queen-size bed, and yes, a generic mountain landscape print above the headboard. But he lost the bet with himself. It was a misty sunrise with a wolf on a rocky ledge.

The floor felt slightly spongy underfoot, and a musty smell permeated the air. Max dropped his bag on the bed and flicked on the ancient TV experimentally, unsurprised when it emitted only static. He used the bathroom. He'd seen worse. A lot worse. He walked back into the main room. Exhaustion suddenly hit him like a wave. He collapsed onto the bed, the springs creaking in protest, and was asleep within minutes.

———

When he awoke, the digital clock on the nightstand showed 8:47 p.m. in angry red numbers. The storm still raged outside, rain pelting the window. Feeling restless, he decided to check out the Crooked Nail. Might as well make it a clean sweep through town.

He stepped out into the rain, pulling up his hood. The Sunrise Cafe's windows were dark now, just the CLOSED sign glowing. Patty and the grill man had earned their rest. In the empty parking lot, a security light cast a bright cone beneath the corner-mounted camera, creating a pool of moth-filled light.

The bar was a short walk up the street on the same side of the road as the motel. He could see, or more accurately, hear, its sign, a massive, rusted nail bent into a horseshoe shape, creaking as it swung in the rain. He started walking on the shoulder.

Across the street from the bar was a multi-use stone building. A small light lit up a signboard. Grimswood Professional Building. Dr. Mia Johnson, Family Medicine. Pearson's Dental Care. Everett & Sons, Attorneys at Law. U.S. Post

Office. Jill's Hair & Nail Salon. Cumberland Tax Prep. Johnson County Extension Office.

All the cornerstones of small-town life were crammed under one roof. They were just missing a funeral home to make it a one-stop-shop for birth, death, and everything in-between. Maybe that was around the back or in the basement. The building stood as a testament to rural efficiency—or perhaps desperation.

The road itself was deserted, though the bar's parking lot told a different story, filled with a hodgepodge of trucks and worn-out sedans. The small street-facing windows, clouded by years of cigarette smoke and neglect, leaked dim light as Max approached the door.

Pushing it open, he stepped inside and shook off the rain. The bar's interior lived up to its name in every sense. The floor slanted noticeably, giving patrons the unsettling sensation of being perpetually off-balance, as if they'd stumbled onto the deck of a slowly sinking ship. Shadows clung to every corner while the air was warm, scented with a fug of salt, smoke, and beer.

The bar itself was a long, scarred wooden affair that looked like it had weathered a century of elbow leaning, fist pounding, and drink spilling. Behind it, a wall of liquor bottles reflected the weak overhead light, their labels faded and dusty. Three unmarked taps stood sentinel in the middle of the span. Max guessed a regular, a light, and maybe another regular. He doubted there was an import.

A handful of patrons hunched over their drinks, each seemingly intent on maintaining their own bubble of solitude. The pose of a serious and dedicated drinker. Max recognized the trucker from the Sunrise Cafe on one of the stools near the door. His posture hadn't changed, only the type of drink in front of him. In one corner, an ancient jukebox wheezed out a Hank Williams tune, the mournful twang a fitting soundtrack to the scene.

The bartender, a burly man with forearms like tree trunks and a beard that could hide a family of squirrels, gave Max a cursory nod as he approached. "What'll it be?" he asked, his voice surprisingly high and reedy, like a piccolo played offkey. The incongruity between his imposing physique and his voice was jarring, adding another layer of surrealism to the already off-kilter atmosphere.

Max slid onto a stool, bracing himself as it creaked ominously beneath him but held. "Whiskey. Neat," he said, his eyes scanning the rest of the room. A dartboard hung on one wall, its surface so pockmarked it looked like it had survived a firing squad. Nearby, a stuffed deer head stared glassy-eyed into the middle distance, tinsel still draped around its antlers from some long-forgotten Christmas.

In the far corner, a group of men hunched over a poker game, their faces obscured by the smoke from their cigarettes. The occasional clink of chips and muttered curses were the only sounds that broke through the haze.

As the bartender slid Max's drink across the bar, a sudden burst of raucous laughter erupted from a booth near the back. Max turned to see a group of men, each of their vests or caps adorned with a company logo which Max couldn't make out, slapping the table in mirth at some shared joke.

Max turned around and took a sip. The whiskey burned going down, but Max welcomed the warmth. He couldn't shake the feeling that, like the deer on the wall, he was being watched. But every time he glanced around, he saw only the same tableau of small-town despair and quiet desperation.

The Crooked Nail, like a lot of small-town bars he'd found himself in over the years, was more than just a bar. It was a refuge for the lost, the lonely, and those looking to forget—or to hide. As he signaled for another drink, Max wondered which category he fell into.

He felt that slight itching feeling on his neck again. He took another casual look around the bar and this time found another familiar face from the Sunrise Cafe—the blonde woman from the booth sat alone at the far end of the bar, nursing her own drink. Their eyes locked for a moment and then she looked away. Max settled onto his creaky stool, sipped his second whiskey more slowly, and turned his attention to the baseball game playing silently on the TV above the bar. Pirates versus Brewers. As the innings passed, the bar grew rowdier. Or, at least the company men in the one booth did. Max was about to call it a night when he noticed two men, clearly deep in their cups, approach the blonde woman. One tall and one short, like a pair of mismatched salt and pepper shakers, the tall one's head freshly powdered with dandruff, the short one red-faced and spicy with the night's drinking.

"Hey there, sweetheart," the taller one slurred, leaning uncomfortably close. Max suppressed a shudder. He would bet the man's breath wasn't any better than his hair hygiene. "What's a pretty thing like you doing all alone?"

The woman didn't flinch or even look up from her drink. "Enjoying the solitude. You're ruining it."

The shorter man laughed. "Ooh, she's got a mouth on her. I like that in a woman."

"How about I buy you another drink and you can join our party over there?"

"I'm not interested," she said, still not raising her eyes. "Please leave me alone."

The taller man's face darkened. "Now that ain't very friendly. We're just trying to be nice."

Max finished his drink and settled his tab, watching the situation unfold. The bartender seemed more interested in wiping down the already clean counter than intervening. The men edged closer, the shorter one against her back pressing her into the bar. The taller one pushing in from the left.

"I said, leave me alone," the woman repeated, an edge creeping into her voice. "Are you guys stupid, drunk, disabled or all three?"

"Come on, don't be like that," the taller man said, reaching out to grab her arm.

Max began to ease off his stool. But before he could take a step, the woman moved. Fast. Very fast.

Her hand shot up and out as if she was waving away a fly. He grabbed his cheek in surprise, checked his hand, then leaned forward to try again. That was a mistake. She grabbed his wrist. A twist. A pull. His momentum betrayed him. He stumbled forward. She slid out of the way, then placed her hand on the back of his neck and pushed. Hard. His face bounced off the bar with a crack and an explosion of blood from his nose.

She didn't pause. She used the force of her push to pivot off the stool. Her leg swept low. A graceful arc. It caught the shorter man behind the knees. He folded backwards. She gave him a push. His head met a table's edge with a dull thud. He crumpled to the floor.

Seconds passed. The bar fell silent other than Willie singing about a Whiskey River. Two men down, each groaning in pain. The woman stood unruffled, her expression a mixture of annoyance and contempt. She looked around the room, maybe wondering if anyone else wanted to give it a try. No one moved.

The woman calmly picked up her purse, dropped a few bills on the bar, and walked out, the door swinging shut behind her with a loose clatter.

CHAPTER SEVEN

The ancient air conditioning unit rattled to life with a wheezing cough, startling Max from his fitful sleep. He blinked, disoriented, as the dim gray light of dawn filtered through the threadbare curtains. The musty smell of the motel room hit him anew, a pungent reminder of where he was.

Grimswood. Stuck.

Max fumbled for his phone on the nightstand, squinting at the screen. Still early. Just after six. Still no service. He sighed, tossing it back onto the scratched surface. So much for checking in with Vic.

Swinging his legs over the side of the bed, Max grimaced as his feet touched the cold, slightly damp carpet. He stood, stretching his arms overhead until his back gave a satisfying pop. The room felt claustrophobic, the walls seeming to press in on him.

Max padded into the bathroom, the cold tiles sending a shiver up his spine. After relieving himself, he grabbed one of the rough white towels from the rack, its texture reminiscent of sandpaper against his skin. He returned to the main room.

With a grunt, he nudged the small, rickety table and its mismatched chairs into the corner, clearing a space by the front window.

He unfurled the towel onto the floor. The absurdity of his actions did occur to him as he smoothed out the wrinkles in the towel with his foot. Perhaps it was akin to using a band-aid on a broken bone, but it felt better to have a barrier, any barrier, between his skin and the carpet.

Max dropped to the floor and began his routine: push-ups, sit-ups, squats. The familiar routine helped clear the fog from his mind, his muscles warming as he moved through the exercises. By the time he finished, a light sheen of sweat covered his skin, and his breath came in controlled, even pants.

———

The shower sputtered to life reluctantly, water trickling out in an anemic stream. Max stepped under the lukewarm spray, ducking his head to avoid the low-hanging showerhead. He lathered up quickly with the small bar of soap and tried not to touch the mildewed plastic curtain.

As he toweled off, Max caught his reflection in the spotted mirror. The face that stared back at him looked tired, the lines around his eyes deeper than he remembered. He ran a hand over the stubble on his jaw, deciding a shave could wait. It wasn't like he had anywhere important to be.

Dressed in fresh clothes, Max stepped out of his room. The air was heavy with moisture, the scent of wet earth and decaying leaves filled his lungs. Dark clouds hung low on the horizon, but for now, the rain had stopped. Puddles dotted the motel's parking lot, reflecting the gray sky like dull mirrors.

He glanced toward the office as he passed. Through the smudged window, he could see the clerk, hunched over his desk, head bowed as he pored over his book. The man looked like he'd been frozen in place since the night before.

———

The bell above the Sunrise Cafe's door jangled as Max pushed it open, the warm aroma of coffee and fried food once again washing over. The diner was significantly busier than the previous day, a low hum of conversation filling the air. Patty looked up from behind the counter, flashing him a harried smile.

"Mornin', hon," she called out, juggling a coffeepot and a stack of plates. "Sit anywhere you like. I'll be with you in a jiffy."

Max nodded, his eyes scanning the crowded space. Most of the stools at the counter were occupied, as were the booths along the walls. He recognized a few faces from the day before. The trucker from the bar, nursing a steaming mug, staring straight ahead. Maybe he didn't sleep, just shuttled between a stool at the cafe and a stool at the bar. The elderly couple was also present, sharing a newspaper as they picked at their breakfast. The deputy he'd spoken to at the roadblock sat at the far end of the counter. Max made his way over, sliding onto the empty stool next to him. The creases in the deputy's uniform were sharp enough to cut paper.

"Morning, Deputy," Max said, nodding in greeting.

The man turned, recognition flickering in his eyes. "Well, if it isn't our stranded traveler. How'd you fare last night?"

Max raised an eyebrow. "Have you ever slept at the Crossroads, Deputy?"

The deputy let out a low chuckle, shaking his head. "Can't say I have. But I've heard enough stories about those mattresses that I'd rather sleep in my patrol car." He leaned in conspiratorially. "Is it true that one of them still has the imprint of Jesse James after he hid there in 1874?"

Max nodded, a wry smile tugging at his lips. "I wouldn't be surprised. I swear mine came with a handwritten note warning about smallpox from the previous guest."

"Wouldn't surprise me," the deputy snorted. "That place hasn't changed in 30 years. I swear, the dust bunnies have squatter's rights by now."

"Then I probably shouldn't elaborate any more on my night," Max said, his tone dry. "Any news on the roads?"

The deputy shook his head, a grim expression settling on his face. "Nothing good, I'm afraid. Bridge to the south is still out. Crew's working on it, but it'll be at least another day, maybe two. And up north?" He let out a low whistle. "Multiple washouts. They're saying it could be up to a week before that's passable."

Max felt his stomach sink. A week. He'd have to find a way to contact Vic, let her know what was happening. "Thanks for the update," he said, trying to keep the disappointment out of his voice. "Since I'm here for a while, what do you recommend for breakfast?"

The deputy's face brightened. "Can't go wrong with Patty's biscuits and gravy. Or if you're feeling adventurous, try the buckwheat pancakes. They're a local favorite."

Max took a menu as Patty bustled over, coffeepot in hand. She flipped over a mug that sat on the counter and filled it without asking. "Be with you in a sec, hon," she said, already moving on.

As Max turned to survey the room again, his eyes landed on another familiar face. A few more days in town and maybe everyone would be familiar. The blonde woman from the bar sat in the same booth as yesterday, a couple of empty plates scattered across the table amongst a notebook and sheets of loose paper. Her hair was slightly disheveled, the silver streak catching the light as she bent over what looked like a map.

Making a split-second decision, Max stood, coffee mug in hand, and approached her table. "Mind if I join you?" he asked, gesturing to the empty seat across from her.

She looked up, her eyes narrowing slightly. For a moment, he thought she might refuse, but then she gave a curt nod, making no move to clear the cluttered surface.

"Max Parish," he said as he slid into the booth, setting his mug down in a small clear space. That was the latest name he'd been using since his dust-up down in Texas. He'd left there on good enough terms that a new alias hadn't been necessary. Not yet. "Busy morning?"

The woman shrugged, her attention already back on the paper in front of her. "Been here a while," she said, her voice clipped.

Patty appeared at their table, notepad in hand, nonplussed by his seat swapping. "Ready to order, hon?" she asked Max.

Before he could respond, the woman across from him spoke up. "It's hard to fuck up eggs," she said, not looking up from her map. "I stick with that, at least for breakfast. The rest of it I can barely comprehend. Red-eye gravy? Grits? Reminds me of baby puke."

If Patty was put off by these comments, she didn't show it. The corner of her mouth might have twitched but Max wasn't sure if it was up or down. A smile or a frown. Maybe she was used to the woman. She appeared to be practically paying rent on the booth.

Max couldn't help but chuckle. "I'll take the eggs then," he told Patty. "Over easy, with toast and bacon."

As Patty walked away, Max turned his attention back to his tablemate. "Not from around here, then?" he asked.

"No," she replied, her tone making it clear she wasn't interested in any more small talk.

Max sipped his coffee and looked out the window. He was comfortable with silence. Nothing moved outside. There were no new cars in the Crossroads parking lot. He imagined Jeb turning a page in his book. Eventually, he returned his attention to inside the cafe. His eyes fell on the largest piece of paper on the table. It was a topographical map, covered in a maze of contour lines and symbols. He reached out, picking it up to get a better look.

The woman's hand twitched, as if she wanted to snatch it back, but she restrained herself. Instead, she reached across the table, turning the map around in his hands. "You had it upside down," she said, this time a hint of amusement in her voice.

"Thanks," Max said, studying the now-correctly oriented map. "You stuck here, too?"

She shook her head. "No. Why?"

Max briefly explained about the road closures, watching as she listened with only half interest. When he finished, she simply said, "No, I'm here by choice."

That piqued his curiosity. "Really? Why?" he asked, unable to imagine voluntarily spending time in a place like Grimswood.

For the first time since he'd sat down, the woman met his eyes directly. Her eyes were a pale blue or light gray. The intensity in her gaze caught him off guard. He leaned back slightly.

"My sister," she said, her voice low and tight with an emotion Max couldn't quite place.

The loaded words hung in the air between them. Max opened his mouth to respond, but before he could, Patty returned with his breakfast.

"Here you go, hon," she said, setting the plate down in

front of him. The yellow yolks gleamed under the diner's fluorescent lights. The bacon was crisp, its salty aroma making Max's stomach growl.

"Can I get you anything else, Riley?" Patty asked, turning to the woman across from Max.

Riley. So that was her name.

Riley shook her head, gesturing to her still-full coffee mug. "I'm good, thanks, Patty."

As Patty walked away, Max picked up his fork, suddenly aware of how hungry he was. He cut into one of the eggs, watching as the yolk spilled out onto the plate. "Your sister," he said, looking back up at Riley. "What happened?"

Riley's jaw tightened, her fingers tracing a contour line on the map. For a moment, Max thought she might not answer. But then she spoke, her voice barely above a whisper.

"She disappeared. A week ago."

CHAPTER EIGHT

M ax set his fork down, his appetite suddenly diminished. "I'm sorry," he said, the words feeling inadequate even as they left his mouth.

Riley's eyes snapped up to meet his, a fierce determination he had no trouble identifying burning in them. "Don't be sorry," she said. "I heard you talking to that cop. If you're stuck here. Help me find her."

"Speaking of. Have the local authorities been involved?"

"They've been worse than useless," she said, her tone frustrated and bitter. "They think Sarah just took off, maybe got lost hiking. But I know my sister. Something's wrong."

Max leaned back, studying Riley's face. The intensity of her gaze, the tension in her shoulders—this wasn't just worry. This was fear, mixed with a desperate sort of hope. He thought about the storm and the lack of cell service.

"What makes you so sure?" he asked carefully. "With all the rain and the spotty cell service...is it possible she's just out of range?"

Riley's hand clenched into a fist on the table and the words rushed out. "I never liked this plan. I never wanted her to go. She's experienced in the woods, but Jake could be so single-minded about his brother's case, I worried it might make him blind to the dangers. They had a sat phone and a beacon. The deal was that she'd check in once a day. If there was trouble, they'd activate the PLB." She paused, swallowing hard. "The first two days, I received the short messages as planned, but then nothing. Radio silence."

Max felt a familiar stirring in his gut, a mixture of curiosity and caution. He'd been down roads like this before, and they rarely led anywhere good. But the urgency in Riley's voice, the raw emotion in her eyes—it was hard to ignore.

"I'm sorry," he said again, then quickly continued. "If I'm going to help at all, you're going to have to back up. Who's Jake?"

Riley took a deep breath, her fingers tracing the contours on the map. "Jake Cotter. He's my sister's boyfriend and the brother of Vance Cotter."

"And Vance Cotter is...?" Max prompted.

"The reason we're all here," Riley said, her voice tight. "Vance disappeared in the Monongahela National Forest on a solo hike three years ago. He was a very experienced hiker and outdoorsman. Bordered on being a survivalist, actually. But he vanished without a trace, and Jake's been obsessed with finding out what happened ever since."

Max leaned back, processing the information. "What about the initial search and rescue efforts?"

Riley shook her head. "Extensive. They combed the area for weeks. Search and rescue teams, volunteers, even brought in dogs and helicopters. Nothing. It's like the forest just swallowed him up."

"And since then?" Max asked.

"Friends and family have organized follow-up searches every year. Jake's been back countless times. There have even been a few internet sleuths who've taken an interest in the case."

Max's brow furrowed. "Internet sleuths?"

Riley looked at him, a hint of surprise in her eyes. "You don't know about this? Cold cases are a thing on the internet. Amateur detectives pick apart unsolved mysteries, share theories, sometimes even do their own investigations."

"Huh," Max mused, filing away this piece of information. "And they're interested in Vance's case?"

"Not just Vance's," Riley said, her voice lowering. "Turns out Grimswood is ground zero for more than just Vance Cotter. Quite a few hikers have gone missing or are suspected of being missing after passing through here and entering the Monongahela."

"How many are we talking about?"

"I've been able to find seven over the past 25 years."

"Is that a lot?"

Riley's eyes met his again, hard and determined. "Reddit and the internet swear there's more, but that's seven too many for me and I don't want to add Sarah and Jake to the list."

Max's mind raced, trying to process all the new information. Something about this place or about Vance Cotter tickled at the back of his mind. He didn't spend a lot of time on the internet and when he did it was not in Reddit chat rooms. A half-remembered story, perhaps, or a case he'd heard about in passing.

An image popped into his mind. A name printed above the entrance to an ice rink in West Roxbury. He'd spent hours there as a youth for practices, tournaments, and games.

"Cotter," Max said, more to himself than to Riley. "As in the Boston Cotters?"

Riley's eyebrows raised slightly, a mix of surprise and wariness crossing her face. "You know about the family?"

Max nodded slowly, more memories coming into focus. "Hard not to if you've spent any time in Boston. I grew up in Southie. Their name is everywhere—buildings, parks, charity foundations. You probably can't walk more than a mile in the city proper without passing something they built or put their name on."

Riley's posture stiffened slightly. "That's right. Vance and Jake are part of that family. Though Vance...he always tried to distance himself from all that."

"I remember now," Max said, the pieces falling into place. "There was quite a stir when Vance disappeared. It wasn't just another missing hiker—it was a scion of one of Boston's most prominent families vanishing without a trace."

Riley nodded, a pained expression crossing her face. "It was a circus for a while. News vans, reporters camping out in the forest, helicopters buzzing overhead. Vance's disappearance was the lead story on national news for days. The family's prominence only amplified the attention."

"And nothing came of all that?" Max asked.

"Nothing concrete," Riley sighed. "Days turned into weeks. Summer into fall. Seasons into years. Vance was just gone. Lots of theories, lots of speculation, but no hard evidence. Vance had created a following on YouTube with his outdoor and nature videos. Some people thought he staged his own disappearance for publicity or to escape family pressure—to break away from the Cotter name and make it on his own. A dedicated group is convinced he's still alive living under a new identity. Others suggested he might have run into trouble with wildlife or fallen into a ravine. There were even wild theories about kidnapping for ransom, given the family's wealth, or him stumbling into some kind of government conspiracy. The internet went wild with it all."

Max leaned back, taking it all in. "But you don't believe any of that."

Riley shook her head firmly. "No. Vance was experienced, careful. He wouldn't have taken unnecessary risks, and he certainly wouldn't have put his family through something like this intentionally. And Jake...Jake's convinced there's more to the story. That's why he's been so obsessed with finding answers."

"And now Jake and your sister Sarah are out there, following in Vance's footsteps," Max said, understanding dawning.

"Exactly," Riley said, her voice tight with worry. "Jake's spent the past year researching and planning this latest expedition, trying to retrace Vance's last known route. He thought he'd found some new lead, something about a place called Grave's End. Sarah...she went along to keep an eye on him, to make sure he didn't do anything reckless."

"Any idea what this new lead might be?"

Riley picked up the map again, her finger circling a particular area. "Have you ever heard of Grave's End?" she asked, her voice barely above a whisper.

Max shook his head, leaning in to get a better look at the map. "Can't say that I have. What is it?"

Riley's finger tapped a spot on the map. "It's a place deep in the Monongahela. Not on any official maps but mentioned in local legends and speculated about in online hiking forums I've found. Some say it's just a myth, a campfire story to scare tourists. But others..." She trailed off.

"Others what?" Max prompted.

Riley refocused on him. "Others say it's real. A place where the forest is different, where compasses spin and GPS fails. Where people go in, but don't come out."

It sounded farfetched, the stuff of horror movies and urban legends. But he'd seen enough in his life to know that sometimes, just sometimes, the legends had a kernel of truth.

"And you think this Grave's End might be connected to the disappearances?"

Riley nodded. "I think it's my best lead. I'll be honest, it's really my only lead other than the trailhead they started at. If Jake and Sarah were heading there, or at least to the general area where it's supposed to be, that's where I need to start."

He knew he should walk away, tell her to leave it to the professionals. But something about the mix of strength and desperation in Riley's eyes pulled at him. Max hesitated, weighing his options. But sometimes you just know. Sometimes he chose to get involved and sometimes the situation chose him. He had no woodland experience, he knew he was more of a city mouse, but he was stuck here, at least for a few days. And if Sarah and Jake were really missing...could he just turn his back on Riley when she was asking for help?

"All right," he said finally. "I'm in. Tell me everything you know about Grave's End."

CHAPTER NINE

Riley leaned back in the booth. The morning rush was now in full swing, the hum of conversation and the clatter of cups and silverware was loud, still she lowered her voice, "This isn't the place for that conversation. There's someone you need to meet, someone who knows a lot more about Grave's End than I do."

"Lead the way," he said, leaving a few bills on the table to cover his meal.

Max dipped his finger in the phone's coin slot as they passed. Still empty. The bell jangled behind them as they stepped into the humid air. The sky remained overcast, heavy with the promise of more rain. They crossed the street, their shoes squelching in puddles that hadn't yet evaporated from the previous downpour.

As they approached the Crossroads Inn, Max noticed the same vehicles in the parking lot. No one new had arrived, and no one had left. The town remained as isolated as it had been the day before.

Riley led Max past his room and the broken vending machine to the second door from the end. She rapped her knuckles against the peeling green paint, the sound echoing in the empty lot. Shuffling noises came from inside, followed by the creak of bedsprings. After a moment, the door opened a crack, held by a security chain. A young man with tousled brown hair and a neatly trimmed beard peered out, squinting against the daylight. Max recognized him as Riley's companion from the Sunrise yesterday, the one engaged in an intense discussion with her.

"Riley? What's going on?" he asked. Then he caught sight of Max, and his eyes widened, darting between the two visitors with growing alertness.

"We need to talk, Ethan," Riley said, her tone leaving no room for argument. "This is Max. He's offered to help."

Ethan hesitated, then closed the door. There was a light rattle of the chain, then the door opened wider. "Come in, I guess."

Max followed Riley into the room, immediately hit by the now-familiar musty smell of old carpet and stale air. The room was identical to his own—same sagging bed, same generic artwork, same feeling of decay barely held at bay. But where Max's room was sparse, with only his duffel bag as evidence of occupancy, Ethan's was cluttered with maps, notebooks, and what looked like scattered mountaineering equipment.

Ethan cleared a stack of papers from one of the chairs by the small circular table under the window and gestured for Max to sit. Riley perched on the edge of the unmade bed, while Ethan leaned against the dresser, arms crossed.

"So," Ethan began, his voice cautious, "what exactly are we talking about here? Wait," he held up both hands, "don't answer that yet. I can't have this conversation in my underwear." He leaned over and grabbed some clothes off a haphazard pile near the bed and disappeared into the bathroom. He returned a minute later in jeans and a T-shirt. His hair now wet and mostly flat on his head. "Okay, go ahead," he said, resuming his stance against the dresser.

"We're talking about finding Sarah and Jake. Max here has some experience that might be useful."

Ethan's eyebrows rose. "Experience?"

Max forced himself not to look at Riley. They hadn't discussed this nor did he have any practical experience that might help with a search and rescue op in the deep woods. But if this is how she wanted to play it, or needed to play it, to convince Ethan, he would go along.

Max shifted in his chair, the plastic creaking beneath him. "I used to work in private security. Did some search and rescue work, too. Typically more urban scenarios but many of the same principles apply."

"And you just happened to get stranded in Grimswood?" Ethan's tone was skeptical.

"The bridge is out to the south, and the road's washed out to the north," Max explained. "I'm stuck here for a few days at least. The entertainment options are limited."

"This is not about entertainment."

Max held up a palm. "You're right. Poor choice of words. My point is I might as well make myself useful. Always been my motto."

"And how has that worked out for you?" Ethan's tone remained clipped.

Max shrugged. "It's gotten me in some trouble in the past, but on balance I think the ledger shows me in the positive."

Ethan nodded slowly, then turned to Riley. "And you trust him?"

Riley's jaw tightened. "I trust that we need all the help we can get. More people means more options. We can cover more ground."

"It can also mean going slower. You okay with that?"

"Now you sound like Hatfield."

"You want me to trust this guy, but you don't trust Hatfield. A man with infinitely more knowledge and experience for the current situation."

The tension in the room was palpable. Max could sense an undercurrent of unspoken history between Riley and Ethan, something beyond just their current disagreement. Plus, who was Hatfield?

Before he could interject, Riley continued, "Can we focus on what's important? Max wants to know about Grave's End."

"Are you sure we have time for this?"

"Ethan, please..."

Ethan sighed, running a hand through his wet hair. "All right. What do you want to know?"

Max leaned forward, elbows on his knees. "Everything. Start with the basics. What is Grave's End, and why do you think Sarah and Jake might have gone there?"

Ethan moved to the table, pushing aside some equipment to unroll a large topographical map. The paper crinkled as he smoothed it out, weighted down by a battered compass and marked with a handful of colorful sticky notes.

"Grave's End," Ethan began, his finger tracing a large circular area on the map, "is supposedly a place deep in the Monongahela National Forest. Rumors put it somewhere around here. It doesn't appear on any official maps, but it's mentioned prominently in local legends, old diaries and journals at least as far back as the 1830s, and even a few older primary source accounts from early settlers."

"Jeremiah Grim?"

Ethan glanced up, maybe in surprise, then continued, "No, nothing from him specifically. From what I understand, he was a businessman and entrepreneur, not an explorer, but a few generations down the line, his great-great-grandson talks about it."

"And what makes it special?" Max asked.

Riley spoke up. "People disappear there."

Ethan shot her a look. "That's the legend, yes. Or part of it, but it's more complicated than that." He turned back to Max. "The stories describe it as a place where the normal rules don't apply. Compasses can't hold north, GPS fails, people get turned around even when they think they're walking in a straight line."

Max's brow furrowed. "That sounds like it could just be the result of magnetic anomalies or dense forest cover. A West Virginia Bermuda Triangle."

"That's what I've been saying," Ethan nodded and glanced at Riley now. "There are rational explanations for most of the phenomena associated with Grave's End. But..."

"But what?" Max prompted.

Ethan hesitated, now looking at Max. "But there are aspects of the legend that are harder to explain. Reports of strange lights, unexplained sounds, even sightings of...things that shouldn't exist."

Riley stood abruptly, pacing the small space between the bed and the wall. "This is why we're getting nowhere. We keep getting bogged down in ghost stories and Bigfoot sightings when we should be out there looking!"

"Riley," Ethan's voice was gentle but firm, "we've been over this. We can't just charge into the forest without a plan. It's dangerous, and it won't help Sarah or Jake."

"And how is sitting here helping?" Riley snapped.

Max watched the exchange, noting the way Ethan's eyes followed Riley's movements, the mix of concern and frustration in his expression. "Would it have helped to be out in the woods during that rain? That would have just put us at risk, too."

"Okay," Max interjected, trying to defuse the growing tension. "Let's back up. Why do you think Sarah and Jake went to Grave's End in the first place?"

Ethan turned back to the map, his finger circling a specific area. "Jake thought he'd found a connection between Grave's End and his brother's disappearance. He'd been poring over Vance's journals, watching his last videos, cross-referencing them with the historical accounts and local legends. He became convinced that Vance had stumbled onto something big."

"What kind of something?" Max asked.

Ethan shook his head. "Jake wasn't sure, or, if he was, he didn't share the details with me. Vance never said anything either. I know that for a fact. I went over the same material. There's a lot of oblique references, almost teases. Vance knew the power of his name and YouTube platform. He was ginning up interest, but he also knew he'd need proof. Jake believes that's why he went into the Monongahela. And if there was something big to announce or to find in there, it probably has to do with Grave's End. At least, that's what Jake also believed. He was excited, more energized than I'd seen him in years."

"And you've known him a long time?"

"Roommates freshman year at Dartmouth and we both work at the foundation."

Max didn't need to ask what foundation.

Riley stopped pacing, her arms wrapped tightly around herself, and brought them back to the business at hand. "And Sarah went with him to keep him safe. To make sure he didn't do anything stupid."

The irony of the statement hung heavily in the air.

Max leaned back in his chair, processing the information.

"So, we have two missing people, potentially in an area of the forest known for strange occurrences and previous disappearances. What's been done so far in terms of search efforts?"

Ethan and Riley exchanged a look, and Max sensed he'd again touched the electrified third rail and at least part of the source of their earlier argument.

"That's...complicated," Ethan said slowly. "Officially, Sarah and Jake aren't missing persons yet."

"Bullshit," Riley blurted and resumed her pacing.

"It hasn't been long enough," Ethan continued, "and given their experience and the nature of their trip, the authorities are reluctant to mount a full-scale search."

Riley stopped again and sat back down on the bed, her fists clenched in her lap. "Which is why we need to go out there ourselves. Every day we wait could just be another day we're too late."

"And every day we rush in unprepared is a day we could end up needing rescue ourselves," Ethan countered. "We need to be smart about this, Riley."

Max held up a placating hand, sensing a tired argument was about to reignite. "Okay, I think I'm getting the picture. But there're still a lot of holes. How about we start with the details of Sarah and Jake's plan? What did they tell you before they left?"

Outside, more rain began to fall, drumming softly on the motel's metal roof. In the distance, thunder rumbled, a low, ominous sound that seemed to echo the tension in the room.

CHAPTER TEN

Max leaned forward in his chair, the plastic once again creaking under his weight. He watched as Ethan and Riley exchanged glances, a silent communication passing between them. Ethan sighed and moved to sit on the edge of the bed next to Riley. This was something they could agree on, Max thought.

"Honestly? Not much," Ethan said. "Jake was...excited. More excited than I'd seen him in years, like I said. But he was also secretive."

Riley nodded. "Sarah told me they were going to Grave's End. Jake was convinced he'd find answers about Vance there, or at least somewhere along the way."

"Convinced how?" Max asked.

Ethan's shoulders slumped slightly. "That's just it. We don't know. Jake had been obsessed with finding Vance for so long, and suddenly he seemed to have this...certainty. But he wouldn't share the details."

Max could feel the frustration radiating off Riley and could see the worry etched in Ethan's face. Whatever personal issues these two might share or arguments they'd had since arriving in Grimswood, it was clear they both cared deeply for Jake and Sarah. "Okay, so what do you know for sure?"

Riley stood and began to pace again. Her shoes making soft thuds on the worn carpet. Max realized she was one of those people who thought best in motion. "We know the day they started," she said. "Sarah sent me a text when they hit the trailhead."

Ethan nodded, reaching for a notebook on the cluttered bedside table. He flipped it open, revealing pages filled with scribbled notes and diagrams. "We were able to backtrack to the trailhead they used from the metadata in the text message. We visited the location first thing and found their car there, undisturbed."

"And the follow-ups from Sarah? The sister check ins she promised? Did those have GPS coordinates?" Max asked, remembering their earlier conversation.

"Right," Riley said. "Sarah sent those initial two check ins. We have the GPS coordinates for both."

"So," Max said slowly, "you have a starting point and two more data points. That's something, at least."

"Maybe not enough." Ethan reached for the topo map again, this time pointing to a large red circle drawn on the map. "Their last known location. Taking into account the average distance two fit people could travel...this would be the primary search area. Or, the starting point." Max studied the map. The area that Ethan had previously indicated might include Grave's End clipped out of a portion of this other, more definitive circle. "But remember, the Monongahela covers almost a million acres across 10 counties. It's like shoving someone out the door in New York and telling them London is to the east. You can head confidently in the general direction and still likely miss the mark by thousands of miles."

Max let the numbers and geography sink in. "Okay, good point. Let's put it aside for now. Any ideas why Jake was so certain about Grave's End? If it's just a local legend, how was he so sure he knew where to find it? How did he know he was headed in the right direction?"

Ethan and Riley exchanged another look, this one tinged with what Max thought might be embarrassment.

"We...we think we might have figured that out," Ethan said hesitantly. He stood, moving to the table where the map was still spread out. His finger traced a path from the marked trailhead through the two known GPS points. "We believe Jake might have gotten his hands on some kind of map."

Max raised an eyebrow. "A map? Of what? To what? Grave's End?"

Riley nodded. "We think so. But not just any map. Jake was hopeful, almost zealous about getting answers, but he wouldn't just grab a printout from any internet chat room. We think he got it from a local...well, I guess you'd call him a hermit. That's what he appears to call himself. Maybe he's actually a recluse. Who knows? Someone with firsthand knowledge. Someone Jake would trust or at least believe."

"A hermit," Max repeated. "And how did Jake find this hermit?"

Ethan shook his head, frustration evident in his voice. "We don't know. Not for sure. Jake didn't tell us how he found out about this guy, or how he managed to get information from him. Best guess? We think they connected online. I found a username jotted in the margin of one of Jake's notebooks." He paused and dug around in his pile of notes, maps, and documents and then handed Max a small notebook. Then took it back and opened it to a specific page near the back and pointed at some notations on the side. "There. The only note like that in any of Jake's things that I could find." Max looked at the small, cramped handwriting:

WVhermithiker889, local?, map? "I had a friend crack Jake's laptop, and we found the username along with activity by Jake in a hiking forum. WVhermithiker889 is a prolific poster on the forums, especially about the area around Grimswood. They both added to a thread about the Monongahela but didn't appear to have any direct conversations, not on that forum, but something made Jake write down that handle. They might have linked up on the dark web or a secure chat room."

"A hermit was using the dark web?"

"The guy just might not like people. Doesn't mean he's a Luddite. All we know is that in the weeks leading up to their trip, Jake became more and more excited, more certain. He kept mentioning 'new information' he'd gotten, but he never elaborated. He just told us that we'd see when he had answers. I think he was okay with building up his own hopes, but didn't want to falsely give hope to anyone else until he was sure. This WVhermithiker guy is the only really new thing I saw in his notes. I know Vance's case pretty well. Nothing else jumped out."

Max leaned over the table. He studied the map, noting the markers for the trailhead and the two check-in points were clearly labeled. "Why would this guy break out of his self-imposed seclusion to give Jake this information?" Before either of them could answer, Max waved them off. "Forget it. Let's put the why aside. That's not a question we need answered right now. Obvious next question: have you talked to this...recluse? Maybe he could shed some light on what Jake was planning."

The silence that followed his question was answer enough, but Riley spoke anyway, her voice tight. "We've tried. But it's...complicated."

"Complicated how?" Max pressed.

"We can't find him...or her, I suppose. The locals...they're oddly protective of this person. Secretive, even. Every time we've tried to get any information about him, we've hit a wall," Ethan said.

"It's like they're afraid of him," Riley added. "Or for him. We can't get a straight answer on where he lives. Or if he even exists."

"But you think Jake was able to gain his trust and get some sort of map?"

"Yes. Jake could be very persuasive. And if he thought this person might have information that would help bring Vance home? He'd be relentless, too."

Max looked between them, noting the dark circles under their eyes, the tension in their postures. They were exhausted, physically and emotionally, running on fumes and hope.

"Okay," Max said, straightening up. "You're right. It might not be much, but it *is* a start. But we need to find a way to get to him. For simplicity, I'm going to assume a man for now. If your guess is correct, he might be our best lead." Max didn't want or need to add it was their only lead.

"I think we all agree on that, but how?"

"Leave that to me. I also have friends who are good with computers. In the meantime, I agree with Riley, we need to finish any prep work and get moving. I assume you guys have gathered every bit of information you can about the area around those GPS coordinates. Terrain, weather patterns, any local landmarks or features that might be significant."

Ethan nodded, already reaching for another notebook. "I've been compiling data on the region. Topographical maps, geological surveys, historical accounts. The terrain is tough, undulating and varied, but it won't be a surprise."

"Riley, let's get a solid weather forecast. We need to cover some ground but if waiting a few hours avoids doing it in a monsoon, I think that would be better. Second, I'll need some gear."

She nodded and said, "I've got extra in my truck."

"In my size?"

"Okay, got me there."

"See if Patty or Jeb—"

"Jeb?"

"The front desk clerk. See if either know of a place, an accessible place, where I can do some shopping."

"What are you going to do?"

"Dig out this hermit."

CHAPTER ELEVEN

Max pulled his jacket collar up as he stepped out of Ethan's room, his mind churning with the information they'd shared. He paused at the edge of the covered walkway, scanning the parking lot. Old habits. Know your surroundings. Have an exit plan. A new vehicle had appeared since his arrival, a weathered Ford F-150 with a gun rack visible in the rear window, parked at the far edge of the lot, near the office. A friend of Jeb's? The truck's faded green paint was splattered with mud. Through the shadows and rain-streaked windshield, he couldn't make out if anyone was inside

Max fished in his pocket for his room key, the cold metal a stark contrast to the humid air. As he entered his own musty sanctuary, he reached for his phone to call Lawrence, then remembered the lack of service. He double-checked. No bars. He cursed under his breath, tossing the useless device onto the bed.

The Sunrise Cafe beckoned from across the street. Break-fast. Lunch. Dinner. Public phones. Max zipped his jacket to his chin and made a dash for it, puddles splashing under his feet. The bell above the door jangled as he entered.

Patty looked up from behind the counter, a knowing smile on her face. "Forget something, hon?"

Max nodded, fishing in his pocket for some bills. "Any chance you can break a twenty for the payphone?"

She chuckled, pulling change from the register. "Thought those were going extinct, but I suppose they still have their uses. Funny, I never got around to calling the phone company to take it out. Now I'm glad I didn't. You'd be surprised how much I make on that relic between the sparse service out here or batteries going dead. Last time Ma Bell called about it, I told them to take a hike. I was keeping it."

The coins felt oddly heavy in Max's hand as he approached the ancient payphone near the entrance. He lifted the receiver, grimacing at the faint stickiness, and heard a dial tone. He punched in Lawrence's number from memory. A recorded voice demanded seventy-five cents for the call. Max fed three quarters into the slot, hearing each one register with a metallic ding. The line clicked, then began to ring. He didn't expect Lawrence to answer. This wasn't the shop phone. This was his personal phone. Very few people had the number and if he didn't recognize the incoming number, he likely wouldn't pick up. He didn't and after ten rings, voice-mail kicked in. No message, just a pause and a beep.

"It's me. No cell service, I'm calling from a payphone. I'll call back in two minutes."

While he waited, he glanced out the door. The F-150 was still there. Otherwise, the whole tableau looked the same. He wondered if the trucker had moved to his bar stool yet. He picked up the phone and dialed again.

"World's best barber and information merchant, how may I direct your call?" Lawrence's familiar voice crackled through the line.

Max couldn't help but smile. "I need to speak to the proprietor about a delicate matter."

"Max, my man!" Lawrence's tone shifted. "To what do I owe the pleasure? Last I heard, you were road-tripping it back to the land of fall foliage and maple syrup."

Max leaned against the wall, keeping his voice low. The breakfast rush had died down, but a few stragglers still nursed coffee at the counter. "Yeah, about that. I've hit a bit of a snag in West Virginia. Place called Grimswood."

"Grimswood? Sounds like the setting for a Stephen King novel."

"You're not far off," Max said, glancing around to ensure no one was paying attention. "Listen, I need your help. And probably Eddie's too."

There was a pause on the other end of the line. Lawrence was well aware of Max's penchant for finding himself in the middle of a maelstrom. "I'm listening."

Max gave Lawrence a quick rundown of the situation—the bridge and washed-out roads, Riley and Ethan, the missing hikers, Grave's End, and the mysterious hermit who might hold the key to it all. As he spoke, he could almost picture Lawrence's furrowed brow, the way he'd be tapping a pencil against his desk in the back room of the barber shop as he processed the information.

"Let me get this straight," Lawrence said when Max finished. "You're stuck in some backwoods Appalachian town with no cell service, no internet, and you've decided to play search and rescue for a couple of strangers?"

"When you put it that way, it does sound a little crazy," Max admitted.

"A little? Max, my friend, this is full-tilt bonkers. Even for you."

Max snorted. "That's your definition of civilization? No cable. No internet. Welcome to the borderlands."

"That's most people's definition these days," Lawrence replied. "I've heard about places like that. Didn't think they still existed. Even The Gambia has internet these days."

Max knew he was supposed to ask. Lawrence loved his minutiae. He gave it a second then caved. "The Gambia?"

"The smallest country on the African mainland and it's one of the few countries in the world that includes an article in its official name."

"Thank you, professor. Although the situation here is temporary. They'll be back online in a few days."

"Uh-huh," Lawrence said. "Why do everyone's problems have to be your problem? And let me ask you something else, Max. Have you ever even hiked before? Do you know the difference between an oak and a maple tree? Can you read a map? I'm pretty sure your survival skills only stretch to finding the next Dunkin'. If there's no cable, can't you just read one of your old paperbacks and wait for the roads to clear?"

"Finished the last one yesterday. I haven't spotted a bookstore or library yet."

"That might be the most disturbing thing you've told me about Grimswood so far." Lawrence was a big fan of the benefits of public libraries. There was a pause, then Lawrence sighed. "All right, what exactly do you need from me and Eddie?"

"I need you to find this hermit," Max said. "Someone's already tried digging into his whereabouts via Jake's laptop but came up empty. They think the pair might have communicated using the dark web."

Lawrence chuckled. "Someone might have tried, but not me and not Eddie. Even the dark web leaves footprints, my friend. Faint, but they're there."

Max felt a surge of hope. "So, you think you can find him?"

"I didn't say that since I assume ideally you want all this in the next fifteen minutes," Lawrence cautioned. "If we had a few days or a week even, I bet we could track him through the dark net, but still, we've got a few angles we can work. Man's gotta eat, right? Maybe we can get a handle on him that way. Or through utilities—light, power, that sort of thing."

"That's more than I had five minutes ago," Max said.

"You do come up with interesting problems, Max," Lawrence said, a mix of exasperation and amusement in his voice. "All right, leave it with us. We'll see what we can dig up."

"Thanks, Lawrence. I owe you one."

"You owe me several, but who's counting? Stay safe out there in the wilderness, city boy."

The line went dead, and Max hung up the receiver. He turned to find Patty watching him, one eyebrow raised.

"Everything all right, hon?" she asked.

Max nodded, forcing a smile. He wondered how much she'd overheard. And if it mattered. "Just checking in with a friend. Thanks for the change."

CHAPTER TWELVE

Max stepped out of the diner, the bell jingling behind him. The rain was finally letting up and, though there was no hint of sun, the stolid gray sky was a welcome change after the relentless deluge of the past few days. He paused for a moment, taking in a deep breath of the damp, earthy air. It made him think of Vic and Vermont. A worm of guilt churned in his stomach. Why was he doing this? Again. Getting involved in other people's problems. Rushing into a potentially dangerous situation. Why? For what? No immediate answers jumped to mind. At least none that he wanted to consider in the Sunrise Cafe parking lot.

As he started to cross the street toward the motel, his eyes were again drawn to the Ford F-150 parked in the lot. He hadn't noticed it earlier, but now he could clearly see the U.S. Forest Service shield on the door and the government license plate. Just as he approached, a shadow shifted in the cab and the driver's door swung open.

A tall man in his early 50s stepped out, his salt-and-pepper hair slightly disheveled. He wore the green uniform of a

Forest Service officer, the badge on his chest catching what little light filtered through the clouds.

"Are you Max?" the man called out, his voice carrying easily across the empty parking lot.

Max stopped halfway to his car, muscles tensing. He hadn't told anyone his name here. Or had he? Jeb hadn't asked. Nor had the deputy. Maybe he'd mentioned it to Riley. Or Ethan. He turned slowly, keeping his guard up. "That's me. And you are?"

The man approached, his stride purposeful but not threatening. "Buck Holcomb. I'm the district ranger for this area of the Monongahela National Forest." He extended a hand.

Max shook it, noting the firm grip and callused palm. The hand of a man used to hard work outdoors. "Are you looking for me?"

Buck's eyes scanned the area before settling back on Max. "Word travels fast in a small town like Grimswood. Especially when strangers start asking questions about missing hikers and local legends."

Max's eyebrow raised. "And that's why you're here? To find out what I know?"

"Not really," Buck admitted. "I'm sure I know everything you do and more. It's more to give you a friendly warning."

"A warning?" Max crossed his arms. "Are you the sheriff in this tale? Letting me know I have until sunset to get out of town?"

Buck sighed, leaning against his truck. "Look, I know why you're here—"

"I'm not sure what you heard, but I'm not here by choice. I'm here because some hopped up long-haul trucker hit a bridge support to the south and all this rain washed out my detour to the north."

"Okay, fair enough, but I know you've been talking to

Riley and Ethan. I know about Sarah and Jake. And I know about Vance Cotter's disappearance three years ago."

Max remained silent and waited for Buck to continue.

"I was here for that search, too," Buck said, his voice tinged with what sounded like regret. "We combed every inch of those woods. Brought in dogs, helicopters, the works. Found nothing."

"And you think the same thing's happened to Sarah and Jake," Max said.

Buck nodded. "It's a possibility we have to consider. But here's the thing, Max. These woods...they're dangerous. Even for experienced hikers. The terrain is treacherous, the weather unpredictable. And then there's Grave's End."

"What do you know about it?"

Buck's eyes met Max's. "I know it's a myth that's gotten people into trouble. Folks come here chasing stories and end up underestimating the real dangers of the wilderness."

"But there's more to it than just stories, isn't there?" Max pressed.

Buck was silent for a long moment, his eyes darting to the misty forest visible beyond the town's edge. He sighed heavily. "Look, what matters is that people are missing. The 'why' or 'how' doesn't change the fact that these woods are treacherous, even for experienced hikers."

Max realized that wasn't exactly an answer but might be all he'd get. "So that's your warning? Stay out of the woods?"

"My warning," Buck said, his voice low and intense, "is to be careful. These forests...they're unforgiving. It's easy to get turned around, to lose your bearings. That might sound like an overreaction standing here in a parking lot, but I promise you, it's the truth. And when that happens, things can go south fast.

"Let me tell you something else. More than 1600 people, probably more than that, go missing from national parks or other public lands each year. Hikers, canoers, day trippers. Children, God help me. One second they're there, the next they're gone.

"There is no big FBI or national database to track these cases. Hell, half the time the jurisdiction alone isn't clear and time gets wasted figuring out whose supposed to be in charge. And there's always the question of who is going to pay. People don't like to talk about that. It's an ugly truth but that doesn't make it any less true. Large searches can cost hundreds of thousands a day. That will wipe out a county budget real quick."

Max felt the weight of Buck's words settle in his gut. Buck's words carried the weight of experience. The disappointing experiences of having seen such disappearances firsthand.

"I appreciate the concern," Max replied, "and I understand the reality you laid out, but I can't just sit back and do nothing."

Buck nodded, a look of understanding crossing his face. "I get it. I do. It's the volunteers who make most rescue ops possible. Just...if you do go out there, be prepared. Really prepared. And don't go off alone. These woods have a way of swallowing people up, and I'd hate to see another name added to the list of the missing."

The intensity in Buck's voice was unmistakable. This wasn't just a routine warning; it was the plea of a man who had seen the forest's dangers firsthand.

"Why are you telling me this? Why come out here?" Max asked. "Why not just let me stumble around in the dark like everyone else?"

Buck pushed off from his truck, reaching for the door handle. "Despite what some folks around here might think, I want to find Sarah and Jake as much as anyone." He paused, one foot in the cab. "Just...watch your step. In more ways than one."

With that, Buck climbed into his truck and started the engine. Max watched as the F-150 pulled out of the lot and disappeared down the misty street, its taillights glowing dully in the gray light. Max stood there for a moment and pondered Buck's warning. That's what it was, however he wanted to couch it.

Max turned toward his room. Through the grimy office window, he caught sight of Jeb, the clerk, staring at him intently over the top of his ever-present Civil War book. Their eyes met for a brief moment before Jeb quickly looked down, pretending, at least, to be engrossed in his reading once more.

"What was that all about? Was that Buck Holcomb?" Riley asked. She was standing in the doorway, looking off down the road.

"Yup. He was welcoming me to town and encouraging me to leave at the same time."

"Word travels fast in Grimswood. I got the same speech a few days ago. You gonna listen?"

"About as much as you did."

"Good. Want to go shopping?"

CHAPTER THIRTEEN

"Where are we going?" Max asked, breaking the silence that had settled between them since leaving Grimswood. The silver Camry wound its way along the curving road, its suspension absorbing the occasional bump from loose gravel that had washed onto the asphalt during the recent downpours. The transmission whined as she accelerated around a curve. The car appeared solid and well used, but also in need of some maintenance. Max sat in the passenger seat, watching the dense forest pass by in a blur of green and brown.

"The proud town of nearby Elkton. We can get there via local roads. Patty came through for us. Made some calls to the head of the local volunteer search team. Hank Ramsey. Turns out her second cousin's husband's nephew or some such thing is involved. You know how it is in small towns—everyone's connected somehow."

Max nodded. It didn't work that way just in small towns. He knew cities and neighborhoods could also work that way. Half the people he knew in Southie growing up were related in some way if you went back a few generations. "And he's willing to help?"

"He told her the fire department in Elkton keeps some extra equipment for volunteer teams that might end up in woods overnight. Said we were welcome to check it out. Borrow it, if needed." Riley's lips quirked up in a half smile. "Maybe for a donation."

"I've got no problem with that," Max replied. He had more cash than he knew what to do with, thanks to Lawrence's investing strategies. Never mind where that seed money might have come from originally. He didn't dip into it often and when he did, he tried to spread it around where it might do some good.

"We can also pilfer some of Ethan's supplies," Riley added. "He brought enough for at least three people, probably with redundancies within those."

Max chuckled. "Yeah, he struck me as the type to keep plenty of spares around."

Riley's smile tightened, the muscles in her jaw visibly clenching. Max sensed he was nearing that invisible trip wire again. He went quiet, and Riley followed suit.

For the next fifteen minutes, they drove in silence through a tunnel of woods that pressed in close on both sides of the road. The trees loomed overhead, their branches creating a canopy that filtered the weak sunlight into dappled patterns on the windshield.

The radio, which had been playing a block of classic George Jones, faded to static. Riley reached out and snapped it off. "Sorry," she said. "Ethan and I...we have history. It's a long story."

Max nodded, knowing better than to pry further. But there was something else he was curious about. "I saw you at the bar last night," he said carefully.

Riley's eyebrow quirked up. "Oh?" Maybe she'd been waiting for him to ask.

"Those guys...they deserved what they got."

A ghost of a smile flitted across Riley's face. "Oh, no doubt."

He noticed the ring on her left hand and remembered the guy's reaction when he tried to lean in with his pickup line. The ring was slim and gold with a small, rounded detail on top almost like a shark's fin. "Nice ring. Do you need to use it a lot."

The quick smile again. "Not a lot but it comes in handy." She took her hand off the wheel and used her thumb to turn the ring slightly. "My dad gave one to my sister and a matching one to me when we went off to college."

"Self-defense jewelry."

"Best present I ever got."

Max hesitated, he wasn't sure if she was kidding or not, then pressed on. "I don't need the Ethan story, but how about you? I feel like I should at least know your last name before heading off into the woods with you."

Riley was quiet for a long moment, her eyes fixed on the road ahead. Just as Max thought she wasn't going to answer, she spoke.

"Keller. Riley Keller. I grew up in Newton, same as Sarah. But we couldn't have been more different as kids." Riley's voice became more relaxed as she talked. "Sarah was all sunshine and smiles, captain of the debate team, straight-A student. Me? I was the troublemaker, always getting into scraps, sneaking out at night."

"Having fun."

"That's what I would have said at the time." She paused, a fond smile playing on her lips. "But Sarah...she never gave up on me. Even when our parents were at their wits' end, she'd be there, patching me up after a fight or helping me study for a test I'd forgotten about."

Max listened intently, watching as emotions played across Riley's face like shadows. He could picture the sisters in the leafy, affluent suburbs of Newton, distinctly different from his own upbringing on the streets of Southie.

"When I turned 18, I enlisted. Army. It was...an escape, I guess. Not that I had many other options given my grades. But it was a good way to channel all that restless energy into something productive." Riley's knuckles whitened on the steering wheel. "Did two tours in Afghanistan. It was...not productive."

Max nodded silently.

"When I came back, I was a mess. PTSD, nightmares, the whole nine yards. And there was Sarah, once again, picking up the pieces." Riley's voice cracked slightly. "She'd just finished nursing school. Insisted on moving in with me, helping me through the worst of it. Said it was good practice for her career."

Riley fell silent for a moment, lost in memory. The car rounded a bend and a shaft of sunlight broke through the trees, illuminating the silver streak in her hair.

"Is that when..." Max gestured vaguely toward her hair.

Riley's hand unconsciously went to the silver streak. "Yeah. Started showing up not long after I got back. Doctors said it was stress related. Sarah used to joke it made me look distinguished."

She took a deep breath before continuing. "Anyway, it was Sarah who got me into martial arts. Said I needed a healthy outlet for all my pent-up energy and hypervigilance. Turns out, I had a knack for it. Started competing, even opened my own dojo."

"And now you're here, looking for her," Max said.

"She's always been there for me. Always. And now...now it's my turn to be there for her."

———

The car crested a hill, and suddenly the woods opened up, revealing a sprawling valley below. In the distance, a small town—Elkton, Max presumed—nestled against the base of a mountain.

"We're almost there," Riley said, her voice regaining its earlier businesslike tone.

The Camry rolled into Elkton, its main street presenting a different face from Grimswood's worn-down charm. Here, freshly painted storefronts and neatly trimmed trees lined the sidewalks, giving the town an air of tidy prosperity that seemed at odds with the rugged wilderness surrounding it.

Riley navigated through the light mid-morning traffic, her eyes scanning for signs to the fire department.

"There," Max pointed, spotting a redbrick building with a large garage door.

As Riley pulled into a streetside parking lot, Max turned to her. "Whatever it takes, we're going to find her," he said.

Riley met his gaze "Goddam right we are," she replied.

———

Riley and Max entered the fire station through an open garage door, the smell of oil, rubber, and canvas immediately filling their nostrils. The interior was cavernous, with high ceilings and concrete floors that amplified their footsteps. One bay was empty, while the other housed an old, almost antique fire engine. Its red paint was faded but still gleaming, brass fittings polished to a shine. The truck seemed more suited for a parade than fighting fires.

A row of lockers stood along one wall, their doors adorned with faded nameplates. A few had family photos taped to their fronts. The opposite wall was lined with neatly organized equipment: coiled hoses, axes, and other fire-fighting paraphernalia. Despite the signs of recent use—a coffee mug on a desk, a half-finished crossword puzzle—the place appeared empty.

Their eyes were drawn to four various-sized packs hanging on the far wall. They approached, examining each one before selecting the pack that seemed best suited for Max's size. Together, they began to inventory its contents: a neatly rolled foam pad, a compact tent, a tightly compressed sleeping bag, water bottles, an emergency whistle, a comprehensive first aid kit, waterproof matches, a utility knife, a headlamp, a flash-light, and a water filtration system. Each item was meticu-lously packed, a testament to the care and experience of the volunteer team. Or the necessity, and potential danger, of one being missing.

"Pretty comprehensive," Max commented, turning the water filtration system over in his hands.

Riley nodded, her eyes scanning the contents they'd laid out on the floor. "Standard stuff for search and rescue. Though I'm glad to see that water filter. Didn't expect that. Dehydration can be a killer out there."

"Speaking from experience?" Max asked, glancing at her, remembering her time overseas.

Riley's jaw tightened slightly. "Let's just say I've seen what happens when you're not prepared."

Max nodded. "At least we're starting off on the right foot," he said, replacing the items as neatly as he could.

As he zipped up the pack, the sound of tires on gravel drew their attention. Through the open bay door, they watched a dusty Chevy Silverado pull up. A man in his late 50s climbed out, his movements fluid despite his age. He was tall and lean, with sun-weathered skin and salt-and-pepper hair peeking out from under a worn baseball cap.

"Hank Ramsey?" Max asked.

"That's right."

"I'm Max. This is Riley. Sarah's sister," Max replied, shaking Hank's hand. "Thanks for letting us borrow some equipment." He gestured to the bag at his feet.

"Of course. I hate to see folks go out there unprepared."

"You live in Elkton?"

Hank nodded, his eyes crinkling at the corners as he smiled. "Born and raised. Teach geography and environmental science over at the high school. Been doing that for about 25 years now. The search and rescue work? That's my summer gig and weekend warrior routine." He laughed softly. "Keeps me busy and out of trouble. Plus, it's a way to put all that map reading and terrain knowledge to good use outside the classroom."

Riley stepped forward, her posture straightening almost imperceptibly. "How long have you been leading the search team?"

"Going on fifteen years now," Hank replied, his tone becoming more serious. "Seen my fair share of lost hikers and tough situations. But don't you worry, we take every search seriously, whether it's a kid who wandered off a trail or..." he paused, his eyes meeting Riley's, "...or something more complex."

"So you were around for the search of Vance Cotter?" Max asked.

"That's right. We were called out quick. Most of the locals ended up pitching in at some point. I helped coordinate the first hasty teams with Silas."

"What do you think happened out there?"

Hank's eyes hardened, his gaze fixed on the line of search packs. "The wilderness doesn't forgive mistakes," he said. "It's not malicious, but it's not merciful either." There was no laughter in Hank's voice now.

"Vance was no newbie in the woods. He had plenty of experience," Riley said, a little edge in her voice, "and respect."

Hank shrugged. "No disrespect. Mistakes happen."

"What about wildlife? Bears? Mountain lions?"

"I don't go into the woods without my gun. There's a reason for that but unless you stumble onto a bear and her cubs, black bears aren't usually a problem. We don't have grizzlies." He shrugged again. "Mountain lions are officially extinct on the eastern seaboard, according to the government. Coyotes, wild boar, wolves. They're all pretty shy and typically stay away from humans. And if something like that had happened..." he paused, side eyed Riley, "animals don't have the best table manners."

"You would have found evidence."

"We would have found *something*. One team found an area of disturbance, I think that's what the official report eventually called it. But no blood. No evidence of remains. He was just gone like the others. He just happened to have a different last name. Got more attention, but the same result."

"You know about the others," Max said and regretted the question almost as soon as it was out of his mouth. Of course he did. It was written in the lines on his face. He wasn't just talking about Vance.

"Buck and I have talked about it a bit. At least five, maybe more."

"Seven," Riley said.

Hank didn't question her, just nodded. "There are various numbers floating around."

"You think that's a lot for the Monongahela?"

"It's not a little. That's for damn sure."

CHAPTER FOURTEEN

As Hank's words faded, the atmosphere in the garage seemed to shift and a silence fell over them. Talking about the dead. Whispering about ghosts. Max was familiar with ghosts. The kind that haunted dreams and whispered in the dark, their voices a mix of accusation and plea. He'd learned to carry their weight. He glanced at Riley, noting the tightness in her jaw, and knew he wasn't the only one. She had her own demons lurking in her head, different perhaps, but no less real.

Clearing his throat, Hank gestured toward the pack, clearly eager to move the conversation in a different direction. "I talked to Buck Holcomb on my way over. You're heading into a rough area. That gear will serve you well out there," he said. "But what about clothes? You folks got proper attire for the conditions?"

The abrupt change of subject was jarring, but Max felt a sense of relief at the return to practical matters.

Riley and Max exchanged glances. "I came from Texas," Max admitted. "I have a few things, but maybe not the right things."

Hank's brow furrowed as he considered their situation. "You're gonna need layers, that's for sure. Late August, early September in the Monongahela can be tricky."

He paused, his eyes taking on a distant look as if visualizing the forest. "During the day, temps can climb into the 80s, maybe even 90s in the lower elevations. But at night? It can drop into the 40s, especially up in the higher parts of the forest."

Max nodded, taking in the information.

Hank continued, "And don't let the summer fool you. We can get rain any time of year, and when it comes, it often comes hard. You've seen that firsthand the past few days. The forest canopy helps out there, but you'll want waterproof gear.

"And the fog..." He shook his head. "It can roll in quick, especially in the mornings or after rain. Can make visibility a real challenge."

He turned back to Max. "So yeah, you're gonna need those layers. Moisture-wicking base layer, insulating mid-layer, and a waterproof outer shell. What about boots and a good jacket?"

"I have boots," Max said. "But a good jacket...any places in town where I might buy some things?"

Hank shook his head. "Not really. Most folks go up to the Walmart in Clarksburg for gear these days. Put all the little places out of business over the last 10 years. Can't get there now though, with the bridge being out."

Max's eyes fell on Hank. He was two, maybe three inches taller, but Max was a little wider in the chest and shoulders. It might all even out. Beggars and choosers and all. "How about you?"

"What about me?"

"Do you have some clothes I could...rent? For a donation to the volunteer fund."

Hank hesitated, his hand unconsciously running along the sleeve of his shirt. For a moment, it seemed he might refuse. Then, with a slight nod, he began to shrug it off. "Suppose I could help you out. Missus is always on me to clean out my closet."

———

The gravel crunched under the tires of Riley's Camry as they pulled into Hank's driveway. A neat, white-painted house stood before them, its front porch adorned with hanging baskets of colorful flowers. The scent of freshly cut grass hung in the air. A small John Deere tractor stood by the edge of the attached garage. A chore finished, but not completed while he ran down to the fire station.

Hank led them up the porch steps, the old wood creaking slightly under their feet. As he opened the door, warm, cinnamon-scented air wafted out to greet them.

"Martha," Hank called out, "we've got company."

A petite woman with silver hair and kind eyes appeared from what Max assumed was the kitchen. She wiped her hands on her apron, leaving faint traces of flour. Max thought she looked like the quintessential grandmother from a Norman Rockwell painting transplanted to the hills of West Virginia. He wondered briefly if she always looked like that on a weekday afternoon, or if it was for their benefit. But as he watched her warm smile and effortless movements, he decided no, Martha always looked like this. It wasn't an act; it was simply who she was.

"Well, hello there," she said, her voice warm and welcoming. "I'm Martha. I just pulled some cookies out of the oven. Would you like some? Maybe some coffee to go with them?"

Max opened his mouth to accept, but Riley spoke first.

"Thank you, ma'am, but we're in a bit of a hurry. We appreciate the offer, though."

Martha's smile dimmed slightly, but she nodded in understanding. "Of course, dear. You must be here about those missing hikers. Patty called. Such a terrible thing."

Hank cleared his throat. "Martha, I'm going to take them upstairs. See if we can't find some proper gear for the young man here."

As they climbed the stairs, the scent of cinnamon faded, replaced by the musty smell of old wood and the faint aroma of mothballs. Hank led them to a small bedroom that had been converted into a makeshift storage space. Cardboard boxes labeled with neat handwriting lined the walls, and a large cedar chest sat at the foot of an old brass bed.

Hank opened the chest, releasing a whiff of cedar and memories. "Let's see what we've got here," he said, rummaging through the contents.

Over the next twenty minutes, they pieced together outfits suitable for the Monongahela's unpredictability. Max found himself the new owner of a pair of sturdy, water-resistant hiking pants, two moisture-wicking base layer shirts, a warm fleece mid-layer, and three pairs of thick wool socks. Hank even produced a pair of gaiters to protect Max's lower legs from brush and debris.

"These should keep you dry and comfortable," Hank said. "The rain shell has a hood, too."

Max tried a few things on, just to be sure. The clothes fit well enough, each piece carrying the slight stiffness of infrequent use, but the unmistakable quality of gear meant to last.

"How does it feel?" Riley asked, eyeing Max's new attire critically.

Max rolled his shoulders, testing the range of motion in the layers. "Good. A little loose, but comfortable. I feel... ready."

Hank nodded approvingly. "That's the idea. Now, let's head back downstairs. I've got one more thing for you."

In the living room, Hank disappeared into a closet, emerging with a well-worn waxed canvas coat. "This here's been with me on more searches than I can count," he said, holding it out to Max. "Plenty of pockets for gear, and it'll keep you warm and dry through a hurricane. And I mean that quite literally. You take care of it and it'll take care of you."

Max slipped on the coat, feeling its weight settle on his shoulders. It smelled of the outdoors—a mix of pine, earth, and something indefinable that spoke of countless hours spent in the wilderness.

"Hank, I can't take this," Max said, his hand running over the weathered material.

"You can and you will," Hank replied firmly. "Where you're going, you're gonna need it more than I do. The rest you can keep, but maybe bring this back if you get the chance."

Max nodded, reaching for his wallet. He pulled out a thick wad of cash, holding it out to Hank.

Hank's eyes widened slightly at the sight of the money. He held up his hands, shaking his head. "Now, I can't take that. It's too much. This is just neighbors helping neighbors."

"Please," Max insisted. "We agreed. If not for the clothes and gear, then consider it a donation to the search and rescue team. For future searches. I'm sure you could use some new equipment."

Hank hesitated, then slowly reached out and took the money. "I appreciate it. We'll put it to good use."

They said goodbye to Martha and made their way back outside, the midday sun casting short shadows across Hank's neatly manicured lawn.

"Anything else we should know before we head out?" Riley asked Hank, her voice tight with barely contained impatience. They were late to meet Ethan at the Sunrise, which meant they were also letting more time pass before they could start into the woods. Max could almost feel it like static coming off her skin.

Hank's expression grew serious. "Just remember, the forest out there...it's not forgiving. Stay alert, stay together, and don't take any unnecessary risks. You want to be damn careful in those woods." His voice carried a note of something Max couldn't quite place. Hope? Doubt?

As they climbed back into the Camry, Max caught sight of Martha watching from the window, her smile doing nothing to hide the underlying expression of concern and something that looked almost like fear. He raised a hand in farewell, and she responded with a small, tentative wave before letting the curtain settle back into place over the window.

CHAPTER FIFTEEN

The Sunrise Cafe was in the midst of its post-lunch lull when Max and Riley arrived back in Grimswood. The clatter of dishes from the kitchen had subsided to a rhythmic hum of the dishwasher, punctuated by the occasional clink of a coffee mug being refilled. A few patrons nursed soda or coffee at the counter, engaged in low conversation with Patty, who wiped down the already clean counter. She gave them a wave and a smile as they entered.

Ethan sat in the same booth near the back, a spread of maps covering the table. His empty plate had been pushed to the side, a half-empty coffee mug leaving a faint ring on one of the maps.

As they approached, Ethan glanced up, his brow furrowed. "Took you long enough," he said, his tone tinged with annoyance.

Riley slid into the booth across from him, Max following suit. "We got held up. But we're here now."

Ethan nodded, his fingers drumming on the table. "I've got the initial route planned out," he said, pointing to a red line snaking across one of the maps. "Based on the information we have, this seems like our best bet."

Max leaned in, studying the map. The line wound through a maze of contour lines and cryptic symbols, terminating at a point marked with an X. "And after that?"

Ethan shook his head. "That's where we go blind. I've been over it a dozen times, but after that second known location from Sarah's call, we're in the dark."

Riley's jaw tightened. "Any good news?"

"Weather should improve for the next few days," Ethan replied, though his tone suggested that wasn't much comfort. "Which only means a fifty percent chance of torrential rains instead of the usual eighty percent."

"I'm not waiting any longer."

"I know," Ethan said, his eyes meeting hers. "We go at first light. It's our best shot."

A moment of understanding passed between them. Riley reached out, touching Ethan's hand briefly. "Thanks."

Ethan cleared his throat, looking back down at the maps. "But after that second known location, we have the same problem. Where did they go? I've looked at the surrounding areas and there are likely paths, but...I can't be sure."

He ran a hand through his hair, frustration evident in his voice. "Our chances of success would be much, much better if we knew what they knew. Even then...it's not 100 percent we'll find them."

Both Riley and Ethan turned to Max. His job was the hermit.

Max nodded, understanding the unspoken question. "Let me go check on that," he said, sliding out of the booth.

He made his way to the payphone near the entrance, fished out some coins, and dialed.

The phone rang three times before a gruff voice answered.

"Took you long enough. I thought you said this was a rush job?"

If Lawrence was joking around it meant good news.

"You found something?"

"We can't lock it down from up here, but we've got two possibilities for you to check out. Eddie thinks both are high probabilities based on the data we have."

"What do you have?" Max leaned against the wall, his free hand absently tracing the graffiti etched into the wall next to the phone. "I'm all ears."

"All right, so we've been digging into property records, satellite imagery, and looked at delivery patterns from Amazon and UPS. As far as we can tell, no local store does deliveries. We've narrowed it down to two possible locations for your hermit."

Max straightened. "Go on."

"First location is an old property about fifteen miles northwest of Grimswood. It's not hooked up to any town services, but here's the kicker—property taxes are still being paid, like clockwork, every year."

"By whom? Could be someone just paying on the land. Lives somewhere else," Max said.

"Hold your horses," Lawrence replied. "They are paid by a trust. We cross-referenced with satellite imagery. There's definitely a dwelling on the property. Looks well maintained too, not some rundown shack. More than one building. We can see at least one truck in the sat images."

"Also owned by the trust."

"That's right."

"Okay, I agree that's worth a look. Tell me about the second location."

"This one's interesting. It's completely off grid, like the first one, also owned by a blind corporate trust registered in Delaware. That's a dead end. It's about twenty miles east of

Grimswood. Dirt road. The definition of the middle of nowhere. No official records of habitation, no building permits, services, etc. Heavy canopy cover, but it looks like *something* is there."

"Abandoned?"

"That was our first thought, too, but we noticed something odd in the local delivery patterns."

"Abandoned buildings don't get deliveries."

"Yeah, get this. There's a Walmart distribution center about fifty miles from Grimswood. They make regular deliveries to a store in Clarksburg, a few towns over, right? But once a month, like clockwork, there's an additional stop on their route. It's always the same spot, just off a dirt road that doesn't show up on most maps."

Max's brow furrowed. He didn't need to ask how Lawrence got inside Walmart's systems. His half-brother Eddie was a computer hacking savant. Nothing short of the NSA could keep Eddie out. "A hermit getting Walmart deliveries?"

"Hey, even recluses need toilet paper," Lawrence said. "But seriously, it's a substantial delivery each time. We're talking enough supplies to last a month for one or two people."

"Any idea what's in these deliveries?"

"Mostly non-perishables, some basic electronics. Batteries, that sort of thing. Oh, and get this—a lot of external hard drives. Like, an unusual amount."

Max's mind raced with the implications. "Sounds like someone who's doing a lot of data storage. Or maybe sharing large files?"

"That's what we thought too," Lawrence agreed. "Could be your guy is into some heavy-duty online activity. Mining for bitcoin. Running a server for a site. Maybe that's how Jake made contact."

"Anything else stand out?"

"Well, there's a mix of survival gear and tech stuff. Water purification tablets, propane tanks, solar chargers. Preservation supplies like vacuum sealer bags. Oh, and a steady supply of coffee and pet food."

"Pet food?"

"Yeah, suggests your hermit might have a furry friend. Or maybe he just really likes kibble," Lawrence said.

Max nodded, processing the information. "Sounds like someone prepared for long-term isolation but still very much connected to the digital world."

"Exactly," Lawrence confirmed. "Whoever this is, they're not just hiding from the world. They're watching it."

Max glanced over at Riley and Ethan, still hunched over their maps. "Hold on one second, Lawrence." He hustled back to the table and grabbed a pen and one of Ethan's small pocket notebooks and headed back to the phone. Patty gave him an odd look as he passed, then shook her head. He picked up the receiver. "This is good, Lawrence. Really good. Give me the addresses or the coordinates for both locations. One of the guys here has detailed maps, we'll find them." Lawrence read them out and Max copied them down. "Thanks, Lawrence. I owe you again."

"I'll add it to your tab. Be careful out there, Max. I can't get your back this time. Makes me a little nervous. And a little jealous to miss out on the adventure. Just...watch yourself, okay? And keep us posted."

"Will do. Thanks again, Lawrence."

Max hung up the phone, the plastic clicking loudly in the quiet diner. He stood there for a moment, processing the information Lawrence had given him. Then, almost without thinking, he picked up the receiver again and dialed another number.

"Hello?"

"It's me."

"Still stuck?"

Max felt himself smile at the sound of Vic's voice. "Yeah, still here in Grimswood. Cell phones are still out but the diner pay phone works."

"Making yourself useful?"

The way she said it, Max knew immediately. "You talked to Lawrence, didn't you?"

The pair had never actually met in person but had still somehow become fast friends.

"Yes, I got worried when I didn't hear from you." There was a pause, then, "Be careful."

Max leaned against the wall, feeling the cool surface against his forehead. He appreciated that Vic didn't press him for details or question his decision. She understood his need to help, to try.

"How's Bailey doing?" Max asked, changing the subject.

"Better. The vet says he's on his way to a full recovery. He's already trying to chase squirrels again."

Max chuckled, picturing the coonhound hobbling after the furry tree rats that surrounded the property. "Sounds like he's back to his old self."

"Almost. He still whines when he hears certain noises. The vet says it might take time for the psychological scars to heal."

He understood all too well how some wounds went deeper than the physical. "How's the lodge?" he asked. Vic owned The Cliffside, an old-school motor lodge in a small town in Vermont just over the Massachusetts border. It was one of her many small-business ventures.

"Quiet. It's that lull between summer vacationers and the fall leaf-peepers invading. I've been using the downtime to repaint some of the rooms."

"Let me guess, you're doing it yourself instead of hiring someone."

"You know me too well," Vic replied, and Max could hear the smile in her voice. "Why pay someone when I can do it myself?"

"Because you're supposed to be the owner, not the handyman?"

"I prefer 'jack of all trades,' thank you very much. Plus, my preferred handyman is away."

"You could have Rob help."

"Rob's unavailable for the time being."

"What happened?"

"He volunteered to help with the town's Founder's Day fireworks display."

Max felt a mixture of amusement and concern. "Rob and explosives? That doesn't sound like a great combination."

"It wasn't. He claimed he watched a bunch of YouTube tutorials on pyrotechnics."

"Oh no."

"Oh yes. Everything was fine until he decided to check why one of the mortars wasn't firing."

Max winced. "Please tell me he didn't look down the tube."

"No, thank God. But he did try to re-light it manually. With a lighter. While leaning over it."

"How bad?"

"Could've been worse. The thing went off right as he was bending down. Singed off his eyebrows and gave him some nasty burns on both hands."

Max shook his head. "So I'm guessing Rob's not allowed near fireworks anymore?"

"Or matches. Or lighters. Or anything more incendiary than a glow stick. The town manager threatened to make him take a safety course before he's allowed to so much as light a birthday candle."

"How's he doing now?"

"Both hands are wrapped up like a mummy. Can't do much of anything for himself. Sally from the diner has been bringing him meals. I think he's milking it a bit now, to be honest."

Max chuckled. "Sounds like Rob. So no help from him for a while then?"

"Nope. He can barely hold a spoon, let alone a paint-brush. No one asks how he handles the bathroom."

Their conversation continued, touching on the mundane details of life back in Vermont. Max found himself relaxing as they talked, the tension of the past few days easing from his shoulders.

As they spoke, the diner's ambient sounds faded into the background. The clink of dishes from the kitchen, the low murmur of other patrons' conversations, even the hum of the refrigerator behind the counter—all of it receded, leaving only Vic's voice in his ear.

"Oh, before I forget," Vic said, "Mrs. Abernathy stopped by looking for you."

Max groaned. "Please tell me you didn't give her my cell number."

"And deprive myself of the entertainment when you get back? Not a chance."

"You're evil, you know that?"

"I prefer delightfully mischievous," Vic retorted.

There was a pause. Max realized that hearing Vic's voice had grounded him, reminding him of the life he'd built back in Vermont. He had people waiting for him. People who might come looking if he went missing. Eventually Max said, "I should get going," noticing Riley and Ethan looking his way from their booth.

"All right," Vic replied. "Just...be careful, okay? I need my night manager back in one piece."

"Yes, ma'am," Max said, a smile tugging at his lips. "I'll check in when I can."

"You'd better. And Max?"

"Yeah?"

"Good luck."

The line went dead, leaving Max holding the receiver, the dial tone a low hum in his ear. He placed it back in its cradle, taking a moment to compose himself before heading back to the booth.

CHAPTER SIXTEEN

The Camry bounced and whined as they wound their way through the dense forest, following the coordinates Lawrence had provided. Ethan had plenty of maps. He had been able to pick out the location, or at least the approximate location, of both sites and was guiding them from the back seat.

"It should be coming up on the left," he said, now leaning forward from between the seats.

As they rounded a bend, a sprawling property came into view. A sturdy log cabin stood at its center, a touch of smoke curling lazily from the chimney. Max could see where the wood differed slightly as the house had been repaired and added to over the years. The afternoon light glinted off solar panels on the roof, a modern touch against the rustic backdrop.

Riley slowed the car to a crawl. "This can't be right," she muttered.

Max squinted through the windshield. A high fence surrounded the property, its top bristling with coils of razor wire. Yellow signs dotted the perimeter at regular intervals, their bold black lettering clearly visible: NO TRESPASSING - VIOLATORS WILL BE SHOT.

"Friendly bunch," Ethan remarked.

As they inched closer, the fence seemed to stretch endlessly in both directions before disappearing into the woods again. Beyond it, the property bustled with activity. A large vegetable garden sprawled to one side of the cabin, its neat rows bursting with late-summer produce. On the other, a series of outbuildings dotted the landscape.

"Look," Max pointed, "chicken coops."

Sure enough, a flock of hens pecked at the ground near one of the structures, overseen by a watchful rooster. Farther back, they could make out what looked like a greenhouse, its glass panels reflecting the morning sun and a paddock for larger animals. It reminded Max of the Amish farms from his time on Prince Edward Island in Canada.

"This is no hermit," Riley said. "This is a full-on homestead."

A chorus of barking erupted, and three large dogs appeared from behind the cabin, racing toward the fence. Their powerful bodies moved with purpose, hackles raised as they fixed their eyes on the unfamiliar vehicle.

"I think that's our cue to leave," Max said.

Riley nodded, but before she could put the car in reverse, movement near the cabin caught their attention. A man emerged, shotgun in hand. Even from this distance, his stance radiated wariness.

"Definitely not our guy," Ethan murmured. "Too confrontational."

Riley began to back up slowly. The dogs paced along the fence, their barks echoing through the damp air.

As they retreated, Max caught sight of something that cemented their decision. Near the cabin's porch, a woman stood watching them, a toddler balanced on her hip. An older child peeked out from behind her skirt.

"Family," Max said quietly. "That doesn't feel right. This isn't the place."

Riley continued to back up, one eye on the dogs and one eye on the mirror. They drove in silence for a minute, the tension gradually easing as the homestead disappeared from view. Finally, Ethan broke the silence.

"Well, that was a bust."

Riley sighed and took her foot off the gas. The Camry rolled to a stop on the lonely road, her fingers drummed on the steering wheel. "Not a complete bust. We have more information, and we know where not to look now."

"True," Max agreed. "And it reinforces something about the area. You didn't learn anything with casual questions because people out here value their privacy. Our hermit might have similar security measures."

"Great," Ethan muttered. "So we might be walking into a fortress."

"Or worse," Riley added, her voice tight. "If that's how regular folks live out here, imagine what a true recluse might have set up." She hit the gas, and they started moving again.

Max gazed out the window, watching the trees blur past. "We'll cross that bridge when we come to it. For now, let's focus on finding the second location. See what we see."

———

Ethan guided them back to paved roads and a few minutes later they rolled back through Grimswood, this time heading in the opposite direction. The tired town center unspooled quickly through the windshield. A small hardware store, its windows displaying a jumble of tools and gardening supplies. Next door, a tired-looking laundromat, a lone customer visible through its foggy windows. Farther down, a small library stood nestled between an antique shop and a shuttered building that might have once been a movie theater, its marquee long-since blank. At the end of the row, a faded sign announced 'Grimswood General Store,' the peeling paint suggesting it had seen better days. Its porch was adorned with stacked bags of pet food and a rusting ice chest. Then, the familiar Crossroads Inn and the Crooked Nail followed by the two-story block of the professional building.

As they approached the Sunrise Cafe, its windows reflected a sudden burst of golden light. The clouds had finally broken, allowing the sun to peek through for the first time in days. The unexpected brightness made them all squint.

"Well, I'll be," Riley murmured, her eyes on the sky.

"I'd almost forgotten what the sun looks like," Ethan said.

"Feels weird, doesn't it? After all that rain."

"Maybe it's a good sign," Max said.

They passed the cafe, its sun-drenched windows now offering a clear view inside. It was mostly empty inside. Max spotted the trucker on his stool. Patty stood behind the counter, her hand shielding her eyes as she peered out, watching their car move down the street.

Then Grimswood was gone, and they were back in the tunnel of trees. They drove on, Ethan with two maps spread open on the back seat. Twice they had to backtrack, Ethan apologizing then insisting they turn where no road seemed to exist.

"This can't be right," Riley muttered, peering through the windshield at a solid wall of greenery.

Max scanned the tree line, then pointed. "No, he might be right. There. See that gap?"

Barely visible, a narrow dirt track snaked between two large oaks. Branches hung low, obscuring the entrance.

"Looks like someone goes out of their way not to trim back that brush," Ethan said.

"That's probably the point," Max replied. "If you're trying to stay hidden, you don't want to be easy to find."

Riley eased the Camry onto the track. Immediately, branches scraped against the sides of the car, their fingers leaving trails in the dust on the windows. The suspension groaned as they navigated around potholes and over exposed roots.

"Good thing we didn't bring anything bigger," Ethan commented, wincing as a particularly loud scrape echoed through the car. "A truck would never make it through here."

For nearly a mile, they crept along the overgrown path. The forest pressed in close on both sides, the newly-arrived sun barely penetrating the thick canopy above. Then, suddenly, they were through. The trees gave way to a small clearing.

Riley brought the car to a stop and they all leaned forward, taking in the scene before them.

A small, weatherworn house stood in the center of the clearing, its ashen planks blending seamlessly with the surrounding forest. The roof sagged slightly in the middle and vines crept up one side, as if nature was slowly reclaiming the structure.

To the left of the house, a shed or small barn listed to one side, its doors hanging crookedly on rusted hinges. On the right, a second smaller building that might have once been a workshop stood, its windows dark and grimy.

Behind the house, barely visible, Max spotted the metal roof of what looked like a greenhouse glinting in the sunlight.

"This is more like it," Max said. "A casting director couldn't have done better. It definitely feels like a hermit's place."

"Or a psycho killer," Ethan said.

"Nah," Max replied. "What would a psycho killer do with a greenhouse?"

They sat in silence for a moment, the only sound the ticking of the Camry's cooling engine. No signs of life stirred in the clearing. No dogs barked. No chickens clucked. The stillness was almost oppressive.

"No dogs," Riley observed. "That's a relief."

Max remembered Lawrence's words. "No loose dogs, at least. The delivery manifest mentioned pet food."

"Great," Ethan said.

They exchanged glances, then slowly opened their doors. As they stepped out, the forest seemed to hold its breath. Their footsteps on the packed earth sounded unnaturally loud in the quiet clearing. The air smelled of wet loam and damp wood, with an underlying mustiness that spoke of decay and neglect. A gentle breeze rustled the leaves overhead, sending drops of water and dappled shadows dancing across the ground.

They stood there, taking in the scene. The house showed no signs of recent activity. No smoke curled from the chimney. No lights shone in the windows. The small garden to the side looked slightly overgrown, vegetables waiting on their vines.

"Looks deserted," Ethan whispered, as if afraid to break the silence.

Max didn't reply but agreed. It *felt* empty.

Riley nodded, her eyes scanning the tree line. "But recently. Look at the path. It's been used."

Max followed her gaze. The narrow track that led to the house from the outbuildings and garden was clear of debris, unlike the overgrown driveway they'd come in on. Someone had been here, and not too long ago.

"The last delivery was two weeks ago," Max said and took a step toward the house. "Only one way to find out."

The porch steps creaked under his weight as he approached the front door. Paint peeled from the weathered wood in long strips, curling like pale fingers. The windows on either side were grimy, their curtains drawn.

Max raised his hand, hesitated for a moment, then rapped his knuckles against the door. The sound echoed through the clearing, startlingly loud.

They waited, the seconds stretching out. No response. No sounds from inside.

Max tried again, louder this time. "Hello? Anyone home?"

His voice seemed to be swallowed by the surrounding forest.

He turned back to Riley and Ethan, who had followed him onto the porch. "What do you think?"

Riley's hand hovered near her hip. A habit from her time overseas or she carried a concealed weapon. Her eyes were bright with a shininess that Max recognized. He felt the same anticipation in his chest.

"Could be out. Or hiding," she said.

Ethan shifted nervously. "Or watching us right now."

Max nodded, considering their options. The sun was sinking lower, casting long shadows across the clearing. They didn't have much daylight left.

"We came all this way," he said finally. "Might as well take a look around. But stay alert."

Max cast a final look at the silent house before stepping off the porch. As the trio fanned out across the property, an uneasy prickle crawled up his spine. The forest loomed around them, a thick, almost impenetrable wall. Did it want to keep them in or keep them out?

CHAPTER SEVENTEEN

The trio headed toward the dilapidated shed. No one said it out loud but sticking together seemed like the best plan for now. The structure was larger than it had first appeared, its siding stretching nearly twenty feet in length back toward the encroaching tree. Two wide hanging doors dominated the front, their paint peeling and wood splintering. Max reached for one of the doors, surprised by how easily it swung open despite its decrepit appearance.

"That's odd," he muttered, running his hand along the edge of the door. "These hinges are practically new."

Inside, they found themselves in a small, dusty antechamber. Old tools hung on the walls, and a workbench covered in cobwebs occupied one corner. But it was the interior wall that caught Max's attention. A second set of doors, these made of thick, solid wood and in remarkably good condition, blocked their path. A heavy new padlock secured them shut.

"Now we're getting somewhere," Riley said, her eyes scanning the room.

Ethan pointed to a small window set into the interior wall. "Look there."

Max approached the window. A thin curtain on the inside covered most of the window, but not all of it. Through a narrow slit where the fabric didn't quite meet the frame, Max caught a glimpse of the room beyond. His eyes widened.

"You're not going to believe this," he said, stepping back to let them look.

Riley peered through the gap. "Looks like some kind of server room. I can see racks of equipment and...blinking lights. Computers are not my thing, but that's not what I'd expect to see in an old barn."

Ethan took his turn at the window. "Definitely some kind of server farm. I can see cooling systems, cable management...This is a serious setup. And look over there," he pointed toward the opposite wall, "in the corner. Smile everyone."

A small, blinking red light was barely visible behind a stack of rusty paint cans.

"Security camera," Riley muttered. "Clever hiding spot."

Max ran a hand through his hair, his mind racing. "A hidden server room in the middle of nowhere. What could our hermit be running that needs this kind of infrastructure?"

He glanced around the small room. There wasn't much else to see. He walked back and studied the padlock. No use trying to get through it without some specialized tools. "Let's keep looking."

Max circled around to the exterior of the shed, his eyes searching the walls. The rear of the shed was a different story entirely. A sleek solar array covered most of the roof, its panels gleaming in the fading sunlight. Next to it, a small but sophisticated satellite dish was mounted. He spotted another window, set higher up on the side of the building.

"Riley," he called out. "Think you can get a look if I boost you up?"

She nodded, jogging over. Max interlaced his fingers,

creating a step for her. With a grunt, he lifted her up to the window.

Riley wiped away some of the grime from the window with her sleeve and pressed her face to the glass. "It's even more impressive from this angle. I can see the whole layout now. There are three full server racks. I can see thick bundles of cables running between them, all neatly organized. There's a small workstation in the corner with multiple monitors. And listen—" She paused, pressing her ear closer to the window. "I can hear the hum of cooling fans. They've got some serious climate control in there. This isn't just some hobbyist setup. It's professional grade, like something you'd see in a tech company."

Max lowered her back to the ground, his mind racing with possibilities. "Maybe it is a tech company."

"What do you mean?" Riley asked.

"The guy is getting regular special deliveries from Walmart. He's off the grid, but he's not poor. Maybe the servers are running a business."

"Maybe," Riley said, but her expression said she doubted it. "Feels hinky."

"Everyone thinks geniuses are crazy."

"Who's calling this guy a genius? I'm still calling him a hermit. A very strange hermit."

"Let's check out that greenhouse," Max said.

———

They made their way to the greenhouse, the lower glass panels clouded with dust and overgrown vines. But as they drew closer, Max noticed a faint humming sound.

"Listen," he said, holding up a hand.

Riley pressed her ear to the greenhouse wall. "Sounds like...fans? Maybe a pump?"

Max tried the door. There was no fancy padlock, but there was a deadbolt. He cupped his hands around his eyes and peered through a relatively clean section of glass. Inside, rows of lush plants thrived under artificial grow lights. A complex system of tubes and wires ran between the planters, suggesting an automated hydroponic setup.

"Whatever's growing in there, it's not just tomatoes and cucumbers," he said, stepping back.

Ethan ran a hand through his hair, looking bewildered. "So we've got a high-tech operation disguised as a rundown hermit's shack. But why? And where's the hermit?"

Riley's eyes darted between the buildings and the silent main house. "Only one way to find out."

———

As they headed back toward the main house, Max paused at the last small outbuilding. "Might as well check this one too," he said, reaching for the door handle.

No lock and no surprises. The door swung open easily, revealing a cluttered but ordinary interior. Unlike the other structures, this shed seemed to be exactly what it appeared to be.

"Well, this is refreshingly normal," Ethan remarked, stepping inside.

The walls were lined with sturdy wooden shelves, each one laden with an assortment of gardening tools, spare parts, and supplies. Rakes, shovels, and hoes leaned in one corner, their handles worn smooth from use. A workbench ran along one wall, its surface covered in an assortment of hand tools—hammers, screwdrivers, pliers and wrenches of various sizes.

Riley picked up a coil of rope hanging from a hook. "At least some of this fits the hermit image," she said, running her fingers over the rough fibers.

Max nodded, his eyes scanning the room. He spotted bags of fertilizer stacked neatly beside containers of pesticides and herbicides. A small refrigerator hummed quietly in the corner, likely used for storing seeds or other temperature-sensitive items.

"Looks like basic homesteading supplies," he observed. "Canning jars, pruning shears, even some traps for small game."

Ethan pointed to a shelf near the back. "Check it out—there's even some homemade preserves. Looks like strawberry jam, maybe some pickles. Makes me sort of hungry."

They stepped back out and Max closed the door, the normalcy of the shed somehow more unsettling in light of their other discoveries.

CHAPTER EIGHTEEN

The front door was locked, but the back door wasn't. The back door wasn't even closed. It stood open a crack. They all paused on the threshold then Max nudged the door wider with his elbow, revealing a small, cluttered kitchen space. They paused again, but there was no response, no vibrations of movement. The house was empty. Max spotted a plate and a fork crusted with dry bits of food in the sink. A pair of dog bowls sat on the floor against the wall.

"Looks like no one's been here for a while," Riley said, her voice still hushed.

Max walked to the refrigerator and opened the door. The interior light flickered on, revealing a sparse but practical assortment of items. Mason jars filled with homemade preserves lined the door shelves. On the main shelves, he spotted a block of homemade cheese, a carton of eggs likely gathered from free-range chickens, and some foraged wild berries in a recycled container. A few bottles of cloudy liquid, maybe homebrewed kombucha, sat next to a pitcher of what looked like fresh juice.

He pulled out a carton of milk, not from the farm, probably from the delivery runs. It was three-quarters full. "The expiration date is tomorrow. Been empty a couple of days, at least, I'd say. But not that long. Still some water in the dog bowl, too."

They moved cautiously through the house. To the left, a narrow hallway led to what appeared to be a bedroom and bathroom. Riley and Ethan peeled off in that direction to search. To the right, Max found himself in a sitting room at the front of the house that looked out over the barn and surrounding property.

It was a cozy space centered around a woodstove against a wall in the middle of the room. Bookshelves lined the front half of the room, floor-to-ceiling, crammed with a mix of well-worn paperbacks and hefty academic tomes. Max stepped over and glanced at the spines, mostly local histories and gardening books, plus a mix of classic and contemporary fiction. A comfortable-looking armchair sat in one corner, a reading lamp positioned beside it. Max could see himself spending long, pleasant hours reading his own books in a chair like that.

The back half of the room was more bewildering.

And Max had a sense that any answers they might find here would come from there. If they could make sense of it.

The space was dominated by a high-end computer tower with dual monitors on a swivel stand atop a large desk. An ergonomic chair was pushed against the desk. Every other available surface surrounding the desk was covered with papers, books, photos, and other scraps related to the nearby Monongahela National Forest. Stacks of dusty tomes, maybe overflowing from the bookcases, teetered in precarious piles on the floor. Various maps were pinned to the walls, their surfaces marked with cryptic symbols and citations. Sticky notes and index cards with more notes and addenda were taped on top. Bits and pieces overlapped like a mad scientist's fever dream.

Max didn't touch anything but let his gaze sweep over it all, trying to get some sense of order or approach. He believed it wasn't total chaos. He could almost sense some underlying, if haphazard, organization. He saw scattered printouts detailing past searches, including several related to Vance Cotter's disappearance. He saw other groupings centered around other presumably missing individuals. There was a section on the history of the Monongahela. Bits on local legends. Pages torn from maps and atlases detailing weather patterns and geological formations. Still, despite the tornado of paper, something nagged at the back of his mind. It felt as if something was missing, but he couldn't quite place what it was.

Ethan walked in, his eyes wide. "Whoa," he breathed, wandering around the cramped space. He stopped abruptly in the center of the room, his gaze fixed on a spot above the computer setup. "The map is missing."

"What?" Max asked, following Ethan's line of sight.

Ethan pointed at a space over the monitors. It wasn't completely blank, but it was less dense with paper than other areas around the room. Now that Ethan pointed it out, Max felt it was almost conspicuous against the clutter surrounding it.

"The focal point. If this were me, and thank God it's not, but some principles still apply, I would put my main focus, my main interest right there. I'd see it all the time when I sat at the desk. It would be a reminder."

"Yes, I think you're right," Max muttered. "That's what was bothering me."

"Now, the question is, what was it?" Ethan moved closer to the desk and started poking around, lifting up papers and moving books, but careful to put them back in their original place. Then he pulled down some of the papers over the monitors. These he placed in a stack on top of the keyboard. "Yup. You can see two small nail marks. Something was hanging here."

Max kept out of the way and let him ride his intuition.

"Check this out." Ethan pulled out something from behind the desk and turned to face Max. He was holding a corkboard, 24 x 36 inches. It was empty. "It was behind the desk, against the wall." He walked past Max to the window and bent over the corkboard, examining it carefully. "Whatever was up there, was there for a while. You can see where the sun or light discolored the edges of the board that weren't covered up." He abruptly put the corkboard down and left the room without a word.

Left alone, Max's attention was drawn to a framed photograph on the desk. He picked it up, noting how the image had faded slightly with age. It showed a young man and woman standing in a forest clearing, their smiles bright despite the photo's washed-out colors. Max glanced around, realizing it was the only personal photo in the cluttered room. He took out his phone. He might not be able to call anyone, but it still had its uses. He snapped a photo of the photo and set the frame back down as Ethan returned, his arms full of maps from the car.

"I'm thinking..." Ethan muttered, spreading the maps out on the floor. He held each one up to the blank space on the corkboard, comparing sizes and shapes.

On the fifth attempt, Ethan's eyes lit up. "Bingo!" he exclaimed, holding up a US Bureau of Land Management official map. It fit neatly into the sun-faded outline on the board. "We might be in business."

"Clever," Max nodded, impressed.

"It gets better," Ethan said, his voice excited. "You can sort of see from the push pin indentations and wear over time where he'd marked it up." He laid the map flat on the desk, running his fingers over its surface. "Give me a few minutes."

As Ethan bent over the map, Riley appeared in the doorway. "Find anything?" she asked.

"Maybe." Max filled her in on their discovery. "Anything in the bedroom?" he finished.

"It's pretty spartan. See for yourself."

Max and Riley left Ethan to his work and made their way down the narrow hallway to the bedroom. The door creaked open, revealing a simple, almost monastic space.

A single bed with a thin mattress occupied one corner, its iron frame rusted at the joints. A small nightstand held a lamp and a well-worn Bible. The opposite wall housed a simple wooden wardrobe, its doors slightly ajar.

"Not exactly living in luxury, is he?" Max said.

Riley opened the wardrobe, riffling through the limited selection of clothing. "Mostly practical stuff. Lots of flannel, work pants. Wait a second..." She pulled out a garment bag from the back. "There's a suit in here. Decent quality, too."

"For blending in when he needs to?" Max suggested.

"Maybe. It's nice, but old." Riley zipped the bag closed. "Found some medications in the nightstand drawer. Nothing exotic, no prescriptions, just some over-the-counter pain relievers and allergy meds."

Max's attention was drawn to a small frame on the dresser. Another photo. He picked it up, studying the image. It showed a family of four, posed in front of a backdrop of dense forest. Was it taken right outside this house? Max couldn't tell. The father stood tall and proud, his broad shoulders and weathered face suggesting a life of outdoor work. His dark hair was peppered with gray at the temples, and laugh lines crinkled the corners of his eyes. One arm was wrapped around his wife, a petite woman with warm eyes and honey-blonde hair pulled back in a loose bun. Her other hand rested on her daughter's shoulder. The kids were the same ones from the photo in the other room. They were younger in this photo by maybe a decade, but the resemblance was strong. The girl, probably around eight or nine, had inherited her mother's hair color and her father's mischievous grin. She beamed at the camera, revealing a missing front tooth. The son, a teenager with his father's strong jawline and his mother's kind eyes, stood slightly apart, caught in that awkward phase between child and adult.

He turned to tell Riley, but before he could say anything, Ethan's voice called out from the front room. "Guys, I think I've got something!"

They exchanged a glance. Max carefully replaced the frame on the dresser, and they hurried back to join Ethan.

———

Ethan sat cross-legged on the floor, a triumphant gleam in his eyes. "I think I've got it," he said, gesturing for them to come closer. Max and Riley peered down at the map. Ethan had placed a sheet of tracing paper over it, on which he'd re-created the faint marks and indentations.

"See these clusters?" Ethan pointed to several areas he'd circled. "They correspond to known disappearances, including Vance's last known location."

Max leaned in, studying the markings. "And these lines connecting them?"

"That's where it gets interesting," Ethan replied. "They form a pattern. And if you follow it..." His finger traced a path across the map, ending at a spot he'd marked with an X. "This is where I think our hermit believed Grave's End to be."

Riley's breath caught. "That's not far from Sarah and Jake's last known coordinates. From her second check in."

The three of them stood in silence, the weight of Ethan's discovery settling over them. Outside, the sun had dipped below the tree line, casting long shadows across the overgrown yard. The forest seemed to press closer, as if listening to Ethan's theory.

"Guys," Ethan said, "I think we have our map."

———

Max lingered in the front room, his eyes sweeping over the chaos of papers and maps one last time. The empty space above the computer monitors nagged at him. Who had taken the map? And why?

As Riley and Ethan made their way back through the house, Max followed slowly, his mind churning with possibilities. Had the hermit removed it himself, protecting his hard-won theory of Grave's End? Or had someone else been here, seeking to erase that same information?

The floorboards creaked under his feet as he moved through the narrow hallway. The musty scent of old books and neglect hung in the air, mingling with the faint odor of unwashed dishes from the kitchen.

Riley paused at the back door, her hand on the knob. "We should go," she said, her voice barely above a whisper. "It'll be dark soon."

As Ethan followed Riley outside, Max's gaze drifted across the worn linoleum floor to the dog bowls. Where was the dog? Then something else caught his eye—a series of dark spots near the back door, almost hidden in the floral floor pattern. He frowned, kneeling to get a closer look.

The spots were small, each no larger than a dime, and appeared to be dried onto the floor. Max's pulse quickened as he gently touched one with his fingertip. It was hard and slightly raised, like a scab.

"Max?" Riley's voice called from outside. "You coming?"

"Just a second," he replied, rising to his feet.

Max moved to the sink, his eyes scanning the cluttered counter. He found a dish towel hanging from a cabinet knob and turned on the faucet. The pipes groaned, but clear water sputtered out. He wet a corner of the towel and returned to the spots on the floor.

Kneeling once more, Max carefully dabbed at one of the dark marks. The damp cloth came away with a reddish-brown stain. His stomach tightened as he realized what he was looking at.

Blood.

The missing map now took on a more sinister significance. This wasn't just about protecting information—something violent had happened here. Or maybe he was jumping to conclusions. Surely accidents, especially on farms or homesteads, happened all the time.

"Max!" Ethan's voice this time. "Everything okay in there?"

He looked down at the bloodstained cloth in his hand, then back at the inconspicuous spots on the floor. Should he tell Riley and Ethan what he found? Or would it only add to their worry and slow them down? Whatever had happened here, it was clear that finding Sarah and Jake had become even more urgent.

Max tossed the dish towel into the sink. As Max pulled the door shut behind him, he couldn't shake the feeling that they were no longer just searching for missing hikers. They were walking into something more complex—and potentially deadly.

CHAPTER NINETEEN

"What's our next move?" Ethan asked as Riley guided the Camry back down the narrow road.

"Dinner," Max and Riley answered in unison. That broke some of the tension.

Ethan leaned forward from the back seat. "We need to talk to Hatfield."

Max noticed a fleeting expression flash across Riley's face. "Who's Hatfield?" he asked.

"He's a local guide," Riley explained. "Used to be the district ranger before Holcomb. Owns an outfitting company now. Runs hiking, camping, fishing trips into the Monongahela."

Ethan added, "He's about the only one who's taken us seriously about Jake and Sarah being missing. He's agreed to join our search and might even get a few others to help. Hatfield's actually the most sought-after guide in the area. People say he can navigate the Monongahela blindfolded."

Max's memory clicked. "I think I saw you three talking at the cafe. Older guy? Skinny?"

Riley nodded. "That's him."

"More eyes and local knowledge could help," Max said.

Riley remained silent, focused on driving. As they reached the end of the dirt road and turned back toward Grimswood, Max noticed a change in Riley's demeanor. The earlier agitation had transformed into the familiar bristling energy he'd come to associate with her. As they accelerated toward town, she said, "Let's have him meet us at the Crooked Nail. Now that we have a map, or at least a direction, a theory—whatever you want to call it—I want to leave at first light."

———

The Camry's headlights cut through the gathering dusk as Riley steered them back into Grimswood. The town seemed even quieter than usual, if that was possible. Max spotted a lone figure shuffling along the sidewalk by the abandoned movie theater, collar turned up against the growing chill. Now that the clouds had lifted, the temperature had dropped, and Max was reminded of Buck Holcomb's warning about the sometimes extreme temperature fluctuations in the forest.

Riley pulled into the Crossroads Inn parking lot. The light was on in the office, but Max couldn't see if Jeb was at his post or not. As they exited the car, Riley spoke up, "Let's meet at the Crooked Nail in an hour," her voice cutting through the silence. "I could use a shower and..." she didn't finish the sentence, just turned and walked off toward her room.

Max and Ethan watched her retreating back, then looked at each other and nodded in agreement. As they headed to their respective rooms, Max glanced across the street. The Sunrise Cafe's windows were dark, the CLOSED sign clearly visible. He frowned, realizing he wouldn't be able to use the payphone. He'd hoped to call Vic one last time before heading into the woods. Maybe talk to Lawrence too, see if he could dig deeper on the second property, figure out the owner or, barring that, at least more of the homestead's history.

Inside his room, Max stripped off his clothes and stepped into the shower. The water pressure hadn't changed overnight. It was weak, but it was hot, and he let it wash over him, easing some of the tension from his muscles. As he dried off, his mind wandered back to the spots he'd found in the hermit's kitchen. The sight of those dark stains nagged at him, raising more questions than answers. How recent was the blood? Was it the hermit's or someone else's? Was it an accident or intentional? Was it connected to Sarah and Jake's disappearance? And where was the damn dog?

Dressed in fresh clothes, Max settled on the bed and picked up the Dennis Lehane novel he'd finished the previous week. He reread a few chapters, letting the familiar prose wash over him and distract him from the questions swirling in his head.

When it was time to leave, Max stepped outside, nearly colliding with Ethan. Max raised an eyebrow.

"I got Jeb to let me use the office phone to call Hatfield. He said he'd meet us," Ethan said. "Ready?"

Max nodded, and they fell into step beside each other. As they passed Riley's room, they could hear her moving around inside.

They walked down the quiet street toward the Crooked Nail, a companionable silence between them. The massive, rusted nail bent into a horseshoe shape creaked as it swung in the evening breeze.

Max pushed open the heavy wooden door. The bar was crowded, a sea of flannel shirts and worn baseball caps. Cigarette smoke hung in the air, mingling with the sharp scent of spilled beer and the underlying musk of too many bodies in too small a space.

Somehow, they managed to snag a small table near the back. The surface was sticky with countless spilled drinks, and Max had to peel his sleeve from the wood when he leaned on it.

A Hank Williams Jr. song blared from the jukebox, making conversation nearly impossible. But as it faded out, replaced by something mellower—Patsy Cline, Max thought —he turned to Ethan.

"So," Max said, leaning back in his chair. "What's your story? How'd you get mixed up in all this?"

Ethan's eyes darted around the room before settling back on Max. He took a deep breath, as if preparing to dive into deep water.

"I grew up in Philadelphia," Ethan began. "Not near the Liberty Bell or on the Main Line. North Philly. And not the gentrified part. Dad split when I was young, Mom worked multiple jobs to keep us afloat. We never had much."

Max nodded, he'd spent some time in the city and Ethan's upbringing echoed some of his own with his aunt and cousins in South Boston.

He paused, his eyes going a little glassy. "Our neighbor-hood was rough. I learned to duck at the sound of gunshots before I learned long division. Mom did her best, but she was stretched thin. My older sister practically raised me." Ethan's fingers absently traced patterns on the sticky table surface. "We lived in this tiny two-bedroom apartment above a bodega. The smell of frying empanadas would wake me up every morning. Sometimes, that was the only good thing about my day." He shook his head, as if clearing away old memories.

"But books...books were my lifeline. I'd spend hours at the local library. It was small, but to me, it was a palace. The librarian, Mrs. Chen, she'd always save the new arrivals for me. Said I was her best customer." A soft smile played on his lips at the memory.

"And I was good at school," Ethan continued. "It was my escape, you know? Had this English teacher in high school, Mr. Ramirez. He saw something in me, pushed me to apply to colleges I thought were way out of my league. Got into Dartmouth on a full ride. Surprised the hell out of me, but not Mr. Ramirez. That's where I met Jake, like I told you before."

"And the Cotters took you under their wing?"

"Yeah," Ethan said, his voice softening. "They did. Invited me home for holidays, helped me get internships. After graduation, they offered me a job at the foundation. Been there ever since."

Max opened his mouth to ask another question, but a movement caught his eye. Riley approached their table, a small smile playing on her lips.

"Telling the origin story again, Ethan?" she asked, sliding into the empty chair.

Ethan shrugged. "Max asked."

A waitress finally made her way to their table, notepad in hand. She was a middle-aged woman with frizzy red hair pulled back in a messy ponytail, her tired eyes framed by crow's feet that deepened as she forced a polite smile. "What can I get you folks?"

"What's on the menu?" Max asked.

The waitress sighed, as if she'd answered the same question a thousand times. "We've got burgers and fries. Or cheeseburgers and fries. Pickled eggs on the bar for a buck apiece, and free peanuts from the barrel by the pool table. Domestic beer, light or regular. No imports."

They exchanged glances. "Three cheeseburger plates," Riley said. "A round of drafts. You can keep the pickled eggs and community peanuts."

If the waitress was offended, she didn't show it, just scribbled a note on her pad and spun away.

Max turned back to Ethan. "So, you've known the Cotters for a while then?"

Ethan nodded. "Yeah, they're the only family I've got left, blood or not. After losing Mom to cancer and my sister in that car accident, the Cotters practically adopted me. With Vance gone and now Jake and Sarah missing..." He trailed off.

"We'll find them," Riley said.

The conversation lulled as the juke kicked up and an argument broke out near the pool table. The waitress returned with their food. The burgers were greasy but satisfying, the fries crisp and salty. They ate in companionable silence for a few minutes, the din of the bar washing over them.

As Max wiped his hands on a paper napkin, he noticed Ethan checking his watch.

"Hatfield should be here soon," Ethan said.

"What else can you tell me about him?" Max asked, taking a sip of beer.

Riley and Ethan exchanged a look. "He's...intense," Ethan said carefully.

"Intense how?"

"Hatfield's been in these woods longer than anyone," Riley explained. "He knows things, sees things others don't."

"Or thinks he does," Ethan added, earning a sharp look from Riley.

"I don't care about his personality or his personal beliefs. If he can help us find Sarah and Jake, I'll put up with all of it. It's also not like we have a lot of choice. He's practically the only one in town who will talk to us."

Max raised an eyebrow. "You two don't seem to agree on him."

Riley sighed. "Hatfield's got some...unconventional ideas about the forest. About Grave's End. Or the rumors of it."

"Such as?"

Before Riley could answer, the bar's front door swung open and a tall, lean man stepped inside. He moved with the fluid grace of a predator, each step soundless despite the creaky floorboards. A thin scruff of salt-and-pepper beard partially covered his jaw. His eyes, the pale blue of a winter sky, were sharp and alert, scanning the room with the practiced ease of a hunter. When they landed on their table, a flicker of recognition passed over his face. He began making his way over, navigating through the crowded bar without touching a single person, like water flowing around stones in a stream.

This man was confident and capable, Max thought. And maybe a little dangerous.

"Speak of the devil," Ethan muttered.

Hatfield stopped at their table, his presence commanding attention without a word spoken. He nodded at Riley and Ethan before turning his piercing gaze to Max.

"You must be the newcomer," he said, his voice gravelly and low. "Heard you might be joining our little expedition."

Max met his gaze steadily. "That's right. Name's Max."

Hatfield's eyes narrowed slightly, as if assessing Max's worth. After a moment, he said, "Clint Hatfield." He pulled out the empty chair and sat down.

"All right then," he said, leaning forward. "Let's talk about what you're really getting yourself into, Max."

CHAPTER TWENTY

"Do you have any background in search and rescue ops? Specifically woodland terrain?" Hatfield asked, his gravelly voice barely audible over the twang of a country song.

"No," Max replied honestly.

Hatfield leaned forward, put his callused hands flat on the table. "Got a pack? Gear? Don't let the Monongahela fool you. This is not going to be an easy Sunday afternoon hike. Not where we're planning to go. You need to be experienced. I can't take the time to teach you out there. You need to be able to handle yourself."

Max felt the implicit warning, but he wasn't about to be dissuaded. "I've got gear. I'll pull my weight. I won't slow you down. I'm here to help."

Hatfield glanced at Riley, then Ethan. They both gave slight nods. He sighed, recognizing he was outvoted, but decided to give it one more shot.

"Let me tell you about a guy named Charlie," Hatfield began, his voice taking on a storyteller's cadence. "Cocky son of a bitch, claimed he was practically birthed by the White

Mountains back in New Hampshire. Spent a couple days here, might've sat at this very table." He tapped the sticky surface for emphasis. "All the locals, including myself, tried to tell him this place was different. He laughed, shrugged, bought a few rounds. Hiked into the Monongahela the next morning."

"And how is Charlie doing today?" Max asked, already suspecting the answer. "Still shuffling along this mortal coil?"

Hatfield's eyes hardened. "He shuffled off in pieces. A month later, we found his bones. Or some of them. Probably a bear attack, he was picked clean and scavenged right down to the marrow."

Max knew Hatfield was being intentionally harsh and graphic to scare him off, but he found it in poor taste given they were searching for Jake and Sarah. He glanced at Riley, but she seemed unfazed. Maybe she'd seen worse in Afghanistan. Or maybe Hatfield had already tried the same tactic on her.

Max raised his beer. "May we avoid Charlie's fate."

He caught a faint hint of a grin from Riley. Hatfield rolled his eyes, an expression he seemed to have perfected over the years.

"If I'm the guide, I'm responsible for your safety," Hatfield said, his tone flat and rehearsed.

"I'm in good shape. I won't complain. I won't slow you down," Max insisted.

Hatfield peered under the table at Max's feet. "What about boots? Your feet are the most important thing on this trip. If those go, it brings the whole thing down. You need support and tread."

Max stuck out a foot from under the table. Hatfield examined it, then grudgingly nodded. "Those should work."

Ethan excused himself to use the bathroom. Riley stood up, asking about another round. Max agreed to one more, while Hatfield asked for water. As Riley headed to the bar, a sudden lull fell over the Crooked Nail. Someone had plugged a new round of quarters into the jukebox, and the afterwork crowd had thinned out, leaving behind only the low hum of conversation and the occasional pop of colliding pool balls.

Hatfield's blue eyes bore into Max. "Why do you care? Ethan told me you're stuck in town until the bridge is fixed."

"Because I do isn't a good enough answer?" Max replied.

"Not really. Complete strangers don't get involved in other complete strangers' business. Not like this. What do you want?"

"Just to help. If I can. It's as simple as that."

Hatfield stared at him, clearly struggling with Max's response. "Any time someone says it's simple, it tends to be the opposite." He paused, then continued, "You don't know Riley or Jake or the Cotters? You really have no personal connection to this?"

Max turned the question back on him. "You're going out there. Do you?"

Hatfield looked away, his jaw clenching. "I was the district ranger when Vance went missing. I led that search, at least in the beginning." He met Max's gaze again. "I won't lose another member of that family. I owe them that much."

"What about the other missing people?"

A thin, humorless smile crossed Hatfield's face. "Chatting with the locals?"

"Cable TV isn't working at the motel. Not much else to do. Gotta pass the time."

"Do you know how big the Monongahela is?"

"Ethan mentioned it's roughly the size of Rhode Island?"

"He might have exaggerated, but not by much. It's fucking huge, over a hundred thousand acres with very few groomed trails. It's raw, visceral, and powerful. People often forget how ruthless Mother Nature can be. Take away all the progress and creature comforts most people have come to expect, throw them at the mercy of Mother Nature, and not all of them are going to come back out alive. Simple statistics."

Max leaned forward, his voice low but firm. "You're not going to scare me off. I'm in it until the end."

Hatfield leaned back, lifted his hands slightly. "I'm not trying to scare you. I'm trying to prepare you. I've led a lot of search and rescue ops. Did you know that most of them find a body? Often it's just not the one they're looking for."

As Ethan and Riley returned to the table, the conversation shifted to expedition details, but Max couldn't shake the weight of Hatfield's words. Despite his words a moment ago, he was nervous. Hiking off into the wild, even with a guide, was far out of his comfort zone.

———

Riley pushed her empty plate aside. "We found something today, Clint. A map."

Hatfield's eyebrows rose. "A map? Where?"

"At...well, we don't know his name. We think he and Jake were in communication. Online," Ethan said.

Hatfield's eyes narrowed. "A local? And you found him? Met up with him?

"We found his property," Max said. "Never did find him. Place was empty. Looked like it had been for a few days. Door was open."

Hatfield looked at each of them in turn, his silence heavy. "And there was a map sitting on the kitchen table waiting for you?"

"Well, sort of," Ethan replied. "We found where a map used to be."

"Interesting," Hatfield said. "And this shadow map...what did it show?"

Ethan leaned in, lowering his voice. "We think it might lead to Grave's End."

Hatfield's face remained impassive, but Max noticed a slight tightening around his eyes. "Grave's End," Hatfield repeated, the words hanging in the air between them. "You're still intent on chasing after that?"

"No, we are *intent* on finding Sarah and Jake. Our best lead is Jake and Jake's best lead was Vance's mysterious upcoming announcement. Jake believed it had to do with Grave's End," Riley said. "It's not a choice. We have to find them."

Hatfield sighed, the sound barely audible over another boot stomper from the juke. If he looked angry or anxious before, now he just looked tired. Maybe resigned.. "I've known these woods my whole life," he said. "There are things out there...things that can't be explained by your typical forest ecology or geology."

Max leaned back in his chair. "What kinds of things?"

Hatfield's gaze swept over each of them in turn. "People go missing in these woods. I've told all of you that. More than once. And it's not just getting lost or animal attacks or general human stupidity. It's like the forest...takes them."

Ethan shifted uncomfortably in his seat. "Come on, Clint. You can't seriously believe—"

"I've seen things," Hatfield cut him off. "Things that don't make sense. Compasses spinning wildly. GPS devices failing for no reason. Experienced hikers getting turned around in areas they know like the back of their hand."

Hatfield pulled out his brass compass, its case smooth from years of handling. "My father carried this through these woods for 30 years before me. Said as long as I trusted it, I'd never truly be lost. But even it acts strange sometimes in certain spots."

He leaned in, his voice dropping lower. "There are places where time seems to move differently. You think you've been walking for an hour, but your watch says it's been five minutes. Or the other way around."

Riley raised an eyebrow. "That could just be the disorientation of being in the woods. Dehydration. Panic."

Hatfield shook his head. "I'd say the same thing if I heard it secondhand, but it's more than that. I've seen it myself. There are spots where fog appears out of nowhere, thick as pea soup, even on clear days. It'll be confined to a small area, like it's trapped there. And the temperature—" He paused, taking a sip of his water. "I've found pockets of cold in the middle of summer that'll freeze the sweat on your back. No explanation for it."

Max watched Hatfield carefully, noting the tension in his jaw. He realized with a start that the man was scared. "Anything else?"

Hatfield's gaze grew distant, his voice low and measured. "The animals...they behave strangely in certain areas. Sometimes, the forest falls dead silent, as if every creature is holding its breath. Other times, typically shy animals become unnaturally bold, or usually harmless ones turn aggressive."

He paused, his expression grim. "There are spots where the air pressure shifts dramatically. It can disorient you, mess with your head. And there's one section," his voice dropped lower, "it's the worst. I refuse to take groups anywhere near it."

Hatfield looked up, his eyes meeting each of theirs. "We think we're so advanced, that we understand everything. But the Monongahela has been here for millennia. We've only scratched the surface of its mysteries. We don't have all the answers. Not even close."

The table fell silent, Hatfield's words settling heavily over them. The ambient noise of the bar seemed to fade away, leaving them isolated in a bubble of uneasy contemplation.

Riley leaned forward, her elbows on the table. "But you'll still help us, right? You'll guide us?"

Hatfield was quiet for a long moment, his fingers drumming a slow rhythm on the table's scarred surface. Finally, he nodded. "I'll take you as far as I can. But understand this—once we're out there, my word is law. You do what I say, when I say it. No questions, no arguments. It's the only way I can keep you safe."

Max studied Hatfield's face, searching for any sign of doubt or deception. He found none. Whatever Hatfield believed about the forest, his conviction was genuine.

"All right," Max said. "When do we leave?"

Hatfield stood to leave. "First light," he replied. "Meet me at the trailhead. And pack smart and light—where we're going, you might need to be quick on your feet."

CHAPTER TWENTY-ONE

The second round of drinks disappeared quickly. There wasn't a lot left to say and first light would come early. Max reached for his wallet, but Riley held out a hand.

"I've got this," she said. "It's the least I can do, considering your help."

Max nodded, pulling out a few bills for the tip instead. They stood, making their way through the thinning crowd toward the exit. The old brass hinges protested as they pushed through the door. The night air was cool and smelled like rain mixed with car exhaust. Thin clouds strafed the night sky but nothing promising more rain. Maybe the start of the hike would remain dry. The dusty, yellow glow from the Crooked Nail's windows faded as they walked across the gravel parking lot. The massive, rusted nail swayed in the night breeze. Ethan trailed a few steps behind, his eyes fixed on his phone.

"Good news," he said. "Looks like cell service is back."

Max glanced over his shoulder to respond when a shadow moved between two parked pickup trucks. His instincts screamed a warning, sending a jolt of adrenaline through his body. Time seemed to slow as two burly figures emerged from the darkness.

One man lunged at Ethan, his meaty fist connecting with the back of Ethan's head. Ethan crumpled to the ground without a sound.

"Hey!" Max shouted, but his attention quickly shifted to the man advancing on him. Fight or flight. The familiar sensation washed over him, and Max felt a guilty thrill of anticipation and excitement.

The attacker was tall and broad shouldered, with a shaved head and a thick neck. A scar on his upper lip gave him a perpetual sneer. He grinned, revealing tobacco-stained teeth.

"Looks like we got ourselves some out-of-towners who don't know when to mind their own business," he growled.

Max took a step to the side, creating distance between himself and Riley. He caught a glimpse of her squaring off against Ethan's assailant, her stance low and ready. He'd seen her handiwork before. He put his attention back on his guy. She would be fine.

As the scarred man approached, Max felt the world around him sharpen into crystal clarity. Every sense cranked up—the crunch of gravel under his attacker's boots, the smell of stale beer and cigarettes, the cool night air on his skin. He hated how much he loved this feeling, dancing along the razor's edge between danger and elation.

Max didn't fight it this time. These guys had made the choice. They'd pushed him. So he embraced it. He was a fighter, always had been. And right now, Ethan and Riley needed that fighter. Here, in this moment, his purpose was clear. Protect his friends. Survive. Win.

The scarred man was fast, but undisciplined. He swung first, a telegraphed wild haymaker that whistled past Max's ear. Max ducked under the punch and then came forward, driving his shoulder into the man's solar plexus. The attacker let out a wheezing gasp as the air rushed from his lungs.

Max shuffled back a step and followed up with a quick jab to the man's nose. Nothing hard or disabling, but certainly painful and distracting. It was his preferred punch during the occasional hockey fight as a kid. There was a satisfying crunch and blood began to flow. The man stumbled back, his eyes watering.

"You little shit," he snarled, lunging forward again.

This time, Max was ready for the speed. He sidestepped, letting the man's momentum carry him forward. As the attacker passed, Max grabbed his arm, twisting it behind his back. With a sharp push, he sent the man face first into the side of a nearby truck.

The impact was loud in the quiet parking lot. The man slumped to the ground, dazed and groaning. He didn't appear to be in a hurry to get up. A trail of blood smeared the truck's passenger door.

Max turned to check on Riley, his heart pounding. His brief prior assessment was correct. He needn't have worried.

Riley stood over her opponent, who lay curled on the ground, trying to clutch both his groin and his head at the same time. She was breathing hard, but a wild grin spread across her face. Max knew the feeling. He was sure if someone held up a mirror, he'd find a similar look on his own face.

"You okay?" Max asked.

"Never better," Riley replied, her eyes bright with adrenaline. "You?"

"I'll live. Let's check on Ethan."

They hurried over to where Ethan lay. He was stirring, a hand pressed to the back of his head.

"Ethan? Can you hear me?" Her voice tinged with concern as she knelt beside him.

Ethan groaned, his eyes fluttering open. "What...what happened?"

"You got sucker punched," Max said, helping him sit up. "How many fingers am I holding up?"

Ethan squinted. "Three? No, two. Definitely two."

"Close enough," Max replied. "Can you stand?"

As they helped Ethan to his feet, the sound of an engine roaring to life cut through the night. Max turned to see a battered pickup peeling out of the parking lot, gravel spraying in its wake. Their assailants making a getaway.

"Friends of yours?" Max asked Riley.

She shook her head. "Never seen them before. But I get the feeling this wasn't random."

"Definitely not a coincidence. The guy called me an out-of-towner not minding my own business."

"Someone doesn't want us poking around."

"Clearly not, but what live wire did we touch to provoke this response?"

"I don't know. Seems sort of extreme."

Ethan leaned heavily on Max's shoulder. "Can we talk about this somewhere that isn't spinning?"

They made their way slowly back to the Crossroads Inn, the gravel crunching under their feet. The adrenaline began to fade, replaced by a growing sense of unease.

As they reached the motel, Max turned to Riley. "First light?" The unasked question implied, though Max knew what her answer would be.

Riley's jaw set, her eyes hardening. "First light, just like we planned. Whatever's out there, whatever happened to Sarah and Jake, I need to know."

Max nodded. "All right. But first, we need to take care of Ethan. He might have a concussion."

Riley's expression softened slightly as she looked at

Ethan, who was still leaning heavily on Max. "You're right. Ethan, how are you feeling?"

"Like I got hit by a truck," Ethan mumbled. "Room's still spinning a bit."

Max glanced at Riley. They were still outside. "Let's get him to his room," Max said. "We'll need to keep an eye on him tonight."

They helped Ethan to his room. Max turned on the lamp, its soft light illuminating Ethan's pale face.

"I'll go grab some ice," Riley said, heading for the door.

While she was gone, Max checked Ethan's pupils. "They look equal, that's good. But we need to wake you up every couple of hours, just to be safe."

Riley returned with a makeshift ice pack made from one of the thin hotel towels. "Here, put this on the back of your head. It'll help with the swelling."

Ethan winced as he applied the ice. "What about tomorrow? I can still go, right?"

"For now, just rest," Max said.

They got him settled on the bed and he was snoring within minutes.

"I can stay here. I'll wake him up every couple hours to check on him."

"You sure? I can take a shift."

"No, I'm good. You get some rest. You're going to need it. But first, grab some extra supplies from Ethan's stash to add to your volunteer pack." She moved to a large duffel bag in the corner, unzipping it to reveal a treasure trove of hiking supplies. "Let's see what we've got here."

Max joined her, riffling through the bag's contents. "Extra socks, always a good idea," he said, pulling out a few pairs and setting them aside.

Riley held up a compact, high-powered flashlight. "This could come in handy. Ethan's got two, so he won't miss one."

They continued sorting through the gear, occasionally consulting each other on what might be useful. Riley discovered a small bottle of water purification tablets and added it to their pile. Max added a compact solar charger. Riley nodded. "Good find. Here's a spare first aid kit. Never hurts to have an extra."

They also found some high-energy protein bars, a compact multitool, and a small bottle of biodegradable soap. Max spotted a tightly rolled emergency blanket and placed it on top of the pile.

"I think that should do it," Riley said, surveying their haul. "We don't want to weigh ourselves down too much, but these extras could make a big difference."

Max agreed, gathering the items. "I'll add these to my pack." He headed for the door. "Wake me if you need anything.

Max?" she said as he opened the door. He looked back. "Thanks."

––––––––

Max closed the door to his room. The adrenaline was fading, but it left him feeling slightly queasy and restless, like he drank a pot of coffee on an empty stomach. He paced the small space then veered into the small bathroom. He stripped off his clothes and stepped into the shower, letting the luke-warm water—the best the Crossroads Inn could muster—wash over him.

As the water drummed against his skin, he tried to calm his nerves about the impending hike into the Monongahela. He was a city guy, after all. What did he know about navigating dense forests? Hatfield's warnings about the forest's mysteries and Holcomb's cautionary words echoed in his head. The missing hermit, the drops of blood, the aggressive response to their inquiries—what exactly was going on here?

Toweling off, Max flopped onto the bed and reached for his phone: 10:45 p.m. Sleep felt a million miles away. He noticed the service bars had returned—Ethan was right. A series of texts from Lawrence lit up his screen, mostly information they'd already discussed on the phone. But the last message caught his eye:

Eddie cracked the Walmart system. Those deliveries go to an Amos Redding.

Amos Redding. The name didn't ring any bells for Max.

Max tapped the call button next to Vic's name. She answered on the second ring.

"Hey, you," Vic's voice came through, warm and familiar.

"Hey, yourself. How's the inn?"

"Quiet. Repainted the lobby today. Went with a nice eggshell finish."

"Sounds thrilling," Max chuckled.

They talked about nothing important—the weather, a funny commercial Vic had seen, the Bruins prospects for the upcoming hockey season, and the latest antics of the local squirrel clan that Bailey loved to chase. Max felt the tension slowly easing from his muscles, his eyelids growing heavy.

"All right, I should try to get some sleep," Max said, stifling a yawn.

"Good idea. Be careful out there, okay?"

"Always am."

"Are you?"

"Goodnight, Vic."

"Night, Max."

Max set his phone aside and closed his eyes, drifting off almost immediately. His sleep was fitful, plagued by unsettling images. A dense forest, the trees growing impossibly tall around him. The ground shifting and undulating under his feet, like a living entity. Whispers, just on the edge of comprehension. Branches reaching out like grasping fingers. He woke with a start, a minute before his alarm, the details of the dream slipping through his fingers like water, leaving him with a vague sense of unease that clung to him like a shroud.

CHAPTER TWENTY-TWO

Max sat up, rubbing his eyes, fragments of his strange dream still clinging to the edges of his consciousness. He turned off his phone alarm and dressed quickly in the lightweight gear from Holcomb, appreciating the comfort and flexibility of the fabric. He couldn't recall the last time he hadn't worn jeans and a T-shirt.

He stepped outside his room and inhaled deeply, hoping the cool morning air would clear his head. And it *was* cool. He could see the hint of his breath and the fog that clung to the ground, softening the edges of the world. He glanced to his left. The lights in both Ethan and Riley's rooms glowed through the thin curtains.

He needed to check on Ethan, but first coffee. Max made his way across the street to the Sunrise Cafe. The bell above the door jangled as he entered, breaking the early-morning quiet. He paused, surprised to see Hatfield at the counter, bent close to Patty. Their heads were together, voices low, intimate. At the sound of the bell, they straightened abruptly, putting some distance between them.

"Morning," Max said, approaching the counter. There were no other customers yet. He could see the first pot of coffee just finishing.

Patty's cheeks were flushed as she turned to face him. "What can I get you, hon?"

"Coffee and some egg sandwiches to go, please. For three."

As Patty moved to prepare his order, Hatfield cleared his throat. "You can leave your car and luggage in the Sunrise lot. Patty'll keep an eye on things. Just pull around the side. With his nose in his books, Jeb may or may not notice you've checked out."

Max nodded. "Thanks. That's helpful."

Hatfield leaned forward, his expression serious. "Listen, I know you're not from around here. You don't have much experience in the woods. Stay close, follow my lead, and we might all make it back in one piece."

"Even Jake and Sarah?" Max asked, meeting Hatfield's gaze.

"God willing," Hatfield replied.

"You a church going man, Clint?"

Hatfield scratched at his lip. "Maybe not in the traditional sense, but I do believe in a larger plan. The world is just too damn...big and complicated to be just chance. Gotta be something more." Hatfield stood abruptly, maybe embarrassed by his admission, slight as it was. "See you at the trailhead." He nodded to Patty before exiting, the bell chiming in his wake. Max was surprised he didn't hear that sound in his dreams.

Max collected his order from Patty and headed back to the motel. He found Ethan and Riley outside their rooms, loading gear into Riley's car.

"How's the head?" Max asked Ethan.

Ethan managed a weak smile. "Been better but I'm good

to go. No more dizziness, but a dull headache. Feels a bit like a solid hangover."

Riley shot Max a concerned look but said nothing.

They checked out with Jeb, who nodded, but barely looked up from his Civil War tome, and moved their cars to the Sunrise lot. The trio piled into Riley's Camry for the short drive to the trailhead.

———

The small parking area was empty save for Hatfield's truck when they arrived. Mist still clung to the tree line and the air smelled like decaying leaves and wild mushrooms. There was also the hint of woodsmoke, perhaps from a nearby campsite. It mingled, not unpleasantly, with the sharp tang of the blooming mountain laurel.

As they approached, they saw Hatfield wasn't alone. A man stood beside him, tall and lean, with a neatly trimmed beard. He appeared to be in his mid-30s, older than Riley and Ethan but younger than Max. He had deep-set eyes which darted between all of them, watchful and assessing. A series of small, geometric tattoos peeked out from beneath his collar, disappearing down his neck and under his shirt. While his posture remained calm and still, the man's hands never stopped moving, fingers constantly fiddling with a worn piece of paracord.

"This is Jamie," Hatfield said by way of introduction. "He works for me at the outfitting company. He's coming with us."

Riley's eyebrows shot up. "That wasn't part of the plan."

"Plans change," Hatfield replied. "Jamie's got advanced wilderness first aid training and knows these woods almost as well as I do. We might need both."

All the outcomes that statement implied were left unsaid and, before anyone could argue further, the sound of an approaching vehicle cut through the morning stillness. A Forest Service truck pulled into the lot, and Buck Holcomb stepped out, his expression unreadable.

"Thought I might find you folks here," Holcomb said, approaching the group.

"Buck," Hatfield nodded. "What brings you out so early?"

Holcomb's eyes swept over the group. "Checked in with the sheriff this morning. Saw some interesting overnight notes. Seems two locals ended up in the hospital over in Millbrook."

Max felt his stomach tighten.

"Oh?" Riley said, her voice carefully neutral.

"Yeah," Holcomb continued, his gaze settling on Max. "Told the deputy they got jumped from behind outside the Nail. You folks wouldn't know anything about that, would you?"

Hatfield glanced up from where he was adjusting his gear, his eyes narrowing.

Max shook his head. "Can't say that we do."

"Funny thing," Holcomb said, his tone easy. "They got jumped from behind, but all their injuries, and there were many, were to the front."

"Strange," Max agreed, meeting Holcomb's gaze.

A silence fell over the group. Hatfield continued to prep his pack. Jamie fiddled with the paracord. Then, unexpectedly, Holcomb turned and pulled a pack from the back of his truck.

"What's this?" Hatfield asked, straightening up.

"I'm coming with you," Holcomb stated, shouldering his pack.

Ethan's eyebrows shot up. "Is that...allowed?"

"I've thought about it since we talked yesterday," Holcomb said. "Couldn't convince my boss or the sheriff to mount an official search, but no one can stop me from taking some personal days. And if I happen to spend those days in the woods, well, that's my business."

Max studied Holcomb's face. It was clear there would be no arguing with the man. To his surprise, Max found himself glad for Holcomb's presence. He'd only had a brief conversation with the man, but that was more than he'd had with Jamie, and the man's calm demeanor might balance out the group's dynamics again. Plus, another experienced set of eyes could only help.

Hatfield looked like he might object for a moment, but then he simply nodded and unfolded a map. Max recognized it as a copy of the same Land Management Office map that Ethan had matched up to the hermit's corkboard the day before. Hatfield spread it on a picnic table near the trailhead. Everyone crowded closer.

Hatfield reached into his pocket, pulling out a small tin. He popped the lid open and pinched a wad of chewing tobacco between his thumb and forefinger and tucked it into his lip. "The first six or seven miles aren't bad," Hatfield began. "We'll be on groomed park trails for about five of those. Our goal is to reach this point," he tapped a spot on the map, "well before nightfall."

His finger traced a path along the paper. "The last three miles or so are going to be challenging. And this final climb?" He indicated a tightly clustered set of contour lines. "It's short but brutal. Not gonna lie."

Hatfield straightened, his gaze sweeping over each member of the group. "From this point on, I am God to you. What I say goes. If I say we stop, we stop. We drink, we drink. If you're not thirsty, drink anyway. I don't care."

He paused, letting his words sink in, glanced at Holcomb, then continued. "If you have any issues—feet, back, shoulders, pack—you let me know and we fix it. Immediately. Especially feet." His eyes narrowed. "You all might be imagining bears or wolves, but if anything's going to get us in trouble, it's feet. We are unlikely to turn back due to bears, but I've seen many hikes fail due to blisters. Tell me immediately if you need a break or have any other issues. Don't wait. Don't be embarrassed. We will not lose anyone on this trek. Got it?"

Max found himself nodding along with the others. Despite his initial skepticism, he was impressed. He'd heard some good speeches in his youth, playing hockey, and this was a good one. Hatfield had a calm confidence. Max wasn't big on authority, but he was ready to follow Hatfield into these woods.

The man continued, "When we get to that last stretch, the real bitch part, stay connected to the person in front of you. Stick together, don't get separated. There's no trail to follow. You will be following me." He looked at each of them. "Questions?"

The group remained silent. Hatfield nodded.

"All right then," he said, pulling on his pack. "We're burning daylight. Let's move out."

As the now-expanded group gathered their gear and prepared to set off, Max caught Riley's eye. She gave him a slight nod. He shouldered his own pack. It was heavy but manageable. He noticed Ethan wince slightly as he tugged his pack on and adjusted the straps.

"You sure about this?" Max asked one last time.

Ethan nodded. "I'm not staying behind. I'll be fine."

The forest loomed before them, dark and inscrutable, holding its secrets close.

"All right," Max said following Riley down the trail. "Let's go find some answers."

CHAPTER TWENTY-THREE

The forest came alive around them as they set out, the morning stillness giving way to the cacophony of nature. Beams of sunlight pierced through gaps in the canopy, creating glowing spotlights on the forest floor as the mist slowly dissipated and the day warmed. Max glanced down. The trail beneath his feet was a patchwork of textures—packed earth cushioned with fallen leaves, a stretch of exposed roots forming natural steps.

Max breathed in deeply. He was a city boy at heart, but he could appreciate nature. He was aware this was the honeymoon phase of the trip, but he'd enjoy it while he could. He had no doubt it would get worse. They'd only been hiking a couple of hours and only had to choke down one protein bar. It would *definitely* get worse. He adjusted his pack and tried to keep a steady pace.

The groomed trail wound its way through stands of towering oaks and maples, their leaves just beginning to hint at the autumn spectacle to come. Delicate ferns unfurled at the base of moss-covered boulders. A chipmunk darted across their path, pausing to eye the group curiously, maybe a little suspiciously, before disappearing into the underbrush with a flick of its striped tail.

As they pressed on, Max found himself falling into a sustainable rhythm as his boots crunched softly on the gravel, leaves, and packed dirt. The forest seemed to embrace them, the outside world fading away with each step deeper into the green heart of the Monongahela. A passing thought blew through his head as he rounded a bend.

Would it let them go again?

———

Hatfield led the group. His stride loose and confident. He looked as fresh and full of energy as when they first stepped onto the trail. The new guy, Jamie, came next. Occasionally Max could see Hatfield turn and say something to the man, but Max was too far back to hear anything. Next came Riley, close on Jamie's heels. As soon as they hit the woods she was like a dog straining against a leash, eager to get out and run. Ethan followed her, head down and quiet, but keeping pace. Max found himself near the back with Holcomb bringing up the rear.

The trail was well maintained this close to the trailhead. The path itself was a mix of packed earth and fine gravel, wide enough for two people to walk side by side comfortably. Wooden planks bridged small streams, and stone steps had been cut into steeper inclines. At regular intervals, blue diamond-shaped blazes adorned tree trunks, reassuring day hikers they were on the right path. Informational kiosks stood at key junctions, offering detailed topographical maps and highlighting points of interest.

Max let a small gap open up between himself and Ethan and turned to Holcomb. "So, Hatfield used to be a ranger?"

Holcomb nodded, his eyes flicking ahead then back to Max. "Yeah, for quite a few years. He was good at it, too."

"What happened?"

Holcomb was quiet for a moment, considering his words. "It's not really my story to tell, but...there was an incident. A group of hikers went missing. Hatfield led the quick response team."

Max waited, sensing there was more to the story. Holcomb eventually continued, his voice low.

"They found them, or what was left of them. Bear attack, officially. Never found the bear, but it was the right time of year, if the hikers had stumbled onto a mother and her cubs. It was a bad scene. Everyone agreed on that."

"But?" Max said.

Holcomb's eyes scanned ahead before he continued. "But during the search, one of Hatfield's team members was killed. Under...questionable circumstances."

"What do you mean, questionable?"

"The official report, and I've read it, said it was an accident—a fall from a steep ridge. But there were inconsistencies. Some of the injuries didn't quite match up with a fall. And Hatfield was the last one to see him alive."

Max frowned. "Are you saying Hatfield was suspected of something?"

"No," Holcomb said quickly. "But there were questions. About his leadership, his decision-making. Some wondered if he'd pushed too hard, taken too many risks."

"And that's why he quit?"

Holcomb nodded. "He resigned before the investigation concluded. Said he couldn't lead if his team didn't trust him."

"He quit being a ranger, but he didn't quit going into the woods."

"No," Holcomb replied. "It didn't let up its grip."

They walked in silence for a while, the forest growing

denser around them. The easy trail began to give way to a more rugged path. Roots jutted from the earth, and fallen branches required careful navigation.

"You ever ask him about it?" Max asked finally.

Holcomb shook his head. "No need. You can see it in the way he carries himself, the way he approaches every search. He's a man with something to prove."

Max considered this. "And yet, people still trust him to lead them into the woods."

"That's the thing about Hatfield," Holcomb said, his voice a mix of admiration and caution. "He knows these forests better than anyone. You heard his speech this morning."

"It was good."

"I know. That wasn't bullshit. It wouldn't work if it was. He's driven in a way most aren't. Whether that's a good thing or not..." He left the thought unfinished, his eyes fixed on Hatfield's back as they continued down the trail. "Maybe that's why I'm here," he eventually said. "To make up my mind."

———

By midmorning, they paused for a water break. Max leaned against a large oak as he surveyed the group. Hatfield stood apart, consulting a map, his brow furrowed in concentration. Jamie hovered nearby, his fingers working that ever-present piece of paracord with an intensity that seemed at odds with the moment of rest.

Riley helped Ethan adjust his pack, her movements efficient and practiced. Ethan looked pale, his jaw clenched in determination. Max noticed a slight tremor in Ethan's hands as he reached for his water bottle.

A sudden rustling in the undergrowth made Max turn. A

deer emerged briefly from the foliage, its large eyes regarding them warily before it bounded away.

Hatfield folded up the map and approached Max, offering an energy bar. "How're you holding up?"

Max accepted the bar with a nod of thanks. "Pretty good, actually. Feet feel solid, pack's not too bad."

"Done much hiking before?"

"Some, up in Vermont with a friend. Nothing this intense though."

Hatfield's eyes crinkled at the corners, but the smile didn't reach his eyes. "Well, pace yourself. This is not intense. Not yet." He glanced back at the trail they'd come from, then leaned in closer. "Listen, we're entering a part of the forest that can be...tricky. Stay alert. If you notice anything unusual—sounds, smells, anything—you tell me immediately. Understood?"

Max nodded, not sure what to make of his comment. "What should I be looking for?"

Hatfield's gaze swept over the group before settling back on Max. "Anything that doesn't feel right. Trust your instincts." He paused, then added in a lower voice, "And keep an eye on Ethan. He's not looking too good."

As Hatfield moved away, Max felt a prickling on his neck. He looked up and found Jamie watching him. As soon as Max made eye contact, Jamie looked away. Max found himself studying the man more closely. His fingers never stopped moving, weaving complex patterns in the paracord. His eyes, though, were constantly scanning the forest, as if expecting something to emerge from the shadows at any moment.

Max took a bite of the energy bar, the overly sweet taste cloying in his mouth. The forest around them seemed to press in closer, the shadows deepening despite the midmorning sun. He shook off the feeling. He was determined not to let Hatfield or Jamie's paranoia soak into his thoughts. Not without a reason.

"Let's move out," Hatfield called.

As they started to fall back in line behind Hatfield, Max noticed Riley slip something into Ethan's pack—a bottle of pills, perhaps? The gesture was quick, almost furtive. He made a mental note to keep a closer eye on Ethan as they continued their journey. Max also noticed something else. While everyone else had taken up the same positions, Jamie had slipped to the back of the group and now brought up the rear behind Holcomb. Was it by happenstance or design? Other than Hatfield up front, no one had told them how to fall in line. Max didn't have much time to consider the question. The trail ahead quickly narrowed and after a half mile began to climb more steeply. The air grew thinner, and any conversation stalled as the group focused on following Hatfield and navigating the next section of terrain.

CHAPTER TWENTY-FOUR

By early afternoon, they reached a small clearing. A fallen log provided seating and a nearby stream offered fresh water. Hatfield called for a longer break. The clearing was carpeted with a thick layer of moss, punctuated by colorful clusters of woodland flowers that Max couldn't identify.

Max sank onto the log, gratefully shrugging off his pack. As the weight fell from his shoulders, he felt a mix of relief and satisfaction. His muscles ached, a testament to the morning's exertion, but it was a good ache—the kind that came from pushing oneself without going too far. He rolled his shoulders, feeling a few vertebrae pop back into place. His feet were sore, but not blistered, and while his back was damp with sweat, he didn't feel overly fatigued. In other words, he felt like he'd spent most of the day hiking.

As they rested, Hatfield sat slightly apart, his compass balanced on his knee. His thumb traced the familiar groove where the lid had worn thin from countless openings. Max noticed how the ranger checked it almost unconsciously, likely a habit born from years in the wilderness.

Max rummaged through his pack, pulling out a packet of trail mix and a protein bar. Not even 12 hours in and he knew he'd never willingly eat another protein bar ever again. No matter the flavor or brand, the texture was somewhere between cardboard and old bubblegum, with just enough stickiness to remind you that, yes, this was meant to be food. With no other choice until they set up camp and cooked dinner, he unwrapped the bar and eyed the sad, beige rectangle with a mixture of resignation and mild disgust. Fuel was fuel, he reminded himself, even if it came in the form of glorified building material masquerading as nutrition.

He chewed. And chewed some more. After he eventually swallowed, he turned to Ethan, who sat nearby, massaging his temples.

"How're you doing?" Max asked, offering some of the trail mix to Ethan.

Ethan managed a weak smile, accepting a handful of the mix. "I've been better. But I'll manage."

Max nodded and tried to swallow a bite of shingling. It stuck in his throat, and he needed a long drink from his canteen. After a moment, he said, "Tell me more about Jake. How'd you two meet?"

Ethan's eyes lit up, some color returning to his face. "Freshman year at Dartmouth. We were roommates. Couldn't have been more different at first glance. Me, the scholarship kid from North Philly. Jake, the Boston blue blood."

He chuckled, shaking his head. "But we hit it off right away. Jake...he has this way of making you feel like you belong, you know? Like you're exactly where you're supposed to be."

Max listened, noting the present tense. Ethan still believed Jake was alive.

"There was this one time," Ethan continued, "during

finals week. Sophomore year. I was stressed out of my mind, ready to pack it in and head back to Philly. Jake found me at the library at 3:00 a.m., brought me a thermos of coffee and a stack of fresh notecards."

Ethan's smile went a little crooked. "Of course, Vance showed up the next morning unannounced with bagels and more coffee. Vance had this way of...I don't know, amplifying everything. Suddenly it wasn't just Jake and me cramming for a final. Vance was there. It was an event."

Max raised an eyebrow. "Sounds like Vance made an impression."

Ethan nodded. "Yeah, he did. Don't get me wrong, Jake's great. But Vance...he was something else. When people say larger than life, that was him, you know? When he walked into a room, everyone noticed. You couldn't help it."

"Must have been hard, being in his shadow," Max said.

Ethan shrugged. "Sometimes. But Jake never seemed to mind. He adored Vance, looked up to him. We all did, I guess."

As Ethan spoke, Max couldn't help but notice how the conversation had shifted. They'd started talking about Jake, but somehow Vance had taken center stage. Even now, years after his disappearance, Vance's presence seemed to linger, overshadowing everything else.

"Did Vance know?" Max asked. "The effect he had on people?"

Ethan was quiet for a moment, considering. "I think so. He was always aware of his audience, always performing in a way. But it never felt fake, you know? That's probably why his YouTube channel took off. He didn't want to trade on his last name, but he also couldn't hide from it no matter what he chose to do. He had a certain charisma. He was just...Vance."

Max nodded, mulling this over. Charisma, he knew, was a

double-edged sword. It could inspire loyalty and draw people in, but it could also attract unwanted attention, perhaps even danger. He wondered if Vance had ever considered the darker implications. He glanced around the clearing, noting how the others seemed to be listening too, even as they went about their own tasks. Riley, adjusting her bootlaces, kept glancing up, her expression a mix of curiosity and something harder to define. Even Hatfield had drifted nearer, his weathered face inscrutable as he pretended to study his map. Vance's presence—or rather, his absence—would be a constant, invisible companion on this journey. In the Monongahela, Vance Cotter was both everywhere and nowhere at once. Max found himself wondering who they were really searching for. Was it Jake? Sarah? Or was Vance, in his own way, leading them all deeper into the forest, toward some unknown destination?

"Take 10 more minutes, then we're off again," Hatfield barked out.

Max glanced over at Ethan, who had fallen asleep, slumped against the log, his face pale and drawn. Holcomb wandered over, his eyes fixed on the sleeping figure.

"He going to make it?" Holcomb asked, his voice low with concern. "That's a nasty-looking lump behind his ear."

Max hesitated. He wasn't sure, but he felt he owed it to Ethan to have his back. He watched Ethan's hand twitch in his lap as he slept.

"He'll be okay," Riley said, striding over. Max could hear her try to inject an enthusiasm she probably didn't feel into her voice. "He's got youth on his side."

Holcomb raised an eyebrow, clearly not buying it, but he didn't push the issue.

"That last stretch was tough," Holcomb admitted. "The next bit, I'm assuming Hatfield is making for Raven's Ridge, isn't a cakewalk either. But if Ethan's made it this far, he should be able to reach the base camp location." He paused, then added, "Another night of sleep should help."

"He'll make it," she said.

Max nodded, hoping that both of them were right. He studied Ethan's face, noticing the dark circles under his eyes and the tight set of his jaw even in sleep. The young man was pushing himself to his limits, driven by a determination Max couldn't help but admire, even as it worried him.

"We'll keep an eye on him," Max said, more to himself than to Holcomb. "Make sure he doesn't push too hard."

Holcomb glanced at his watch. "Better wake him. We'll be moving out soon."

As Max bent to pick up his pack, a strangled cry erupted from the forest. It started low, almost like a whimper, then crescendoed into something akin to a screaming baby. The sound cut through the clearing, causing Max to instinctively drop into a crouch. For five, maybe ten seconds, the cry grew in volume before fading away, leaving an ominous silence in its wake.

"What the hell was that?" Riley asked, her voice tight.

Hatfield's gaze swept the tree line, his expression unreadable. "Just an animal," he said flatly.

Max caught Holcomb's eye, but the other man looked away, his jaw clenched.

"What kind of animal?" Max asked.

Hatfield didn't answer. Instead, he adjusted his pack, his movements deliberate and controlled. Then the sound came again, seemingly closer this time. It lingered in the air, haunting and plaintive, before fading away.

"Break's over. Let's go," Hatfield announced, his tone brooking no argument.

Max looked down at Ethan. The young man was no longer asleep. If anything, he looked worse than before. His face had drained of what little color it had regained during his short nap. His eyes were wide with a mix of exhaustion and unmistakable fear. As Ethan struggled to his feet, Max noticed it wasn't just his hands that were trembling, but his whole body.

The group fell into line and one by one followed Hatfield deeper into the woods.

CHAPTER TWENTY-FIVE

After another 90 minutes of hiking, difficult, but not the breath-stealing vertical scramble that had preceded it, the group finally emerged onto Raven's Ridge. The trail opened up to reveal a breathtaking vista. A flat, grassy clearing stretched before them, ringed by towering pines. To the east, a pristine lake reflected the late-afternoon sun, its surface rippling gently in the breeze. Beyond the lake, the rugged peaks of the Allegheny Mountains loomed in the distance.

The air here felt different—crisper, somehow cleaner, but maybe that was Max's imagination. He had very few past frames of reference for this tableau. The air smelled of pine and moss. A chorus of birdsong filled the air, punctuated by the occasional cry of a single hawk circling overhead.

Hatfield dropped his pack and surveyed the area, his eyes scanning the tree line before settling on the group. "All right, folks. Drop your gear. This is home for tonight and maybe the rest of the trip. We'll see how tomorrow goes before we make a decision. Let's get camp set up before we lose the light."

He pointed to a spot near the tree line where a natural depression in the ground would provide shelter from the wind. "Riley, Ethan, set up the cooking area over there. Firepit, water station, the works. Make sure the firepit is clear of overhanging branches and at least fifteen feet from the tents."

Riley nodded, already moving toward the designated spot. Ethan followed, his movements slower but determined.

Hatfield turned to Jamie. "You're on latrine duty. There's a good spot about 50 yards that way, behind those boulders. Remember, we're following the Leave No Trace principles. Dig deep and cover well."

Jamie gave a curt nod and headed off, shovel in hand.

"Holcomb, you and I will do a perimeter check. We'll mark the boundaries of our camp and look for any potential hazards or animal signs. You head west," he nodded to his right, "I'll head east and we'll meetup."

Holcomb nodded and headed out.

Finally, Hatfield's gaze landed on Max. He indicated the bags of gear scattered in a rough circle around them. "Start setting up the tents in that flat area by the big oak. Make sure they're at least 200 feet from the water source and not directly under any dead branches."

As the group worked around him, Max stood rooted to the spot, overwhelmed. He stared at his pack, then at the clearing, then back at his pack. Tent poles, stakes, rainflies—the terms Hatfield had casually tossed out during their brief gear check this morning swirled in his head, a jumble of unfamiliar jargon.

He fumbled with the zipper on his pack, not even sure which compartment held the tent. When he finally located it, he pulled out a mass of fabric and metal that might as well have been an alien artifact. He spread it on the ground, looking for some clue as to how it all fit together. Max picked up what he thought might be a tent pole, only to drop it immediately as it unfolded with a metallic snap. He wasn't just in over his head; he was drowning in a sea of canvas and confusion.

Riley approached, a knowing smile on her face. "Need a hand?"

Max nodded, grateful for the help. "Is it that obvious?"

"Only to anyone with eyes," she teased. "Here, I'll show you how to get started. First, find a spot that's relatively flat and free of rocks or roots."

She helped Max clear a small area, then showed him how to lay out the tent fabric and assemble the poles. As they worked, Max couldn't help but notice the efficiency of her movements, the ease with which she handled the equipment.

"You've done this before," he observed.

Riley's hands stilled for a moment. "Yeah, Sarah and I used to go camping a lot when we were kids. Before...well, before a lot of things."

Max waited, but Riley quickly changed the subject. "Why don't you gather some firewood and haul some water from the lake? We'll need both for dinner. Look for dry, dead wood on the ground—no cutting live branches. And make sure to gather different sizes, from small kindling to larger logs."

Relieved to have a task he understood, Max headed toward the lake, empty water containers in hand. As he approached the shore, he spotted a figure floating in the water. It was Ethan, fully clothed and seemingly unbothered by the chill that Max could feel even five feet from the bank.

Max called out, "Ethan? You okay?"

Ethan's head turned toward him, water droplets flying from his hair. "Yeah, this is the best I've felt all day. Come on in, the water's fine."

Skeptical, but thinking the water might soothe his aching feet, he dropped the containers, removed his boots and socks, and rolled up his pant legs. He waded in and almost gasped at the coldness. The shock of it hit him like a linebacker, knocking the breath from his lungs. It felt as if his feet had plunged into liquid nitrogen, the cold so intense it bordered on burning.

"Fine? It's freezing!"

Ethan laughed, the sound echoing across the lake. "Feels great to me. Cleared my head right up."

"That's probably because you can't actually feel your extremities."

But Max noticed that Ethan *did* look better. His eyes were clearer, more alert than they had been all day. The pallor that had haunted his features since getting jumped outside the Nail seemed to have faded. After his feet went numb, Max decided it might not be a bad idea to rinse his sweaty hiking clothes. He stripped down to his underwear and gave the clothes, and his socks, a quick rinse in the lake. He then took a deep breath and dropped his head into the water. He came up sputtering but had to admit he did feel a little better. He wasn't sure it was a cure for a concussion, but it might be as good as aspirin.

"How are you holding up?" Max asked, shaking his head then carrying his damp bundle to the shore before wading back to his waist.

"Better. Really," Ethan replied, lazily treading water. "The hike was rough, but this helps. It's like...I don't know, like the water's washing away all the cobwebs in my brain."

A fish jumped nearby, its splash creating ripples that lapped gently against their legs. Suddenly, Ethan asked, "Why do you think Holcomb really joined us?"

The question caught Max off guard. "He said he wanted to help, didn't he? Maybe he's still carrying some baggage from the search for Vance."

Ethan shook his head, water dripping from his hair. "I'm

not so sure it's that simple. I did some digging when we first got to Grimswood. Trying to figure out who we needed to talk to. Who might help us. There are rumors about Holcomb. He might not exactly be the friendly park ranger he pretends to be."

"What do you mean?"

Ethan opened his mouth to respond, but before he could, they heard footsteps approaching. Holcomb emerged from the tree line, his eyes scanning the lake before settling on them. His sudden appearance sent a flock of small birds scattering from a nearby bush.

"Everything all right here?" Holcomb called out, his voice carrying easily across the still water.

Ethan's demeanor instantly changed. He plastered on a smile and called back, "Just fine. Cooling off after the hike."

Holcomb nodded, his expression unreadable. "You feeling okay? You look okay."

"Yes, sir."

"All right then, don't stay in too long. That lake run off is cold and hypothermia will sneak up on you. Also, be careful—the lake bottom can drop off suddenly in some spots."

As Holcomb continued on his perimeter march, the crunch of pine needles under his boots fading into the distance, Max caught Ethan's eye. The younger man's face had closed off, the brief moment of openness gone.

"We should head back," Ethan said, wading toward the shore then collecting his shoes and walking barefoot back toward camp.

Max followed, his mind churning with questions. What had Ethan been about to say? And why did Holcomb's presence shut him down so quickly?

CHAPTER TWENTY-SIX

Back at the campsite, activity was in full swing. The six tents were set up and Riley had a fire going, the flames casting a warm glow over the area. Jamie was setting up a clothesline between two trees and, when he was done, Max added his clothes before ducking into his tent and pulling on dry gear. He then returned to the lake and filled the water buckets for dinner and washing.

When he returned to camp, Hatfield was once again hunched over a map spread out on a flat rock, making notations with a pencil. The sun was sinking lower on the horizon, casting long shadows across the clearing. The temperature was dropping rapidly despite the fire. Someone, probably more than one person, had dragged some logs out of the pines and positioned them near the fire.

As Max approached with the water, Riley looked up. "Perfect timing. Can you fill the big pot and get it over the fire? We need to boil it before using it for cooking or drinking."

Max nodded, once again glad to have clear instructions. As he worked, he kept an eye on Ethan, who had retreated to his tent. The young man emerged a few minutes later in dry clothes.

The camp slowly came together as the last light faded from the sky. Stars began to appear overhead, more numerous and brilliant than Max had ever seen in the city. There weren't any sirens, or horns, or the white noise of people living close together like there would be in the city, but the night was alive with sounds—the crackle of the fire, the hoot of an owl, the rustle of small animals in the underbrush.

As they gathered around the fire for a simple dinner of rehydrated stew and instant mashed potatoes, the group was mostly quiet. The exertion of the day dampened any attempt at long conversations, with only the occasional murmur or request to pass a salt packet or the stew pot breaking the silence. The stew, while not gourmet, was hot and filling and tasted heavenly to Max after a day of protein bars and gels. Hatfield had even produced a small bottle of hot sauce, which was passed around to add some extra kick to the meal.

As they finished eating, Hatfield spoke up. "All right, folks. Before we turn in, let's talk about tomorrow." Hatfield pulled the map out of his vest pocket and laid it flat on the ground near a small electric lantern someone had added by the fire. He used the lantern to hold one corner of the map down and added his compass to the opposite corner. He pulled out a small pocket-sized flashlight that he turned on and pointed at the map.

The group huddled around, their faces illuminated by the dual light sources. Hatfield traced a finger along a series of concentric circles he'd drawn earlier.

"I've divided our search area into quadrants," he explained. "We know from Sarah's contact with Riley the first two days, the general direction the pair were headed. We assume that was still their plan. Based on some assumptions," Hatfield glanced at Ethan, "and...probabilities, we developed the quadrants. We'll work in teams of two, each taking a section. The goal is to cover as much ground as possible while maintaining visual or audio contact with at least one other team."

Riley leaned in, her brow furrowed. "What's our search pattern within each quadrant?"

Hatfield nodded. "Good question. We'll use a grid pattern. Each team will move in parallel lines about 50 feet apart, then shift over and come back the other way. Like mowing a lawn, but much, much slower."

"How slow are we talking?" Max asked. Even a novice like Max could see the search area was large. Too large to really cover with six people in less than a week.

"In terrain like this? Maybe half a mile an hour, if we're thorough," Hatfield replied. "It's painstaking work, but it's the best way to ensure we don't miss anything."

Holcomb spoke up. "What about markers? We don't want to get turned around out there."

"Right," Hatfield said. "Each team will carry bright-orange surveyor's tape. We'll mark our paths at regular intervals. This serves two purposes: it helps us maintain our search pattern and provides a trail back if we need to retrace our steps quickly."

He paused, looking around the group. "Now, this is crucial. If anyone finds anything—and I mean anything—you stop immediately and call for the rest of us. Don't touch it, don't move it. We document everything in place first."

"What exactly are we looking for?" Ethan asked, his voice tinged with a mix of hope and apprehension.

Hatfield's expression grew serious. "Anything that doesn't belong in the woods. Bits of clothing, gear, disturbed earth, unusual markings on trees. Hell, even if something just feels off, we investigate. Trust your instincts out here. If they were hurt or ran into trouble, their first priority would have been shelter. We believe both Sarah and Jake were experienced enough to know that. This section," he indicated a quadrant in the upper northwest section of the map, "is known to include some caves. That's a three- or four-hour hike. I don't expect to make it that far tomorrow."

Hatfield didn't say the words out loud, but Max knew that it was the area indicated on the hermit's map that Ethan believed might be Grave's End.

Hatfield didn't say it, but Holcomb did. "Why Grave's End? I've only been near there a few times in my career. It's not groomed for a reason. It's difficult terrain even for experienced hikers. Looking at their heading from the last known points, there are many other trails they could have taken."

Ethan spoke up. "We believe Jake found some evidence or had a strong belief that Vance was headed in that direction when he disappeared."

Holcomb frowned. "That's far from the original search, if I remember correctly."

"You're right," Hatfield said.

There was a beat of silence as the group digested that and the implications before Riley asked, "And if we find a sign of Sarah or Jake?" Max could practically hear her teeth grinding. The deeper they went into the woods, the higher her anxiety climbed.

"Then we switch gears and we might speed up," Hatfield said. "We go from a search pattern to tracking. But let's not get ahead of ourselves. Tomorrow is about thorough, methodical searching."

He put the compass in his pocket, moved the lantern and folded the map before looking at each of them in turn. "Any other questions?" The group remained silent. "All right then. Before we turn in, we need to secure the camp. Food goes in the bear canisters and up in those trees." He pointed to a pair of sturdy oaks a hundred feet or so from the tents. "We'll hang them at least ten feet high and four feet out from the trunk."

Riley and Jamie volunteered for the task, working together to hoist the canisters. Meanwhile, Max and Ethan collected the pots and dishes and headed to the designated washing station. They used biodegradable soap and strained the wash water through a fine mesh to collect any food particles, which went into a sealable bag to be packed out with them.

Holcomb made a final sweep of the campsite, ensuring no food wrappers or scented items were left out. "Remember," he called out, "no food, toothpaste, or anything scented in the tents. That includes lip balm and medications."

Hatfield doused the fire, plunging the camp into darkness broken only by the scant lantern light and soft glow of the overhead stars.

"Get some rest," Hatfield said. "We break camp and start the search at first light."

———

Max lay in the dark in his sleeping bag, acutely aware of the thin fabric of the tent separating him from the wilderness. The darkness outside felt thick, almost sentient, as if the trees themselves were leaning in, whispering secrets just beyond his comprehension. He'd traveled extensively in recent years, but always gravitated toward cities, their bustling energy and concrete landscapes a familiar comfort.

The closest he'd come to this was his time on Prince Edward Island, but even that paled in comparison to the raw, untamed essence of the Monongahela. Here, in the heart of the forest, he felt both exhilarated and unnerved.

The night sounds filtered through the tent—the rustle of leaves, the distant hoot of an owl, the occasional snap of a twig under an unseen animal's foot. This deep immersion in nature stirred something primal within him. He was tapping into a part of himself long dormant, awakening senses dulled by urban living.

Whatever secrets the woods held, whatever answers they sought, lay somewhere out there in the vast expanse of the Monongahela. His last conscious thought before he fell asleep was wondering whether they were truly prepared for what they might find.

The screaming started sometime after midnight.

CHAPTER TWENTY-SEVEN

Max jolted awake. He scrambled out of his sleeping bag and fumbled with the tent zipper, heart pounding. Cold air hit his face as he stumbled out.

Chaos reigned in the clearing. Dark shapes darted between tents. Headlamps and flashlight beams crisscrossed wildly. The screams bounced and echoed, impossible to pinpoint.

"What's happening?" someone shouted. Holcomb?

No answer. Just more screaming.

Max spotted Hatfield, head lamp blazing, a gun in his hand. The ex-forest ranger's face was taut, his gaze sharp as he scanned the tree line before running in that direction.

More figures rushed past. More crashing sounds. Muffled curses. Branches snapping.

Max didn't move. He needed light. He ducked back into his tent and fished his phone from his pack, clicked on the flashlight. The beam seemed feeble against the overwhelming darkness.

The screaming stopped abruptly. Cut off like a radio unplugged mid-song. The sudden silence was jarring, almost as unsettling as the screams themselves. Silence fell, broken only by distant shouts and footsteps fading into the forest.

The campsite was suddenly empty, everyone careening through the surrounding woods. Max was alone. He strained his ears. A splash. Faint, but unmistakable.

He moved quickly toward the lake, trying to find the thin path he'd used earlier, branches whipped his face. Roots grabbed at his feet. He stumbled, caught himself, pushed on.

The trees parted and he stepped out close to the lake's edge. Starlight glimmered on the water's surface. A hunched shape huddled by the shore, half hidden in the reeds.

Max froze. Human? Animal? He couldn't tell.

He waited, barely breathing. The shape stirred, rose up.

Max aimed his light. The beam caught a pale face, wide eyes.

"Ethan?" Max called softly. He approached slowly.

Ethan didn't respond. His shirt was torn. Blood streaked his arms and face.

Max touched his shoulder. "Can you hear me?"

No reaction. Just a blank stare.

"Come on," Max said. He gently took Ethan's arm, led him carefully through the trees and back to camp.

The clearing was deserted. He could hear movement and occasionally see a light along the tree line as the others ran about. Max sat Ethan on a log near the dead fire. He grabbed the first aid kit near the wash station and a bucket of leftover water.

"What happened?" Max asked. He opened the kit and removed some gauze and a tube of antibiotic cream. He also grabbed a foil first aid blanket. Ethan was shivering and Max didn't want to wait to restart the fire. He returned to Ethan.

He hadn't moved, just stared down at a spot between his knees. Max unwrapped the blanket and draped it over Ethan's shoulders then gently used the gauze to dab at the worst of the cuts on the man's forehead.

Ethan blinked slowly. "I...I saw him."

"Who?"

"Vance."

Max paused. "Vance Cotter?"

Ethan continued on as if he hadn't heard Max. "He was in the trees. I got up to go the bathroom and he was just there. Staring at me. His face was so pale. So white in the night. Hey, that rhymes." Ethan looked up and gave a wan smile. Max took the opportunity to check his eyes. Both pupils were dilated and large, but equal size, though Ethan's entire demeanor appeared unfocused and skittish.

"Where?"

"Where what?"

"Where did you see Vance?"

Ethan glanced around for a moment then raised a scratched and bloody arm. "There, by the designated latrine."

"But I found you down by the lake." The lake was 75 yards in almost the opposite direction. "You were screaming. Do you remember?"

Ethan nodded. "I was asleep. Then I got up. Then I saw Vance. He told me to look in the water. So that's where I went, but it was cold. So cold."

Max dabbed antibiotic cream on the cut. Ethan didn't flinch.

"Did something attack you?" Max asked. He wasn't sure what to make of Ethan's story. Maybe different questions could tease out something that made more sense.

"Attack me? No. I don't think so. I just...felt wrong. Like I wasn't myself."

Footsteps approached. Riley burst into the clearing, breathing hard.

"Max? Is that...Ethan?" She rushed over. "What happened? We've been searching everywhere."

"I found him by the lake," Max explained. "He doesn't remember much."

Riley knelt beside Ethan, took his hand. "God, you're freezing. Is that blood? Are you okay? Was that you screaming? You scared us all half to death."

Ethan's eyes focused on her. The sight of her, or maybe her familiar voice, seemed to bring him back a bit. "Riley? I'm sorry. I don't know what came over me."

Jamie and Holcomb filtered back into camp. Hatfield arrived last, holstering his gun.

"Report," he barked.

"Easy," Riley said. "Ethan's here. Max found him."

Hatfield's eyes narrowed. His face remained intense, but his voice was more controlled. "What happened?"

Ethan shrugged helplessly. "I can't explain it."

"You said you saw Vance?" Max prodded.

"I did?"

"Yes. Just now. You told me you woke up to go the bathroom and saw him, or his face, in the woods."

Ethan's cheeks colored and he looked down. "That doesn't sound...I'm sorry, I don't remember that. One minute I was asleep, the next I was in the lake, screaming. I remember the cold mostly."

"Sleepwalking?" Holcomb suggested.

"I used to as a kid, sometimes, but it hasn't happened in years."

"Maybe," Hatfield said, "the stress could have brought it on. But I've never heard of sleepwalking that violent."

Holcomb approached, frowning. He lifted one of Ethan's

arms and then examined his ripped shirt. "Those weren't normal screams. They sounded...inhuman."

An uneasy silence fell over the group.

"Could it be related to his head injury?" Max asked.

Riley nodded. "Possible. Concussions can cause all sorts of weird symptoms."

"Or maybe it's something else entirely," Jamie muttered.

Hatfield shot him a warning look. "Let's not jump to conclusions. For now, Ethan needs rest. We all do. Let's get him back to his tent."

———

The camp gradually settled into an uneasy quiet. Max helped Riley guide Ethan back to his tent, the young man's eyes almost closing as they walked. They managed to work him into the sleeping bag; he was snoring before they left the tent.

"I'll grab my stuff and sleep in here. Keep an eye on him until morning," Riley said.

"Becoming a bad habit. Make sure you get some sleep, too."

"I've never needed much."

As they zipped up the tent flap, Jamie materialized out of the darkness. Holcomb was nowhere to be seen, likely back in his tent, but Hatfield stood nearby. Even in the dark, Max could see the coiled intensity in the man.

Max's gaze immediately fixed on Jamie's hand. He wasn't carrying a firearm like Hatfield nor was his ever-present paracord visible. Instead, he gripped a wicked-looking knife with a serrated edge and a matte black blade that seemed to absorb what little light there was.

But it wasn't the knife that captured Max's full attention. It was Jamie's next words.

"There's a problem with the food," he said.

Max blinked, startled. It was the first time he'd heard Jamie speak directly, not under his breath or off to the side to Hatfield. His voice was surprisingly soft, with a slight rasp, as if he wasn't used to using it.

Hatfield looked at the younger man for a beat. "Show me."

Max followed the pair to where they'd hung the bear bags earlier. As they approached, he could make out shapes scattered on the ground. When they got closer, his stomach dropped.

The bags were in tatters, shredded beyond repair. Their contents lay strewn across the forest floor—energy bars, dehydrated meals, trail mix, some torn open and further scattered on the ground.

"What the hell?" Hatfield breathed. There was a note in his voice Max hadn't heard before—worry, tinged with fear. Hatfield crouched, examining the remnants of a bag. "How did this happen?" No one had an answer. At least not one they wanted to say out loud.

Max stared up at the branch where they'd hung the canisters. It was at least ten feet off the ground like Hatfield requested. He'd watched Jamie and Riley as they'd hoisted them up.

A chill ran down his spine as a thought occurred to him. Maybe the better question wasn't how this happened, but what did this? What kind of animal could reach that high and cause this much destruction?

As if reading his thoughts, Jamie spoke again, his soft voice, barely above a whisper. "No bear did this."

The group fell silent, the implications of Jamie's words hanging in the air. Whatever had attacked their food supply wasn't a normal forest predator. And suddenly, the vast wilderness surrounding them felt a lot more threatening. The screams, Ethan or not, took on a new dimension.

Hatfield straightened up. "We need to salvage what we can. And tomorrow, we're going to have to figure out how to ration what's left."

CHAPTER TWENTY-EIGHT

Max's body ached in places he didn't know could ache. The predawn light filtered through the tent fabric, casting everything in a soft-gray hue. He groaned as he sat up, his muscles protesting every movement.

Outside, the camp was already stirring. The smell of coffee wafted through the air, a beacon of normalcy in the aftermath of last night's chaos. Max emerged from his tent, rubbing the sleep from his eyes.

Ethan sat on a log by the rekindled fire, his face pale and drawn. A pot of oatmeal bubbled in a small pot hanging over the fire. Max grabbed a tin mug of coffee and settled beside him.

"How are you feeling?" Max asked.

Ethan shrugged, wincing at the movement. "Like I got hit by a truck. Again."

"Do you remember anything about last night?"

"It's all a blur," Ethan said, his voice barely above a whisper. "I keep seeing flashes—the tent, the water, the trees, but nothing makes sense."

Max nodded. "The face?"

"Yes," Ethan said softly. "That's one part I'd like to forget."

Max sipped his coffee. The bitter liquid was a comfort. They sat in silence, even as Max's head swirled with questions about the events of the night before.

Riley came out next, took a slug of coffee, and sat on the log next to Ethan. Holcomb was next, looking as tired and sore as Max felt. Hatfield and Jamie were last, emerging from the woods near the washing station and walking over to the fire. Both men looked like they'd been up for hours, and Max wondered if Hatfield slept or just plugged himself into a tree to recharge.

"We need to talk about the food situation," Hatfield said.

"What about it?" Holcomb asked.

Hatfield explained to Riley and Holcomb what they had discovered about the food supplies the previous night.

"How long will what's left last us?" Riley asked.

"If we ration carefully, maybe three days," Hatfield replied. "Four if we're lucky."

"Maybe we should consider heading back, re-supply, get Ethan some medical attention," Holcomb said.

"What? No." Riley responded, an edge in her voice. "I'm not going back. We've already wasted enough time waiting on the weather. My sister and Jake could be hurt or suffering. If we still have enough for three days, I'm taking three days. If Ethan's not up for hiking, he can stay here, maintain camp."

"I'm good," Ethan said.

He couldn't sound further from good, Max thought. A heavy silence fell over the group. Max glanced up, noticing dark clouds rolling in over the distant mountains. The brief respite of clear skies wouldn't last much longer.

"We stay the course for now," Hatfield said and cleared his throat. "Everyone eat. We can't waste anything, then we've got work to do before we pack out. Riley, Ethan, you're on water duty. Filter what we need for the day. Max, Jamie, break down breakfast, clean the pots. Holcomb and I will sort through what's left of the food and plan the route for the day."

———

The group ate quickly and dispersed to their assigned tasks. Max found himself working alongside Jamie to douse the fire and clean the breakfast dishes. As they worked in silence, Max couldn't help but feel uneasy. He typically appreciated quiet efficiency, but after the previous night's events, he felt a pressing need to know more about this late addition to the group; a man that he was, at least partially, trusting with his life in this wilderness.

Crouching next to Jamie, Max rinsed the group's coffee cups and silverware. The chirping of birds in the surrounding trees seemed to emphasize the silence between them.

"So," Max said, "how long have you been working with Hatfield?"

Jamie didn't look up from scrubbing the oatmeal pot. "Years," he said. The word barely carried over the sounds of the forest, as if Jamie was unaccustomed to speaking above a whisper.

Max waited, but Jamie offered nothing more. The gurgling of the nearby stream feeding the lake filled the void.

"Must've seen some interesting things out here," Max pressed.

Jamie's hands paused momentarily. "Yep."

Max watched Jamie's methodical movements. The man's face remained impassive, a mask of concentration—or perhaps concealment.

"Any advice for a newbie like me?" Max tried once more.

Jamie finally glanced at him, his eyes unreadable. "Watch your step."

Before Max could probe further, Hatfield's voice sliced through the air. "Let's move, people! We're burning daylight."

Hatfield pulled his battered brass compass from his vest pocket and checked their bearing. The morning light caught the worn script etched into its case: From this point on, I am God to you. What I say goes. That seemed about right to Max. As they packed up, Max noticed Hatfield observing them closely. The guide's gaze seemed to hold a mixture of assessment and something else—concern, perhaps?

"Time to head out," Hatfield announced 10 minutes later, shouldering his pack. "Jamie, you're on point with me. Holcomb, bring up the rear and watch our six with Max."

Max couldn't help but wonder if Hatfield was deliberately separating them. He watched Jamie move to the front, the piece of paracord appearing in his hand. The man's silence said something, but what exactly it was remained a mystery. With a last glance at Jamie's retreating back, Max took his position at the rear of the group, ready for whatever the day might bring. Or, so he hoped.

———

The forest seemed different in the daylight—less menacing, but no less mysterious. The group moved in staggered pairs, spreading out when they crossed wider fields or open forest, then coming together when they funneled into more narrow areas or thin game trails, eyes scanning the underbrush for any sign of Sarah or Jake.

Max fell into step beside Holcomb, the ranger's steady pace a counterpoint to the uneven terrain.

"Can I ask you something?" Max said, ducking under a

low-hanging branch as they followed a twisting route within earshot of the stream.

Holcomb nodded, his eyes never leaving the vague path ahead.

"Why are you really here? It's not just about guilt over never finding Vance, is it?"

Holcomb was quiet for a long moment, the only sounds their boots crunching on fallen leaves.

"Everyone deserves to be found," he finally said.

"The other missing people," Max pressed. "Is that what this is about?"

Holcomb's jaw tightened. "Like I said, everyone deserves to be found. Can we leave it at that?"

They walked in silence for a while, the forest growing denser around them. Max's mind wandered back to the previous night.

"What do you think happened to the food?" he asked. "Did you notice there were no tracks?"

Holcomb's steps faltered for a moment. "I noticed."

"So, what does that mean? What could have done that without leaving a trace?"

"I don't know," Holcomb admitted, his voice low, eyes leaving the ground and looking ahead. "And that's what worries me."

A twig snapped somewhere to their left. Both men froze, eyes scanning the underbrush. After a tense moment, a squirrel darted across their path, disappearing into the foliage.

"This forest," Holcomb said, resuming their trek, "it's old. Older than any of us can really comprehend. And old places, they have a way of keeping secrets."

"What kinds of secrets?"

Holcomb shook his head. "The kind that don't like being discovered."

They crested a small rise, the trees thinning slightly. Ahead, Max could see Riley and Ethan, their heads bent close in conversation. Hatfield and Jamie were farther ahead, in a shallow valley, 10 yards apart, their heads swiveling side to side, taking in their surroundings.

"You've been out here a long time, walked a lot of these trails," Max said. "Have you ever seen anything...unexplainable?"

Holcomb was quiet for so long that Max thought he wasn't going to answer. Then, so softly Max almost missed it, he said, "Once. Maybe twice."

He waited, giving Holcomb time, but he remained quiet, walking and scanning the underbrush. Five minutes later, Hatfield called for a break. The group gathered in a small clearing, passing around water bottles and what remained of their trail mix.

As Max chewed on a handful of nuts and dried fruit, he couldn't shake the feeling that they were being watched. He scanned the tree line, half expecting to see eyes glinting back at him from the shadows.

But there was nothing. Just trees and shadows and the endless greens and browns of the forest. Yet the feeling persisted, a prickling on the back of his neck. He didn't dismiss it. Long, hard years had taught him to lean into that feeling and pay close attention.

Ethan approached Max, his face ashen yet resolute. "I keep hearing something," he whispered. "Like whispers. But when I try to focus, they vanish."

Max studied the younger man's face. Maybe that wasn't determination. Maybe it was exhaustion. There were dark circles under Ethan's eyes and a feverish glint that hadn't been there that morning.

"Maybe you and I should head back to camp," Max suggested. "You look like you could use some rest."

Ethan shook his head vigorously. "No. We must keep going. We have to find them." He paused, then shook his head again as if dislodging an unwelcome thought. Without another word, he trudged back to where he'd left his pack on the ground.

Max glanced over toward Riley, but she was saying something to Holcomb. She must have noticed Ethan's deterioration. Was she so determined to find her sister that she would sacrifice Ethan in the process? Before Max could press the issue, Hatfield gave the signal to move out. As they fell back into formation, Max couldn't help but wonder what other surprises the forest might have in store for them. The clouds overhead grew darker, and Max pulled his pack's straps tighter around himself. A chilling thought crept into his mind that their mission might not end by rescuing Jake and Sarah, but instead add their own names to the growing list of the Monongahela missing.

They resumed their hike, but it felt more like trudging now. Max found himself stumbling frequently, his boots catching on roots and rocks, nearly toppling him. He noticed the others struggling as well, all except Hatfield, who somehow looked as fresh as ever. The man was made of stone. Max felt he could sleep for days. And this was all after just a single day. Given Ethan's earlier state, Max marveled that he was still upright.

Max tried to push back the fatigue and focus on the search, then suddenly a shout echoed from ahead.

Max turned to Holcomb, who was walking nearby, off to the left. "What was that?"

"C'mon," the older man said, quickening his pace. "They've found something."

CHAPTER TWENTY-NINE

Hatfield had dropped to one knee, his weathered hands hovering over something on the forest floor. The rest of the group formed a ragged semi-circle behind him. They had veered off the main trail, pushing through dense underbrush to reach this unremarkable patch of forest. Max scanned the area, seeing only a tapestry of moss-covered logs, ferns, and leaf litter typical of the Monongahela. Towering oaks and maples stretched overhead. Yet Hatfield's intent gaze suggested he had spotted something significant, invisible to Max's untrained eye. How? Max wasn't sure.

"What is it?" Riley asked, her voice tinged with a mixture of hope and apprehension. Maybe she was having similar thoughts.

Hatfield stood, brushing dirt from his hands. "We've got signs of a camp. Recent, by the looks of it." He gestured to a slight depression in the grass, barely visible beneath a scattering of fallen leaves. "See that? That's where a tent stood."

"How recent?" Max asked.

"Probably within the last week or so. The grass hasn't fully sprung back yet."

He moved a few feet to his left, crouching down again. With a practiced sweep of his hand, he brushed away a layer of leaves and forest debris, revealing a circular patch of earth. "And here's our firepit." Hatfield dug his fingers into the ground, coming up with a handful of sodden ash. "These ashes are still damp. If it had been a month or more, they'd have dried out or washed away completely."

Max leaned in, trying to see what Hatfield saw. Now that it had been pointed out, he could just make out the faint outline of where a tent might have been, the grass slightly flatter, forming a vague rectangular shape.

"Could it be Sarah and Jake's camp?" Ethan asked.

"No way to be sure," Holcomb said. "But it's the first solid lead we've had." Hatfield stood again, his eyes scanning the surrounding area. "The timing fits. But we can't be certain yet. Let's spread out and see what else we can find. Ideally, we'll get a better sense of where they went next." The group began to fan out, their movements cautious and deliberate. "Remember," Hatfield called, "go slow, look for any signs—broken branches, discarded items, anything out of place."

The group nodded, pairing off without discussion. This time Max found himself walking alongside Riley.

They walked in silence for a while, eyes scanning the underbrush, the adrenaline of finally finding something washing away the fatigue, at least temporarily. But the reprieve was short-lived. There was no quick follow-up. No second lead. They kept looking, working methodically outward, but the energy fizzled.

"Tell me about them," Max said, breaking the silence. "Sarah and Jake."

Riley's pace slowed, her eyes unfocused as if looking into the past. "Sarah's always been the responsible one. Even when we were kids, she was the one making sure I didn't do anything too stupid."

Max nodded but said nothing. He did notice she doggedly stuck to the present tense. Her hope in a happy ending hadn't fizzled.

"Jake...he's different. Intense, you know? When he focuses on something, it's like the rest of the world disappears."

"Like with Vance?"

Riley sighed. "Yeah, but it's not just that. Jake gets fixated on things. Before Vance disappeared, it was rock climbing. He'd spend hours researching gear, planning trips. He even built a climbing wall in their apartment."

"In their apartment? Sounds dedicated."

"That's one word for it," Riley said with a wry smile. "But he wasn't all intensity. When he wasn't obsessing over something, when he managed to turn it off, he could be...sweet. Thoughtful. He once spent a week learning to bake just so he could make Sarah's favorite cake for her birthday."

Max stepped around a large boulder. "How did Sarah handle his obsessions?"

"She was patient. More patient than I would've been. I think she saw it as part of who he was, you know? And with Vance's disappearance...I mean, can you imagine? I think she understood why Jake couldn't let it go."

They fell silent for a moment, the weight of the missing brothers hanging between them.

"What about Holcomb and Hatfield?" Max asked, changing the subject. "What do you know about them?"

Riley shrugged. "Not much more than you, I imagine. Hatfield used to be a ranger, now he's a guide. The best and most sought after in these parts, so the locals say. Holcomb's the current ranger. His wife likes to bake and play home-maker. The pair of them seem to know these woods better than anyone else."

Max studied her face, searching for any sign that she knew more. "That's it?"

"Hatfield can be a stubborn ass and never seems to get tired?" She flashed a small grin then dropped it. "Why? Should I know more?"

Max hesitated, his mind juggling two revelations: Ethan's cryptic warning about Holcomb's past and Holcomb's own disclosure regarding Hatfield's controversial exit from the Forest Service. "No, I guess not. Just curious."

They continued their search, eyes combing the forest floor for any signs of human disturbance or presence. Though the tree canopy obscured most of the sky, Max sensed the air growing thick with humidity. The rivulets of sweat trickling down his back served as a barometer of the changing weather. More rain was coming.

The changing weather wasn't Max's only concern. As he trudged behind Riley, his stomach growled insistently. It was loud enough that he was sure it scared away any small game in the area. The meager ration of oatmeal from breakfast felt like a distant memory. His body, pushed by the hike, burned through calories at an alarming rate. The loss of almost half their food supply loomed large, transforming what should have been a well-provisioned search into a race against dwindling resources. Max made a silent pact with himself to push through the hunger and to ignore the occasional starbursts flickering at the edges of his vision. They couldn't afford to deplete their supplies any faster, not when every protein bar and dehydrated meal might mean the difference between success and failure—or worse. He tightened the straps on his pack, the physical discomfort a welcome distraction from the rumbling in his gut.

Soon, the pair pushed through a thick patch of mountain laurel, its leathery leaves slapping against their arms and faces, and stumbled into a small clearing, where a shallow stream cut through the forest floor, its bright, burbling waters a contrast to the silence that had fallen over the group.

The others were gathered at the water's edge. Ethan sat on a moss-covered log, his shoulders slumped, while Jamie stood apart, his fingers working the frayed piece of paracord as he stared up at the distant mountain peaks. Hatfield crouched by the stream, his weathered face etched with lines of frustration as he studied his map.

Holcomb, meanwhile, paced the perimeter of the clearing, his eyes constantly scanning the tree line. Every few steps, he'd pause, head cocked slightly as if listening for something beyond the ambient sounds of the forest.

The initial spark of hope ignited by the discovery of the campsite had sputtered out, replaced by a palpable sense of disappointment. The Monongahela wasn't giving up its secrets easily. Max glanced again at Hatfield. They were back to relying on their guide, rumors, and a hermit's map.

As they approached the group, Riley briefly put a hand on Max's arm, maybe sensing the group's collective morale. "They're alive, Max. They have to be."

Max kept his gaze carefully neutral. Somewhere out there, Jake and Sarah were waiting to be found. And something else was waiting too, something that had shredded their food bags and left no tracks.

CHAPTER THIRTY

"We're moving out," Hatfield announced abruptly, rising to his feet and folding his map with quick decisive movements. "We're heading through Raven's Gap."

The sudden declaration broke the silence that had settled over the group as they rested by the burbling stream. Max looked up. "Raven's Gap?" he asked, straightening up from his position of leaning against a moss-covered boulder. His muscles barked in response, already aching from the half day of exertion.

Hatfield nodded, his stony face set with a scowl that might have doubled as determination. "It's the lowest pass through the Monongahela foothills. It'll get us to where we need to be faster than skirting around."

"Do you think Sarah and Jake took the pass?"

"I don't know, but if you're right and they were headed toward Grave's End, they would have to pass through the ravine. Raven's Gap is the fastest way to get there."

Riley persisted, her brow furrowed. "Is it safe? We're already low on supplies."

"Safe enough," Hatfield replied, his tone clipped. "It's our best shot at covering ground quickly. And we need to get to that northwest quadrant if we want to stay on schedule. Especially with low supplies."

Without waiting for further discussion, Hatfield turned on his heel and strode into the forest. Jamie, silent as ever, looked them over, then fell into step behind him.

The remaining four exchanged uncertain glances. Ethan sat slumped on a fallen log, his face pale and drawn. Holcomb had stopped pacing the perimeter, but stood apart, his eyes still scanning the tree line.

"What do you think?" Ethan asked, his question directed in Holcomb's direction.

Holcomb paused and looked at each of them before he replied. "If Hatfield says we move, we move. He knows these woods better than anyone. That's why you wanted him along."

With a collective sigh, they gathered their packs and set off after Hatfield and Jamie. Ten steps outside the clearing and out of sight of the brook, the forest swallowed them, transforming from an open woodland into a claustrophobic maze of towering trunks and grasping underbrush. Shafts of afternoon light, now scarce and fleeting, barely penetrated the canopy above, casting the group in an eerie, emerald twilight.

As they walked, Max found himself once again beside Holcomb. "You've been through Raven's Gap before?"

Holcomb nodded, ducking under a low-hanging branch. "Once or twice. It's not an easy trek, but Hatfield's right—it's the fastest way to get to where we're going."

"And where exactly are we going?" Max asked.

Holcomb's eyes darted around before settling back on Max. "There's a place locals call The Gardens—it's a...well, it's sort of hard to describe. It's a unique feature of the park that you just have to see for yourself. If Jake and Sarah needed shelter, they might have gone there. It's also on our route to Grave's End, based on the map we're following."

They walked in silence for a few minutes, the only sounds their labored breathing and the crunch of leaves underfoot. Ahead, Hatfield and Jamie were barely visible through the trees.

"You okay back there?" Hatfield's voice carried back to them, gruff but tinged with concern.

"We're managing," Riley called back, her voice strained.

As they pressed on, the terrain began to change. The ground became rockier, the incline steeper. Max's boots slipped on loose stones, and he had to grab onto tree trunks for balance.

"Watch your footing," Holcomb warned. "It only gets trickier from here."

———

They trudged on for another hour, each step a battle against gravity and the precarious terrain. The narrow pass wound between weathered outcrops of Devonian-era sandstone, their layers telling a silent story of the ancient Appalachian uplift. Stunted red spruce and yellow birch, twisted by relentless winds, clung tenaciously to the rocky soil. As they climbed, the carpet of ferns and mosses that blanketed the forest floor gradually thinned, giving way to hardy mountain laurel and tenacious blueberry shrubs clinging to the increasingly rocky terrain.

Max's thighs screamed in protest, his calves knotted with fatigue. Every labored breath felt insufficient in the thinning air, heavy with the sharp scent of spruce and the musky odor of sun-warmed lichen. Sweat plastered his shirt to his back, chilling him as the wind funneled through the pass, carrying with it the promise of more rain from the valleys below.

A quick glance at his companions revealed similar states of exhaustion—faces flushed, shoulders slumped, feet dragging on the loose shale. If he was suffering, so were they. As they crested the pass, the forest opened up, revealing a sweeping vista of ridges and valleys cloaked in a patchwork of hardwoods and evergreens. The descent began, gentler but no less treacherous, as gravity now threatened to pull them stumbling down the slope.

When Hatfield's gruff voice finally called for a halt in a small clearing on the lee side of the pass, Max all but collapsed on the trail. His legs twitched uncontrollably as he sat, grateful for the momentary reprieve. Around him, mountain ash and fire cherry trees offered sparse shade, their leaves rustling in the constant breeze that swept across the exposed mountainside.

Max realized with a mixture of frustration and awe that despite hiking since almost dawn, they had covered surprisingly little ground. First the slow search around the discovered campsite and then the unforgiving landscape of the pass had dictated their pace, turning what might have been an easy day's journey in gentler terrain into an arduous crawl.

He unwrapped a protein bar, grimacing, but also savoring, the now-familiar cardboard texture as needed fuel. Nearby, Hatfield and Holcomb huddled over the map, their voices low but carrying in the stillness of the forest.

"Morton's Hanging Gardens Ravine is just ahead," Hatfield said, pointing to a spot on the map. "Usually, just called The Gardens. It's unlike anything you've ever seen."

Ethan chimed in. "I've heard stories. A living ceiling, right?"

"That's right. Vegetation growing downward from overhanging rocks. It creates a sort of natural ceiling." Hatfield's voice trailed off, the usual gruffness replaced by a hint of wonder. Max found himself leaning in, his curiosity momentarily overriding his fatigue. Max caught Riley's eye. She offered a weary but genuine smile, which he returned, both seemingly rejuvenated by this glimpse of Hatfield's softer side.

The moment was fleeting. Five minutes later, Hatfield's customary brusqueness returned as he ordered them back on their feet. As Max forced his aching body to stand, he couldn't help but grin. The brief show of enthusiasm from their stoic guide had, oddly enough, bolstered his spirits more than any rest could have. It was reassuring to know the man was not completely made of granite.

As they continued their trek after the brief respite, the forest began to change more dramatically. The ground became rockier, with loose sandstone and shale fragments sliding under their boots. The air grew noticeably cooler and damper, carrying a faint, mossy, earthy scent that reminded Max of a greenhouse. Suddenly, the red spruces and eastern hemlocks parted, revealing a sight that made Max stop in his tracks, his breath catching in his throat.

"Welcome to The Gardens," Hatfield said.

CHAPTER THIRTY-ONE

Max stood awestruck, his eyes trying to take in every detail. Before them stretched a vast ravine, its walls a vertical garden of impossibility. Ferns and small trees sprouted from the rock face above, their foliage hanging down like a living curtain. Shafts of sunlight filtered through gaps in the vegetation, creating a dappled, green glow that danced across the ravine floor.

Small waterfalls cascaded from the plant-covered ceiling, their droplets catching the light like falling diamonds. The floor of the ravine was a mix of smooth river stones and dark, damp loam, supporting its own ecosystem of shade-loving plants.

"It's...incredible," Max said. His words feeling almost inadequate to describe the scene before him.

Ethan stepped up beside him, and for the first time that day, the pallor of fatigue was absent from his face. His eyes widened, drinking in the scene before them, a spark of wonder replacing the exhaustion that had haunted his features. For a moment, he looked like the eager, anxious friend Max had met back at the Crossroads Inn, rather than the worn-out hiker he'd been all day.

"Now I understand why people get drawn deeper into these forests. Stumbling on a place like this...it makes you want to see what other wonders are hiding out here," he said.

The group stood in silent awe for several more minutes, each lost in their own thoughts as they took in the breathtaking ravine. Max noticed Riley's eyes scanning the ravine floor, no doubt searching for any sign of her sister. Holcomb's gaze was fixed on the rock walls, his brow furrowed as if trying to decipher some hidden message in the hanging foliage. Jamie, as usual, stood slightly apart, his fingers knotting and unknotting the paracord. The wonder of The Gardens seemed to effect even the stoic Hatfield; however, the moment of collective wonder was fleeting. As if suddenly remembering their purpose, Hatfield's face hardened once more, the seasoned guide reasserting control, and he gathered the group around him.

"We'll split up like we did earlier to cover more ground." He showed them the map and pointed out features and sections for each member to explore. "The ravine's structure creates some unusual acoustics, so we'll use whistles to signal each other. Three sharp blasts mean you need help immediately." He handed each of them a small silver whistle. "And be careful where you step. The stones can be slippery, and the hanging vegetation can obscure your path. Stay alert and don't take any unnecessary risks."

———

With areas assigned, the group spread out into the strange upside down landscape. As the most experienced hikers and guides, Hatfield and Holcomb had taken the farthest areas from where the group entered The Gardens. Jamie was next, setting off at a trot toward a large mass of boulders that dominated the middle section. Max, Riley, and Ethan took the closer and less challenging sections.

Five minutes after dispersing, Max found himself alone, picking his way through a section near the eastern wall of the ravine. The constant background noise of trickling water filled his ears, occasionally punctuated by the soft plop of water droplets falling from the hanging foliage. The entire place hummed with life. And everything was slightly damp, covered in a perpetual sheen of moisture. For a brief period during his youth, his brother Danny had kept a pet turtle named Sheldon in a terrarium in their shared room. Max felt as if he were walking through Sheldon's old habitat, only on a massive surreal scale.

Max did his best to scan the area for clues and listen for a possible call for help while he simultaneously tried not to break an ankle or fall on his ass due to the slick, moss-covered stones. It wasn't easy. He picked up a thick, wet branch to help him balance. The play of light and shadow through the hanging vegetation created a vertigo effect, making distances hard to judge and surfaces hard to see clearly.

The more he explored his small section of The Gardens, the more he became convinced that Jake and Sarah might have passed through, but unless they were desperate, they hadn't stayed. It might be hospitable for foliage and ferns, but it wouldn't be comfortable for humans. It was too wet and too rocky.

He ducked under a low-hanging curtain of ferns, emerging into a small grotto formed by the overhanging rocks. The space felt almost sacred, like a natural cathedral. Max's footsteps echoed softly as he scanned the area for any signs of human presence.

As he rounded a bend, something caught his eye—a flash of color, there and gone, but it had seemed out of place among the natural greens and browns. What was it? He stopped and let his focus go soft. Something had grabbed his attention, but he'd lost it. He closed his eyes, inhaled deeply, then opened them, allowing his gaze to sweep slowly across the landscape. There. Something pink off to his left, at eye level. Maybe just a flower, but maybe something else. His gut said it was something else. Something significant. His heart rate quickened as he moved closer, carefully picking his way across the uneven ground.

Suddenly, three sharp whistle blasts pierced the air. Max spun around, momentarily disoriented as the sound bounced off the ravine walls, seeming to come from all directions at once. He took off in what he hoped was the right direction, his boots slipping on the damp stones.

As he pushed back through the curtain of ferns, his foot caught on a hidden root. Max went down hard, the breath knocked from his lungs as he hit the ground. For a moment, he lay there, dazed. The damp rocks and soil felt cool on his skin. He was tempted to close his eyes and let himself relax. Then, gritting his teeth against the pain in his ribs, he pushed himself up and pressed on.

Three more whistles. It was easier to hear the sounds out in the main section. He pivoted left and ran as fast as he dared on the slick stones. He came around the large set of boulders that Hatfield told them marked roughly the middle of The Gardens and found Holcomb kneeling beside Jamie on the ground. Blood seeped from a gash somewhere on Jamie's head and spread out around him. The man's eyes were closed, and his face was very pale. His pack had slipped from his shoulders and lay twisted beside him. Holcomb's pack was nearby, half unzipped. He'd taken a T-shirt out and placed it under Jamie's head. The pale material was already discolored with blood.

Holcomb was about to blow his whistle again when he spotted Max.

"What happened?" Max asked, breathless from his run. He tried not to think about the pulsing pain in his ribs.

"I don't know," Holcomb replied. "I'd finished my sweep and was heading back to the rendezvous point when I came across him. He hasn't said anything. I'm afraid to move him."

Just then, Jamie opened his eyes and blinked. "I can hear you," he said, but his eyes remained unfocused.

"Okay. Good," Max said, "do you remember what happened?"

"I...I'm not sure. I was searching, found an opening." He tried to raise his head but stopped and then pointed back toward the boulders. "I was going to check it out when I heard a sound, turned, and...boom. Here I am."

The others arrived in quick succession, a flurry of questions and concerns filling the air. Riley immediately dropped down next to Holcomb and assessed Jamie's injury. Max had another glimpse of what Riley must have been like as a soldier.

Her movements were swift and precise. "Everyone back up, give him some space," she ordered, her voice calm but authoritative.

She leaned over Jamie, making eye contact. "Hey, Jamie, I'm going to check you over, okay? Can you tell me where it hurts the most?"

Jamie winced. "My head...and my back."

Riley nodded, then turned to the group. "Jamie, you were our medic. Do you have a first aid kit?"

There was a pause but then he said, "Yes, in my pack. Front pocket. On top."

"Ethan, grab it for me."

As Ethan scrambled toward the nearby pack, she addressed Holcomb, "Good call on not moving him. We need to stabilize his head and neck."

She carefully probed Jamie's head with her fingers until he hissed with pain. The wound was behind his right ear. "Max, I need you to maintain manual C-spine stabilization. Hold his head steady, like this." She demonstrated the proper hand placement.

Max moved into position, gently cradling Jamie's head.

Riley opened the first aid kit Ethan had retrieved. She pulled out a package of gauze and tore it open with her teeth. "Jamie, I'm going to apply pressure to stop the bleeding. It might hurt, but I need you to stay as still as possible."

She pressed the gauze firmly against the wound. Jamie hissed again in pain but remained still.

"Hatfield," Riley called, "we need to elevate his legs to prevent shock. Use a pack or something similar."

As Hatfield took off his own pack and placed it under Jamie's feet, Riley continued her assessment. She gently took off one of his boots. "Jamie, can you wiggle your toes for me?" She watched carefully as he did so. "Good. Now, squeeze my hands." She placed her hands in his.

"Good," she nodded "Okay, it doesn't appear there's any spinal injury, but we still need to be careful. He probably has a concussion. We need to get him out of here."

"There's no cell service," Holcomb said, frustration evident in his voice.

Riley's brow furrowed in concentration. "All right, we need to improvise a stretcher. Hatfield, you know these woods best. What's our fastest route back to camp? We can reassess our options when we're safely there." Riley turned back to Jamie. She replaced the now-soaked gauze with a fresh piece, securing it with medical tape. "Hang in there, Jamie. We're going to get you out of here."

"Are you sure you want to backtrack now?" Hatfield asked.

"Are you kidding?" Ethan said.

"No, I'm not kidding. Jamie's stable. We hiked all the way up here. You know it wasn't easy. Let's let Jamie rest and recover and finish the search of The Gardens. Then we can head back."

The rest of the group glanced at each other. Max could see the conflict written on Riley's face. She wanted to keep looking for her sister, but she also didn't want anyone else to get hurt.

"I don't know," Holcomb said. "Between what happened last night and whatever happened here, it feels like maybe we get out, re-supply, and try again later. Maybe I can get the Forest Service involved."

"I…I can walk. I don't need a stretcher. Just give me some time. Finish the search."

There was a beat of silence but that settled it. Hatfield took charge again.

"Max, help Jamie get back to the entrance. Find him a comfortable spot to sit," he said. "But don't let him sleep. Keep him talking, watch for signs of a concussion. The rest of us will finish the search."

CHAPTER THIRTY-TWO

As the group dispersed to continue their search, Max caught Riley's arm. "Riley, wait. There's something I need to tell you."

Riley turned, her brow furrowing at his tone. "What is it?"

"Just before the whistles, I saw something. A flash of color—pink, I think—something out of place in all this green." He gestured at the lush foliage surrounding them.

"Pink?" Riley's said. "Like what? Clothing?"

"I'm not sure. I didn't get a close look. I was picking my way in that direction when Holcomb blew his whistle. But it's there and I think it's worth checking out."

"No, you're right. Anything unusual is worth it," Riley said. "If it's nothing, no harm, no foul." The others were out of sight and Max could tell she was anxious to get going. She squared her shoulders. "Show me."

"I'll be right back," Max told Jamie, who had risen to a seated position and was pulling his pack closer. Jamie nodded in acknowledgment, then began riffling through his pack with an unusual intensity, muttering softly to himself as he emptied its contents onto the ground.

Max frowned, but then quickly led Riley partway back along the path he'd taken earlier, his eyes scanning the walls of the ravine, afraid he would miss the nook he'd ducked into, but then he spotted the hanging curtain of fern. He gently pushed it aside and stepped through, making room for Riley.

"I don't want to leave Jamie too long. He doesn't look exactly right. Walk about a hundred yards and look left, about eye high."

"Pink?"

"Yeah, a sort of mottled pink or light red, I think. It's roughly the size of a baseball, but irregular—like a smeared handprint or a torn piece of fabric."

———

Max returned to Jamie and found that he'd re-packed his bag and was trying to stand but having trouble getting up off his knees. The frayed piece of nylon paracord was gripped in one fist. The intensity he'd seen in Jamie's eyes a few minutes ago was gone, replaced by a vague emptiness. Blood was dripping down the side of Jamie's neck. Max gently guided him back to a sitting position.

"Let me take one more look at that wound before we leave," Max said. He knew head wounds, while rarely fatal, could bleed profusely. Rummaging through the open first aid kit which Jamie hadn't repacked, Max searched for something specific. His past experience running his own crews on dangerous jobs had taught him the value of hemostatic bandages. To his relief, he found what he was looking for.

"This should do the trick," he said, pulling out a QuikClot bandage. Gently, he removed the current bandage, now nearly saturated with blood. The wound was a jagged gash about two inches long, the edges already starting to swell and bruise. After a moment's consideration, Max also grabbed some antibiotic spray.

"This might sting a bit," he warned Jamie, who nodded stoically. As Max began spraying the wound, Jamie hissed in pain. Max then carefully applied the clotting bandage, hoping it would stem the persistent bleeding.

"So," Max said, trying to keep Jamie alert and distracted from the pain, "what brought you out here anyway? You don't strike me as the amateur detective type."

Jamie flinched slightly as Max applied the bandage. Max didn't expect Jamie to respond but maybe the stinging pain had cleared his head. He did reply and sounded lucid. "Money, mostly. Hatfield pays well. More than I'd make in two weeks of regular guide work on my own or with another outfit."

"You do this often? Search and rescue?"

"Not that often, thankfully. Normally, it's fishing or spotting for hunters. Starting fires and cleaning up their beer cans. It ain't my dream job, but I'm outside and it pays the bills. Mostly. And sometimes...when you do get a callout for an SAR and get a result? Bring them home. It feels good, you know? Like you're worth something."

Max nodded as he finished dressing the wound. "So, Jamie, if money wasn't an issue, what would be your dream job?"

Jamie's eyes drifted past Max, losing focus in the dappled light of the ravine. "I...I always wanted to be a marine biologist. Study whales, you know?"

Max blinked, caught off guard. If Jamie had said he wanted to be an astronaut or a Bollywood dancer, it might have been less surprising. "Whales? That's quite a leap from mountain guide."

A ghost of a smile touched Jamie's lips. "Yeah, I know, but

you asked. There's just something about them. Their songs, the way they move through the ocean. So massive, yet so graceful. They seem almost...impossible, right?" He paused, his fingers absently working the piece of paracord. "I grew up a few counties over. Never even seen the ocean in person. Maybe it's just the unknown. Maybe if I stepped in the ocean the whole thing would fall apart."

"What stops you?" Max asked, genuinely curious. "From pursuing marine biology?"

Jamie shrugged, wincing slightly at the movement. "Life, I suppose. College isn't cheap. Took a job as a guide to save up, and just...never left." His gaze swept across the hanging gardens. "The mountains have their own kind of pull, you know?"

The last few words sounded sleepy and almost slurred. Max leaned in, concerned, and gave him a gentle slap on one cheek. "Hey, stay with me. Tell me more about the whales. What's your favorite species?"

"Whales? Oh, yeah. Humpbacks. Their songs...did you know they change them? Learn new ones." Jamie blinked slowly, his gaze becoming unfocused. "I think...I think he lied."

Max's brow furrowed. "Who lied? About what?"

But Jamie's eyes had slid closed, his body suddenly going limp as he collapsed to the side. Max shook him gently, then more urgently. "Jamie? Jamie!"

As Max's fingers searched for a pulse, a deep, guttural rumble reverberated through the ravine. He jerked his head up, squinting through the dense canopy. The once-dappled light filtering through the hanging foliage had dimmed, replaced by an eerie, greenish gloom.

Through gaps in the living ceiling, Max saw roiling masses of charcoal-gray clouds, their underbellies tinged an unnatural sickly yellow. They churned and boiled across the sky as if pursued by some unseen force. He could feel his ears pop as the air pressure dropped along with the temperature.

Max glanced back at the unconscious Jamie, then toward the depths of the ravine where the others had disappeared. The hanging vegetation started to sway in the wind, creating shifting shadows that seemed to move with a life of their own. Leaves and small twigs torn loose swirled in miniature cyclones.

As the first heavy drops of rain began to fall, splattering against the stones and sending ripples across shallow pools, Max realized they were in for more than just a passing shower. This could be dangerous, maybe life-threatening if they were caught in a flash flood. The drops quickly became a steady patter.

He stood, cupping his hands around his mouth. "Hatfield! Riley! We need to get out of here!"

His voice echoed through the ravine, distorted by the unusual acoustics. For a moment, there was no response. Then, faintly, he heard a whistle. Someone had heard him or reached the same conclusion.

Max turned his attention back to Jamie, checking his pulse again. It was steady, but light, and he remained unresponsive. What had he said right before he passed out? What had he meant about someone lying? He pushed the question away. Not something he'd get an answer to now. Right now, he had to find better shelter than this exposed ravine.

A flash of lightning split the sky and, for a brief second, illuminated The Gardens in a blue-white light. The following thunder was so loud and so close that Max felt it in his bones. The deep bass sound bounced off the stone walls. Small pebbles, shaken loose by the vibrations, clattered down the rocky slopes.

The wind was really picking up now, whipping the hanging vegetation into a frenzy. Small branches and leaves rained down around them. Max hunched over Jamie, trying to protect him from the debris. He realized they couldn't stay here. They were too exposed. Max shrugged off his pack and maneuvered his arms around Jamie's limp body. Gritting his teeth, he hoisted the unconscious man onto his shoulders in a fireman's carry. His tired muscles screamed in protest. He staggered under the sudden weight and his feet threatened to slide out from under him on the rain-slicked stones. He took two shuddering steps, almost tipped over, but then found his balance. He didn't know how far he'd make it, but he had to try. He had to do something.

In the distance, he heard shouts—the others were getting closer. But so was the storm, the thunder was now a constant ominous rumble at his back. As another fork of lightning split the sky, Max couldn't shake the feeling that they were trapped in the maw of some ancient, awakening beast.

CHAPTER THIRTY-THREE

Max's boots slipped on the wet rocks, and he fought to keep his balance. Jamie's limp form felt heavier with each passing second. Rain pelted Max's face, blurring his vision and making it nearly impossible to see more than a few feet ahead. He felt like he was fighting against a current. The more the rain pelted him, the slower he moved. Each step threatened to send both he and Jamie sprawling. Another bolt of lightning lit up the canyon walls followed by a clap of thunder so loud it made Max's ears ring. He watched more rocks and dirt fall from the walls. The wind howled through the ravine like a banshee scream, transforming the once-tranquil Gardens into a maelstrom of thrashing vegetation and stinging rain.

If the others were coming, Max could no longer hear them over the storm. He kept moving forward, ignoring his screaming legs. He kept his eyes down and focused on the next step. The world narrowed to the small patch of ground in front of him and the dead weight across his shoulders. Finally, on the verge of collapse, his legs burning, he looked up. Through the curtain of rain, Max spotted Holcomb and

Riley already at the entrance to The Gardens. Buck rushed forward to help, taking Jamie's legs while Max supported his upper body.

"Over there!" Buck shouted over the storm, nodding toward a stand of trees.

Max helped carry Jamie toward the meager shelter. Just as they reached the tree line, he saw Hatfield and Ethan scramble out of the ravine and join them under the canopy. Max huddled with the group under the canopy, his chest heaving as he caught his breath. The storm seemed to lash out in one final furious attempt. Max watched the wind bend the tree branches at impossible angles. Leaves and twigs whipped through the air. He could hear the trees groan under the assault.

The trees provided little protection from the deluge. Max felt soaked to the bone. When he looked down at Jamie, he found the man's eyes open, staring skyward. The QuikClot bandage was saturated through, and rivulets of pale pink water traced down Jamie's neck as rain mixed with blood. Jamie tilted his head up, letting the rain wash over his face. To Max's surprise, his expression was almost peaceful.

For a minute or two, Max feared the storm might succeed in tearing apart their meager shelter. But then, as quickly as it had intensified, the storm ebbed. The wind's howl faded, and the rain slackened to a steady patter then stopped completely.

As quickly as the storm had moved, Max noticed the group now moved much more slowly, their earlier urgency sapped by the rain and the fruitless search. He approached Riley, who was digging through her pack.

"Find anything?" he asked quietly.

Riley glanced around before reaching into her bag. She pulled out a pink bandana with a Boston Red Sox logo. "It's

Sarah's," she whispered. "She never went anywhere without it. Sort of her good luck charm."

"Why would she leave it?"

"I don't know," Riley replied, quickly stuffing it back into her pack. "Found it snagged on a branch. Could be intentional, could be an accident."

Max wanted to ask why they were whispering, but he felt it too—that creeping sense that something was wrong, something neither of them fully understood. Not yet.

The trek back to camp was slow and arduous. Max watched Jamie walk unsteadily, requiring support and constant vigilance. Hatfield led the way, while the others took turns helping Jamie.

When Holcomb rotated back, Max seized the opportunity for a blunt interrogation. "Did you hit Jamie with a rock?"

Holcomb's eyes widened. "What? No. Why would I do that?"

Max watched the older man's face carefully but couldn't pick up anything. He couldn't tell if the man was lying or being truthful. "I don't know, but it's clear you, Hatfield, and Jamie are holding something back."

"I didn't hit Jamie," Holcomb insisted. "I don't know him and have no reason to hurt him."

Max let it go, but this time he did pick up something. Jamie's words echoed in his mind: He lied. Who had Jamie meant? Max recalled Jamie also mentioned his participation in search and rescue missions. Surely, he would have encountered the local forest ranger during those operations. Jamie also led his own guided expeditions occasionally. So why was Holcomb lying about knowing him?

As they neared the camp, Max heard Ethan break the silence. "What now? We found nothing in The Gardens."

"We regroup," Hatfield said. "Assess our supplies, tend to Jamie's wound, and plan our next move."

"Next move?" Riley asked. "We're no closer to finding Sarah and Jake."

Max noticed she didn't mention the bandana to the group.

"We don't know that," Hatfield replied. "Sometimes what you don't find is just as important as what you do."

Max caught Riley's eye, seeing his own skepticism mirrored there.

"Let's just get back to camp," Holcomb said. "We all need rest and some hot food."

Max's mind turned over the events of the last two days. Ethan's late-night vision, the ripped-up food bags, the pink bandana, Jamie's injury, Holcomb's denial—pieces of a puzzle that didn't quite fit together.

As they trudged on and neared camp, Max noticed the group had lapsed back into silence, each seemingly lost in their own thoughts.

Max glanced at his companions. Everyone was wet. One was bleeding. All five looked exhausted. And he suspected at least two were lying.

CHAPTER THIRTY-FOUR

Max practically stumbled into the campsite. The forest surrounded them. What had previously felt protective, a quiet space to set up camp, now felt like a dark wall of shadows that was alive. And quietly watching. He'd never felt so exposed, so vulnerable. The city had its dangers, but they were familiar, predictable. Out here, he felt like a stranger in a strange land. He needed food and rest. He wanted a hot meal and a dry bed, but he knew that wasn't going to happen. Not right away. This was camping.

The group dispersed wordlessly, not needing Hatfield to distribute the chores this time. They fell into their assigned roles. Hatfield and Holcomb set about rekindling the fire, while Riley and Ethan fetched water from the nearby stream. Max helped Jamie to his tent, then turned his attention to gathering branches for firewood. He deposited the bundle near the firepit and Hatfield gave a grunt that might have been thanks.

"Check the guidelines on the tents. If the storm passed

over, they might be a bit battered. And then get on your gear. Lay it out to dry. You don't want any mildew or mold."

Max nodded and moved on to checking the tents. The storm had battered them, and he found himself re-securing guidelines and stakes with numb fingers. Despite Hatfield's grumpiness, he was happy for the task. It made him feel a little more in control and it kept his hands busy and his mind focused. He knew from past experience that idle hands could lead to darker thoughts. He carefully and methodically went through his pack and laid out anything damp in his tent in hopes that it might dry. He then changed into dry clothes and joined the others around the fire. Everyone looked more comfortable after changing, but no less weary.

———

Holcomb hung a pot of water over the fire to boil and they passed around the meager foil packets of their remaining rations. The crackle of the flames and the distant hooting of an owl were the only sounds that broke the heavy silence as they all waited to see if a watched pot really would or wouldn't boil.

Slowly, as if waking from a dream, the group began to show signs of life. Hatfield took out his map and asked Holcomb a question. The other man leaned over and put a finger on the map. Riley asked Jamie something.

Max then turned to Ethan, who sat hunched, elbows on his knees. "How are you feeling?"

Ethan looked up, his eyes sunken, still rimmed with dark circles. "I'm okay," he said, his voice lacking any conviction.

"You are a bad liar, my friend. You want to head back in the morning?" Max asked.

Ethan hesitated, then shook his head. "I'll be fine. Just need some rest."

"You and me both. That was not easy today. My legs are shot."

Ethan showed a thin smile. "Look at you. Then look at me and imagine how I feel. I spend 10 to 12 hours of my day behind a desk or on a phone. The last time I hiked for fun was, well, never, but I remember having to complete an orienteering day for a scout badge at some point in high school."

"I grew up in the concrete jungle of South Boston. I've rarely been out of sight of an electric pole."

The water did boil, and they took turns filling their bowls and mixing in the food packets. They again fell into mostly silence as they ate.

Once they were finished, Hatfield cleared his throat. "Given our situation—low supplies, injuries—we should consider turning back. We haven't found any signs of Jake and Sarah in this area. Maybe we should ditch the map and head toward more popular hiking spots. There are some linking trails that could get us there in six or seven hours." He glanced at Holcomb, who nodded.

Max saw the logic in that plan, but he knew more than Hatfield. He glanced at Riley, who had remained silent throughout the meal and Hatfield's proposal.

Without a word, Riley stood and disappeared into her tent. She returned moments later, clutching something in her hand. She held it out for all to see—a pink bandana with a Boston Red Sox logo.

"I found this in the ravine," she said, her voice barely above a whisper. "Actually, Max spotted it first, right before the whistling and the storm. It's Sarah's. She never went anywhere without it."

Hatfield's eyes narrowed as he studied the bandana. "That changes things," he said, slowly. He took out the map again and laid it near the fire for everyone to see. He traced a route. "If we bypass The Gardens, but keep the same heading, we can make it here," he pointed, "what you believed was their target." He paused to consider it and looked around. No one said anything. "We might have enough to make one more push. Out and back. We can leave Jamie and Ethan here to watch each other. We can move faster without them. The four of us can leave at first light. Any objections?" He paused, got nothing, then added, "Let's plan on it, but sleep on it. Be ready." With that, Hatfield refolded the map and retreated to his tent

Max turned his attention to Jamie, who sat across from him. He looked better after some food. Ethan, on the other hand, seemed to have deteriorated further, his face gaunt in the firelight.

"Get some rest, both of you," Max said. He looked at Riley and Holcomb. "Let's do shifts. Wake them every couple of hours to check on them, but we'll each get four solid hours of sleep. Holcomb you go first, then I'll go, then Riley."

They all nodded in agreement. As the group dispersed, Holcomb remained by the fire, staring into the flames. Max lingered, watching the ranger. Holcomb seemed to have aged years in the past two days, his shoulders slumped and his neck bowed.

Sensing Max's gaze, Holcomb looked up, his eyes reflecting the dancing flames. "These aren't the woods I know," he said.

Max retreated to his tent. Inside the cramped space, he collapsed onto his sleeping bag, not bothering to fully undress. He set the alarm on his watch to relieve Holcomb and check on Ethan and Jamie, then lay there as the forest whispered secrets just beyond his grasp. In the hazy space between wakefulness and sleep, Max could almost convince himself he understood what it was saying, only to have its meaning slip away like smoke through his fingers.

Sleep, when it came, was a feverish descent into a surreal twisted landscape. Max found himself wading through a forest of flesh-like trees, their bark pulsing with an unseen heartbeat. The trunks twisted upward, merging into a canopy of grasping hands instead of leaves, their fingers obscuring a sky that rained embers. He tried to call out for Sarah and Jake, for Riley and Ethan, but his voice emerged as a flock of black birds, their wings beating frantically before dissolving into ash. The ground beneath his feet was a writhing carpet of roots that seemed to reach for his ankles. With each step, the forest grew denser and lusher. It became hard to breathe. He felt like he was choking, then drowning in a silent verdant sea.

He woke with a start to the buzzing of his watch alarm, heart hammering against his ribs. His shirt was damp with sweat, his mind still half-trapped in the nightmare. He forced himself up and out of the tent.

Holcomb sat hunched by the dying fire, poking at the embers with a stick. He looked up as Max approached.

"Anything?" Max asked, his voice rough with sleep.

Holcomb shook his head. "Quiet. Too quiet, maybe." He stood, joints cracking. "No animal sounds for the last hour."

"Get some rest," Max said. "I've got it from here."

The ranger nodded, hesitating. "That Jamie... check his wound. The bandage looked soaked through when I checked an hour ago."

After Holcomb disappeared into his tent, Max moved first to Ethan's tent. He was curled on his side, breathing, shallow but steady. His skin felt clammy to the touch.

In the next tent, Jamie's condition had worsened. Sweat beaded on his forehead despite the night chill, and when Max gently peeled back the bandage, the wound looked angry and inflamed. Jamie didn't stir. His face showed that Max wasn't the only one to have dark dreams. He pressed the back of his hand to the man's forehead—definitely feverish. Max worried about infection setting in. He hesitated, torn between waking Jamie and letting him rest. He decided to let the body work, but made a mental note to check again in an hour.

Returning to the fire, he added another log and settled in for his watch, the forest pressing in around him. He stared at the orange flames and craved the sunrise that might wash away the lingering tendrils of his own strange dreams.

But daylight only brought more problems.

CHAPTER THIRTY-FIVE

The next morning, Max emerged from his tent to find Holcomb and Hatfield huddled around the remnants of last night's fire. He rubbed his gritty eyes and settled onto a log. After Riley had relieved him, he'd slept deeply—or at least didn't remember his dreams. Holcomb worked methodically, feeding the meager flames with small sticks and bark, a pot of water waiting nearby. Max hoped it was for coffee. Across from him, Hatfield sat studying his map, face creased in concentration. Ethan and Jamie were nowhere to be seen—still sleeping, Max hoped. They needed all the rest they could get. A rustling from the left drew his attention as Riley emerged from the woods carrying a bear-proof food bag. She dropped it by the fire and began rummaging through its contents. Then she stood abruptly, her expression shifting to something that made Max's stomach tighten. Fear? Anger? Despair? Whatever it was, it meant trouble.

"We have a problem," she said, holding up the sack and dropping it again. "Most of our food is gone."

"Not new news. We learned that yesterday," Hatfield said,

not looking up from the map, but turning his head to spit a stream of tobacco into the dirt.

"No, you don't understand. Even that is gone. Or, mostly gone."

"What?" Hatfield said, finally looking up. "How is that possible?"

Riley picked up the sack again and emptied it on the ground. A few packets of ready-to-eat meals dropped out. Very few.

Holcomb looked at the collection and frowned. "Did anyone hear anything last night?" The group exchanged glances but shook their heads. Holcomb continued, "And you two did your checks on Jamie and Ethan?"

"Yes," Riley said. "I didn't do a perimeter check, stayed by the fire, checked on both Jamie and Ethan every hour or so. I didn't see or hear anything unusual. It didn't feel off, you know?"

Max thought back. He'd done much the same as Riley and nothing had pinged on his radar. But would it? His Spidey sense wasn't exactly attuned to the woods. He'd likely spot a tail or feel something hinky in the city, but he was so far out of his element, he wasn't sure what was normal or not.

Holcomb nodded then looked at Max. "Same," he said.

"It was a little quiet, but I didn't think too much of it," Holcomb said. "Why target the food twice?"

"Maybe we didn't get the message the first time," Hatfield replied. He picked through the remaining packets, then dropped them back in the pile.

Jamie emerged from his tent, his face pale and drawn. He stumbled slightly as he approached the group.

"What's going on?" he asked, his voice hoarse. He was wearing a T-shirt and jeans and no shoes despite the early-morning chill. His forehead glistened with sweat.

Riley frowned, he really did not look good, but then quickly filled him in on the missing food.

"We need to figure out our options," Holcomb said. "This food won't last the day between us."

"The lake's right there," Riley said. "We could try fishing."

"With what?" Max asked. "We don't have any gear."

"We could improvise," Jamie suggested. "Use some string from the tents, bend a safety pin or small piece of metal for a hook."

Hatfield shook his head. "That would take time we don't have and energy we can't spare, and there's no guarantee we'd catch anything substantial."

"What about hunting then?" Jamie asked, swaying slightly.

"Sit, before you fall over," Max said, pointing at another log.

Holcomb sighed. "Same problem. We're not equipped for it, and the noise might scare off any game in the area. Plus, none of us are experienced hunters."

The group fell silent, the gravity of their situation sinking in.

"I've got a couple protein bars in my pack. Some trail mix," Max said. He'd forgotten to empty it out and add it to the sack when they'd returned to camp.

Hatfield frowned at him, clearly annoyed he'd broken protocol, but then Jamie piped up. "Unless someone emptied my bag, I probably have the same."

"Ditto," Riley said.

In this case, their negligence might be a blessing in disguise. They each went to their tents and then returned and dumped their findings in the pile. Three MRE camp meals. Four protein bars. A 100-calorie pack of almonds and two chocolate energy gels with caffeine. It wasn't much but it was more than they'd had before.

They boiled the pot of water and then thinned and

stretched out one ready-made meal as far as it would go. Max was hungry enough that even the few spoonfuls of beef stroganoff tasted heavenly.

As they scraped the bottoms of their bowls, Max turned to Jamie. "How are you feeling? You mentioned something yesterday before you passed out."

Jamie's brow furrowed. Max saw his eyes glance quickly around. Hatfield and Holcomb had wandered off. Riley was going through Ethan's pack looking for steaks or maybe ribs. She pulled out a bar of dark chocolate and held it up. Not a terrible consolation prize.

"I did? I'm sorry, everything from yesterday is a blur. What did I say?"

Max studied Jamie's face, searching for any sign of deception. "You said something about someone lying. Do you remember that?"

Jamie shook his head slowly, eyes on the ground. "I'm sorry, I don't. My head's still pretty foggy."

Max wasn't sure whether to believe him or not. Jamie did look terrible—his skin was clammy, and his eyes were glassy with fever or infection.

"Let me take a look at that wound," Riley said, approaching Jamie.

As Riley examined the injury, her frown deepened. "It's infected. We need to clean it out properly."

She retrieved the first aid kit and pulled out a small knife. She held the blade in the fire then further sterilized it with an alcohol wipe from the first aid kit. She turned to Jamie. "This is going to hurt, but we need to drain the infection."

"This is some Civil War-era shit," he said, but nodded.

"Be ready to catch him if he passes out." Max moved over next to Jamie. This close he could smell the wound. Riley was right. They had to drain it. He also would need antibiotics but those would have to wait.

"On three. One, two." She didn't wait. She made three quick cuts and opened the wound. Pus oozed out, and Jamie, his knuckles white as he gripped the log beneath him, moaned.

"Sorry," Riley murmured. She probed the wound gently, forcing out more pus and blood, then cleaned the area as best she could before applying a fresh bandage. "We're lucky Holcomb brought such a well-stocked kit. Here, take some Tylenol for the pain and fever. You should rest."

He dry-swallowed the pills. "I think I'll soak in the lake first," Jamie said. "Cool off a bit." He stood, swayed a little, caught himself, and then headed off toward the narrow path that led to the lake.

"I'll go with him," Ethan offered, emerging from his tent, squinting against the morning light then putting a hand over his eyes to block it out completely. "Make sure he doesn't drown."

"Tell him not to get the bandage wet. We don't have that many more," Riley called.

———

As Jamie and Ethan made their way to the lake, Riley turned to Max. "I'm worried about Ethan. Jamie looks terrible and needs help but Ethan is also hurting and doesn't look it, so he's going to push it, but if he has a concussion then more strenuous hiking is the last thing he needs."

Holcomb and Hatfield returned to the firepit.

"Neither of those boys look too good," Hatfield said.

"We need to decide whether to stay or go," Holcomb replied. "Our supplies are dwindling, and we have two injured who need medical attention."

"I don't disagree with any of that but I'm still not leaving," Riley said firmly. "Not without finding Sarah and Jake."

"No one is saying we abandon the search," Hatfield said.

"You know that every day, hell, every hour is critical," Riley shot back. "While we are restocking and getting a comfortable amount of food, my sister could be dying."

A shout from the direction of the lake interrupted their discussion. Ethan came stumbling back, his face pale.

"You need to see this," he panted.

CHAPTER THIRTY-SIX

The group followed Ethan to the edge of the campsite then onto the path through the thin strip of woods prior to the lakefront. Twenty yards into the woods, he stopped and pointed to either side of the trail. Scattered on the ground were several of their missing food packets, torn open and empty.

"What the hell?" Hatfield said, squatting down and examining a container. "Sliced open with something sharp."

"But not eaten," Max said.

"Hard to tell, but yes, not all of it, certainly."

"It looks...deliberate," Holcomb said, crouching next to Hatfield and flicking through the scraps. His eyes narrowed. "Wait here." He stood and hustled back up the trail toward camp. He returned two minutes later. "I found two more like this over by the tents and the fire. I bet there are more. I bet it forms a circle."

"Why?" Riley said.

Holcomb looked at Hatfield. It was clear he already knew the answer.

"This is bait," he said. "Someone's trying to lure animals into our camp."

In other words, Max thought, someone or something doesn't want us searching any further. Max thought about the implications and his suspicions deepened.

"But who would do that?" Ethan asked. "And why?"

———

Ethan continued down to the lake to check on Jamie. The others returned to the campsite, the mood even more somber than before.

"We need to get help," Holcomb said. "Someone needs to go back and alert the authorities."

"I'll go," Hatfield volunteered. "I know the fastest routes down. If I push hard, I can make it before dark and get a rescue operation started."

Riley looked skeptical. "Are you sure that's the best idea? You're our most experienced guide."

"Holcomb can handle things here," Hatfield replied. "He knows the map. He knows where you want to go. And right now, speed is of the essence."

The group debated for a few more minutes before agreeing to Hatfield's plan. No one had a better alternative. Hatfield would get back to the trailhead and Grimswood as fast as he could and alert the sheriff and get a formal search operation going, including a medivac helicopter to get Jamie and Ethan out.

Hatfield pulled out his compass, the brass case catching the dim light filtering through the canopy. "Due east to the ranger station," he said, nodding to himself and watching the needle settle. His thumb traced the burnished script as he snapped it shut. "Never failed me yet."

As Hatfield prepared to leave, Max pulled him aside. "Be careful out there. Something doesn't feel right about all this."

Hatfield nodded grimly. "I know. Keep your eyes open, Max. Even if you're a city boy, trust those instincts."

City or country. Trail or asphalt. Some things transcended setting. Danger was danger. Fear was fear.

With a final check of his gear, Hatfield set off down the trail, quickly disappearing into the dense forest.

The remaining group watched him go, each lost in their own thoughts about what the day might bring.

———

Ethan returned from the lake, carrying his shoes, his legs wet to the knees. "I don't feel so good. My head's killing me and I'm seeing double."

Riley guided him to a log. "Sit down. Those are classic concussion symptoms. You need to rest."

"But the search—" Ethan protested.

"You're in no condition to hike," Max said. "We can't search and also take care of you. You and Jamie stay here. We'll handle the search today."

As if on cue, Jamie returned from the lake, looking marginally better but still unsteady on his feet.

"What's the plan? Where's Hatfield?" he asked, lowering himself carefully onto a nearby rock.

Holcomb filled both Ethan and Jamie in on the plan for Hatfield to get help, then laid out a map on a flat stone. "As for the rest of us, we need to cover as much ground as possible. I think we should split up."

Riley's head snapped up. "Split up? After everything that's happened? That's asking for trouble."

"I don't like it either," Holcomb admitted, his face grim. "And wouldn't recommend it in normal circumstances, but we are far from normal right now. We're running out of time and options. If we split up, we can cover twice the area."

"And if something happens to one of us?" Riley challenged. "We'd be alone out there, with no backup."

Max watched the exchange. He tended to agree with Riley. Splitting up on a job never ended well for someone. Holcomb sighed, running a hand through his hair. "I know the risks, Riley. Trust me. But you said it yourself, every hour that passes..."

"I get it," Riley interrupted. "But we're already down two people. Three if you count Hatfield going back. If we lose anyone else, this whole search could fall apart, if it hasn't already."

Holcomb nodded, considering. "What if we compromise? We stick together until we get through The Gardens. We've already searched that area pretty well. Once we reach the area where Grave's End is supposed to be, we split up to cover more ground but stay close. The area doesn't look that large. We might not have direct line of sight, but we wouldn't be far apart."

Riley mulled it over, her eyes flicking between the map and their injured companions. "Okay," she said finally. "But everyone takes a whistle and bear spray or something to defend themselves with."

"Agreed," Holcomb said. He turned to Max. "You okay with this plan?"

Max nodded. "I can manage. So Ethan and Jamie stay put?"

"They stay here," Riley said firmly. She looked at the two men, but neither put up a fight. "Rest, stay hydrated, and keep an eye on the camp. If anything seems off, use the emergency whistle. You have bear spray?"

"I have some," Jamie said.

"Get it out. Have it handy. It works on more than just bears."

"You?" She looked at Ethan.

"I've got a knife. And my razor wit."

"Try to rely on the knife."

With the plan settled, he couldn't shake a feeling of dread. He looked at his companions—Riley's determined face, Holcomb's wary eyes, Ethan's pained expression, and Jamie's feverish gaze—and realized that finding Sarah and Jake was no longer their only goal. Survival itself was now at stake.

CHAPTER THIRTY-SEVEN

The dense canopy overhead filtered the weak morning light, casting fuzzy shadows across the sodden forest floor. Max, Riley, and Holcomb had been hiking for hours, their boots sinking into a carpet of waterlogged leaves and moss. They'd passed the remnants of the campfire. Had that only been yesterday? Then skirted around The Gardens through a parallel ravine that was less scenic and steeper, but more direct. A persistent drip-drip-drip was nature's soundtrack as water collected on leaves and branches before falling to the ground. As they paused to catch their breath, a fat drop landed squarely on Max's nose, causing him to blink in surprise and wipe his face with an already damp sleeve.

Max wiped sweat from his brow. His stomach growled, loud enough that he thought the others might hear, but perhaps they were distracted by their own appetites. He glanced at his companions. Riley led the way, she had from the start, plowing ahead and showing signs of fatigue. Her pace hadn't slowed since they'd left camp, and Max couldn't help but admire her resilience. Still, he noticed the slight tremor in her hands when they paused occasionally to check the map. He noted the way her shoulders slumped a little more with each passing hour. Her hair was matted with sweat and dirt, the silver streak at her temple now dulled to gunmetal gray. He knew the drive to find her sister was pushing her beyond her limits, and he worried about what might happen if they didn't find Sarah on this trip. Holcomb brought up the rear, his eyes constantly scanning their surroundings, his weathered face betraying nothing of his own exhaustion.

"We should be getting close," Holcomb said, breaking the silence that had settled over them for the past hour.

Riley paused, looking down at the map, then turning to face him. "You're sure you plotted this out right? Because I swear we've passed that fallen oak three times already."

"The terrain all looks similar," Holcomb replied, his tone measured. "It's what makes navigating around this area tricky, but trust me, we're on the right track."

Max stepped between them. "Let's take a quick break. We could all use some water."

And a long shower, hot meal, and a cold beer but none of that was going to happen any time soon. A hike in the woods that made you long for the bed at the Crossroads and crave a burger at the Sunrise had gone seriously sideways.

They found a small clearing and paused to rest. Max leaned against a weathered, angular boulder, while Riley sat on a gnarled tree root. Holcomb took off his pack, but remained standing, stretching his back. As Max took a swig from his water bottle, a twig snapped in the distance. Sharp and loud. Almost deliberate. His head jerked up, eyes scanning the tree line.

"Did you hear that?" he asked.

Riley nodded, her body tensing. "Could be an animal."

"Maybe," Holcomb said, his hand moving to the knife at his belt. "But let's stay alert."

They fell silent. The forest seemed to hold its breath, the usual background noise of birds and insects noticeably absent.

Another snap, closer this time, followed by the rustle of leaves.

"There," Max whispered, pointing to a dense patch of underbrush.

The foliage trembled slightly, but nothing emerged.

"Probably a deer," Holcomb said, his voice low but steady. "They're common in these parts. Skittish things."

Max nodded, but he hadn't seen a deer recently, even at a distance. He recapped his bottle and picked up his pack. As they resumed their hike, he couldn't shake the feeling that whatever was out there was far from skittish. The way the underbrush had moved, the deliberate snapping of twigs—it felt more like they were being stalked than simply stumbling upon easily startled wildlife.

"What kind of animal moves like that?" Max whispered to Riley as they fell into single file, following Holcomb up a narrow section that barely resembled a trail.

Riley shrugged, her eyes constantly scanning their surroundings. "Bears can be pretty stealthy when they want to be. So can mountain lions."

"Great," Max muttered. "Just what we need."

As they pressed on, the sense of being watched intensified. Shadows seemed to flicker with intent but then always disappeared when they turned to look. Each snapping twig or rustling leaf set their nerves further on edge.

"The ridge we're looking for should be just ahead," Holcomb said, his voice, whether he recognized it or not, was pitched low. "The map shows a steep incline just ahead."

Riley, who had re-taken the lead, nodded. "I can see it. The terrain's getting rougher."

They began to ascend, the forest floor giving way to loose rocks and gravel that Max was becoming accustomed to. The slope grew steeper, forcing them to sometimes use their hands for balance as they climbed. There was no talking. They needed all their strength and concentration to manage the shifting, uneven ground. There was only the sound of the wind, their ragged breathing, and their scuffing footsteps.

As they neared the top of the ridge, Max noticed the right side of the trail dropping off sharply. The edge was partially obscured by thick undergrowth, but glimpses through the foliage revealed a dizzying drop to the ravine below.

Max realized there was a reason this section of the vast national park was less traveled and less documented on maps. It was wild, dangerous, and unpredictable. The terrain seemed to resist human intrusion, as if the very land itself was trying to keep its secrets hidden.

Suddenly, a clatter of rocks broke the tense silence. Max looked up to see Riley lose her footing on a patch of loose stones. She stumbled, arms windmilling wildly as she fought to regain her balance. Her hand shot out, grasping at a nearby shrub, but the plant's shallow roots gave way instantly.

"Riley!" Max shouted, lunging forward.

But he was too far behind. With a startled cry, Riley toppled backward, vanishing over the edge of the cliff they'd been skirting.

Max scrambled to the edge, Holcomb close behind.

"Riley!" he shouted. "Can you hear me? Riley!"

Her voice came back, strained and filled with pain. "I'm here! I fell—I can't—Max, help!"

Twenty feet below, Riley clung to a narrow ledge, her body pressed against the rocky slope. The descent wasn't a sheer vertical drop—but close to it—a near-vertical incline of loose scree, jagged rocks, and sparse vegetation. Her feet scrabbled for purchase on the crumbling edge, sending small cascades of pebbles tumbling into the void below. The ravine stretched down at least another hundred feet, its bottom obscured by low-hanging mist. An uncontrolled fall from this height would almost certainly be fatal, or at the very least, cause severe, life-threatening injuries.

Blood trickled from a gash on Riley's forehead, leaving a bright red trail down her dirt-smeared face. Her eyes were wide with shock and fear, her knuckles white as she gripped the narrow ledge.

"Hold on!" Max called down. "We're coming to get you!"

He turned to Holcomb, who was already shrugging off his pack. "I've got some rope," Holcomb said. "We can rig up a harness."

They worked quickly. Every second felt like an eternity, knowing Riley was down there, one slip away from disaster.

"Okay," Holcomb said, double-checking the makeshift harness. "You're going down, Max."

"Me? Shouldn't you go?"

"You're younger and stronger. And she trusts you. That trumps my experience. I'll anchor you and guide you from up here." Holcomb's voice was steady, authoritative. "Listen carefully. Keep your body perpendicular to the rock face. Use your legs to push off, not to climb. Let the rope do the work. Test each hold before you put your weight on it. If you start to slip, don't panic—just grip the rope and I'll stop your descent. Got it?"

Max nodded, absorbing the instructions. There was no time for second-guessing.

"Remember," Holcomb added, "slow and steady wins the race. Riley needs you calm and focused."

Taking a deep breath, Max stepped to the edge. He gave Holcomb a final nod before leaning back into the harness and beginning his descent. The rock face loomed before him, but he forced himself to focus on Holcomb's instructions, moving deliberately and testing each hold before committing his weight.

As he neared Riley's position, something caught his eye. Just below her ledge, partially obscured by shadows and vegetation on the side, but visible from above, was what appeared to be an opening in the rock face. He paused and felt Holcomb jerk the rope. No time to consider it now. He reached Riley and secured the rope around her waist.

"I've got you," he said. "Just hold onto me, okay? We're going back up together."

Riley nodded, wrapping her arms around Max's neck. As a passenger, she could help with balance but not with the climbing itself. As they began their ascent, Max quickly realized how challenging this would be. Every movement was a struggle against gravity and exhaustion. His muscles screamed in protest as he inched them upward, one painstaking step at a time.

The rock face was more treacherous on the way up, loose stones and crumbling earth giving way under their combined weight. More than once, Max felt his foot slip.

"Steady!" Holcomb's voice called from above. "Take it slow!"

Sweat poured down Max's face, stinging his eyes and making his grip on the rope slippery. He gritted his teeth, forcing himself to focus on each movement. Hand over hand. Inch by inch. Still, the top seemed to recede with every effort, as if the cliff was stretching upward, mocking their attempt to conquer it.

After what felt like an eternity, Max's hand finally grasped the edge of the cliff, and he heaved himself and Riley over the lip. They collapsed onto solid ground, chests heaving, bodies trembling with exertion and residual fear.

Holcomb rushed to help, pulling them farther from the edge. All three lay there, catching their breath, the realization of how close they'd come to disaster sinking in.

"There's something down there. A cave, I think," Riley said. Her voice was still shaky.

"I saw it," Max replied. "Off to the left, a little farther down."

"And there are markings around it—symbols carved into the rock."

"I missed that."

"And something else. Did you see the pitons?"

"What are those?"

"Sort of spikes that mountain climbers hammer into the rocks."

"Why?"

"Helps them climb more safely. They can attach ropes and carabiners."

"No, why would they be there at all?"

"Access," Holcomb said.

Max tried to think it through. Could that be the entrance to Grave's End? Is that why it had remained hidden all these years? Had Riley's fall inadvertently led them to what they'd been searching for?

CHAPTER THIRTY-EIGHT

Max sat up. His arms and legs tired and twitchy from the effort of climbing back up. "That cave entrance, could it be what we're looking for? Grave's End?"

Holcomb shook his head. "Unlikely. There are numerous cave systems throughout the park. The Monongahela is riddled with them."

"Really?" Riley said.

"Oh yeah," Holcomb replied. "The park's geology is perfect for cave formation. Millions of years ago, this area was covered by an ancient sea. As the water receded, it left behind layers of limestone. Over time, rainwater and groundwater seeped through cracks in the rock, slowly dissolving the limestone and creating extensive cave networks. There's a big exhibit and a few caves open to the public near the main entrance in Riverstone."

"But couldn't this particular cave be significant?"

"It could be," Holcomb conceded. "But if we're trusting the map—and we've been following it this far—it says no. We're close, but this isn't it. Odds are it's just what it looks like. A small cave that might have been used thousands of years ago by some distant ancestor."

"We should mark it though," Riley suggested, glancing at Max. "Just in case."

Holcomb shrugged. "Sure."

They agreed, noting the location on their map before getting to their feet, packing up their gear, and continuing their hike. The terrain remained challenging, with steep inclines and dense undergrowth. After what felt like hours of effort but was less than a couple of miles, they reached the spot indicated on their copy of the hermit's map.

"This has to be it," Riley said, her voice tinged with frustration as she looked at the map Holcomb held, then back up at the view in front of them. "But I don't see anything unusual. What makes this place special? Why would you name it Grave's End?"

They had climbed partially up yet another steep hill and stood at the edge of more dense forest. Max had never visited the Amazon or the rainforests, but this is what he imagined: a wall of unyielding trees and green. Towering oaks and hickories formed the foundation around a patchwork of moss-covered rocks and fallen logs, bursts of laurel and thick brambles.

"I agree," Max said. The verdant landscape looked like many others that they'd passed in the last three days. Dazzling and inspiring but also now monotonous. His brain had stopped seeing it. He forced himself to slowly scan the area and look at it fresh but still came up empty. "Maybe we're looking at it wrong," he said. "If this place is supposed to be hidden, it wouldn't be obvious. There wouldn't be a flashing sign, or people would have found it already."

Holcomb nodded. "Sure. Good point. Let's spread out and search the immediate vicinity. But stay close."

They fanned out, maintaining roughly fifty yards between

them, each taking a section of the green wall while keeping one another in sight. Max walked along the forest's edge, then carefully stepped inside the perimeter of trees. As he pushed through the undergrowth, something caught his eye—a flash of pink against the ocean of green.

Perhaps he was primed to spot it after finding Sarah's bandana earlier, or maybe it was simply the stark contrast against the verdant backdrop. Whatever the reason, it snagged his attention. He moved closer.

There, caught on a sharp bramble, was a small tuft of pink fabric.

"Hey," he called out, voice tight with excitement. "I think I found something."

Riley and Holcomb hurried over, navigating through the thick underbrush. Max carefully extracted the fabric from the thorns, holding it up for inspection.

"It's not much," he said, "but it's definitely not natural."

Riley eyed the fabric pinched between Max's fingers, her expression a mixture of hope and worry. "That could be from Sarah's backpack or jacket," she said. "I think half her wardrobe is some shade of pink. She's been a bit obsessive ever since our mom died of breast cancer."

They began to explore the thicket more thoroughly, spreading out but staying within earshot. Max bobbed and weaved between branches and vegetation, wincing as thorns and bark scratched at his exposed skin. As he forced his way through a particularly thick patch of brambles, he suddenly stumbled into a small clearing.

There, looming before him, were two massive boulders leaning against each other, creating a narrow passage between them.

"Guys," he called out, his voice echoing slightly in the enclosed space. "I think I found it."

"Where are you?" Riley's voice came back from somewhere on his right. "Keep talking, we'll follow your voice."

Max, feeling a bit foolish but knowing it would help, began to recite:

Shall I compare thee to a summer's day?
Thou art more lovely and more temperate:
Rough winds do shake the darling buds of May,
And summer's lease hath all too short a date...

He continued through Shakespeare's *Sonnet 18*, his voice guiding Riley and Holcomb through the thicket. As he finished, they emerged into the clearing, leaves and twigs caught in their hair and clothes.

Riley raised an eyebrow, a smirk playing at the corners of her mouth. "Shakespeare, huh? Didn't peg you for a poetry buff, Max."

Max shrugged. "What can I say? I'm a lover, not a fighter. It was the first thing that came to mind."

Their playful exchange was cut short as they turned and took in the sight of the boulders. The massive rocks loomed over them, their pockmarked surfaces telling a silent story of centuries withstanding the elements. Max thought back to the previous day's violent storm. How many storms had soaked these boulders? Max looked at his hiking companions and knew they could feel it too. A sense of discovery mingled with a prickly sense of unease.

"It looks like a door, doesn't it?" Holcomb said.

Riley stepped forward, her hand reaching out to touch the stone surface. "This has to be the entrance to Grave's End," she said.

Max studied the passage. It was so narrow that they would need to turn sideways and possibly remove their packs to squeeze through. The thought of shimmying through that tight space made his heart rate quicken, a touch of claustrophobia creeping in.

"No wonder it's remained hidden for so long," he said. "Unless you stumbled upon it directly, you'd never know it was here."

Holcomb nodded. "Nature's perfect camouflage."

As they stood there, each lost in their own thoughts, a cool breeze seemed to emanate from the opening. It carried with it the musty scent of unexplored depths and something else—something older and more unsettling.

It felt like both an invitation and a warning all at once, but underneath it all, there was an unmistakable scent that he recognized. It smelled like death.

———

Riley went first, quickly turning sideways and inching her way farther in. The sound of fabric scraping against stone filled the air as she disappeared into the darkness.

Holcomb hesitated at the entrance, studying the narrow opening. He shrugged off his pack and held it at his side. "Too tight for a full carry," he muttered, his voice echoing slightly. Even without the pack on his shoulders, his larger frame required effort to navigate the tight space. His grunt of discomfort echoed back to Max.

Taking note, Max removed his own pack before stepping forward. He turned sideways almost immediately, the rough stone pressing against his chest and back. With his pack clutched in one hand, he inched forward, wincing as the rock scraped against his clothes and the canvas of his bag.

The passage was even tighter than it had looked from the outside. Max had to flatten himself against the stone, feeling every ridge and bump in the rock face. He wasn't typically claustrophobic, but in that moment, with tons of rock surrounding him, it was hard not to imagine the boulders suddenly shifting, trapping him forever in its stony embrace.

He pushed forward, inch by agonizing inch. Sweat beaded on his forehead and trickled down into his eyes. The cool stone offered no relief; instead, it seemed to mock his struggle. Max forced himself to keep moving and fought against the urge to turn around. The others had obviously made it, so he could too. His head was turned the wrong way to see, but he could sense the void just ahead. With a final push, he squeezed through the last section of the passage and stumbled into an open area.

He brushed himself off, took in a gulping breath, and then looked around. It was a natural amphitheater, its walls rising in a perfect circle of weathered stone. The ground sloped gently downward, covered in a thick carpet of emerald moss that seemed to glow in the filtered sunlight. At the center stood a single ancient tree, its gnarled branches reaching out over the clearing like protective arms.

"This is incredible," Max said as he tried to take in the scene.

They'd seen many beautiful sights and vistas during their often brutal hikes. But this place was different. The feeling that had been growing since they first approached the boulder entrance now intensified. Max could not only smell and feel it but see it as well. An ancient power seemed to crackle through the air like static electricity, invisible yet undeniably present.

Riley stepped up beside him. He glanced over at her to see if she felt it, too. "It's beautiful," she said softly. "But... empty."

Max took in the slump of her shoulders and realized she had pinned a lot of hope on reaching Grave's End and being reunited with her sister.

Holcomb cleared his throat. "There are a lot of places to get lost here. Let's take a look around before we jump to conclusions."

CHAPTER THIRTY-NINE

They spread out, each taking a section of the amphitheater to search. Holcomb moved along the perimeter, eyes scanning the rocky walls and pockets of forest. Riley focused on the ground, carefully walking a grid in search of any signs that Sarah and Jake might have left behind.

Max, meanwhile, found himself drawn to the ancient tree at the center of the clearing. Its imposing presence seemed to demand attention, and he felt compelled to investigate it more closely. As he approached, he noticed something peculiar about its bark.

Up close, the surface wasn't as rough as he'd initially thought. In some areas, the bark appeared unusually smooth, almost polished by time. Max ran his fingers over it, feeling the contrast between the deeply furrowed sections and the smoother patches.

As he studied the bark more closely, he began to see patterns emerging. Swirls and shapes seemed to form and dissipate before his eyes, like images in clouds. He saw what

looked like faces, animals, and abstract symbols, all inter-
twining and morphing into one another.

Max blinked hard and shook his head, trying to clear his
vision. When he looked again, some patterns remained while
others had vanished. He couldn't be sure if the shapes were
truly there, etched by centuries of growth and weathering, or
if his exhausted body and mind were finding meaning in the
randomness of nature.

He turned away and the spell was broken. It was just a
tree. An old, elegant tree. Nothing more. But...he wanted
some distance. His eyes swept over the amphitheater's walls
until he spotted a rocky outcropping near the top that looked
like a promising vantage point to survey the area.

He made his way up. The climb was steep but manageable. As he neared the top, he paused to catch his breath,
wiping sweat from his brow with the back of his hand.

From the top, he looked down on Grave's End and immediately spotted it—a subtle depression or disturbance to the
right of the tree sheltered by the edge of the lower rock bowl.
Max squinted, trying to make out more details but he wasn't
an expert in this sort of thing.

"Holcomb," he called down, "I think I see something.
Can you come take a look?"

Holcomb made his way up and joined Max on the ledge,
following his pointing finger.

"There," Max said. "See that patch of ground? It looks
different from the rest."

Holcomb studied the area, then nodded. "Good eye.
That's definitely remnants of a campsite. The moss is flattened in a roughly rectangular shape—about the size of a two-
person tent."

"Jake and Sarah?"

"Could be. Let's take a closer look."

They made their way back down. Max called out to Riley

as they neared the bottom, "We found something. Possible campsite."

Riley's head snapped up. She was slowly walking the perimeter but had started on the opposite side. "Where?"

Holcomb led them to the spot. Up close, the signs were a little more difficult to discern but Holcomb pointed out certain things.

"See here," Holcomb said, crouching down and gesturing to the flattened moss. "This rectangular area is where the tent stood. It looks to be the right size for a two-person tent. The compression is still visible, which means it's recent."

He moved a few feet to the left. "And look at this," he said, brushing aside some leaves and dirt to reveal a small, blackened patch of earth. "This is where they had their fire."

Riley knelt beside him, her fingers hovering over the burnt earth as if it might still contain some heat.

Holcomb continued, "There are also some subtle changes in the vegetation. See how these small ground plants are bent at an unnatural angle? That's likely from repeated foot traffic."

He stood up and scanned the area. "And over there," he pointed to a nearby tree, "you can see some scuff marks on the bark. Probably from a rope they used to hang their food to keep it away from animals just like we did."

Max watched as Riley absorbed every detail.

"How recent do you think this is?" she asked.

Holcomb considered for a moment. "Not an exact science and we had all that rain, but I'd say very recent."

"This is it," Riley said. "They were here."

"Easy," Holcomb cautioned. "We don't know that for certain."

"But it has to be them. Who else would camp here?"

Max stepped back, letting Riley and Holcomb continue their discussion. He took in the entirety of Grave's End, his mind shifting gears as old instincts kicked in. He'd spent years planning heists, studying buildings and security systems. Now, he applied those same skills to the natural amphitheater surrounding them.

It had been a while since he'd exercised those particular muscles, but the familiar thought patterns slowly returned, like a pianist's fingers finding their place on long-untouched keys. His eyes scanned the rocky walls, looking for irregularities, hidden alcoves, or anything out of place.

If I were hiding something, where would I put it? he thought.

He methodically divided the area into sections, analyzing each one for potential use. The ancient tree at the center, the mossy ground, the steep rocky walls. Max cataloged each feature or detail and made mental notes, but nothing jumped to the top of the list. There were workable opportunities, but each had flaws or drawbacks. Max glanced back at the rocky outcropping he'd climbed earlier. Maybe a different perspective would help.

"I'm going to take another look from up top," he called to Riley and Holcomb.

He made his way back up the steep incline, his legs barking with each step. At the top, once he'd caught his breath, he repeated the same process he'd done down below and this time his eye caught something he'd missed before. Near the far end of the amphitheater, partially hidden by shadows and vegetation, was a subtle change in the rock face. It was well concealed from the ground, but from this higher vantage point, he could make it out. Alarms bells clanged in his head.

A cave entrance.

This is what they were searching for. He wanted to yell to the others and run over to the entrance, but he didn't. He took it slow for a few more minutes and studied it more carefully, noting its position relative to other landmarks. As his gaze slowly traced the entrance, something glinted in the dappled sunlight. It was small, barely noticeable. He couldn't make it out, but, like the pink tuft of cloth, he felt it didn't belong.

Now he did call down to the pair and added, "Holcomb, bring your binoculars."

Five minutes later, he was tightening the focus on a small camera.

Now he had a new question to consider. Was that persistent feeling of being watched due to the camera or something else. He held them out to Riley. "Straight ahead then shift left and up five degrees."

"What the hell? Who put that there?" She handed the binoculars to Holcomb. He peered through. "Maybe the hermit?"

"Could be. Judging by some of the things we saw at his place, he has the technical expertise, but if you look at all the other things in his office and the fact that he appears to mostly live online, why would he trek out here to set up cameras? I'm not sure he's ever set foot here. I think maybe that's why he needed Jake and maybe Vance. Have you felt anything since we arrived here?"

She looked at him. "Like someone's breathing down my neck."

"Exactly. Do you think that could be the reason?"

She considered the question. "Could be, except I felt it before we got to Grave's End. It's just stronger here."

Max thought she had a point. He'd felt it before, too. When had it started? The first day? When they'd made camp on the ridge? He couldn't pin it down. But Riley was right, it was getting stronger, as if Grave's End was amplifying the effect.

"Huh. Looks like a wildlife camera," Holcomb said.

"Pretty expensive one, too. I've seen some around. Occasionally we get scientists asking to put them in the park for research purposes."

"Can't be transmitting, right? No cell connection out here," Max asked.

"Some of them use satellite connections but that's rare or at least expensive to connect and transmit. Slow, too. Drains the battery faster, as well."

"And it's unlikely whoever set that up is coming out regularly to charge it."

"Sure, but you're not asking the most obvious question," Riley said. "Why even set it up in the first place?"

CHAPTER FORTY

The sun had crept lower on the horizon. Long shadows reached halfway across the bowl of Grave's End. Max leaned against an oak tree and studied the dark clouds that circled the peaks of the nearby Alleghenies. Riley paced along the top of the rock ridge, her agitation clear, though her footsteps were muffled by the thick ground moss. Holcomb sat on a flat rock and massaged his lower back. Max noted the dark circles under his eyes. This hike was pushing everyone to their breaking point.

Riley paused her pacing, scanning the area one last time before making her way down the ridge. She navigated carefully over loose rocks, sending small pebbles tumbling ahead of her as she descended to join the others.

"We need to decide our next move," Max said once she reached them. "It will be dark soon and hiking back to camp will be difficult."

Riley brushed dirt from her hands. "They have to be here somewhere. We can't just leave."

"And we can't abandon Ethan and Jamie, either," Max replied.

"I'm not suggesting we abandon them. We're all on the same team, but we know where Ethan and Jamie are. We're here now. We should stay and find Sarah and Jake."

"Easy," Holcomb said, standing up. "I agree."

"With who?" Riley asked.

"Both of you. We need to consider all the possibilities. And balance our effort. We still have three hours of solid light. As long as we get most of the way back before full dark, the last part of the hike into camp is wooded, but not difficult. So let's focus our attention here, for now. Agreed?" He looked at each of them. They nodded and Holcomb continued, "Now, where else might they have gone?" He pulled out the map and laid it on the flat rock in front of him.

Riley walked closer and peered down. "There's nothing else nearby. No other points of interest. We are hemmed in by the canyon and the mountains." She paused. "Whatever happened, happened here. I can feel it."

"What if they found something we haven't?" Max asked. "Maybe they stumbled onto another clue and followed it deeper into the forest. Maybe not the foothills of those mountains, but away from this place."

Holcomb considered it then shook his head. "Possible, but unlikely. At least on the way in. We've been following the trail pretty closely. If they veered off course, or made it here and then reversed course, I think we would have seen signs."

"What about up here?" Max indicated the surrounding forest. "We haven't checked it out as thoroughly as down below."

"That's possible."

"So let's spend a half hour, spread out, and search it."

They split up, each taking a section of the upper ridge.

Max walked slowly and carefully, zigzagging 10 to 15 yards in and out of the tree line. The prickling sensation of being watched had faded, but he still pivoted every few steps, scanning the surrounding shadows. Twenty minutes later, he'd made it back to the flat rock. Holcomb was waiting and Riley appeared a minute later. He could tell by the looks on their faces that they also had come up empty.

"There was one spot. Ground was kicked up a bit, but likely just animals," Riley said and shrugged.

"So we're back to the cave," Max said.

Riley's jaw clenched. "It's our only lead."

"Agreed," Holcomb said. "But we need to be smart about this. We can't all go in."

Max nodded. "Two of us should check it out. The third keeps watch and maintains a link to the outside."

"I'm going in," Riley said, her tone leaving no room for argument.

Max and Holcomb exchanged glances. "Actually," Max said, "I think it should be Holcomb and me."

Riley's eyes flashed. "Like hell. That's my sister in there."

"Exactly," Holcomb said gently. "Which is why you need to stay out here."

"What's that supposed to mean?"

Max stepped forward. "It means we need someone level-headed in there. Someone who won't take unnecessary risks."

"I can be level-headed," Riley protested.

"Maybe," Max said. "But can you guarantee that if we find something...difficult in there, you won't lose focus?"

Riley opened her mouth to argue, then closed it.

"Besides," Holcomb added, "we need your military training out here. You're our best line of defense if...something goes wrong."

"Fine. But if you're not back in an hour, I'm coming in after you."

They gathered their gear and then hiked around and approached the cave entrance from the side, careful to keep out of view of the camera.

Max stood behind a large boulder, his eyes fixed on the small device. "What do you think? Should we do something about that camera?"

Holcomb frowned, considering. "It's tempting to disable it, but that might alert whoever placed it that we're here."

"Could we take it?" Max suggested. "Might give us some clues."

Holcomb shook his head. "Same problem. We don't know if removing it would trigger some kind of alarm or alert."

"So we ignore it?" Max asked.

Holcomb nodded. "For now. Let's focus on the cave. It's going to capture us one way or another, but I can't imagine it's instantaneous. Not out here. There will be a lag. We can deal with the fallout later if we need to."

They crept closer to the entrance, staying low and using the natural cover of the terrain. No reason to get caught on camera earlier than necessary. As they approached, Max noticed how the opening seemed to blend into the rock face.

"Look at that," he said. "It's partially hidden."

Holcomb ran his hand along the edge of the entrance. "Clever. They've used vegetation and weaved it into some kind of netting for better coverage."

Holcomb pulled back the edge of the netting and peered inside. "Looks narrow. We'll have to go single file."

Holcomb had a headlamp. Max didn't, but he handed him a small, slim flashlight from his pack. "Redundancy is the difference between a story and a statistic."

They did one final gear check. "Ready?" Holcomb asked as he tightened a strap.

Max took a deep breath. "As I'll ever be."

They slipped around the netting and inside. The passage

was tight, forcing them to duck and weave around protruding rocks. Their lights cut through the gloom, revealing rough stone walls slick with moisture.

"Watch your step," Holcomb warned. "The ground's uneven."

They moved slowly, carefully picking their way through the tunnel. The air grew thicker and smelled of rock and minerals.

After about fifteen minutes of cautious progress, the passage dipped sharply and the flow of water increased along the edges of the passage. Holcomb held up a hand, signaling Max to stop.

"Look," he said, pointing his light farther ahead.

Max squinted. "Is that...?"

"A collapse," Holcomb confirmed. "And a recent one, by the looks of it."

They approached the pile of rubble cautiously. Max scanned the debris. There was a small gap near the top but not wide enough for either man to squeeze through. As he scanned the edges, his light caught on something out of place.

"There," he said, crouching down. He reached out and plucked a wrapper from between two rocks. "It's a protein bar wrapper."

Holcomb leaned in for a closer look. He took the wrapper and turned it over. "Expiration date isn't for another six months. It's recent."

"We need to find another way in," Max said.

Holcomb nodded. "Let's head back. No point in wasting more time here."

They retraced their steps, emerging from the cave to find Riley pacing anxiously where they'd left her.

"That was too fast," she said as soon as she spotted them.

"There's been a collapse. We couldn't get far."

Riley's face fell. Holcomb held up the wrapper. "We also

found this. Do you know if your sister or Jake preferred a certain brand?"

Riley took the wrapper and turned it over in her hands. "I don't know. It's possible." She looked at the pair of them. "We need to find another way in."

"I had the same thought. But is there one?" Max asked. They both looked at the veteran forest ranger.

Holcomb scratched his chin. "Cave systems like this usually have multiple entrances. Water finds a way in, it finds a way out. We just need to locate it."

"How?" Riley asked.

"We follow the topography," Holcomb explained. "Look for depressions in the ground, listen for running water. Cave entrances often form where surface water disappears underground."

They spread out, searching the area around Grave's End. The sun had dipped below the horizon, leaving them in the gray twilight of dusk. Max found himself straining to see, his eyes playing tricks on him in the fading light.

A shout from Riley grabbed his attention. "Over here!"

Max and Holcomb hurried over. Riley stood at the edge of a small clearing, pointing at the ground.

"Look," she said. "The vegetation is different here."

Max knelt down, examining the area. The grass was indeed different—lusher and greener than the surrounding area. Interspersed were patches of moss and small, moisture-loving plants he didn't recognize.

"It's like a little oasis," Max said, running his hand over the verdant growth.

Holcomb crouched beside him, nodding. "Good eye, Riley. This definitely indicates a nearby water source." He glanced around. "Could be a sign of subsurface drainage. Moisture availability can create these pockets of thriving vegetation."

"So there might be a spring or underground stream?" Riley asked.

"Exactly," Holcomb said. "Let's follow this greener patch and see where it leads us."

They followed the line of lush vegetation, pushing through thick underbrush. The ground sloped gently downward, the grass growing increasingly damp under their feet. Suddenly, the foliage parted, revealing a small clearing.

"Look," Max said, pointing ahead.

Before them lay a shallow pool, perhaps ten feet in diameter. The water was crystal clear, fed by a small spring bubbling up from the ground. Delicate ferns and vibrant moss ringed its edges.

"Where does it go?" Riley asked, noticing there was no visible outflow.

Holcomb circled the pool, his eyes scanning the surrounding rock face. "Here," he called, waving them over.

At the far end of the pool, partially hidden by overhanging vines, a narrow crevice split the rock. The pool's water flowed down into the dark opening.

Max pushed aside the vines for a better look. The crevice was about four feet wide, descending into darkness. The water's surface, visible for a few feet, was black and still in the fading light.

"An underground stream," Holcomb said. "This could be our way in. Underground rivers often carve out passages."

Riley frowned. "How deep is it?"

Max picked up a long branch and carefully probed the water. After a moment, he felt the bottom. "It's about four, maybe five feet deep. I can just scrape the bottom with this branch."

He handed the branch to Riley, who was a few inches shorter. She tested it herself and nodded. "So we'd be wading, maybe swimming in spots."

"Depends on how far it goes," Holcomb added. "The depth could change as we move deeper into the passage."

Riley bit her lip, considering. "It's not ideal, but it might be manageable. At least we wouldn't be completely submerged right away."

Max peered into the dark water, a mixture of anticipation and apprehension on his face. "Still, we don't know how long the passage is or where it leads. We could be walking into a dead end."

Holcomb nodded. "True, but it might be our best shot at finding another way into the cave system. We'll need to be careful, though. Underground waterways can be unpredictable."

"Okay, this is a possibility, but it might not be the only possibility. Let's keep looking and see if there's a...drier way in."

"I think we should clear each opportunity as we find it. Why double back?" Riley said.

Before he could answer, a sharp crack split the air. Chips of rock exploded from the cliff face inches from Max's head.

"Get down!" Riley shouted, instinctively dropping to a crouch.

More shots rang out, bullets pinging off the rocks around them. They pressed themselves into the surrounding cliffside, but there was little cover.

"Where's it coming from?" Max yelled.

"Can't tell," Holcomb shouted back. "The echoes are making it impossible to pinpoint."

Another bullet whizzed past, uncomfortably close. Riley glanced at the water-filled crevice, then back at her companions. No words were needed. Max knew she was right. They were pinned down and if they didn't move soon, they would be picked off one by one. The water was their only choice.

Riley jumped sideways into the pool.

"Go!" Holcomb yelled as he ran forward toward the edge of the small clearing. Max saw a clod of dirt explode by the man's feet. He didn't wait for more. He turned and followed Riley into the pool. The water was cold and the shock of it briefly drove the air from his lungs. He recovered and pushed hard until he was inside the tunnel, then he stopped and turned back. Holcomb was in the water, but still exposed and moving slowly. So slowly. Each step felt like an eternity. Finally, Max was able to reach out and grab the older man and pull him into the dark.

He held onto Holcomb as they moved deeper in, then he let go and both men paused to catch their breath.

It was very dark away from the pool and the mouth of the tunnel. "Riley?"

"Here."

The voice came from a few feet away, just in front of him, but Max couldn't see anything.

"You okay?"

"Five by five."

"Okay. I guess we're exploring this now."

"I guess so."

"Lead the way."

He heard the sounds of sloshing movement. He gave her a moment and then he followed. The passage grew more narrow. Max could feel the rough stone scraping his shoulders and grabbing at the edges of his pack as he followed Riley.

Suddenly, the current picked up. Max felt himself being pulled along, unable to resist the flow. The passage now widened slightly, but the water moved faster. Ahead, he heard a roar growing louder.

"Falls!" He tried to shout, but water filled his mouth.

They were swept over the edge, plummeting through darkness. Max hit the water hard and went under. The pack on his back felt like an anchor. He remained calm and let his natural buoyancy tell him which way was up then he kicked hard to the surface; he broke the surface disoriented and gasping for air. When he could breathe, he looked around. He realized he could suddenly see, a little at least, mostly in shades of gray. There must be cracks somewhere letting in the light. He was relieved to find Riley treading water nearby.

"Holcomb?" he called out, scanning the churning pool.

A shape floated facedown a few yards away. They both swam over quickly, turning Holcomb onto his back. His eyes were closed, his skin pale, a gash visible on his forehead. They struggled toward the shore, dragging Holcomb's deadweight through the current. Behind them, a dark trail bloomed in the water spreading like ink across parchment.

Riley pressed her hand against Holcomb's neck, searching for a pulse. "He's bleeding. Bad."

CHAPTER FORTY-ONE

"If he's bleeding, then he's alive," Max said.

They dragged Holcomb onto the thin, rocky shore. He was pale and limp, blood seeping from a wound they couldn't yet locate.

Riley knelt beside Holcomb, her hands moving swiftly over his body. "We need to find the source of the bleeding. Help me remove his jacket."

They unwound the straps of his backpack, put it aside, and then carefully peeled off the soaked jacket. As they worked, the metallic scent of blood mingled with the damp smell of the cave.

"There," Riley said, pointing to a gash on Holcomb's side, just below his ribs where his shirt was torn. "Looks like he caught it on a rock during the fall."

"Not enough."

"What?"

"You saw how much blood was in the water. That scrape wouldn't produce that much, neither would the cut on his forehead."

Riley nodded and her expression hardened. She began

methodically checking Holcomb's body from top to bottom, her hands moving with practiced efficiency. She didn't have to search far. When she reached his left shoulder, she paused. "Here."

"Where? What?" Max couldn't see anything obvious in the cave's low light.

Riley tore the fabric of Holcomb's shirt and pulled it away from his shoulder, revealing a small, round hole about the size of a dime just below his collarbone. It was blue and black at the edges but only oozed a small amount of blood.

"Entry wound," she said, her voice clinical. "Help me turn him."

They carefully rolled Holcomb onto his side. Max felt his stomach churn.

Where the bullet had exited, it had carved out a ragged crater of flesh the size of Max's fist. Torn muscle and shredded tissue created a grotesque flower pattern, its petals of mangled skin stained crimson. Blood pulsed from the wound with each of Holcomb's shallow breaths, mixing with the water that dripped from his clothes.

"Exit wound," Riley said. "I saw too many of these in Afghanistan. The bullet tumbled as it passed through. That's why there's so much damage on this side. You were right. This is where most of the blood loss is coming from." Max had to look away for a moment. Riley continued, "Holcomb is lucky, in one respect. The bullet passed through the soft tissue of his shoulder, missed major arteries and bone. But he's still losing a lot of blood."

She pressed her hands against the wound. "This needs to be our priority. The other injuries can wait."

"What do we do next?"

Riley's eyes darted around the cavern. "We need to elevate his legs, slow the blood flow to the wound. Use your pack."

Max reached for his backpack and quickly checked the

inside. He noted with relief that while the exterior was soaked, the waterproof lining had mostly done its job. As he positioned the pack under Holcomb's feet, he said, "Most of our stuff should be dry, or at least salvageable."

Riley nodded, rummaging through her own pack with one hand, the other still pressed firmly against Holcomb's side. "Thank God for small mercies. The first aid kit's barely damp."

She pulled out the kit, its contents protected by a watertight seal, and tossed it to Max. "There should be a QuikClot bandage in there. Find it."

Max fumbled through the kit, his hands shaking slightly. He was beginning to feel the effects of the sudden swim in the icy water. He found the package and tore it open.

"Okay," Riley said, "on three, I'm going to move my hands. You need to apply that directly to the wound. Ready?"

Max nodded, positioning himself.

"One, two, three."

As Riley moved, blood welled up from the gash. Max pressed the bandage firmly against it, feeling the warmth of Holcomb's blood seeping through.

"Hold it there," Riley instructed. "The clotting agent should help with the worst of it." She dug through the first aid kit, then patted her pockets. "Dammit."

"What?"

"Over the sand box, everyone, men and women, used to carry tampons. Perfect for bullet wounds—sterile, absorbent, designed to expand and apply pressure." She shook her head. "Have to improvise." She pulled out a roll of gauze. "We'll have to pack the entry wound. It needs pressure from the inside out."

Riley carefully rolled the gauze into a tight cylinder. "Hold him steady." She worked the gauze into the entry wound, her movements precise and methodical. "This isn't ideal, but it should help slow the bleeding."

Riley secured both wounds with more pressure bandages, using nearly all the medical tape from the kit.

"That's all we can do for now," Riley said, sitting back on her heels. Her voice was steady, but Max could see the slight tremor in her hands, either from the cold or from memories of other similar field treatments under fire.

Max nodded, he pulled out and unfolded the foil first aid blanket from the pack and draped it over Holcomb. "How long until he wakes up?"

"There's no way to know," Riley replied. "Could be minutes, could be hours."

"We can't stay here," Max said finally. "Holcomb needs proper medical attention and we're still in danger. Whoever did that," Max said, pointing down at Holcomb, "is still out there or, worse, coming after us."

Riley nodded. "Agreed. But we can't move him in this condition."

"So what do we do?"

Riley stood, then went to the edge of the pool and washed the blood from her hands. She wiped her hands on her pants and turned. "One of us needs to explore, find a way out."

For the first time since their arrival over the falls, they took a moment to check out their surroundings. The cavern was long and tall, its ceiling lost in shadows beyond the reach of their flashlights. The waterfall that had carried them here cascaded down one wall, its roar now a familiar background noise. The water churned in a deep pool before finding an outlet, becoming a swift-moving underground river that disappeared into a dark tunnel.

To their right, a narrow fissure split the cavern wall, wide enough for a person to pass through sideways. A steady breeze emanated from it, suggesting it might lead to the surface. Behind them, almost hidden behind a curtain of stalactites, another passage gaped like a black mouth in the rock face. Their flashlight beams were swallowed by its darkness, making it impossible to determine its direction or depth.

Phosphorescent fungi clung to the damp walls, casting an eerie pale-blue glow that mixed with the harsh beams of their flashlights and the paler, softer light from unseen overhead cracks. Stalactites hung from the ceiling like nature's chandeliers, water droplets clinging to their tips before falling into the pool below with soft, echoing plops. The air was cool and carried the rich scent of wet stone and mineral deposits.

Near where they had dragged Holcomb, the cavern floor sloped upward, creating a relatively dry area strewn with smooth river rocks and fine, black sand. It was an otherworldly landscape, beautiful in an alien way.

"I'll go," Max said.

"No," Riley shook her head. "I should go. I have more experience with this kind of thing."

"Exactly why you should stay with Holcomb. If his condition changes, you'll know what to do. I can handle a little spelunking."

Riley hesitated, then nodded. "All right."

"Three choices," Max said, his voice echoing slightly. "Follow the water, try the fissure, or explore that back passage."

"Follow the water," Riley replied without hesitation.

"All right." He changed clothes first. He couldn't do anything about his wet boots, but felt better with the warmer, dry clothes. "I'll be back as soon as I can," he said. "If Holcomb wakes up..."

"I'll take care of him," Riley assured him. "Just find us a way out of here."

Max nodded, then turned toward the tunnel carrying the

water away. He paused, looking back at Riley. "Wait, what about going back the way we came?"

Riley frowned, considering. "The waterfall?"

They moved to the edge of the pool, shining their lights upward. The falls roared, but as they studied it, Max realized it wasn't as formidable as it had seemed during their chaotic descent.

"It's not as high as I thought," Max said. "Maybe twenty feet?"

Riley nodded. "The darkness and the current made it scarier in the moment. We might be able to scale the sides."

"If one of us could get a rope up there, it could help with the current," Max suggested.

"It's an option," Riley agreed. "But it won't be easy and Holcomb won't be able to make the climb in his condition."

Max sighed, running a hand through his damp hair. "You're right. We should still explore other options."

Riley rummaged in her pack, pulling out a piece of chalk. "Here, take this. Mark your way as you go."

Max took the chalk, tucking it into his pocket. He checked the dwindling supplies in his pack—an extra pair of socks, one energy bar, and a bottle of water.

Max stepped into the tunnel that carried the underground river, relieved to find a narrow ledge running along the right wall. It was barely three feet wide, but the surface was mostly level, worn smooth by countless years of flooding and receding waters. The setup reminded him of the storm drains beneath South Boston—concrete channels he'd used more than once to slip in and out of buildings unseen. But where those had been angular and artificial, this passage was organic, carved by water and time.

His flashlight beam caught the rippling surface of the water to his left. The river moved swiftly but silently, deeper than it looked, its black surface occasionally broken by swirling eddies. The ceiling dropped lower, forcing him to duck his head in spots, but the ledge remained consistent.

Max paused every few minutes to mark the wall with chalk. The tunnel twisted and turned like a drunk trying to follow his sober friend home—sometimes tracking the water's path precisely, other times wandering off on its own dark tangents before inevitably stumbling back to the river's course.

He marked each junction meticulously, not wanting to risk getting lost in this stone maze. The sound of the river became his constant companion, sometimes a distant murmur, other times a rushing presence at his feet, but always there, pulling him forward through the darkness.

After an hour of careful navigation through narrow passages and small chambers, Max paused to rest. He leaned against the damp wall, taking a small sip from his water bottle. The silence was overwhelming, broken only by his own breathing and the burbling white noise of the nearby water.

Then another noise caught his attention. It was faint, barely audible over the ambient sounds of the cave. Max held his breath, straining to listen.

There it was again—a murmur, like voices carried on the wind. But there was no wind here, deep underground.

He tried to still his breathing and listen more closely. The sound wavered in and out like a weak AM radio signal. Were those human voices? Or was his mind playing tricks on him, conjuring sounds from the random echoes of the cave?

He pushed off from the wall, moving toward the source of the sound. The tunnel widened slightly, opening into a larger chamber. The murmurs grew louder, more distinct, yet still maddeningly unclear.

Max swept his flashlight around the chamber, the beam

catching on something. A backpack partially hidden by a rock.

The murmurs continued, unabated and unintelligible. Max strained to make out words, to identify the voices, but they remained soft and sibilant, just beyond his comprehension. He began to wonder if he was truly hearing anything at all.

Had the darkness, the isolation, and the stress finally gotten to him? Max rubbed his eyes with the back of his free hand and tried to clear his head. When he opened them again, the voices were still there. So was the backpack. He walked over and touched the black padded strap. It felt real, even if it looked old. The strap was dry and cracked in places. How had it gotten down here?

He sat on the rock. He was tired. Beyond tired. He felt like he could sleep for three days even just lying on this rock. He didn't dare close his eyes. It was all too tempting. He stood back up.

"Where are you two?"

CHAPTER FORTY-TWO

Sarah pushed herself up to a sitting position. Just that small bit of jostling to her ankle made her wince in pain. She took several deep breaths as her stomach did a few nauseous backflips. The air was distinctly cooler and damper down here and she shivered in her T-shirt. Sitting up had also done little to improve her headache. A dull ache pulsed behind her eyes and radiated down her neck. She gently touched the back of her head and found a discomfortingly large and tender bump. In short, she was a mess.

And she had other problems.

Her gaze drifted back to the camera, its red light blinking in the gloom. It felt as if it were watching her and judging her. She was an unexpected and unwelcome intruder in this ancient space. Questions tumbled through her mind. Who? What? Why? Who placed it there? What was it recording? Why had someone placed it there? And most pressingly, was someone watching her right now? She felt a shiver that had nothing to do with the chilled cave's air.

Her first instinct was to disable it. But as she reached for a nearby rock, she hesitated. What if the camera was her only connection to the outside world? What if it was a scientific thing or part of a rescue operation, placed here by park rangers or search teams looking for lost hikers just like her?

She closed her eyes and tried to think through the fog of pain and confusion. Save herself later or protect herself now? If it was part of a rescue operation, destroying it could mean cutting off her only chance of being found. But if it wasn't... she thought of Jake's scattered belongings.

She opened her eyes, decision made. For now, she would leave the camera intact until she knew more, but she would do her best to stay out of its line of sight. She maneuvered around in a circle to better survey her dim surroundings more carefully. The cavern was larger than she'd initially thought, stretching at least 50 feet in diameter. The ceiling arched high above her, stalactites hanging like stone icicles, their tips glistening with moisture. To her left, a natural pillar of rock rose from floor to ceiling, creating a shadowed alcove behind it. It looked like it might be just out of the camera's field of view. Perfect.

Sarah attempted to stand, careful of her ankle, but as soon as she put any weight on her left foot, agonizing pain lit up her leg from her ankle to her hip. She collapsed back to the ground, sweat popping on her brow and her breath coming in short, ragged bursts.

She took a moment to compose herself and let the pain fade. When it had backed off to a dull roar, she carefully slid over on her butt until she could reach her phone. The screen was cracked but otherwise the phone appeared to be all right. The battery was at 47 percent—not great, but not dire. Not yet. Before she dimmed the flashlight to conserve power, she aimed the beam at her ankle. Her stomach churned at the sight. In the hours since her fall, her ankle had swollen to nearly twice its normal size, the skin mottled with angry purples and sickly yellows. When she tried to rotate her foot, more pain washed over her. She could feel the bones grinding in ways they shouldn't. This was bad—possibly, even probably, a break, definitely a severe sprain.

Sarah knew she needed to stabilize the injury, to fashion some kind of splint from her backpack, but that would have to wait. Right now, she wanted to get out of sight of the camera. Gritting her teeth, she resigned herself to crawling. She collected her pack. Other than one jagged rip where a pocket had torn, it looked largely unaffected. She dragged it along with one hand while trying to minimize the impact to her ankle.

As she inched her way across the cavern floor, a sound beyond the pounding of blood in her ears caught her attention. Water. Not the sporadic drip-drip-drip of moisture seeping through rock, but a consistent steady flow. She paused, retrieving her phone to illuminate the source of the sound.

The beam of light revealed a small stream emerging from a crack in the far wall of the cavern. It cascaded over rocks in a miniature waterfall before pooling in a clear basin about ten feet across. The sight of the water made Sarah acutely aware of how thirsty she was. How long had it been since she'd had anything to drink?

Now that she saw it, she was powerless to resist. She altered her course. When she finally reached the water's edge, she dipped her hands into the cool liquid, bringing them to her cracked lips. Then she paused. Her initial impulse to drink was tempered by a nagging voice of caution. Even in her pain-addled state, she recalled warnings about drinking untreated water. Cave water could harbor dangerous bacteria or parasites. But she also knew that dehydration posed an immediate threat to her survival and clear thinking.

She weighed her options. She had no means to boil the water, no purification tablets, those were in Jake's pack, not even a cloth to use as a makeshift filter. The water looked clear, and its constant flow was a good sign. In the end, the risk of dehydration outweighed the potential danger of the untreated water.

She brought a small amount to her lips first, tasting it cautiously. The water was crisp and clean with no discernible odd flavors. She needed the water. She began to drink more deeply, savoring each swallow as it soothed her parched throat.

After drinking until her stomach sloshed, she cupped more water in her hands and splashed it over her face. The shock of cold against her skin helped clear the fog from her mind, washing away some of the grime and sweat. She thought the icy water might soothe her ankle but didn't want to untie her hiking boot.

Her thirst quenched and face clean, Sarah resumed her painful journey to the alcove. When she finally reached it, she allowed herself a moment of relief. The space behind the pillar was deep enough for her to sit with her back against the cool stone, completely shielded from the camera's view.

As she sat, Sarah again took stock of her situation. She was injured, alone, and lost in a cave system she knew nothing about. But she wasn't entirely without resources. She had her phone, though the battery wouldn't last forever. There was water nearby, so dehydration wouldn't be an immediate concern. She had at least a few protein bars in her pack, so she wouldn't go hungry for a bit. Her crawling journey had been short but had taken a lot out of her. She felt her eyes get heavy. She would just close them for a minute, gather her strength, and plan her next move. Just for a minute...

CHAPTER FORTY-THREE

Sarah's eyes snapped open, her heart pounding. For a moment, she couldn't remember where she was. The darkness pressed in around her. It was deep and opaque and felt endless. She felt the panic rise, but then her eyes began to adjust, she saw shades of gray and it all came rushing back—the fall, her ankle, the blinking red eye of the camera. She was in a cave, hidden behind a rock pillar.

Her hand instinctively reached for her pack, seeking the familiar comfort of her pink Red Sox bandana. Her fingers found the torn fabric where it should have been tied and her heart sank. Lost. Somewhere between the campsite and here. The bandana that had seen her through nursing school, through every hiking trip with Jake, through those endless nights at Mom's bedside. Gone. A small loss among everything else, but somehow it hit harder than her throbbing ankle and aching head.

A low rumble reverberated through the stone beneath her. At first, she thought it was her empty stomach, but the sound grew louder, more insistent. What was it? It faded but then came back with a crack and low boom. Thunder, she realized.

A storm somewhere above her. The thunder continued at regular intervals. That must have been what woke her up.

Sarah shifted, wincing as pain shot through her swollen ankle. Fumbling in the darkness, she found her phone. The cracked screen flickered to life, momentarily blinding her. 5:47 p.m. She'd been out for hours.

Another growl of thunder shook the cave, and Sarah felt a tremor run through the rock. A faint pattering reached her ears, growing steadily louder. Rain. It was pouring outside and the sound was filtering down through cracks in the cave system.

The air grew heavy with moisture and Sarah shivered. Her T-shirt clung to her skin, damp with sweat and cave dew. She hugged herself, trying to generate some warmth, but the chill seemed to seep into her very bones.

A sound rose above the background noise of the rain. She leaned forward and peeked around the pillar. A flash of movement caught her eye. The camera. Its lens whirred softly as it panned across the cavern. Sarah's breath caught in her throat. She pressed herself farther into the shadows of her alcove. She still didn't know if it was friend or foe, but some instinct told her to stay hidden, at least for now. She hadn't anticipated it being able to move, and she prayed the camera's range didn't extend to her hiding spot.

The mechanical eye swept back and forth, searching. Sarah's muscles tensed, ready to move despite the pain if the camera turned her way. But after what felt like an eternity, the lens stilled, pointing once more at the main chamber.

Sarah let out a shaky breath. She was safe, for now. But she couldn't stay hidden forever. Her stomach growled, reminding her of the protein bars in her pack. She took one out and ate half of it. It tasted like paste and wood chips. The wrapper crinkled loudly in the quiet cave, and Sarah hastily stuffed it back into her pack before she gobbled the rest of it down. She had to be smart. She sat in the dark and tried to think of what to do next. She was hydrated, rested, and had some food in her stomach. She needed to know more about her surroundings and about any possible way out.

The pattering of rain grew louder, and Sarah noticed a thin stream of water trickling down the cave wall nearest to her. It snaked its way across the floor, joining other rivulets to form small pools. The cave floor sloped gently away from her alcove toward the underground stream she'd drunk from previously. They were just small trickles now, but Sarah knew that if the rain continued, the water level would rise. A flash flood down here would be fatal.

Another rumble of thunder shook the cave, louder than before. Small pebbles skittered across the ground, dislodged by the vibration. Sarah's eyes widened as another worrying thought struck her. If the storm was this intense, could it destabilize the cave system?

As if the very thought had conjured it, a deafening crack split the air. Sarah instinctively covered her head as a shower of rocks and debris rained down from the ceiling. Dust filled the air, making her cough and her eyes water.

When the dust settled, Sarah used her phone's flashlight and peered out from her alcove. Her heart sank. A pile of rubble now blocked the tunnel she had fallen through. It would have been a challenge to get back up and out that way, but it had been an option. Now it wasn't. She wouldn't be getting out the same way she came in.

Panic clawed at her throat, threatening to overwhelm her. She forced herself to take deep breaths, ignoring the twinge in her ribs. Panicking wouldn't help. She needed to think, to plan.

She glanced toward the camera. It remained motionless, its red light blinking steadily. Sarah weighed her options. She could stay hidden, conserve her energy, and hope for rescue.

But with the tunnel collapsed, how would anyone find her? If they were even looking. And if the water level kept rising...

No, she decided. Air and water were getting in, which meant there had to be a way out. But first, she needed to deal with that camera.

If the camera was recording, staying hidden was pointless—whoever was watching would see her eventually. But if it was just a live feed, disabling it might work in her favor. A 'good guy' might come to investigate why the feed went dark. A 'bad guy' might do the same, but at least they wouldn't know she was there.

Now felt like the right time to act. If someone was watching the live feed, they'd likely just finished a regular check. The odds of catching them off-guard were as good as they'd ever be.

The storm that had possibly sealed her exit had also provided her with ammunition. Sarah felt around in the darkness, her fingers closing around several baseball-sized rocks. She collected four, used the front of her T-shirt to hold them, then carefully crawled out of her alcove.

Positioning herself in front of the camera, Sarah squinted up at it. The device was mounted high on the cave wall, its blinking red light a taunting target. She took a deep breath, visualizing the trajectory in her mind. With a grunt of effort, she hurled the first rock.

It sailed wide to the left, clattering against the cave wall. Sarah muttered a curse. Baseball had never been her thing. Really any sport involving a ball hadn't been her thing. No excuses, she told herself. She adjusted her aim. The second throw was closer, grazing the edge of the camera mount.

Sarah wound up for her third attempt. The rock arced through the air, and for a heart-stopping moment, she thought it would hit. But at the last second, it dipped, missing the lens by mere inches.

Sarah closed her eyes, took a steadying breath, and focused all her frustration and fear into her throw. She opened her eyes and let it fly. A sharp crack echoed through the cavern. The camera's red light flickered once, twice, then went dark.

Sarah allowed herself a small smile of triumph. Whatever happened next, at least she'd bought herself some privacy— and perhaps a crucial advantage.

With the camera dealt with, it was time to explore. She eyed the far side of the cavern, where shadows hinted at possible tunnels or passageways. Getting there would be a challenge with her injured ankle, but she had no choice.

Sarah took a deep breath, steeling herself for the pain to come and started to move before she could think about it too much. She scooted forward on her bottom, using her good leg to propel herself. Each movement sent jolts of agony through her ankle, but she pressed on, gritting her teeth against the pain.

She paused every minute or so to rest and shine the light around the space, taking in details she had missed before. Halfway across the cavern, near a large, flat section of raised rock that resembled a primitive dining room table, the beam of her phone's flashlight swept across the rock's base and caught on something that made her pause. She detoured slightly and inched closer.

There, half hidden by a small rock, was a cigarette butt. Sarah frowned. She hadn't noticed it during her initial panicked exploration of the cave. She picked it up, turning it over in her fingers. The filter was crushed, but the paper was barely degraded. It couldn't have been there long.

Someone else had been here, and recently. But who? And why? Her mind raced with possibilities.

Pocketing the cigarette butt, Sarah continued her slow journey across the cavern floor. Her clothes were soaked now, a combination of sweat and the increasing dampness in the air and running across the rocks. The thunder had passed, but it must still be raining. The sound of rushing water grew louder as she moved, and Sarah realized with a jolt that the small stream she had drunk from earlier had swollen to a fast-moving current.

As she caught her breath near the far wall, Sarah's light caught on something else. A small metallic glint reflected off her beam. Curious, she inched closer, her fingers probing the rough cave floor until they brushed against something smooth and cold.

Sarah carefully pried the object free from the sandy grit. It was a button, no larger than her thumbnail. The metal was tarnished, but she could make out an unfamiliar insignia etched on its surface. Sarah turned the button over in her palm. Who did this belong to? And why were they in this cave?

A loud crack echoed through the cavern, making Sarah jump. It was not thunder this time. A chunk of rock crashed to the ground nearby, missing her by inches. The cave trembled and Sarah could hear the ominous sound of shifting stones.

Panic gave her strength. Ignoring the screaming pain in her ankle, she put the button and her phone in her front pocket then half crawled, half dragged herself toward the nearest shadow that hinted at a tunnel. Water lapped at her legs, rising faster now. The stream had become a torrent, fed by unseen cracks and fissures throughout the cave system.

As Sarah reached the tunnel entrance, a deep, grinding noise filled the air. She looked back just in time to see a large section of the cavern ceiling give way. Rocks and debris crashed down, sending up a cloud of dust and spray. The camera and with a pang, she realized, her pack disappeared beneath the rubble.

Sarah didn't wait to see more. She pulled herself into the tunnel, her arms trembling with the effort. The passage was narrow, forcing her to wiggle forward on her stomach. Sharp rocks dug into her skin, but she hardly noticed. All that mattered was getting away from the collapsing cavern.

The sound of rushing water grew louder, drowning out the thunder of the storm and the rumble of the shifting rocks. Sarah's fingers scrabbled at the smooth stone, desperate for purchase as she felt a surge of water at her feet.

The flood was coming.

Sarah redoubled her efforts, ignoring the pain that lanced through her body with every movement. The tunnel seemed endless, a throat of stone threatening to swallow her whole. Her lungs burned, her muscles screamed for relief, but she kept going. The tunnel began to tilt up slightly. She passed a smaller passage to her right, too small for a human, but large enough to drain off the water. She felt a small moment of relief as the water drained away.

Just as Sarah felt her strength giving out, her hand reached into empty space. The tunnel opened up into...something. She couldn't see what lay ahead in the darkness.

With one final effort, Sarah pulled herself forward. She tumbled out of the tunnel, falling for a heart-stopping moment before landing with a splash in shallow water. The shock of cold made her gasp.

Panting, Sarah pushed herself up to her knees. She fumbled her phone out of her pocket, praying it had survived the journey. The screen flickered to life, casting a weak glow around her.

The light revealed secrets older than the forest above—and far less forgiving.

CHAPTER FORTY-FOUR

Sarah's eyes adjusted to the dim light. She slowly struggled to her feet, keeping her weight off her bad ankle and leaning against the cave the wall for balance. She touched the screen to turn the flashlight on and shone it about. The space was tight and oppressive, its low ceiling barely clearing her head. Rough-hewn walls pressed in from all sides, their uneven surfaces slick with moisture. The air was stagnant. The phone's light cut through the gloom, casting long, dancing shadows that seemed to writhe in the cramped space.

"Oh my God," Sarah whispered. The sound of her own voice helped push back the darkness. She'd used another trick she'd picked up in hospitals—talking through the tough cases, even when alone, kept the panic at bay.

Along the walls, small, uniform alcoves were carved into the living rock. As her light swept across the nearest recess, it illuminated a pile of what could only be described as dust with purpose. Fragments of bone poked through the powdery remains, a femur here, the curve of a skull there. Lives long past.

"What is this place?" she whispered. Keep talking, she told herself. Don't let the dark win.

The sight transported Sarah back to a family trip to Rome years ago. She had been 10 or 11 years old. They had visited the catacombs, descending into a world of perpetual twilight. The memory was vivid: the cool, damp air against her skin, the echoing of their footsteps in narrow passageways, and the pervasive scent of ancient stone.

Sarah remembered how she had clutched Riley's hand tightly as they navigated the twisting corridors. "It's like a giant maze," her big sister had whispered. Sarah had squeezed her hand, grateful for the contact.

The walls of those Roman catacombs had been lined with niches, stacked from floor to ceiling, each recess holding the remains of the long-dead. Bones, yellowed with age, had been visible in some of the open tombs. The flicker of their guide's lantern had made the shadows dance, giving an unsettling illusion of movement to the resting bones.

The cavern she was now in bore an eerie resemblance to those Roman chambers, but with a crucial difference. Where those catacombs had felt like a place of reverent rest, this space radiated something different. Something unsettling. What had happened here? What had gone on at Grave's End?

She half limped, half hopped forward on her bad ankle. Her time asleep had stiffened up her ankle. Which made it slightly easier to walk if she put her weight on her heel. She knew she was risking further injury with each step but she also didn't see any other choice. As she slowly moved deeper into the cavern, the contents of the niches began to change. In one, she saw the remains of a skeleton, its bones still articulated but beginning to crumble. In the next, wisps of fabric clung to more intact remains.

Then, startlingly, her light fell upon a figure shrouded in crisp, white fabric. The body beneath the wrappings was clearly intact, the shape unmistakably human. Sarah's breath caught in her throat as she realized what she was seeing—a recent burial in this ancient crypt.

"No, no, no," she breathed, her hand over her mouth to stifle a scream.

She counted seven more bodies, each laid out with care in their stone niches, sharing space with the ancient dead. Some appeared older, their shrouds discolored and sunken in places where decomposition had taken its toll. Others looked unsettlingly recent, their wrappings still pristine.

The air was thick with the musty scent of decay, undercut by something sharper—a chemical smell that Sarah couldn't quite place. It was as if someone had tried to mask the odor of death with modern embalming techniques.

The cavern wall bent slightly to the right. As she limped forward, her light caught something in the corner—a pile of backpacks stacked haphazardly against the wall. Some were newer and barely scuffed, others worn and faded. Sarah's breath hitched as she recognized Jake's pack among them, its familiar patches and scuff marks unmistakable even in the dim light. Her mind struggled to process what she was seeing. How was Jake's bag here? She'd seen it outside. She'd searched it herself. She pushed the thought aside. That wasn't the most important thing right now.

"Jake," she murmured, a mixture of hope and dread washing over her.

She slowly limped around the corner, terrified of what macabre scene might await her, but powerless to stop moving despite the pain in her ankle. She had to know.

But there was nothing. This corridor of the catacombs was empty.

Or so she thought at first.

As she drew closer to the far end of the chamber, her gaze fell on the last niche and her breath caught in her throat. This body wasn't wrapped. It lay exposed, limbs askew, as if it had been placed there in a hurry. As Sarah drew closer, her heart began to race. The figure was familiar—broad shoulders, dark hair matted with blood.

"Jake!" Sarah cried out, rushing forward as fast as her injured ankle would allow.

She reached his side, her hands hovering uncertainly over his battered form. Jake's face was a mess of bruises, one eye swollen shut. His wrists and ankles were bound with thick rope, and a dirty cloth was tied tightly around his mouth.

"Jake, can you hear me?" Sarah's voice cracked as she gently touched his cheek.

There was no response. Sarah felt panic rising in her chest. She pressed her fingers to his neck, searching for a pulse. For a terrifying moment, she felt nothing. Then, faintly, she detected a slow, steady beat.

"Oh, thank God," Sarah breathed.

She quickly worked to remove the gag, her fingers fumbling with the tight knot. As she pulled the cloth away, Jake let out a low moan but didn't open his eyes.

"Jake, it's me. It's Sarah," she said, fighting to keep her voice steady. "I'm going to get you out of here, okay?"

Sarah noticed a small pool of blood on the stone beneath Jake's head. Carefully, she turned him onto his side, revealing a large, angry lump at the base of his skull.

"Who did this to you?" Sarah whispered, gently probing the injury.

As she worked to untie Jake's bonds, Sarah's mind raced. Who had brought him here? Why? And what about the other bodies? Were they connected somehow to Jake's search for Vance?

The ropes finally came loose and Sarah pulled them away, wincing at the raw marks they'd left on Jake's skin. She rubbed his wrists gently, trying to restore circulation.

"Jake, please wake up," Sarah pleaded. "We need to get out of here."

A low rumble echoed through the cavern, reminding Sarah of the unstable conditions in the cave system. She glanced nervously at the tunnel she'd emerged from, half expecting to see floodwater pouring through at any moment.

"Come on, Jake," she urged, patting his cheek lightly. "I can't carry you out of here. I need you to wake up."

Jake's eyelids fluttered and he let out another groan. Sarah leaned in close, her heart pounding.

"That's it," she encouraged. "Open your eyes, Jake."

Slowly, painfully, Jake's eyes opened. But instead of relief, Sarah saw raw terror flood his face. His mouth opened in a silent scream, his gaze fixed on something behind her.

Before she could turn, a hand clamped over her mouth. The world spun, then went black.

CHAPTER FORTY-FIVE

Sarah floated in darkness.

Consciousness came in waves, each one bringing brief disjointed fragments of awareness before dragging her back under. Sometimes she heard footsteps, a cloth would cover her face, and she tasted something bitter and chemical. Other times there was only the endless dark, pressing in from all sides.

In one moment of clarity, she felt rough stone against her back, ropes biting into her wrists and ankles. A voice drifted through the haze: "...perfect additions to my collection..." Then darkness claimed her again.

Another time, she heard Jake's voice, weak but urgent: "Sarah? Sarah, can you hear me?" She tried to respond, but her tongue felt thick and useless in her mouth. The drugs pulled her back down before she could form words.

The next time Sarah surfaced, something was different. Her thoughts still felt sluggish, but the oppressive fog that had wrapped around her mind was starting to lift. She forced her heavy eyelids open, blinking against the darkness.

Sarah tried to move and found herself bound tightly to

some kind of stone shelf or ledge. Her arms were secured above her head, ankles lashed together. Every muscle ached, and her injured ankle throbbed with a deep, persistent pain. How long had she been here? Hours? Days?

"Jake?" she whispered. Her throat felt dry. Her voice hoarse. No response.

She turned her head, fighting a wave of nausea. In the dim light filtering from somewhere above, she could just make out Jake's form in a nearby alcove. He appeared to be unconscious, or drugged, or asleep, but similarly bound.

Sarah closed her eyes, forcing herself to think through the lingering effects of whatever drugs were in her system. The ring. She still had her ring—she could feel its familiar weight on her finger. Their father had given matching ones to her and Riley years ago, each containing a carefully concealed small blade that appeared to be purely decorative but was not. "For emergencies," he'd said. She'd never used it all through her college years or the midnight shifts at the hospital, but she kept wearing it, first out of loyalty to her dad and then out of habit.

Twisting against the rope, Sarah managed to rotate her wrists just enough that she could contact the rope against the small blade. The angle was awkward, requiring her to bend her hands painfully and work slowly, but gradually she began sawing through the fibers.

The work was painstaking. Every few minutes, she had to pause to listen for footsteps, her heart pounding at every echo through the cavern. The rope was thick, and the tiny blade made slow progress. But finally, after what felt like hours, she felt the bindings give way.

With trembling fingers, Sarah untied her ankles, then eased herself off the stone shelf. Her legs nearly buckled— whether from the drugs, her ankle injury, or simple disuse, she couldn't tell. She caught herself against the wall, waiting for the spinning sensation to pass.

When she felt steady enough, Sarah made her way to Jake's alcove. He didn't stir as she began pulling at the knots, then giving up and cutting through the rope. Up close, she could see the extent of his injuries—the bruises, the dried blood matting his hair. When the last rope fell away from his ankles, he startled awake, his eyes wild with fear and confusion.

"Shh," she whispered, placing a steadying hand on his shoulder. "It's me. We need to get out of here."

Jake tried to sit up but immediately fell back, his face going pale. "Water," he managed to croak.

Sarah nodded, understanding. Her own throat felt like sandpaper. "I saw some packs earlier, when I first came in," she whispered. "Let me check them. Don't move yet."

She stumbled to the corner where several backpacks were piled, her movements still clumsy from the drugs. Some looked almost new, while others were so weathered and dirty they'd clearly been there for years. She riffled through them one by one. The first pack contained only moldy clothes and useless electronics—an old, blocky Garmin GPS unit with a cracked screen, a camera with a corroded battery compartment. In another, she found protein bar wrappers and an old trail map dated 2016. Relief flooded through her when she spotted her own phone among the pile, its pink case unmistakable even in the dim light. The screen was intact and it still had a charge—small mercies. She put it in her pocket.

She grabbed Jake's pack, the familiar red and black material standing out among the others. She grabbed it, hands trembling as she unzipped the main compartment. Everything was there, untouched—his spare clothes, snacks, first aid kit, and his trusty metal water bottle with all the National Park stickers. She'd teased him about collecting those stickers like a kid with baseball cards, but now the sight of them made her throat tight. She grabbed the bottle and made her way to the small pool of water near the chamber's entrance.

The water was murky but cold. Sarah filled the metal bottle quickly, constantly glancing over her shoulder. The drugs made the shadows seem to move and dance at the edges of her vision. She hurried back to Jake, who hadn't moved from where she'd left him.

"Small sips," she urged, helping him lift his head. "We don't know how long it's been."

Jake managed a few swallows before pushing the bottle away. His eyes were clearer now, more focused. "How did you get free? I watched him tie you up."

"Dad's ring," Sarah said, showing him the tiny blade. "For once his paranoia paid off."

"Sarah," Jake grabbed her wrist, suddenly urgent. "We have to go. He'll be back soon. He has a schedule, he—"

Footsteps echoed through the cavern, cutting him off. Jake's grip on her wrist tightened.

"Hide," he hissed. "Quick!"

Sarah hesitated. After being bound and drugged herself, the thought of hiding in one of the corpse-filled niches made her stomach turn. But Jake pushed her weakly away.

"Please," he whispered. "There's no time. I'll distract him. Just hide."

The footsteps grew closer. Sarah's heart pounded as she limped around the corner. She found an empty niche and squeezed inside, fighting back a wave of panic as her hand brushed against fabric in the darkness.

A figure appeared at the opposite end, wearing a bright headlamp that cut through the gloom. Sarah could make out dark rain gear but couldn't see his face. He moved to Jake first, checking his bonds.

"Did you get these off yourself?" The voice was calm,

almost conversational. "I doubt it. Never happened before, so..." The headlamp moved to where Sarah had been held captive. "How...inconvenient. I like the ones who struggle, but..."

Sarah pressed both hands against her mouth to stay quiet.

"Come on out," he called. "I know you're still here. Let's just skip this part and not play these games. I don't have the time."

Sarah remained frozen, her drugged mind sluggishly racing through options. She could barely walk—fighting seemed impossible. Running might be worse.

The stranger sighed. "Have it your way." Metal gleamed as he drew a gun, pointing it at Jake's head. "Last chance. Come out now, or things are going to get very unpleasant for your friend here."

"Wait!" Sarah called, her voice shaky. She couldn't let Jake die. Not after everything. "I'm coming out. Don't hurt him."

She emerged from her hiding spot, hands raised. The figure turned, training the gun on her chest. The headlamp's glare made it impossible to see his face.

"How did you get the ropes loose?" He seemed genuinely interested in an answer.

Sarah saw Jake's eyes snap open behind the stranger. Despite his injuries, despite the drugs they'd both been given, he lunged forward, tackling their captor's legs. The gun went off, the sound deafening in the enclosed space.

"Sarah, run!" Jake yelled as they grappled.

Sarah hesitated for a split second—Jake stood no chance on his own. She lurched forward, grabbing a rock from the ground. With her good leg braced beneath her, she swung hard at the stranger's hand. The impact jarred up her arm, but the gun skittered across the stone floor. Jake landed a punch that sent their attacker stumbling back. He tripped and went down.

"Come on!" Jake grabbed her hand, pulling her toward another tunnel entrance. This entire place was a web of caverns and connecting tunnels. Sarah let Jake lead. She could feel herself sliding toward shock. She tried to push it back or dodge around it, but she knew it was only a matter of time. Her injured ankle screamed in protest as they ran. Adrenaline and fear overrode the pain. She kept moving. Limping. Hobbling. Getting away. The drugs made everything tilt and spin. She stumbled, nearly falling, but Jake's grip kept her upright. Behind them, she could hear the stranger cursing and getting to his feet.

They reached the tunnel entrance and plunged into darkness.

CHAPTER FORTY-SIX

Jake and Sarah ran into the dark maw of the tunnel. The light from the stranger's headlamp quickly receded. Sarah fumbled her phone out of her pocket and managed to turn on the flashlight as they ran. She knew the battery must be getting low, but she didn't dare check—they had to see. Sprinting blind in the dark wasn't an option. She pointed it ahead of them. The beam cut through the gloom and revealed a branching, twisting decision ahead.

"Left or right?" Sarah said as they came to a fork in the tunnel.

"Left," Jake said and pulled her along.

They ran through caverns and down rock corridors. They passed columns where stalactites and stalagmites had joined in a timeless embrace. In one chamber, delicate soda straws hung from the ceiling like fragile icicles. They skirted around a still, mirror-like pool that reflected their fleeing forms.

Farther on, they squeezed through a narrow passage lined with flowstone that resembled frozen waterfalls, its rippled surface glittering in the beam of Sarah's flashlight.

Each formation blurred into the next. In a different time

and place, she would have stopped and explored each one but then she remembered the catacombs they'd left behind. The air grew thinner and the slope of the ground beneath their feet subtly changed, leading them deeper into the earth.

Sarah's ankle throbbed. Each step felt like landing on a bed of nails. She was gasping with the effort and spots danced at the edges of her vision.

"Jake," she said, "I can't...I need to stop."

Jake slowed. The tunnel behind them was silent and dark. "Okay," he said, "let's rest for a minute."

They ducked into a small alcove off the main passage. Sarah slid down the wall, her legs giving out beneath her. She winced as she stretched out her injured ankle.

After a few moments, Jake broke the silence. "I think we lost him."

Sarah opened her eyes, or thought she did. The darkness was so complete here it was hard to tell the difference. Eventually her eyes adjusted to the subtly different shades of black. She reached out and touched Jake's arm. "Are you sure?" Which felt like a silly question as soon as it left her mouth.

"No," Jake admitted. "But I don't hear anything." He paused and for a moment there was just the sound of their breath slowly returning to normal. Then he said, "What's wrong? You're limping badly. What happened?"

"It's my ankle," Sarah winced. "I fell earlier, before I found you. I slipped on some wet rocks in one of the tunnels. I mostly slid down a slope on my ass and would have been fine, but my foot got caught in a crevice. I don't think it's broken or I wouldn't be able to walk, but it's badly sprained. Maybe some ligament damage. My head took a hit too."

"Always trying to one-up me, huh?"

She thought back to finding him bound and gagged on that stone slab. His face a mess of welts, cuts, and puffy bruises. She was struggling, but he'd also been beaten up pretty good.

"Want me take a look?" Jake continued, but she waved him off.

"Nothing we can do right now, and we can't waste the light. My battery is low. How is your head?"

"Feels like a ringing bell, but I'm okay for now. I think the dark helps. I could use some sleep, but I've felt worse."

"Yeah? When?"

Jake laughed softly. "Remember that story from college? When I thought I could outdrink the entire rugby team? Then woke up two days later in a kiddie pool full of blue Jell-O. Now that was a headache. This? At least I woke up remembering my own name this time."

She'd heard the story before, but she smiled and it lightened the mood momentarily, but the gravity of their situation quickly settled back in. They sat in silence for a while and listened for any sign of pursuit. But the only sounds they heard were the occasional drip of water and their own breathing.

————

As her heart rate returned to normal, Sarah became more aware of their situation. And how dire it might be. They were lost in an unknown cave system, injured, with no supplies and only her dying phone for light.

"Jake," she whispered, "what are we going to do?"

She heard Jake shift in the dark. "I hate to say it, but I think we need to go back."

"Back?" Sarah said. "Are you crazy? That psycho is back there!"

"I know, I know," Jake said. "But I think something else is going on. He didn't do anything to me right away. He left me tied up in that cave. I'm not sure he's chasing us now, either."

"Because he's waiting for us to pop our heads back up."

"Maybe."

"Or, he's enjoying it. He likes the hunt and wants to stretch it out."

"Also, a good guess, but what other options do we have? We could probably find water to drink, but after that? We have no food, no light. Your phone battery won't last forever. We're heading deeper into the cave system. If we keep going, we might never find our way out. We know he comes and goes, so there must be an exit up there somewhere. And those backpacks we saw might have something useful."

"Think they might have a large pepper and mushroom pizza?"

"From Santopiro's?"

"Still warm? With a side of those breadsticks?"

"Might be a stretch but I bet there's something. Chocolate, trail mix. Something."

Sarah wanted to argue, but she knew he was right. They could wander down here for months and not find a way out and die of starvation. Still, she wasn't ready to move just yet. "Okay. But first, tell me what happened to you. How did you end up in that...that crypt?"

Jake shifted beside her. "I woke up early and decided to look around. I couldn't sleep. That place...Grave's End...it was strange. You could feel it, right?"

Sarah nodded. "Like we were being..." She tried to recall the feeling and put it into words. "Observed. Or measured. Like we were being watched by something very old."

"Exactly," Jake said. "I climbed up to the top of that rock formation. What would you call it? A theater?"

"An amphitheater," Sarah said.

"Right. When I got to the top, that feeling intensified. I

tried to tell myself it was nothing. My imagination running wild. I should have listened to my instincts."

Jake paused. Sarah waited, giving him time to collect his thoughts.

"Something hit me from behind," he continued. "Some*one*, I mean. He was wearing some sort of hunting suit. Camo, netting, the whole nine yards. It covered his face and head. He just appeared out of the woods like a tree came to life. A very dangerous and angry tree."

She'd stood up there and she could imagine the sudden terror of the forest coming alive in front of you.

"I was so shocked, I think I just stood there and made a very nice target. He hit me with something," Jake went on. "That was it. Game over. I remember being dragged for a bit, and then...nothing until I saw you." She felt his fingers on her thigh. She took his hand.

Sarah absorbed this information, her mind racing. "Do you think he's connected to your research? To Vance's disappearance?"

Jake shook his head. "I don't know. Maybe. It seems like too much of a coincidence, doesn't it?"

She had no answer to that and wondered if they'd found Vance's body after all this time. It was a high price to pay. "If we're going back, we should do it soon. My ankle...I don't know how much longer I can walk on it."

"Okay," Jake said. "We'll take it slow. Lean on me if you need to."

They emerged from the alcove, Sarah's phone light cutting through the darkness. She forced herself to look. The battery indicator had dipped to 34 percent. The first part was easy, just go straight back, but after that? She hadn't been tracking their movements in her panic to escape. "How are we going to find our way back? We didn't exactly mark our path." She tried to keep the tremor out of her voice.

Jake squeezed her hand. "Old orienteering trick Vance taught me. When in doubt, take two lefts, then a right. That's what we did. So we just reverse it. A left and two rights should eventually get us back."

"Okay," was all she managed. She was happy to reliquinsh the plan to Jake and just concentrate on getting her legs to move. She didn't want to think that getting back might mean running into a pyscho killer, but she also didn't want to die in this cave system. If it had to happen, she wanted to see some blue sky one last time. That became her goal and her mantra as she limped through the dark. Blue sky, blue sky.

———

The going was slow. Sarah's ankle protested with each step, and more than once, they had to stop to let her rest. Jake supported her as much as he could, but Sarah could see the toll their ordeal was taking on him too. His movements were stiff and a grimace of pain flashed across his face whenever he thought she wasn't looking.

As they walked, Sarah's mind wandered to the strange cigarette butt and button she'd found earlier. She debated whether to mention them to Jake but decided against it. They had enough to worry about without adding more mysteries to the mix.

They passed through cavern after cavern, each one frustratingly similar to the last. Sarah began to worry they had taken a wrong turn when Jake suddenly stopped.

"Wait," he whispered.

Sarah froze, her senses straining in the darkness. At first, she noticed nothing but the sound of their breathing and the occasional drip of water. Then, a faint odor reached her nostrils.

"Do you smell that?" Jake asked softly.

Sarah nodded, then remembered Jake couldn't see her. "Yes," she whispered back, fighting the urge to gag. "It's... familiar."

"Decay," Jake murmured. "And something else. Chemical. Like the catacombs."

A chill ran down Sarah's spine as realization dawned. "We're getting close," she breathed, her voice a mix of relief and dread.

They approached cautiously; the musty, slightly chemical odor growing stronger with each step as they neared what they believed to be the entrance to the crypt.

"Stop," he whispered. "The smell's stronger here. I think this is it."

After a moment's hesitation, Jake continued, "Wait here. I'll check if it's clear."

Sarah wanted to protest, but she knew she'd only slow him down. She handed him the phone. "Here, take this. In case you need the light."

Jake took the phone and crept forward, disappearing around the corner. Sarah pressed herself against the wall, her heart pounding in her ears as she waited.

The seconds stretched into minutes. She had to bite her tongue to keep from calling out and was about to follow when Jake reappeared.

"It's clear," he said. "But we need to hurry. No telling when he'll be back."

They entered the catacombs, the scent of decay and damp stone seeming to jump up and cling to them. Sarah's eyes were drawn to the niches lining the walls, the memory of hiding beside one of the shrouded bodies flooding back and making her pause.

"Over here," Jake said, leading her to the corner of the chamber.

They quickly riffled through the bags, setting two aside.

Sarah recognized one as Jake's, but the other...a feeling of dread washed over her.

"Vance?" she said softly, her voice barely above a whisper.

Jake nodded but didn't respond, quickly moving on to more practical matters. Sarah wanted to say something, to acknowledge the weight of this discovery, but held her tongue. If they made it out alive, there would be plenty of time to talk. Survival first.

They stuffed anything useful into the two backpacks: energy bars, a first aid kit, a couple of water bottles to the pair they already had, and a sturdy flashlight. Jake stood, slinging one pack over his shoulder.

"Let me fill all the bottles," he said and headed to the shallow pool near the entrance where Sarah had emerged from the tunnel earlier.

Sarah kept watch, her eyes darting between the various tunnel entrances.

"Okay," Jake said, returning with the filled containers. He distributed them between the two packs. "Let's find a way out of here."

Sarah nodded, forcing herself to focus on the present. She shouldered the second pack, wincing slightly as she adjusted it over her bruised body. The weight of Vance's pack seemed to carry more than just supplies, but she pushed the thought aside. Their escape was all that mattered now.

CHAPTER FORTY-SEVEN

As they moved through the catacombs, Sarah's mind raced. The weight of everything they'd discovered pressed down on her. She found it easier to ignore it all for now. She'd deal with it when they'd gotten out of here. She focused on the next painful step. She knew she needed to tell Jake about the camera, but the words stuck in her throat. What was the point? She knew now who had set them up. No calvary was coming to their rescue. She winced as her injured foot came down awkwardly on a loose rock in the gloom.

She willed away the pain. Take one more step. Then repeat.

The phone battery crept downward. They turned it off when they could, on straightaways or when they paused to rest, which was more and more often. It felt like they'd been walking for hours but it was difficult to hold onto time down in the dark.

Finally, as they reached a small chamber branching off from the main passage they'd been following, she spoke up. "Jake, wait. There's something I need to tell you."

Jake paused, turning to face her. In the dim light of the flashlight, his face was a canvas of shadows, emphasizing the bruises and cuts.

"When I first woke up and couldn't find you, I explored a bit," Sarah began. "I found a cave entrance and made it to a big open cavern. That's where I twisted my ankle. I also found a camera set up in the cavern. It was active, blinking red."

"A camera? Are you sure?"

Sarah nodded. "Positive. I disabled it, but...there might be more."

Jake ran a hand through his hair, wincing as he accidentally brushed against the lump on his head. "We need to be careful. Very careful. I doubt he'd be able to put a lot of cameras down in these passageways, but if," he corrected himself, "when we find a way out, there might be one, that would make sense, we could be walking into a trap. He doesn't have to chase us. He can watch and wait."

"So what do we do?"

"We stay alert. If there are more cameras, we need to find them before he finds us."

They fell silent again. The constant drip of water echoed through the chamber, a reminder of the vast, indifferent cave system surrounding them.

Sarah shivered, not entirely from the cold. The cave suddenly felt much darker, much more dangerous. She and Jake weren't just lost anymore. They were being hunted.

"We should rest," Jake said finally. "We're both exhausted, and we need to think clearly if we're going to find a way out of here."

Sarah nodded. They simply dropped where they were standing and put their backs against the cool stone wall. Jake offered to take the first watch, and Sarah didn't argue. Her eyelids felt like lead, and the throbbing in her ankle had intensified to a constant burning ache.

As Sarah drifted off, Jake's voice cut through the fog of encroaching sleep. "I'll wake you in a couple of hours."

Sarah mumbled an acknowledgment, already half asleep. In her dreams, she wandered through endless tunnels, always just a step behind a shadowy Jake, never quite able to catch up, never finding any light.

When Jake gently shook her awake, it felt like only minutes had passed. She blinked, disoriented in the complete darkness.

"Your turn," Jake whispered. "Two hours, then wake me."

Sarah nodded, fumbling for her phone. She flicked it on. He'd let her sleep far longer than two hours. She started to say something, but Jake was already asleep, his breathing even and steady.

She turned the flashlight off and the darkness dropped back down like a curtain. Sarah's mind wandered, replaying the events that had led them here. She thought of the strange crypt, the bodies in various stages of decay. Who were they? How long had this been going on?

Before she knew it, two hours had passed. She reached out to wake Jake, but hesitated. He looked peaceful, the lines of worry and pain smoothed out in sleep. She decided to let him rest a little longer.

The next thing Sarah knew, she was blinking awake, momentarily confused by the blackness surrounding her. With a jolt, she realized she'd fallen asleep on watch. Panic gripped her as she fumbled for the flashlight, her heart pounding.

"Jake?" she whispered urgently. "Jake, wake up!"

Jake stirred beside her, groaning softly. "What's wrong?"

"I fell asleep. I'm sorry, I didn't mean to—"

"It's okay," Jake interrupted, sitting up with a wince. "No

harm, no foul. We both needed the rest. How long were we out?"

Sarah checked her phone. "Almost ten hours."

"Jeez, we really did need the rest."

Jake nodded, his face grim in the flashlight's beam. "We need to get moving. Find a way out before we lose the light completely."

They gathered their meager supplies, muscles protesting after hours of inactivity on the hard stone floor.

Jake swayed as he stood.

"How do you feel?" Sarah asked.

"Like the Jolly Green Giant chewed me up and spit me out," Jake replied, then added in a more serious tone. "Not great, but probably no worse than you."

Sarah stepped close and put a hand on his forehead. "Oh, Jake, you're warm." He was more than just warm, but she didn't want to alarm him more than necessary.

He shrugged and unscrewed the lid on his water bottle. "I'll stay hydrated. Getting out of here will be the best medicine." Jake paused. "We need a better plan though," he said. "If the back door to this hellhole was close by, we obviously missed the turn. We can't just wander aimlessly."

Sarah thought for a moment, trying to recall any survival tips she'd picked up from her dad over the years of family hiking. "Water," she said finally. "We should follow the water. It has to lead somewhere, right?"

Jake nodded. "Good thinking. And even if it doesn't lead us out, at least we'll have something to drink."

They set off, following the sound of trickling water. The passage twisted and turned, sometimes widening into vast chambers, other times narrowing until they had to turn sideways to squeeze through.

As they walked, Sarah's mind drifted to the world above. "Do you think anyone's looking for us?"

Jake was quiet for a moment before responding. "I hope so. But we didn't exactly leave an itinerary."

They lapsed into silence. The air grew cooler as they descended, a damp chill settling into their bones.

Sarah thought of her sister. "Riley will look," she said, her voice barely above a whisper.

Jake glanced at her, curiosity momentarily overriding his exhaustion. "Your sister? The soldier?"

Sarah nodded. "Yeah. She'll know something's wrong. We have this...connection. Even after everything that happened, it's still there." She paused and gathered her thoughts. "When Riley came back, she was different. Distant. But she always knew when I was in trouble. Like that time I broke my arm rock climbing and didn't tell anyone. She showed up at the ER before I even called her."

Sarah's voice grew stronger, more determined. "Riley won't stop until she finds us. It's just who she is. Stubborn. Relentless."

Jake reached out and squeezed her hand in the dark. "Then we better stay alive until she does."

Sarah squeezed back, drawing strength from the memory of her sister and the hope of rescue. They pressed on, the sound of water guiding their way through the labyrinthine cave system.

***

After what felt like hours of slow, careful walking, they came to a larger chamber. A small waterfall cascaded down one wall, feeding a swift-moving stream that disappeared into a narrow crevice.

"Look," Jake said, pointing. "The water's moving faster here. That's a good sign, right?"

Sarah had no idea, but she nodded, hope flickering in her

chest. They followed the stream, their spirits lifting as the passage began to slope upward. The air felt fresher, carrying a hint of something other than damp stone.

But their optimism was short-lived. The passage ended abruptly in a solid wall of rock. The stream disappeared through a gap barely wider than Sarah's arm.

"No," Jake muttered, running his hands over the unyielding stone. "There has to be a way through."

They searched, probing every crevice, but it was useless. The water had found a path they couldn't follow.

Defeated, they slumped to the ground. Sarah's ankle throbbed mercilessly, and she could feel something deeper than exhaustion tugging at her limbs.

"We should have taken some of the clothes from those packs," she said, shivering in her damp shirt.

Jake nodded, his eyes glassy and distant. "We weren't thinking clearly. Too focused on getting out."

They sat in silence. Sarah could feel herself growing weaker, fatigue and hunger gnawing at her resolve.

"We should eat something," Jake said finally, unzipping a pocket on his pack. He pulled out two energy bars, handing one to Sarah. It was probably a good thing there wasn't enough light to read the expiration date.

She took it, but the thought of food made her stomach churn. She forced herself to take a small bite, knowing she needed the energy.

Jake chuckled weakly as he unwrapped his energy bar. "You know, this reminds me of something I read about World War II rations," he said. Sarah looked up, grateful for any distraction from their grim situation. "The Army developed these chocolate bars for emergencies," Jake continued. "But get this—they deliberately made them taste awful."

"What? Why?" Sarah asked, momentarily forgetting her own tasteless energy bar.

Jake grinned. "So soldiers wouldn't eat them as snacks. One guy said they tasted 'a little better than a boiled potato.'" He took a bite of his energy bar. "Suddenly, this doesn't seem so bad."

Sarah couldn't help but let out a small laugh. "I guess we should be thankful for our marginally less terrible rations."

"Absolutely," Jake agreed. "Though right now, I'd take even that brick-like World War II chocolate."

They shared a moment of laughter, the sound echoing strangely in the cavern. For just a brief instant, the oppressive darkness of the cave seemed to lift a little.

"We should rest again," Jake said. "We're both dead on our feet. We'll think better after some sleep."

Sarah nodded, once again too tired to argue and too tired to fight. The cave was winning. They might have escaped the madman in the crypt, but it might have only put off the inevitable. The cave was slowly squeezing the life from their battered bodies.

As Sarah huddled against Jake for warmth and drifted off to sleep, a faint sound cut through the constant drip of water. Her eyes snapped open. In the distance, echoing through the tunnels, came the unmistakable sound of footsteps.

And they were getting closer.

CHAPTER FORTY-EIGHT

Sarah's heart raced as she listened to the approaching footsteps. She gripped Jake's arm, her voice barely a whisper. "Jake, someone's coming."

Jake tensed beside her. She tried not to think about how hot his skin felt. "How far?" he asked.

"I don't know. Not close but getting closer. It's hard to tell. The sound sort of bounces around."

They held their breath, straining to hear over the constant drip of water. The footsteps echoed through the tunnels, growing louder with each passing second.

"We need to move," Jake said, struggling to his feet. He swayed and she thought he might fall over but he didn't.

Sarah winced as she put weight on her injured ankle. They made quite a pair. "Which way?"

Before Jake could answer, a faint glimmer of light appeared in the distance.

"Run," Jake hissed, grabbing Sarah's hand.

They couldn't run. But they did their best. They stumbled through the darkness as fast as their tired limbs let them. Fear and adrenaline made a powerful cocktail. Sarah bit back the pain as her ankle protested the sudden movement.

"Wait," Sarah gasped, fumbling for her phone. "We need to see where we're going."

"The battery—"

"I know, but we don't have a choice."

The phone's screen flickered to life, casting a weak glow around them. The battery indicator glowed red and showed only a tiny sliver: seven percent.

Ahead, in the dim light, they could see two tunnels branching off from the main passage.

"Which one?" Sarah asked.

Jake hesitated, glancing between the two options. "Left," he decided, pulling Sarah along.

They plunged into the left tunnel, the sound of their ragged breathing echoing off the stone walls. The passage narrowed, forcing them to slow their pace.

"I think it's getting smaller," Sarah said, her voice tight with fear.

Jake didn't respond, pressing forward. The tunnel twisted downward, growing tighter with each step. And then, suddenly, it ended.

"No," Jake muttered, running his hands over the solid rock face before them. "No, no, no."

Sarah turned, ready to backtrack, but froze as she heard the footsteps again. They were much closer now.

"We're trapped," she whispered.

Jake slammed his fist against the stone wall in frustration. "Dammit! We should have gone right."

"We don't know that," Sarah replied, trying to keep her voice calm. "The other tunnel might have led to a dead end too."

"Well, we're certainly at a dead end now, aren't we?" Jake said.

Sarah flinched at his tone. "Keep your voice down," she whispered. "He'll hear us."

"Does it even matter?"

They fell silent. The footsteps had stopped.

Jake swayed suddenly and put a hand against the wall. "Sarah," he mumbled, "I don't feel so good."

Before Sarah could react, Jake's eyes rolled back and he crumpled to the ground.

"Jake!" Sarah knelt beside him, her hands fluttering helplessly over his unconscious form. "Jake, wake up!"

She felt his forehead, alarmed by the heat radiating from his skin. He was burning up.

"Water," she muttered, reaching for her pack. Her hand grasped at empty air. With a jolt, she realized they'd left their supplies behind in their panic to escape.

"No, no, no," Sarah whispered, fighting back tears. "Jake, please wake up. I don't know what to do."

She cradled Jake's head in her lap, stroking his damp hair. She felt helpless. "It's okay," she murmured. "You'll be okay. We'll get out of here." Even if she didn't believe it herself anymore.

The silence stretched out, broken only by Jake's uneven breathing. The sound scraped at her nerves until she couldn't take it anymore. Each one sounded like his last. She found herself talking, her whispers a shield against her worries.

"You know what this reminds me of?" she whispered. "That time we got caught in that freak storm on Mount Baker. Remember? You kept telling these horrible dad jokes while we waited it out." Her voice cracked. "Just a bottomless supply. You said you were just practicing your stand-up for the mountain goats since they were our only audience. God, you and your dad jokes. Three years of dating and I still don't know where you got them all. Your mom swears your father never told a joke in his life. But somehow you've got an endless supply at your fingertips, like you were genetically programmed with them or inherited them from some distant uncle who was a failed comedian."

She squeezed his hand. Still too warm. "Riley would know what to do right now. She always does in a crisis. Three tours in Afghanistan and she still..."

Sarah stopped mid-sentence. The cavern had gone silent.

"I need to check," she whispered. "I'll be right back."

Carefully, she eased Jake's head onto the ground and crept toward the tunnel entrance. Her injured ankle throbbed with each step, but she gritted her teeth and pressed on.

At the mouth of the tunnel, Sarah peered out into the main cavern. Her breath caught in her throat as she spotted a figure standing near the center of the chamber. It wasn't the attacker from before—this man was taller, leaner. He held a flashlight, its beam cutting through the darkness.

Sarah pressed herself against the wall, her heart pounding. Was this friend or foe?

As if in answer to her unspoken question, the man spoke. "Is someone there? Jake? Sarah?"

Sarah clamped a hand over her mouth to keep silent. She forced herself to remain still. How did he know her name?

The man took a step forward, his flashlight beam sweeping the cavern, almost as if he could sense her close by in the dark. But that was impossible. Right?

"Jake? Sarah? If you can hear me, it's okay to come out. We're here to help."

Sarah remained silent, her mind racing as she tried to figure out what to do. It could be a trick. The attacker could have an accomplice.

"Look, I know you have no reason to trust me. But Riley is nearby. We've been looking for you guys for three days now."

Sarah's heart leapt at the mention of her sister, but suspicion still held her back. How did this stranger know about Riley?

As if sensing her doubts, the man continued. "Your sister is a real pain in the ass, you know that? And I wouldn't want to face off with her in a fight. Especially not with that wicked ring of hers."

Sarah's breath hitched. The rings. How could he possibly know about those without talking to Riley?

"She told me you have a matching one from your dad," the man said. "If you're going to jump me in the dark, go easy with that blade, okay? I've got enough scars already."

The tension drained from Sarah's body. No one but Riley knew about the hidden blades in their rings. This man, whoever he was, must be telling the truth.

Slowly, Sarah stepped out of the shadows. "Who are you?"

CHAPTER FORTY-NINE

The roar of the underground falls grew louder with each stumbling step. Max tightened his grip on Jake's arm as the barely conscious man's feet dragged against the rough stone floor. The narrow tunnel pressed in around them, water dripping from unseen crevices above, each drop echoing off the damp walls like a metronome counting down their remaining strength.

"Steady now," Max whispered, more to himself than to Jake. He could feel the heat radiating from Jake's skin even through his soaked shirt—the fever hadn't broken.

Behind them, Sarah limped forward, keeping the flashlight beam focused on the path ahead. The light caught the edges of Max's chalk markings on the walls, many already fading in the cave's perpetual damp. But Max didn't need them anymore. They were close now. He recognized the way.

"Almost there," he said, voice barely carrying over the growing thunder of the falls.

The underground river ran along beside them, black and hungry in the weak light. Max kept them close to the far wall, away from the water's edge. He'd already survived one ride and he wasn't eager to risk another.

Jake mumbled something incomprehensible, his head lolling forward.

"Stay with us, Jake," Sarah urged. Her voice was hoarse, exhausted. She'd been limping badly and fighting her own battle with her injured ankle, but Max noted she hadn't complained once during their slow progress through the tunnels. She was as tough as her sister.

They limped around a bend and the passage widened suddenly and opened into the familiar cavern. The waterfall thundered down one wall, the spray creating a fine mist that filled the air. The beam of the flashlight caught the droplets, making them sparkle like suspended diamonds.

"Riley?" Max called out, raising his voice to be heard over the falling water.

A light blinked across the cavern in response. "Here!" Riley said. "Oh my God, Sarah!"

Sarah's breath caught in a sob at the sound of her sister's voice. She tried to move faster but her ankle gave way. Max felt her stumble against his back. He put an arm out and she grabbed it to steady herself.

"Easy," he cautioned, adjusting his grip on Jake to support them both. "We're safe now. Take it slow."

Riley appeared out of the mist and wrapped her arms around Sarah. The sisters clung to each other, both crying now.

"I knew you'd come," Sarah whispered. "I knew you'd find us."

"Always," Riley replied. She pulled back and examined her sister's face in the beam of her flashlight. "Are you hurt?"

"My ankle," Sarah admitted. "But Jake's worse. He needs help."

Max watched as Riley assessed Jake with the rapid efficiency he'd come to expect from her. Her expression hardened as she took in Jake's condition—the waxy pallor of his skin beneath the scattered bruises, the unfocused glaze in his eyes that spoke of a dangerously high fever. Jake's dark hair was matted with dried blood, and Max had noticed how he'd been protecting his left side during their slow journey through the tunnels, suggesting broken or badly bruised ribs.

"Over here," she said, leading them toward the relatively dry section of the cavern where she'd set up a makeshift camp. "Watch your step—we've got another injured."

"Who?" Sarah asked.

"Buck Holcomb—he's the district ranger," Riley said, then added quickly when she saw Sarah's confusion. "He helped us track you after we found the campsite. But someone..." Her voice tightened. "Someone shot him. He's stable for now, but he needs real medical attention." She looked at Jake's fevered face, then down at Sarah's swollen ankle. "You both do, too."

Holcomb lay nearby, wrapped in an emergency blanket. His face was gray, but his chest rose and fell with steady breaths. He stirred at their approach, his eyes fluttering open.

"You found them," he said weakly.

"We did," Max said, helping Sarah sit down next to Jake.

Riley was already digging through their remaining medical supplies. "We've got some painkillers left," she said, pulling out two packets. "Not much, but it should help."

After watching Jake swallow the pills, Riley tore open an alcohol wipe from the first aid kit. "This might sting," she warned, then began cleaning the gash on his scalp. Her movements were quick but gentle as she worked. "The fever's from infection, probably from this head wound. The antibiotic will help, but we need to keep it clean." She applied the ointment and a bandage, then checked his ribs, her fingers probing carefully.

"Bruised, maybe cracked," she muttered. "Can't do much about that out here." She helped Jake lean back against the cave wall, positioning him so the least injured side took his weight. "Try to stay still and take shallow breaths if it hurts too much." He didn't respond, just closed his eyes.

Then she turned to Sarah. "Your turn. Let me see that ankle." Sarah started to protest but Riley cut her off. "I know you're worried about Jake, but you need to be able to walk out of here."

Max watched as Riley unlaced Sarah's boot and then eased it off, along with her sock, to reveal the puffy, swollen ankle beneath. Sarah hissed in pain but didn't pull away as Riley examined the injury.

"Not broken," Riley said after a moment. "Bad sprain though." She dug through their supplies and pulled out an elastic bandage. "The compression will help with the swelling." She secured the wrap and helped Sarah rotate her foot slightly. "How's that feel?"

"Better," Sarah admitted. "More solid at least."

Riley nodded and pulled out a packet of electrolyte powder, mixing it with some water. "Both of you need to drink this. Slowly." She glanced over at Jake, but he was already asleep, his head slumped chin-first on his chest. She handed the bottle to Sarah. "It's not much, we've had some... supply issues, but it'll help with dehydration."

Sarah took small sips, her hands trembling slightly. Max watched as Riley took the second space blanket from their kit and draped it over Jake, tucking it carefully around him. The metallic material crinkled softly against the constant background roar of the falls. When she was satisfied Jake was as comfortable as possible, Riley settled back against the cave wall next to her sister. For a moment, neither spoke. Then Riley reached out and took Sarah's hand, squeezing it tightly.

"What happened out there?" Riley asked

Sarah described the sequence of events in clipped, exhausted bursts as she sipped at the water. Jake vanishing. His scattered belongings and blood-stained jacket in the woods. Her own search, fall, and injury in the cave system. The camera mounted inside the first cavern. The horror of the crypt in the second cavern, finding Jake, being drugged, and finally their desperate escape into this warren of tunnels.

Riley's face hardened as Sarah finished speaking. "A crypt. In the caves." She glanced at Max. "Someone's been watching. Hunting."

"And they don't want to stop," Max said.

"It explains what's been happening to us. The attacks, Holcomb getting shot, the food sabotage. Someone doesn't want us poking around this area."

Max thought of the local stories, the rumors, the other missing hikers. "How many bodies?"

"I don't know," Sarah whispered. "At least seven, I think. Some were older, just bones, others..." She stopped, unable to continue.

"It doesn't matter right now," Max said. Sarah's face had gone pale at the memory. He didn't want her going into shock. He glanced at Holcomb lying still and then Riley. "What matters is getting everyone out of here. Then we can bring in the FBI, the Forest Service, whoever has jurisdiction over this nightmare."

Sarah paused then reached into her pocket. "There's something else. Before he caught me, I found these." She held out her palm. A crushed cigarette butt and a tarnished metal button caught the dim light.

"The cigarette has been there a while, but not that long. Still has some paper attached to the filter." She turned the button over in her palm. "And this...I found it half buried in the sand. There's some kind of mark or logo on it."

Max picked up the button, studying the design etched

into the metal. The craftsmanship was evident. The mark itself wasn't familiar, but the quality was unmistakable. "This wasn't mass produced."

He glanced at Riley, who had moved closer to examine it. She took the button from Max and turned it over in her hand.

"I don't recognize it, but I agree it doesn't feel like the type of thing you'd find at the local Walmart." Her expression hardened. "So he has connections. Resources. Maybe even a life outside these woods."

"Which means he has something to lose," Max added.

CHAPTER FIFTY

"What's the plan?" Sarah asked. "Do we have one?"

Riley and Max exchanged glances. "We need to get out of here," Riley said. "But with both of you injured, and Holcomb..." She gestured helplessly at the wounded ranger.

"We get out the same way we came in," Max said, nodding his head toward the falls. "It's our best shot. We don't have the time or the supplies to look anywhere else."

Sarah looked at them and then at the waterfall across the cavern. If she thought the plan was crazy, she didn't show it. Maybe she was too exhausted. "How?" was all she said.

"I've got some rope in my pack. Other bits of climbing gear. If we can get a rope secured up there, we might be able to make it work."

It sounded farfetched and feeble even to Max's novice ears, but snuffing out hope at this point wouldn't do anyone any good.

"But first," Max interjected, "you all need rest. A few hours at least."

Sarah opened her mouth to protest, but Riley cut her off. "He's right. Getting out and back aboveground is not going to be easy and that's just the first step. It will only get harder. We're all exhausted and banged up. We'll have a better chance if we rest first."

The events of the past few days had taken their toll on all of them. Max watched as Sarah curled up next to Jake. Riley sat between them and Holcomb, her back against the cave wall.

"I'll take first watch," Max offered.

Riley nodded. "Wake me in two hours."

Max found a position where he could see both the tunnel they'd emerged from and the main entrance to the cavern. As the others drifted into uneasy sleep, he kept his vigil, listening to the endless roar of the falls, thinking about Sarah's story, the timing, and his own growing suspicions.

The next few hours passed in tense silence, broken only by the occasional groan from one of the injured or the constant white noise of the waterfall. Max and Riley traded watches, neither of them truly sleeping during their off hours, too aware of the danger that might still be lurking in the darkness beyond their small circle of safety.

When they finally roused everyone, the task ahead hadn't shrunk any. Jake's fever had dropped slightly, he was still weak, though his eyes were more alert after sleeping and drinking a bottle of the electrolyte mixture. Holcomb's wound had started bleeding again. Riley and Sarah changed the bandages, but they needed to get back to base camp. The first aid kit was largely empty now. Sarah's ankle was tender and swollen but stable.

"We need to fashion some kind of sling," Riley said,

pulling two small sections of rope and a ring of carabiners out of her bag. "Something we can use to help pull them up."

Max nodded, already working with the ropes. "I can make the climb," he said. "Secure the line from above."

Jake spoke up from where he lay propped up against the rocks. "I have some gear, too. Check my bag." He pointed to the left. "More rope and some auto-locking and double pulleys that could help. I have a headlamp, too. Take that. It will free up your hands."

The next hour was spent in preparation. They fashioned a crude harness that could be used to help lift Holcomb and Jake. Holcomb would be more difficult. He was larger and heavier than Jake and he drifted in and out of consciousness. Max tested the knots repeatedly, knowing their lives might depend on them holding.

"Ready?" he asked, coiling the main rope around his shoulder.

Riley nodded. "Be careful up there."

Max approached the falls, eyeing the wet rocks. The climb wouldn't be easy, but he could see enough handholds to make him believe it was possible. The real challenge might be fighting the current once he reached the river level.

He took a deep breath, tightened the straps of his pack, and began to climb. The rocks were slick with spray from the falls, forcing him to test each hold carefully before trusting it with his weight. He was ten feet to the left, but he couldn't avoid getting wet. Water ran down his arms, making the rope heavy and his grip uncertain.

Fifteen feet up, his foot slipped. Max's heart lurched as he swung out over empty space, hanging by his fingertips. Below, he heard a sharp intake of breath and someone gasp. He tried to swallow the panic and remain calm. He let gravity and momentum swing him back to the rocks and after a moment he found a foothold and pressed on.

His arms and legs shaking with effort, he eventually pulled himself up and sat on a thin ledge. He closed his eyes and allowed his breathing to settle and his limbs to stop shaking. Then he looked around more carefully. He inched over and looked into a dark opening as the water rushed out. It wasn't great news. He couldn't see the opposite end, the pool where they'd entered. The amount of rope they had wouldn't reach. Just standing on the edge, he could feel the cold pull of the current around his ankles. They would need support.

He inched back and called down, "I don't think we have enough rope. We're going to have to do this in stages. First, we get everyone up here, then we work our way back up the river to the exit."

Riley nodded. "Okay. An elevator would have been easier, but you can't have everything."

Apparently finding her sister had boosted her spirits.

Max looked around, studying the options, looped the rope around a large rock outcropping, and attached the first pulley. He then dropped the remaining coil with the second pulley and the harness over the edge where Riley snatched it out of the water. She gave a thumbs up.

"Send Sarah up first."

He turned his back and braced his feet against the rocks then gave it a tug to signal he was ready. He felt the jiggle of the rope as they prepped Sarah then a return double tug. He started hauling up the rope. The double pulley reduced the effort required but it still wasn't easy. He took it slow and careful. There was no brake system or redundancy if anything went wrong. Sarah was able to assist, partially climbing as Max pulled on the ropes, but he was still sweating and breathing hard when she climbed over the edge. Holcomb would be much more challenging. Max rested while Sarah dropped the harness back down and Riley and Jake moved Holcomb into position.

"Easy now," Riley said, supporting Holcomb's left side while Jake, despite his own weakness, took the right. The ranger's head lolled forward, his feet dragging as they guided him through the shallow water toward the falls.

"Stay with us, Buck," Jake urged as Holcomb stumbled. Blood had soaked through the latest bandage, a crimson stain spreading across his shirt.

They reached the harness, now hanging just above the water's surface. Riley tested the knots one final time. "This is going to hurt," she warned Holcomb. "But we need you to stay as still as possible."

Holcomb managed a weak nod. "Just...get it done." His skin was pale and clammy, dark circles shadowing his sunken eyes.

The process of getting him into the makeshift harness was agonizing. Each movement drew ragged gasps from the ranger. Twice, his knees buckled, and only Jake and Riley's supporting arms kept him from collapsing into the water.

"Ready?" Riley called up to Max and Sarah.

"Ready!" Max's voice echoed back. He had repositioned himself, legs braced against the rock face, hands gripping the rope. Sarah sat on the ledge beside him, ready to help pull.

Riley gave the rope two sharp tugs. Max pulled hand over hand. The harness tightened, lifting Holcomb's weight from their supporting arms. He let out a strangled cry as the ropes pressed against his wound. But Max didn't stop.

Fifteen feet up, just past the halfway point, Holcomb's head fell forward and his body went completely limp. The sudden shift in weight caused the rope to slip through Max's hands.

"Hold!" Sarah screamed.

Max's arms strained as he fought to get control back. The rope burned against his palms, but he managed to stop the fall after a heart-stopping few feet.

"He's unconscious!" Riley called up.

"Can't...hold this...forever," Max grunted through clenched teeth. His muscles trembled with the effort.

Sarah scrambled closer to help, grabbing the rope and adding her weight to the effort. Together, they began to pull again. The rope creaked ominously as they hauled the dead-weight up the rock face.

Inch by grueling inch, they raised him toward the ledge. Max's arms felt like they were on fire. Sweat ran into his eyes, but he didn't dare let go to wipe it away.

Finally, Holcomb's head appeared at ledge level. Sarah reached out, grabbing his shirt and helping to guide his unconscious form onto the relatively stable surface. Max quickly secured the rope, then collapsed back against the rocks, his hands raw and shaking.

Sarah checked Holcomb's pulse. "It's steady," she reported, relief evident in her voice. "He's breathing normally."

Max nodded, then turned back to the edge. "Okay," he called down. "Who's next?"

After Holcomb's harrowing ascent, getting Jake and Riley up felt almost routine. They were both able to assist in their own climbs, using the rock face for support as Max and Sarah pulled from above. Within minutes, the entire group was assembled on the narrow ledge, catching their breath and watching the water rush past into darkness.

———

Max flexed his hands, trying to restore feeling to his cramped fingers. The rope burns across his palms throbbed.

"Someone needs to get up there," he said, gesturing toward the dark tunnel where the river disappeared. "Secure a line so we can pull ourselves against the current."

"I'll go," Riley said, already shrugging off her pack.

"Riley—" Sarah started to protest.

"I'm the strongest swimmer," Riley cut her off. "And the most rested." She looked pointedly at Max's trembling hands. "We need you down here to help with Holcomb."

Before anyone could argue further, Riley had tied the rope around her waist. "Once I get up there, I'll secure it and give three tugs. Wait for my signal before you start up."

"Be careful," Sarah whispered.

Riley flashed a tight smile, then waded into the current. The water immediately grabbed at her legs and she staggered back. They watched as she angled upstream, fighting for each step until the darkness swallowed her.

The waiting was excruciating. Max held the rope in one hand as he watched the water rush past and over their ledge. Beside him, Sarah held Jake's hand, both of them staring into the darkness where Riley had disappeared. Holcomb lay nearby, his head propped on his pack. The minutes stretched endlessly.

"How long?" Sarah finally asked, her voice barely audible over the rushing water.

Max checked his watch. "Twenty minutes."

"Shouldn't we have felt something by now?"

Their journey down had been fast and frantic and left Max with no impression of the length of the tunnel. He remembered darkness, the pull of the water, and then the drop. But before Max could tell her any of that, the rope twitched in this hand. Then three distinct tugs.

"She made it," Jake said.

Their relief was short-lived as they turned to the unconscious ranger. Holcomb hadn't stirred since his ascent.

"We can't wait for him to wake up," Max said. "And we can't carry him against that current."

"What if we use the harness?" Sarah suggested. "Keep him suspended in the water but secured to the rope?"

Jake shook his head. "The current's too strong. It would spin him like a top."

"What if..." Max paused, considering. "What if we make him float? Use our packs for buoyancy under his arms, keep his face above water. The rope would keep him from washing downstream."

"That might work," Jake said. "My pack can double as a dry bag. It's water resistant and should be buoyant though I've never tried."

They debated briefly but their options were limited. Using their remaining rope, they secured Jake's pack across Holcomb's upper body, creating a makeshift flotation device. They hoped.

"I'll go first," Max said. "Help guide him from the front. Sarah, you and Jake follow, keep him stable from behind."

The water hit Max like a physical blow as he stepped in. The pack on his back, already heavy with wet supplies, threatened to unbalance him. Even with the rope to hold, the current tried to tear his feet from under him. He pushed forward, testing each step before committing his weight.

Behind him, Sarah and Jake eased Holcomb into the water. The pack kept him mostly afloat, but his head lolled frighteningly close to the surface. They formed a human chain, everyone holding the guide rope with one hand while supporting Holcomb with the other.

Progress was agonizingly slow. The cold seeped into their bones. Every few feet, they had to stop and readjust their grips on Holcomb, ensuring his face stayed above water. The rope burned Max's already raw hands, but he forced himself to hold on, alternating hands between the rope and Holcomb.

Time lost meaning in the dark tunnel. There was only the next step, the next foot of progress against the relentless current. Water roared in their ears, making communication impossible. They moved by touch and instinct.

Finally, Max's headlamp caught movement ahead. Riley stood in waist-deep water, wedged between two rocks, reaching for them. Beyond her, Max could see the glimmer of the pool where they'd first entered the cave system.

The last few yards were the hardest. The current grew stronger as the tunnel narrowed. Twice, Max lost his footing, saved only by his grip on the rope. But finally, finally, Riley was there and pulled Holcomb from their grasp, dragging him onto the dry, shallow shelf next to the pool where they'd first taken cover from the gunman.

They collapsed on the rocks, gasping and shivering. Above them, through the cave entrance, Max could see a patch of sky. Night had fallen while they were underground and stars winked down at them, impossibly bright and beautiful.

"The stars," Sarah whispered, her voice filled with wonder and exhaustion. "We made it."

Max nodded, too tired to speak. They'd made it out of the caves, but he knew their ordeal wasn't over. Somewhere out in the dark, someone was waiting. Someone who didn't want their secrets found.

But for now, they were alive.

For now, that was enough.

CHAPTER FIFTY-ONE

Max stared up at the stars. The weather had been cloudy and rainy for most of the trip. He couldn't remember a clear sky. Or the last time he saw the stars this bright. The brief moment of relief at escaping the cave system evaporated as quickly as the water dripping from his clothes. They were still exposed, still vulnerable. His hands throbbed from the rope burns, and every muscle screamed from the effort of pulling Holcomb up the waterfall. He forced himself to confront reality.

"We need to get moving," Max said. "If we stay here, we're target practice."

Riley nodded and slowly pushed herself to her feet. Still a soldier through and through.

Jake lay on the grass, his face pale in the dim light. "What about Holcomb?"

"We can't leave him," Sarah said. She knelt beside the unconscious ranger, checking his pulse again.

"No one's suggesting we do," Max said. "But we're too exposed here." He looked around the cavern. "We need something to carry him on. Some kind of stretcher."

"Maybe use some of our clothes," Riley said. "If we bind them together and find some branches—"

A sharp crack echoed through the cavern, followed by the ping of a bullet ricocheting off rock. Fragments of stone sprayed across Max's face.

"Down!" Riley grabbed Sarah and pulled her into the muddy reeds by the edge of the pond.

Max dove for cover behind a clump of rocks that felt far too small. Jake rolled and scrambled after him, pressing himself into the ground.

"Where is he?" Sarah whispered.

"High ground, I think" Riley said. "That's a guess, but what I'd do. Probably the ridge above Grave's End."

Another shot cracked through the night. This one struck closer, sending up a spray of dirt near Max's feet. He pulled them in closer to his body.

"The brush won't hide us forever," Riley said. "Especially once dawn starts coming. He can keep us pinned down. Just wait us out. Then pick us off."

"He's playing with us," Max said. "He's enjoying this."

A whisper came from the darkness, so close Max nearly jumped. He hadn't heard the injured man move. "Get to camp. Get help." Holcomb's voice was weak but steady. "And get justice for Vance and the others."

Before Max could respond, Holcomb stood and moved past him through the reeds into the moonlight. Holcomb ran in a zigzag pattern across the clearing, a flashlight beam bouncing wildly in his hand. Max had no idea how the man was walking, let alone running.

A shot cracked through the darkness. This time Max saw the flash. Riley was right, he was somewhere at the top of Grave's End. It was four or five hundred yards. Not an easy shot. Not at a moving target. A fourth shot rang out. The light spun through the air but didn't go out. Holcomb's voice carried across the clearing, the words lost in the echo of gunfire.

Max hated it, but there was no choice. Holcomb had made his decision.

"Now!" Max pushed Jake forward. "Don't waste this chance."

They ran, crouching low. Sarah stumbled on her injured ankle. Riley caught her arm, half carrying her sister as they fled. Max kept an eye on Jake.

"This way!" Riley called from up ahead. "Through those trees!"

They crashed through the trees, branches whipping at their faces.

The trees thinned slightly, and Max spotted the massive leaning boulders that marked the hidden entrance to Grave's End. They just needed to squeeze through that narrow passage between the rocks and get back to the main trail that would lead them to camp.

"Everyone through," Max gasped as they reached the boulders. "Single file. Quick as you can."

Riley went first, helping Sarah navigate the tight space. Max heard their labored breathing ahead as they squeezed through. Jake stumbled forward next, Max practically pushing him into the gap and following close behind. The rough stone scraped and grabbed against their wet clothes. The sound of gunfire grew muffled, then faded entirely as they emerged on the other side.

Jake immediately collapsed against a tree, his breathing ragged. "Did...did Holcomb just—"

"Save our lives?" Riley finished. "Yeah."

Sarah wiped tears from her eyes. "We can't just leave him."

"We're not," Max said. "We won't. But we need help. Real

help. We need to get back to camp, find Ethan and Jamie, then—"

"If they're still alive," Jake said.

Riley's face hardened. "They better be."

Max looked back through the boulders. Somewhere on the other side was a killer. Someone who'd been hunting in these woods for years, collecting victims like twisted trophies. "We stick together," he said. "Watch each other's backs. When we make it to camp—"

"That's a big if," Jake said.

"Help is coming. Hatfield will make it," Riley said.

"When we make it to camp, we worry about the next step," Max continued. "We just need to survive the next hour. The next minute if that's too much." He looked at Jake.

Sarah squeezed Jake's hand. "One minute at a time."

"Which way?" Riley asked. "Holcomb had our map."

Max oriented himself. He was a city mouse, but he had a good memory and a good sense of direction. He remembered the path they'd taken earlier. "North. Through that gap in the rocks." He pointed to the left. "The terrain's rough," he said to Sarah and Jake. "I'm not sure which way you came, but that way's our best shot at reaching camp quickly."

"And if he's waiting for us?" Jake asked.

"I don't think he'll be waiting. He won't be ahead of us, but he'll be coming."

"And then we deal with him," Riley said.

Max could hear the edge of violence in her voice and almost smiled. He felt it too. Tired, battered, and exhausted, but very much alive. He could feel that electric wire in his blood. It sizzled. He was alive. And he planned to stay that way.

Riley checked her sister's makeshift ankle wrap. "How is it?"

Sarah tested her weight on it, wincing as she shifted. "The brace helps a little, but it's not good."

Riley scanned the ground around them, then moved quickly to a fallen branch a few yards away. She snapped off the smaller twigs and measured it against Sarah's height. "Try this," she said, handing over the improvised crutch.

Sarah tucked the smoother end under her armpit and leaned on it, taking the weight off her injured ankle. She took a tentative step forward, using the branch for support.

"It'll have to do."

Max pushed off from the tree he'd been leaning against. Like the others, his clothes were still soaked through, weighing him down, but he had no dry alternatives left. They had to keep moving and moving would keep them warm. "Ready?"

They nodded, forming a tight group with Riley on point and Max bringing up the rear. As they moved toward the gap, Max sent up a silent prayer that he wasn't just talking a good game, that Holcomb had bought them enough time. That the ranger's sacrifice wouldn't be in vain.

Above them, an owl called into the darkness. Max saw Jake flinch at the noise. But no answering shots rang out. For now, at least, they moved undetected through the night.

"One minute at a time," Max whispered to himself. "One minute at a time."

———

Riley pushed the pace, but the hike back to base camp was slow and grueling. They moved like wounded animals through the dark forest—Sarah hobbling on her makeshift crutch, Jake weaving between trees with unfocused eyes and skin that burned to the touch, his arm draped across Sarah's shoulders despite her injured ankle. Max brought up the rear, his raw, rope-burned hands leaving occasional bloody smears on tree trunks as he used them for balance. Everyone was exhausted, dirty, cold, and hungry. Only Riley maintained any semblance of her former self, though exhaustion had replaced her usual fluid grace with mechanical precision.

Riley raised her hand, bringing them to a stop at the tree line overlooking their campsite. Through gaps in the branches, they could make out the familiar clearing below. Their tents still stood, pale bubbles against the darkness, looking exactly as they'd left them hours ago. Too perfect?

"Jake needs to rest," Riley whispered, glancing at his fever-flushed face. "Sarah, stay with him here in the cover of the trees. Max and I will check the camp."

Sarah nodded, helping Jake sit against a tree. He didn't protest, which worried Max more than any complaint would have.

"You lead," Max said to Riley. "You've got more experience with this kind of thing."

"Oh, now it's ladies first?" That smile again.

Then she moved forward in a low crouch. They worked their way down the slope, using the trees for cover. The camp slowly came into view—the row of tents, the wash station, the firepit.

Nothing moved.

They waited, watching. Minutes crawled by. A night bird called somewhere in the distance. But no other sound broke the silence.

Riley touched Max's arm and pointed to herself, then the nearest tent. He nodded, understanding. She crept forward. Max kept his eyes on the surrounding trees, watching for any sign of movement.

She reached the first tent, then the second. After checking each one, she turned back to Max and made a slashing motion across her throat. Empty.

Max stood, scanning the campsite. The supplies they hadn't packed were still there, the meager food for Ethan and Jamie. Everything apparently untouched.

But no sign of—

"Who's there?" a voice shouted from the darkness. "I have a gun!"

"Ethan?" Riley called back. "It's Riley!"

A figure emerged from the trees near the washing station. Ethan stepped into the dim light, his hair wild and his clothes covered in dirt and leaves. He clutched a cast iron pan and a can of bear spray in front of him with trembling hands, his eyes wide and unfocused.

"Thank God," he said, dropping his arms. "I thought...I thought it had come back."

Riley stepped toward him. "Where's Jamie?"

CHAPTER FIFTY-TWO

"I have to sit down," Ethan said. He dropped his makeshift weapons and collapsed onto a log near the dead firepit. In the dim light, he looked feral—leaves and twigs matted in his hair, fresh scratches crisscrossing his face and arms.

"Where's Jamie?" Riley pressed.

Ethan pressed his palms against his eyes, as if trying to organize his scattered thoughts. "It's all mixed up. The fever... it just kept climbing. The infection took hold and..." He lowered his hands, his gaze distant. "He stopped making sense. Started talking to people who weren't there."

Drawn by the voices, Sarah and Jake made their way cautiously into the firelight.

"Good to see you, Ethan," Jake said and sank onto a log, his own fever-flushed face a mirror of the horror Ethan had just described.

"You found them," Ethan said to Riley, offering a weak smile. His voice was flat, drained of any energy for surprise or relief.

"Yes."

"I'm glad. I wanted to go, to help search but...I couldn't... I had to..."

"I know," Riley said gently. "Just start from the beginning. What happened after we left?"

"Jamie's fever spiked," Ethan said, his voice cracking. "I used the last of the aspirin, but nothing helped. He just got worse. And then..." He swallowed hard. "Then the noises started."

"What noises?" Riley asked, leaning forward.

"Footsteps. Twigs snapping. Someone circling the camp, just out of sight. Every time I'd look, there'd be nothing there. But as soon as I'd turn away..." He swallowed hard. "Jamie would hear them too, when he was lucid. Said they were getting closer each time."

Max exchanged glances with Riley. She gave a slight nod and began scanning the tree line.

"This went on all night?" Max asked.

"Both nights. There'd be long breaks, hours, and I'd start to think maybe I was going crazy too. Hearing things that weren't there. But then it would come back. Neither of us could sleep. Jamie kept getting worse. The infection spread. I could see the red lines moving up his neck from the wound." Ethan ran his hands through his matted hair. "He started rambling about being watched, about seeing shapes in the dark. The moments between paranoia and clarity shrank."

"When did he disappear?" Riley asked. It was clear that Jamie was no longer in the camp.

"This morning. Or maybe it was afternoon. I must have passed out at some point. Time got...strange." Ethan's hands trembled as he spoke. "The fever had him talking about his father, about swimming with whales. Then he'd snap back, insist someone was watching us from the trees." Ethan reached into his pocket and pulled out a length of frayed paracord. "When I woke up, he was gone. This was all I found. Just laying by his tent."

Riley looked at the cord and frowned. "Nothing else? No signs of struggle?"

"No. Nothing. The way he'd been acting..." Ethan's voice trailed off.

"You think he wandered off?" Sarah asked.

"I should have seen it coming," Ethan said. "Looked for him sooner. Done something. Anything. But my head was pounding, and I couldn't think straight, still can't think straight—" He stopped suddenly, looking around the group. "Where's Holcomb?"

———

Sarah and Max relayed the dual stories. They each kept them simple and concise, but the details were still horrible. Ethan popped up and started pacing before Max could finish.

"So there's a body farm in the caves up there and a madman with a rifle coming after us. Fuck. Why are we sitting here? We need to move. Hide. Do something."

"Easy," Max said and raised a hand. He finished the story, keeping his voice low and steady. He described Holcomb's sacrifice, the mad dash with the flashlight that drew the shooter's fire and gave them time to escape.

Ethan sat back down, his shoulders slumped. His head pitched down between his knees. "So he's dead?" he asked in a muffled voice.

"We don't know for certain," Riley said.

Ethan wrapped his arms around himself, rocking slightly on the log. "But there's someone out there. A real person. With a gun."

"Yes," Max said.

"And he's been watching us. All this time. Maybe messing with us." Ethan's hands trembled as fiddled with the frayed piece of paracord Jamie had left behind.

"It appears that way. Trying to keep us away from the bodies."

"I thought I was going crazy. The footsteps, the sounds in the dark. I kept telling myself it was the concussion, or exhaustion, or..." His voice cracked.

Sarah spoke up. "You weren't imagining things."

"No." Ethan let out a shaky laugh that held no humor. "No, I wasn't. There's just a serial killer stalking us through the woods. That's so much better than losing my mind, right?"

"It means we can fight back," Riley said. "A man can be stopped."

"But why?" Ethan's voice rose. "Why is he doing this? What does he want?"

"I don't think you can explain what he did. It won't make any sense to us," Max said. "Control. Power. Delusion. Psychosis. Take your pick. "

Ethan's face drained of color as the situation fully settled. "Jamie. Oh God, Jamie." He lurched to his feet, swaying. "We have to find him. If—"

"Ethan, sit down before you fall down," Riley said. "You can barely stand."

"But Jamie—"

"We'll find him," Max said. "But first we need a plan and to gather up the remaining supplies. The shooter is behind us for now. But we've also lost our two most knowledgeable guides. We can't just blunder around in the dark."

Moonlight filtered through the branches overhead, casting strange shadows across the clearing. Something rustled in the undergrowth beyond their small circle of relative safety. Everyone tensed.

Just a rabbit, darting between bushes.

Ethan sank back onto the log. "At least now I know," he whispered. He glanced at Jake. "Vance. All those missing hikers over the years. It wasn't the forest taking them. It was him. A monster wearing a man's face."

CHAPTER FIFTY-THREE

"We can't leave Jamie, but we can't stay here," Riley said.

"We don't have to go far," Max said. "Just away from here. Take what we can carry, stay light, stay fast, but move, even a mile, to somewhere he won't immediately find us. Buy Hatfield more time."

"The ridge," Sarah replied. "Where we first made camp. It's defensible, only one real approach, and we can see anyone coming. Jake, do you think you can find it?"

Jake nodded. "I can find it. Half hour hike, maybe a little more in the dark."

"Ethan?" Max said. "Can you make it?"

Ethan picked up the cast iron pan. "Yeah. Just...just give me a minute."

"Jake needs rest, too," Sarah said. She touched Jake's forehead. "The fever's not breaking."

"We'll rest when we're set up somewhere safer," Riley said. "Max, help me grab what we need. Don't take too much. Don't make it obvious we're not using this camp. Be ready in five minutes."

They moved silently through the trees toward the tents. Max kept scanning the darkness, expecting to see a figure emerge from the shadows. Scattered energy bar wrappers created a trail toward Jamie's tent.

Inside Jamie's tent, the sleeping bag was unzipped, one corner soaked with something dark. Max touched it—blood from Jamie's head wound. His green backpack lay open, contents spilled across the floor. Jamie's headlamp sat perched on top, switched on but batteries dead.

"Look at this," Riley said. She pointed to the ground outside the tent. Multiple boot prints crossed and recrossed the area. Some were clear, others partial. Many led nowhere.

"Jamie's?"

"Maybe. But these..." She indicated a bigger set. "Someone else. Heavier. Or maybe taller."

"Not Ethan."

"No.

"Or Jamie stumbling under fever."

"No, not unless the head injury also made his feet get bigger."

They gathered supplies. It didn't take long. There wasn't much left—dry clothes, remaining food, a small medical kit. Max found Jamie's journal wedged under his sleeping bag. The last entry was barely legible, the handwriting deteriorating into scrawls:

Watching. Always watching. From the trees. Can't sleep. Whales don't sleep. They always swim. Have to keep swimming.

"Max." Riley's voice was low. She stood at the edge of camp, flashlight beam focused on a tree. Fresh marks scored the bark, too deliberate for animal claws. Five parallel lines.

"Could be Jamie," Max said. "Trying to leave a trail? Like we did in the caves?"

"I don't know. Maybe. It's weird."

"Maybe that's the point. Just to be weird. Unsettle us."

They rejoined the others. Jake had managed to stand but leaned heavily on Sarah. Ethan still held the pan like a shield.

"Did you see the marks?" Ethan asked. "On the trees. They started appearing after you left. Every night. New ones. Closer each time."

"Which direction did Jamie go?" Riley asked.

Ethan shook his head. "I don't...it's mixed up. I heard noises. Kept checking. Must have fallen asleep. When I woke up..." He gestured helplessly with the pan. "The paracord was just laying there. Like a message."

———

They moved carefully through the dark forest. Max and Riley flanked the group, Sarah hobbling alongside Jake in the middle, occasionally calling out directions, Ethan bringing up the rear. The moon cast strange shadows through the canopy. Every snapping twig made them freeze.

Their progress was like a rusted clock winding down—each movement deliberate and strained, ticking forward with a reluctance that suggested collapse was just a moment away. Sarah's makeshift ankle wrap had already begun to loosen, forcing her to stop every few minutes to adjust it, her face tightening with each adjustment. The group moved as one damaged organism, connected by shared trauma and the desperate need to keep going.

It took almost an hour, but they made it. Along the ridge-line was a depression sheltered by boulders. Riley set up a watch rotation while Sarah tended to Jake. Ethan finally let go of the pan. He'd carried it like a talisman the entire time. Max expected him to sit or lie down in the shelter of the rocks and go to sleep. He sat, but he didn't close his eyes. He dragged the pan within reach and then just stared out into the darkness.

Max went over and sat beside him. Riley had taken the first watch.

"Tell me again. Everything you remember," Max said. "From the beginning."

Ethan stared at his hands. "Jamie's fever got worse. He kept talking about his father, about swimming with whales. Then he'd snap back, insist someone was out there, watching. I checked every noise but found nothing. Just those marks on the trees, new ones each time I looked."

"You said he was lucid sometimes?"

"Less and less. The infection..." Ethan's voice cracked. "I could see it spreading, the red lines moving up his neck. He'd wake up confused, thinking he was somewhere else. Then he'd be clear for a moment, terrified."

"And the night he disappeared?"

"There were noises. Even I could hear them. Or thought I did. Footsteps circling camp. Jamie was agitated, saying they were getting closer. I checked but...everything's blurry after that. When I woke up, he was gone. Just the paracord left behind."

They were quiet for a moment.

Sarah limped over from where she'd been tending to Jake. She handed them two emergency blankets. They'd all changed into dry clothes, but they'd left their tents and sleeping bags behind. "Riley asked me to take a look at your head."

Ethan slid forward a little and bowed his head. Sarah gently parted his matted hair. The moonlight caught the sheen of sweat on his forehead despite the cool night air. His skin had taken on an ashen quality that made the scratches on his face stand out like ink marks.

"That's a hell of a lump," she said, her fingers probing carefully. "But I don't see any other wounds." She pulled back, wiping her hands on her pants. "How's your vision? Any double images?"

"Not anymore. Just hurts."

"Who won the World Series last year?"

"Not the Red Sox."

"Is that a guess?"

"No, their bullpen sucked."

"Okay. Normally, I'd tell you to ice it for twenty minutes at a time and take some acetaminophen – not ibuprofen, that can make bleeding worse." She sighed. "But since we have neither, the best I can offer is try to rest while you can."

Sarah caught Max's eye before turning away. He knew that look—had seen it plenty during his hockey days. She might not be able to see what was happening inside Ethan's skull, but the swelling could be pushing against his brain, causing damage they couldn't assess out here in the wilderness. Max remembered teammates who'd seemed fine after a hit, only to collapse hours later in the locker room.

Sarah made her way back to Jake.

"You and Riley," Max said after everyone had settled. "There's history there."

Ethan glanced toward where Riley stood guard at the edge of their camp. "Ancient history. We're better as friends. Some people just work better that way." He attempted a smile that didn't reach his eyes. "Besides, she never laughs at my jokes."

Max thought about Vic waiting in Vermont, maybe pacing the worn carpets of her mother's old house. Four days. It felt like a lifetime since the rain had washed out those roads, since that bridge had collapsed. He should be there now, painting walls or fixing baseboards at the motel. Safe. Warm. Instead, he sat in the dark woods, hunting—or being hunted by—a killer.

A familiar thrill coursed through his veins, shame followed close behind. Part of him yearned for the quiet safety of Vermont, for Vic's steady presence, and the simple satisfaction of honest work. But another part, a darker part he could never quite suppress, came alive in moments like these. It circled danger like a moth drawn to flame, testing the edges of what was possible, what was survivable.

Max closed his eyes, trying to imagine a version of himself that didn't feel this pull toward darkness. But the night pressed in around him, full of shadows and secrets, and he knew that version of himself was just another fiction.

———

Dawn crept over the mountains, painting the forest in shades of gray.

"He has to be back by now, right?" Ethan said and craned his neck to look up at the sky. "Do you think there will be a helicopter? What are the protocols?"

"I don't know," Riley said. "Not sure if they could land it anywhere."

"But they could get close. Maybe drop people off or pick us up? Like the Coast Guard rescuing people off a sinking ship."

Riley had no answer for that. Ethan just kept looking up.

They waited for full light before approaching the camp, though Max noticed Riley's hand never strayed far from her knife. The hunter was out there—they all knew it—but Jamie's trail grew colder with each passing hour.

"This feels like walking into a trap," Sarah whispered as they crouched at the tree line.

Riley scanned the clearing. "It probably is."

"Then why risk it?"

"Because Jamie's out there," Max said. "If it were me, I'd want someone searching."

They studied the camp. Nothing moved. Everything looked exactly as they'd left it a few hours ago.

"If he's watching," Max said, "he probably already knows we're here."

Riley nodded. "Stay close. Watch each other's back."

They moved into the clearing like soldiers crossing a minefield, alert to every snapped twig and rustling leaf. Riley crouched near a set of prints. "The tracks are useless. Too many, going everywhere. Rain's muddied up anything helpful."

Sarah emerged from Jamie's tent with a troubled expression. "Everything's exactly the same. His pack, gear, supplies —all still there. He didn't take anything with him."

Max surveyed the camp's perimeter. "He's injured, sick, no supplies. Where would he go?"

They searched in expanding circles, staying within arm's reach of each other without discussing it. The lake revealed nothing. The trail back toward town was equally empty. They spiraled out farther. It was all taking too long. Max could feel time bleeding away. Each minute they stayed increased the danger.

"Here!" Sarah's voice called. A broken sapling marked what might be a trail, its pale inner wood gleaming like exposed bone. Beyond it, branches hung at odd angles—some snapped, others pushed aside.

"Someone came through here," Riley said, examining the signs. "Question is, were they running or being chased?"

They followed the trail. Every few yards brought fresh evidence—fabric snagged on thorns, a clear footprint pressed into mud, broken twigs pointing the way forward. Almost too perfect, like signs left by a careful hand rather than a panicked flight.

"It feels wrong," Max said. "Like breadcrumbs in a fairytale."

"Keep going," Riley replied. "But stay alert."

The trail led to a small clearing where the evidence exploded outward. Trampled grass radiated in all directions.

Riley knelt beside a fallen log, scraping at a dark stain with her knife. "Blood."

"Signs of a struggle," Max said, studying the area.

Something glinted in the grass. Max's stomach dropped. He picked up the compass. The needle spun aimlessly, refusing to settle on north. The erratic behavior was probably from rough handling or hitting the ground, not any supernatural force in the forest. Probably.

"What is it?" Sarah asked, peering over his shoulder.

Max turned the compass over, revealing the smear of blood across its brass casing.

"Evidence," Max said, "that someone didn't get as far as we hoped."

CHAPTER FIFTY-FOUR

The hike back to their makeshift ridge camp felt longer than the journey out. Max's neck and shoulder muscles ached from the constant tension of scanning the forest. The morning sun had burned away the mist, leaving behind heavy, humid air that clung to their skin. It was no longer wet and raining but now felt like someone had put them in the oven and was slowly cranking up the heat. Overhead, leaves rustled in a breeze they couldn't feel on the forest floor. It was as if the weather had spun off its axle.

They found Jake awake but pale, propped against a moss-covered boulder. He'd managed to keep down some water but refused the last protein bar Sarah offered.

Max pulled the compass from his pocket and held it up. The needle continued its aimless spinning, catching occasional glints of sunlight that filtered through the canopy.

"Is that..." Ethan pushed himself up from where he'd been sitting, the pan in his lap. "That's Hatfield's compass."

"Found it in a clearing," Max said. "Along with signs of a struggle."

"What's the significance?" Jake asked.

"It was Hatfield's most prized possession," Max said. "Belonged to his father. He never went anywhere without it. Constantly fiddling with it. Like Jamie and his paracord."

"He wouldn't have dropped it," Ethan said. "Not voluntarily." He slumped back against the boulder. "So that's it then. No help coming."

"We don't know that for certain," Riley said. "Like Jamie, we found no body."

"Just a bloody, broken compass." Ethan laughed, a hollow sound that echoed off the rocks. "I'm sure he's fine. Tucked in and sleeping it off in a cave crypt." Max could hear the hysteria in Ethan's voice. He was teetering on the edge. They all were, but Ethan seemed to have one foot dangling over the edge.

Max could really use a cup of coffee, but they couldn't risk starting a fire. Fatigue washed over him as he sat down. He forced himself to eat. He'd need calories for whatever was coming next. He took the last protein bar and carefully broke it up. He ate a piece and offered the rest around. The others shook their heads. He put it back in his bag. "We need to make a decision," he said.

"About what?" Sarah asked.

"What we do next. We can't keep running."

"Why not?" Ethan gestured at the surrounding forest. "Pick a direction and go. Keep going until we hit civilization."

Riley shook her head. "We've got two people who can barely walk. Three, if we include you. Few supplies. We'll be completely out of food by tonight, tomorrow morning at the latest. No real idea which direction might lead to safety other than back to Grimswood. And a killer who knows these woods better than any of us. The longer we stay here, the weaker we get. Each hour, we have less food, less water, less energy."

"So we're trapped," Sarah said.

"Yes," Max replied. "But a trapped animal can still be dangerous."

Jake shifted against his boulder, wincing. "What do you suggest?"

"We can't run. We can't hide—not forever. So we fight."

Silence fell over the group. A jay called somewhere in the distance. Sarah flinched at the harsh noise.

"Fight?" Ethan's voice cracked. "Against someone who's been hunting people in these woods for years? Maybe decades? That's suicide."

"Not if we do it smart," Max said. "Not if we set a trap."

"A trap?" Riley leaned forward, interest sparking in her eyes. "What kind of trap?"

"He's hunting us," Max said. "Using our weaknesses against us. But that goes both ways. He's got patterns, habits. We've seen some of them. The cameras. The way he herds people toward those caves."

"And how he likes to play with his food before he eats it," Ethan muttered.

"Exactly," Max replied. "He's confident. Comfortable. That makes him predictable."

Sarah squeezed Jake's hand. "What are you suggesting?"

"We use his confidence against him. Make him think he's got us exactly where he wants us."

"Then what?" Jake asked.

"Then we spring our own trap." Max picked up a stick and began drawing in the dirt. "Running really isn't an option. We're too hurt, too tired, too lost. Our only chance is to turn the hunter into the hunted. We know he's coming this way. Riley, you've been studying maps of the area. What else can you tell us about the layout around the original campsite?"

As Riley began talking, Max saw the fear in their eyes replaced by something else—not quite hope, but perhaps its desperate cousin. Max just hoped they had enough strength left to see it through.

———

"He has a rifle," Sarah said. "We can't risk anyone being exposed."

"That's why we'll create a ghost camp," Riley replied. "Make him think we're there, but we're not."

"How?" Jake asked. The planning appeared to have revived Jake slightly, leaving him clearer headed but exhausted.

"We set up the camp to look occupied. Sleeping bags arranged like bodies. Keep the fire going. Maybe prop up some jackets, make it look like people sleeping or resting."

"He'll see through that," Ethan said.

"Maybe. Maybe not. He's already underestimating us. He's taken out Hatfield, Holcomb, and Jamie. They were the strongest and most knowledgeable about the woods." Max gestured at Riley's drawing. "We don't have to fake much. It already looks recently abandoned, like we fled in panic, because we did. It doesn't have to fool him for long. It just needs to draw him in enough."

Jake leaned forward. "Where would we be?"

"Hidden," Riley said. "Spread out under cover, but close enough to coordinate. When he comes to investigate—"

"If he comes to investigate," Ethan interrupted. "Sarah's right about the rifle. That's going to be a problem. What if he just starts shooting?"

"He won't," Max said. "I don't think he wanted to shoot Holcomb. Holcomb forced his hand. He likes to get close. To see his handiwork. That's why he has the cave, the crypt. It's not just about killing."

"Well that's a happy thought," Ethan said.

A heavy silence fell over the group.

"What weapons do we have?" Sarah asked finally.

They pooled their resources in the center of their circle. A can of bear spray and the cast iron pan from Ethan. Riley's knife and Sarah's ring. A slim penknife from Jake's pack. A Leatherman tool from Max's borrowed search and rescue pack. Plus, the remains of their climbing gear—ropes and carabiners—if the definition of weapon was stretched.

They stared at the meager pile.

"It's not much against a rifle," Ethan said.

"It's enough if we coordinate," Riley replied. "We might be battered and broken but it's still five against one. We attack from multiple directions, overwhelm him before he can bring the rifle into play."

"We'll need a signal," Jake said. "Something that won't warn him."

"Bird call?" Sarah suggested. "There are enough real birds, it wouldn't stand out."

"Anyone?" Riley asked. Jake made a high-pitched trilling that didn't sound out of place. Ethan answered it with one of his own. The others looked at them.

Ethan shrugged. "Came in handy when sneaking kegs into the dorms during college."

Max looked at their accumulated weapons. "We need to agree now. Everyone has to commit. If we do this, there's no backing out once it starts." Then he looked at each of them in turn to see if they understood what he was really asking.

"And if we don't do this?" Ethan asked.

"Then we wait to die," Max said. "Either from exposure, infection, or a bullet. Those are our choices."

Morning light filtered through the canopy, casting dappled shadows over their faces as they considered their options. A light breeze carried the scent of pine and decay.

One by one, they nodded.

CHAPTER FIFTY-FIVE

Max crouched behind a thick oak, his back pressed against the rough bark. Sweat trickled down his spine despite the cooling air. He'd rubbed mud over his face and could feel it drying and cracking on his skin. The sun had begun its slow descent, casting long shadows through the trees. Perfect cover for an ambush. Or to be ambushed.

Riley had positioned them in a rough circle around the camp. Sarah hunched beneath a fallen log twenty yards to Max's left. Jake, despite his fever and exhaustion, lay concealed in a dense patch of mountain laurel. Ethan had found a spot in the underbrush across the clearing, the cast iron pan gripped tight in both hands. Riley had climbed partway up a maple, using the thick foliage for cover.

Their ghost camp waited in the center of the clearing. They'd arranged sleeping bags to suggest bodies at rest. Sarah's pink Red Sox bandana hung from a branch near the remnants of their firepit, a splash of pink against a world of brown and green. Simple. Almost too simple. But Max remembered Riley's words: He's already underestimating us.

Max flexed his fingers around the utility knife. Its thin handle felt wrong in his grip. He was a planner, then a brawler, someone who trusted in the simple math of fist against jaw, the clean feedback of knuckle meeting bone. But they'd abandoned everything except weapons at their ridge camp. No supplies left to leave behind. No retreat possible. Just five people and their desperation against a forest that wanted to kill them. Times like these called for something sharper than fists.

A crow coasted on a thermal off to the west. It was the only thing moving in the clear sky. A squirrel or a chipmunk chittered something, a warning maybe, from behind him. Then silence fell like a heavy curtain. The constant background noise of the forest simply stopped.

He was here.

Max's pulse quickened. He'd felt this before, the electric anticipation before a job. But those had been his turf—concrete walls, metal doors, security systems he could study and predict. Here, every shadow held potential danger. Every tree could hide their hunter.

He scanned the camp. Nothing moved. The empty tents blazed stark-white in the harsh afternoon sun. The dead firepit gaped black against the sun-bleached earth.

Everything exactly as they'd arranged it.

The silence stretched. A breeze stirred the bandana.

Then a bird call. A happy trilling.

Was that the signal? It sounded right.

Max looked around but saw nothing.

Then the forest moved.

Ten feet from Sarah's position, a tree detached itself from the shadows. The ghillie suit made the hunter nearly invisible —a walking section of woodland come to deadly life.

The hunter paused at the edge of the camp. One hand gripped a rifle, but he made no move to raise it. Instead, he studied the scene before him, head turning slowly. His face was covered but Max thought he might be smiling. As if he wanted all eyes on him.

He turned toward Sarah.

Jake burst from his hiding place and charged across the clearing. Max saw the fever-bright determination in his eyes, no other thought in his mind except protecting Sarah.

The hunter pivoted in one smooth motion and snapped the rifle up. The shot cracked through the air. Jake staggered and then...Max lost sight of him as he started running.

Sarah broke from her cover, a limping pin wheeling dervish of arms and legs, her damaged ankle forcing her into an uneven lurching gait, her father's ring glinting as she slashed at anything in her path. She never got close. He backhanded her away with terrifying strength. The rifle swung toward her fallen form.

Metal rang against bone as Ethan's pan connected with the back of the hunter's head. The impact sent the man stumbling forward, rifle dropping from stunned fingers.

Then Max was in the fog and fury of it. He was inside the hunter's guard, driving his shoulder into the man's midsection. They went down in a tangle of limbs, camo, and artificial foliage.

Max stabbed downward but the blade skittered off with a metallic screech. Body armor under the suit. The hunter bucked, trying to throw him off.

The pan swung again, catching the hunter in the ribs. He grunted—the first sound they'd heard him make—and rolled away.

"Bear spray!" Ethan yelled.

Max barely had time to turn his face away before orange mist filled the air. His eyes and throat burned. Through streaming tears, he saw their attacker was wearing some kind of mask beneath the ghillie suit. The spray that had them all coughing and gagging seemed to have no effect.

The hunter melted back into the forest like smoke. Max stumbled to his feet, knife ready, but the man was gone. Only his rifle remained, dropped during the struggle.

Riley slid her knife into her belt and scooped up the rifle. "Remington 700." She checked the magazine. "Three rounds left."

"Jake!" Sarah's voice broke through the lingering haze of bear spray. She limped toward where he lay crumpled in the grass.

"Cover me," Riley said to Max and handed him the rifle. He watched as she ran through the scattered remains of their camp. She yanked open tent flaps, rummaged through what they'd left behind. Max knew most supplies were gone, taken in their move to the ridge, but maybe there was something they'd overlooked.

She ran back a minute later and dropped to her knees next to Sarah. "How bad?"

"Through-and-through, right shoulder," Sarah reported, her hands already slick with blood, but her voice was steady. "Missed anything vital, but the bleeding—"

"Here." Riley handed her a shirt and opened a small first aid kit that couldn't hold much beyond band-aids. "Max, Ethan, watch the tree line. He might circle back."

Max kept his gaze bouncing between the man on the ground and the circle of trees. Sarah tore the shirt into strips while Riley held pressure on the wound. Jake's eyes were open but unfocused, shock setting in.

"Stay with us," Sarah murmured, working quickly to pack and bind the wound. "Just a little longer."

"Did we get him?" Jake's voice was barely a whisper.

"Got his rifle," Max said. "Made him hurt. He was holding his ribs when he ran off."

"Good."

"Did anyone see which way he went?" Ethan asked.

"He's still here," Max said, gesturing with the rifle. "Watching. This was a trade. The gun for blood. He's telling us he doesn't need it to kill us."

"Great pep talk," Ethan said. "I don't get it. Why not just shoot us all from the trees?" Ethan said.

"Because this is a game to him," Riley said.

"We need to move. We can't stay here. Back to the boulders?" Max asked.

"You need to run," Jake whispered. "Those that can."

There was a beat of silence.

"He's right," Sarah said. "I don't think we'll survive another contact. It's a race now. One of us needs to get out of here and back to town."

"I'm not leaving you," Riley said.

"Do you remember Dad's favorite movie?" Sarah asked.

"Shit," Riley said.

"*Saving Private Ryan*," Sarah said to Max.

"The Niland Brothers," Max said. It wasn't his father's favorite movie, but he knew the story.

The Niland family inspired the story of *Saving Private Ryan*. The four Niland brothers served in World War II. The War Department initially believed that three of the brothers had been killed in action, which led the military to send the last living Niland brother back home to the U.S. under the Sole Survivor Policy, designed to protect the last surviving member of a family.

"One of us has to deal with the old man," Sarah said. "And my ankle is going to have me using a cane for the rest of my life. You have to do it."

Riley looked at her and then turned and walked away a

few paces before turning back around. "Fine, but you better not die."

"We'll do our best."

"We'll do better than that." Ethan patted the cast iron skillet. "I'm staying, too. Right now, I see three Rileys and three Maxes. I'd only slow you down. Now, I want all six of you guys to get the hell out of here and get us a ride out of this hellhole."

CHAPTER FIFTY-SIX

"We should have hit the stream by now," Riley said. She leaned against a tree trunk, her breath coming in short gasps. Sweat plastered her hair to her forehead. The sun was going down. Once it set, things would get tougher. And colder.

Max pulled the crumpled map from his pocket and tried to smooth it against his thigh. His hands shook from exhaustion. "Ethan said to follow the ridge east until we hit water, then north to the main trail and eventually the road." He squinted at Ethan's hastily sketched route. The paper was damp and starting to tear at the folds.

"This place is a godforsaken maze. Did we get turned around? Nothing about this looks like Ethan's map." Riley wiped her face with her sleeve. "I need water."

Max shouldered off his pack and pulled out the empty bottles. They'd been running for hours, at least it felt like hours, crashing through underbrush, scrambling over fallen logs, putting as much distance as possible between themselves and the others.

Between themselves and the hunter.

"There has to be water nearby." He looked around trying to see the forest as an animal might. He thought he saw a thin line through a stand of young maples. "This way."

The ground sloped down and their boots slid on wet leaves. But Max's intuition paid off as they eventually found a thin stream trickling over moss-covered rocks. There was no time, and they had no energy to be picky

Riley kept watch, the rifle ready, while Max filled the bottles. The water was cold enough to make his hands ache. As he waited for each bottle to fill, his mind drifted back to the last time he filled a set of bottles. Jake had been barely conscious, but his eyes were clear when they'd said goodbye. They'd half carried him and Ethan to the hollow beneath a fallen oak, where thick ferns and mountain laurel created a natural blind. Sarah had worked quickly, using broken branches and forest debris to weave additional cover. It wasn't perfect but it didn't need to be. It just needed to last long enough.

They'd left them the pieces of the last protein bar and had filled their water bottles. Sarah had hugged her sister fiercely, whispering something in Riley's ear that made her jaw clench. Then they'd erased any signs of their passage and walked away, leaving the three hidden in their makeshift shelter. The whole time, Max felt the weight of their gamble. Everything hinged on the hunter seeing him and Riley as the real threat. He couldn't risk letting them reach town, couldn't let them expose his killing ground. He would have to come after them.

The water bottle overflowed, shocking Max's hands with fresh cold. He twisted the cap on tight and looked up at Riley. "Ready?"

Max returned the bottles to his pack. His shoulders protested even this meager weight. Beyond the water bottles, very little remained inside—just two short knives wrapped in a torn T-shirt to keep them from clattering, a headlamp with failing batteries, and a flashlight. They'd left everything else with the others, having stripped down to the bare essentials. There hadn't been much to choose from regardless. After the failed ambush, Max could sense an unspoken agreement between them—whatever happened, one way or another, it would all be over in less than twenty-four hours. Either they'd make it back to civilization, or they wouldn't.

They started moving again, slower now. The initial burst of adrenaline had faded, leaving behind leaden limbs and growling stomachs. Every step hurt. Every muscle burned. Max's damp and sweaty clothes clung uncomfortably to his skin. The temperature was dropping with the sun.

"You're shivering," he said to Riley.

"So are you." He looked down at his arms and saw that she was right. That wasn't a good sign. She stepped over a fallen branch. "Keep moving. It helps."

They trudged onward, following the general downward slope of the land. Riley cleared her throat.

"Hey. I need to say something."

"We're going to make it," Max said.

"Probably. But if we don't—" She kept her eyes forward as she spoke. "If I don't, tell Sarah and my dad that I went down fighting. That I didn't give up. Maybe that'll make it a little easier."

"Riley—"

"Don't. Just listen. I've written a lot of these letters. Helped others write theirs. Sometimes they help. Sometimes they don't. But I need to say it."

Max walked in silence for a moment. "What about you?" Riley finally asked. "Anyone need to hear anything?"

Max thought of Lawrence back in his barber shop, waiting for news. But mostly he thought of Vic.

"There's a woman," he said. "She runs this old motor

lodge up on the Vermont border. The Cliffside." He pushed a branch aside. "Just tell her..."

Max fell silent, the words sticking in his throat. What exactly did he want to say to Vic? He thought of her patient acceptance of his restlessness, never demanding explanations for his sudden absences or the scars he brought back. She deserved more than a few hastily spoken words in a dark forest.

"Just tell her I wish we'd had more time. That I wish I could have stopped running." His voice was rough. "She'll understand what that means."

Riley nodded. They walked in silence for several steps before she spoke again. "All right, that's enough of that. Let's focus on making sure no one has to deliver any messages."

"Copy that," Max replied, and they pushed on through the deepening shadows.

A twig snapped somewhere behind them. They turned, muscles tensed. And watched a rabbit skitter across the thin path and back into the brush. They each let out a relieved breath as a gunshot split the air off to their left. It wasn't close, but it wasn't far, either.

They both froze, straining to hear over their own breathing.

The forest had gone quiet.

"Run," Riley whispered.

They ran. Not the desperate sprint of before, but a stumbling jog that carried them through the deepening shadows. Max's toe caught on a root and he pitched forward. Riley grabbed his arm, hauling him up without breaking stride.

"He's herding us," Max said between breaths.

"I know." Riley's voice was a low growl. "But we can't stop."

The undergrowth grew thicker. They pushed through stands of mountain laurel, its thick leaves slapping wetly against their legs. Thorns caught and pulled. Blood ran down Max's forearm from a dozen small cuts. A branch whipped back and caught Riley across the face, snapping her head sideways and pulling her hair loose. The silver streak at her temple was dark with sweat and now blood from a fresh scratch—a new wound crossing an old mark.

They finally broke through into a small clearing and stopped.

The ground ahead disappeared into empty air.

"No," Riley said. She moved to the edge and looked down. The ground dropped away to a field of rocks below. It wasn't a sheer drop, but it was steep and would take time and careful effort to navigate. They would be exposed and easy targets. Max looked left and right. The cliff curved away to either side, hemming them in.

Max turned back toward the forest. The shadows between the trees seemed to writhe and shift. "We walked right into it."

"He knows these woods. Every trail, every cliff." Riley raised the rifle and moved it slowly along the tree line. "But now he has to come at us head-on."

"Last chance to surrender," Max said to Riley.

She chambered a round. "Not in this lifetime."

CHAPTER FIFTY-SEVEN

"Behind the rocks," Riley whispered. She grabbed Max's sleeve and pulled him toward a cluster of boulders near the cliff's edge. It was hardly cover, but it was all they had.

Max's lungs burned as he tried to slow his breathing. Sweat ran down his neck. He reached into the bag and took out one of the short knives while Riley steadied the rifle on the boulder's edge.

A shot cracked through the forest. Very close now. Bark exploded from a tree at the clearing's edge, the sound of impact arriving almost simultaneously with the rifle's report.

"He had another gun all along," Max said. "He's playing with us."

"Shut up and let him play," Riley growled, her finger curled around the trigger. "Just need one clean shot."

Another report echoed through the trees, this one even closer. Leaves drifted down from where the bullet had torn through branches overhead.

Max felt Riley tense beside him.

He emerged from the tree line like smoke solidifying. The

ghillie suit hung in tatters, revealing tactical gear underneath. He moved with fluid grace despite his obvious injuries from their earlier encounter.

"Take the shot," Max murmured.

The rifle was slung over his back. He kept coming forward. He was cocky and confident. Or suicidal. Max didn't really care.

Riley squeezed the trigger. The rifle's report was deafening near Max's ear.

The hunter didn't flinch as the bullet whined past his head.

"Shit," Riley said. "Scope is off. Or, misaligned on purpose." She compensated and fired again.

But this time he did move. He moved very fast. He dodged right and before Max could shout a warning, he was halfway across the clearing and too close for the rifle to be effective. Max rolled to the right as the hunter vaulted over the rocks. His boot caught Riley in the chest, sending her sprawling. The rifle clattered away and over the edge into the growing darkness.

Max was on his feet in a crouch. He faced the hunter and feinted left. The knife slashed in a backhand arc. The hunter shifted. Max felt the blade rebound off body armor. The failed strike threw him off balance.

The hunter caught his wrist and twisted. Pain shot through Max's arm like electricity. The knife fell from dead fingers. A fist slammed into his ribs—hard, precise, devastating. Again. Then a third time. Max's chest locked up. No air. The hunter let go and Max stumbled back, fighting panic. Forced himself to relax. To breathe.

He glanced toward Riley. She lay crumpled and still against the rocks. No help there. He sucked in another breath. Pain, but manageable. He'd survived worse. The hunter was just a man. Survive the next minute. Max set his feet and squared up.

He ducked one blow, moved in close and landed solid body shots. Lefts and rights. Combinations that would have dropped anyone else. The hunter barely flinched. The body armor absorbed everything. Max's knuckles split against the tactical gear. Each punch hurt him more than his opponent. He needed to try something else.

But there was no time. The hunter wasn't a human. He was a machine. Strike. Counter. Strike. Each blow calculated and brutal. Max felt himself being dismantled piece by piece.

Then Max got lucky. A desperate hook caught the hunter above the ear. A soft spot with no armor. His head snapped back. Max surged forward, but the hunter recovered almost instantly. He batted Max away and then an elbow crashed into Max's temple. The world tilted. He staggered.

Max's back slammed against rough bark. A hand clamped around his throat. Iron fingers dug into his windpipe. Black spots bloomed at the edges of his vision. He clawed at the grip. Kicked. Struck. Nothing worked. The armor deflected every desperate counter.

The pressure increased.

Darkness crept in. His lungs burned.

Movement flickered in the shadows. Something emerged —stumbling, shambling, barely upright but moving with terrible purpose. It crashed into the hunter from behind. The iron grip released. Max collapsed, dragging in ragged breaths that felt like swallowing fire.

The hunter sprang up, but Jake kept coming. Blood soaked through his bandages, dripped from his fingertips. His eyes blazed with fever or madness or both.

"Vance," Jake whispered. The word hung in the air like frost.

Jake slammed into him again. They went down hard. The hunter tried to break free, but Jake clung to him like something possessed. Blows rained down. Jake didn't seem to notice.

"Vance," Jake said, louder now. Blood streamed down his face. He climbed to his feet, dragging the hunter with him. Each punch rocked Jake's head back, but he only pressed forward. Driving them toward the cliff. His movements were jerky, mechanical, unstoppable.

"You killed my brother. I'm going to kill you."

The hunter's composure shattered. His arms windmilled. Blows rained down. Jake absorbed it all. Increasingly desperate strikes hammered Jake's wounded shoulder. He made no noise. Made no attempt to defend himself. He simply fell forward, locked his arms around the hunter in a tight embrace.

They struggled at the edge.

Jake kept holding on, driving them both forward.

Then they were gone.

———

Max dragged himself to where Riley lay crumpled against the rocks. Her nose had slid sideways where she'd been kicked. Blood matted her hair from where she'd hit her head on the rocks, but her pulse beat steady under his fingers. The effort of those few feet left him gasping. Each breath sent daggers through his ribs. At least two were broken, maybe more.

He tried to sit up, to assess their situation, but his body refused to cooperate. The adrenaline that had kept him moving was fading, leaving behind a catalog of injuries he could no longer ignore. His throat felt bruised and crushed where the hunter had grabbed him. His left eye was swelling shut. Blood trickled from somewhere on his scalp, running warm down his neck despite the growing cold.

They needed to move. To find help. To get back to town.

But his limbs felt like lead, and Riley hadn't stirred. The thought of standing, let alone walking, seemed as impossible as flying. They weren't going anywhere. No one would be delivering any messages.

He managed to pull himself closer to Riley, trying to share what little warmth remained between them. Her breathing was shallow but regular. Above them, the first stars appeared as the last light bled from the sky. The wind cut through his wet clothes like a knife, raising goosebumps on his skin. He thought of Vic, probably pacing the worn carpets of her mother's old house, waiting for a call that would never come.

Max stared up at the emerging stars until his good eye could no longer stay open. He'd never seen himself making it to a ripe old age. Too many questionable decisions. One was bound to catch up to him. But he'd always envisioned his death alone. Maybe not desperate, but always alone. No friends nearby. He reached out and took Riley's hand. He was happy to be wrong about that. He let go and the darkness swallowed him whole.

CHAPTER FIFTY-EIGHT

The harsh fluorescent light burned through Max's eyelids. He tried to open them, but his body refused to cooperate. Even his eyelids were tired. Sounds filtered in—a steady beeping, the squeak of rubber soles on linoleum, the rustle of paper. Then the darkness claimed him again.

The second time consciousness returned, the assault was gentler. Sunlight filtered through half-closed blinds, casting warm stripes across institutional beige walls. Max blinked, orienting himself. An IV stand loomed beside the bed, its clear tubing snaking down to his arm. Through the room's single window, a brick wall filled the view. A mounted TV played silently in the corner. A cooking show that made his empty stomach clench.

Riley sat in a vinyl chair near the bed, her feet propped on the metal frame. Her face was a roadmap of injuries: nose splinted and bandaged, both eyes blackened, a row of neat stitches along her hairline. A magazine lay forgotten in her lap.

"Welcome back," she said.

Max tried to respond, but his throat was too dry. Only a rasp emerged.

Riley carefully pushed herself off the chair. "Here." She poured water from a plastic pitcher into a small cup and held the straw to his lips. "Small sips."

The water was room temperature but felt like heaven on his raw throat. After a few swallows, he tried again. "Where are we?"

"Cumberland Memorial," Riley said, setting the cup down. "Closest hospital to Grimswood that could handle multiple trauma cases." She settled back into the chair with a wince. "Though they shipped Jake straight to Morgantown—better equipped for that kind of injury."

Max's chest tightened. He had a vision of Jake emerging from the woods. "Did he...?"

"He made it through the first surgery." Riley leaned forward, her elbows on her knees. "He's critical but stable." She rubbed at her temple where the stitches disappeared into her hair. "They're keeping him sedated while the swelling in his brain goes down. Won't know more for a few days."

Max nodded, absorbing this. "Sarah? Ethan?"

"Search and rescue found them. Sarah needed surgery on her ankle. Doctor said torn ligaments. She'll need physical therapy and a cane for a bit, but no permanent damage. Ethan's concussed but mainly needs rest. They're keeping him for observation."

"And you?"

Riley touched her splinted nose. "Not going to win any beauty contests, but that's nothing new. They reset this. That hurt like hell. Might need some plastic surgery later, but otherwise just banged up. Like you." She gestured at his torso. "You've got a couple cracked ribs. They did scans to check for internal bleeding but you're clear."

Max shifted in the bed, testing his injuries. Everything hurt, but in a distant, medicated way. "How did they find us?"

"Patty—the diner owner—got worried when she didn't hear from Hatfield. I guess they're a couple. She called the sheriff and Forest Service. Hank Ramsey led the search team. Buck had told him about Grave's End, gave him a general direction to look. They heard the rifle shots and followed them. Found us just in time." Riley picked at a loose thread on her jeans. "I woke up in the helicopter. Told them where to find Sarah and Ethan."

"I don't remember any of that."

"You were less helpful."

"How long have I been out?"

"Almost two days."

"Clearly I needed more beauty sleep than you."

Despite his playful tone, Max let that sink in. Two days lost. He looked at the window, trying to gauge the time of day, but the brick wall revealed nothing.

"I called her."

"Who?"

"Vic."

"How?"

"They released me yesterday. I was the first one. Took our gear back to the motel. News has started to leak out but most of the details are pretty thin. Your phone was blowing up. I... remembered what you said and eventually answered one of the calls. She wasn't expecting a female voice," Riley smiled. "She's got quite a vocabulary."

Max had to return the smile. "Yes, she does."

"I filled her in. Assured her that you were mostly all right. She was about to jump in a car, but I convinced her to hold off another day." Riley looked at the wall next to the television where a clock hung. "You should probably call her soon."

"Thanks for making the call."

"I'm sure you would have done the same."

There was silence but it was comfortable. He'd been putting it off but finally asked, "Holcomb?"

Riley's face tightened. "They found him in the caves, along with the other remains Sarah and Jake found. Sheriff's called in the state police. FBI's probably next—they'll need help identifying all the remains."

Max closed his eyes. The crypt. The shrouded bodies. How many lives had ended in that dark place?

"Hatfield or Jamie?" he said. He figured he might as well get it all at once.

"Hatfield's not dead, not yet, and you know he's too stubborn to die. They actually found him near the camp. He must not have gotten far before the hunter found him. He's hurt bad though. Really bad from what I understand. They've operated twice. He hasn't woken up yet, but the doctors say his vitals are getting stronger. If he makes it through the next 48 hours, his chances are good."

Max nodded. He could picture Hatfield dragging himself through the dark forest, leaving a trail of blood but refusing to stop. Some people just wouldn't quit, no matter what.

He didn't want to ask, but he had to know. "And Jamie?"

Riley shifted in her chair. "That's...complicated." But there was a hint of a smile on her face.

"Complicated how?"

"He's down the hall. On meds and getting fluids. They found him a couple days ago in Grimswood." Riley leaned forward. "At the post office, of all places. Mailing letters. Naked."

"What?"

"Yup. The sheriff showed me one of the letters. It was full, edge-to-edge, of tiny illegible scribbles. According to him, he walked out of the woods, made it back to town. Said he was simply hot. Didn't feel like wearing clothes. Says he doesn't remember much. Just fragments. Walking for hours. Following water downstream." She shook her head. "Doctor says it's not unusual with that kind of head trauma and infection. The memories might come back, or they might not."

"Is he...okay?"

"Physically? He's recovering. The fever broke and the infection responded to antibiotics. But..." Riley hesitated. "He's different. Even quieter. Keeps talking about going back to school, studying marine biology. Says he's done with the mountains."

Max remembered Jamie's fevered dreams about whales, about always swimming. Sometimes trauma didn't break people, it just pushed them in a different direction.

Riley stood and paced to the window. "The whole area's crawling with law enforcement now. Sheriff says it'll take weeks to process everything."

"And our hunter?"

"They only found Jake at the bottom of that ravine."

CHAPTER FIFTY-NINE

The night nurse had already done her rounds, leaving the hospital corridor quiet except for the soft hum of medical equipment. Max stared at Vic's number on his phone screen before finally pressing dial.

She answered on the first ring. "You're alive."

"More or less."

"Riley filled me in. Most of it anyway. Said you found some things in those caves."

"Yeah." Max shifted in the hospital bed, trying to find a position that didn't hurt his ribs. "Bad things."

"Tell me."

"You sure you want to hear it?"

"Max." Her voice was gentle but firm. "Tell me."

He told her everything. The caves. The crypt. The bodies. The hunter. Jake's desperate charge off the cliff. When he finished, silence stretched between them.

"You know what scares me most?" he finally said.

"What's that?"

"Part of me loved it. Even knowing what was in those caves, what he'd done to all those people...there was this moment when we were setting the trap that I felt so alive. What kind of person does that make me?"

"The kind who runs toward the fire instead of away from it." No judgment in her voice, just understanding. "The kind who helps people."

"Or the kind who can't stop looking for the next adrenaline fix."

"Maybe both." He heard ice cubes clink against glass. "You remember what you said when we first met?"

"That your coffee was terrible?"

She laughed. "After that."

"That I was just passing through. Wouldn't stay long."

"And here we are, almost a year later. You're still running, but you keep coming back."

Max closed his eyes. "I don't deserve you."

"Probably not. But you're stuck with me." Another clink of ice. "You want to know what I think?"

"Always."

"I think there are people who see evil in the world and look away. And there are people who see it and can't look away. You're the second kind. It's not about the adrenaline, not really. It's about not being able to walk past something wrong without trying to make it right."

"Even if it kills me?"

"Even then." She paused. "Though I'd prefer if it didn't."

"The quiet life at the motel isn't enough for me," he admitted. "I try, but..."

"I don't want just the quiet version of you. I want all of you—the guy who fixes my baseboards and the guy who runs toward the fire. Just...maybe fewer killers in the future?"

Max felt something tight in his chest loosen. "I'll work on that."

"Good. Now get some sleep. You look terrible."

"You can't even see me."

"I know you. You look terrible."

"Vic?"

"Yeah?"

"I miss you."

"I know." He could hear her smile. "Come home when you can. Bailey misses you."

"Just Bailey?"

"Maybe I miss you a little too." She yawned. "Call me tomorrow?"

"Promise."

After they hung up, Max lay in the darkness, listening to the quiet beep of the monitors. For the first time since waking up in the hospital, he felt at peace.

———

The plastic lid clattered against the tray as the orderly set down Max's breakfast. "Never gets this busy around here. Not unless there's a big accident on 68." He glanced out into the hallway where voices echoed off the linoleum floors. "And we never get famous people."

"Famous?" Max eyed what appeared to be scrambled eggs. The pale-yellow mass quivered as he shifted the tray. A cup of red Jell-O studded with unidentifiable fruit pieces threatened to break containment.

"You haven't seen?" The orderly—his nametag read Trevor —pulled a folded newspaper from under his arm. "Front page. Above the fold." He carefully placed it on the bedside table within Max's reach, mindful of his broken ribs. "Guess the cat's out of the bag."

The *Cumberland Times-Herald's* headline screamed in bold type: MULTIPLE BODIES DISCOVERED IN MONON-GAHELA CAVES. Max skimmed the article. Most of the details were correct, if incomplete. No names of survivors mentioned. Good.

His gaze caught the photos. The first showed Vance Cotter in hiking gear, smiling at the camera, mountains rising behind him. The second was Holcomb's official Forest Service portrait. The third made Max's hands tighten on the paper.

Trevor paused his methodical folding of spare blankets. "Yeah, that's the only clue they have right now on the IDs of the other bodies," he said. "Found it in one of those old backpacks, they say. Sheriff's asking if anyone can identify them."

A young man and woman stood in a forest clearing. The woman's honey-blonde hair caught the sunlight, her smile bright despite the photo's faded colors. The man stood close by, his face yet unlined by years of grief and searching, his eyes still bright with future plans. The family resemblance was strong in the sharp line of their jaws and the slight tilt of their eyes.

"You okay?" Trevor asked. "You look like you've seen a ghost."

"Just the Jell-O," Max replied. "Never trust hospital Jell-O."

Trevor laughed. "Smart man. Need anything else?"

Max shook his head, eyes fixed on the photo. Trevor's footsteps faded down the hall.

Max read the caption again: If anyone has information about the identities of the individuals pictured, please contact the Cumberland County Sheriff's Office.

A phone number followed.

Max reached for his phone, wincing as his ribs protested. But he didn't dial. He pulled up his photo gallery. He didn't have to scroll far. It felt like a lifetime ago, but it had been only a week since he snapped the photo of the photo in the hermit's cabin. He knew it would match the one in the newspaper.

He knew the story behind that photo now. Understood why the hermit had dedicated so much of his time and effort to searching and studying the nearby Monongahela, searching for the sister who'd disappeared.

CHAPTER SIXTY

Max stared at the old photograph in the newspaper, barely registering the untouched breakfast growing cold beside him. A knock at the door pulled his attention away. A tall man filled the doorway, broad-shouldered but lean, with close-cropped gray hair and a clean-shaven face. He wore a tan sheriff's uniform without a jacket, the badge pinned to his chest catching the morning sunlight filtering through the window. He held his hat in his hand.

"Mr. Parish? I'm Sheriff Tom Whitaker." He stepped into the room. "Mind if I ask you a few questions?"

Max gestured to the chair beside the bed. "Not much else to do in here."

The sheriff settled into the chair, its plastic creaking under his weight. His movements were deliberate, unhurried. He placed the hat, crown facing upward, on the small table next to the chair. He then focused his gaze on Max with pale-blue eyes that had likely seen their share of lies.

"How are you feeling?"

"Like I fell down a mountain. Which I guess isn't far from the truth."

The sheriff nodded. "Doc Schaeffer tells me you'll be released today. Says your injuries are mostly superficial."

"If these are superficial, I'd hate to see serious."

The sheriff's mouth twitched. "Poor choice of words maybe." He shifted in the chair, and Max sensed the casual tone was calculated. "Mind walking me through what happened up there?"

Max gave him the bare bones—being stranded in town, meeting Riley and Ethan, agreeing to help search for Sarah and Jake. He walked through the timeline: their hike into the Monongahela, finding the abandoned campsite, exploring the ravine they called The Gardens. He described how things started going wrong almost immediately—their food supplies mysteriously shredded, strange noises in the night that had Ethan almost catatonic by morning, Jamie's head wound becoming infected and his increasingly erratic behavior before he vanished.

He outlined finding Grave's End, the cave system beneath it, and locating Sarah and Jake inside. Their escape through the underground river, and how Holcomb had sacrificed himself to give them a chance to get away. That part was harder to keep clinical—Holcomb didn't deserve to die alone in those woods. But Max pushed through, describing their retreat to the ridge camp, Jake's fever spiking dangerously high, Sarah barely able to walk on her injured ankle, and the final confrontation at the cliff. He kept his voice steady and factual. He'd had practice with these conversations—knowing to stick to what happened, not how it felt. The sheriff didn't need to know about the way shadows moved in those woods, or how the hunter emerged from them like smoke made solid. Those details could wait for his nightmares.

"That was quite a risk," the sheriff said. "Going into those woods with people you barely knew."

"Seemed like the right thing to do."

"You always do the right thing?"

"I try. In my experience, it's the best way to avoid regrets."

The sheriff looked like he might have an opinion on that but kept it to himself. "Maybe. But being stuck in town didn't mean you had to join their expedition."

"I like to help when I can. Would have wanted someone to do the same for me or my family."

"You got family in these parts?"

"No, just passing through."

"Where'd you say you were from again?"

"I didn't." Max met his gaze. "Boston originally. Living in Vermont now."

The sheriff's eyes narrowed slightly. "You've got experience with this kind of thing?"

"With what? Camping?"

"Sure."

"Just general knowledge. Hiking, camping. Nothing special."

The sheriff let the silence stretch for a moment. "What can you tell me about the man who attacked you? The one you're all calling the hunter?"

"Haven't found him yet?"

"We're working on it."

"Two people went over the side of that cliff, Sheriff."

Whitaker held up a hand. "I believe you. Tell me about him."

"He was strong," Max said. "Trained. Knew how to fight, how to move in those woods. The kind of skills you don't pick up watching YouTube videos. He was well supplied. Up-to-date equipment. Maybe not expensive, but good, quality things."

"That doesn't really narrow it down much out here."

"That's true, but also sort of my point. He's local. Has to be. He knows every trail, every ridge. Even in the dark. And he's been around. Vance Cotter disappeared three years ago and Sarah said some of the...remains looked older than that. This guy is not just passing through."

The sheriff nodded but didn't write anything down. "Anything else?"

"Yes." Max picked up the newspaper from his lap and pointed to the old photograph. "I know who these people are. Or at least, I think I do."

"Go on."

Max told him about the hermit's cabin, though he left Lawrence's involvement out of it. About Jake's online contact, about finding the place abandoned with blood on the floor. He kept his voice neutral, just relaying facts again.

"Why didn't you call the police?"

"We were focused on finding Sarah and Jake. Every minute counted."

"Still could have called it in."

"Maybe. Probably should have. But at the time..." Max shrugged, then winced as the movement pulled at his ribs.

The sheriff studied the photograph. "I know the place you're talking about. Never had cause to go out there myself." He stood, folding the newspaper under his arm and picked up his hat. "I'll check with Bill Tanner. He was sheriff before me. He goes way back. See what he remembers."

"Any updates on the others? Jake?" Max asked.

"Riley and Sarah have been discharged. Ethan should be out today or tomorrow depending on a few more test results. Jake...I won't sugarcoat it. He's not in good shape. Still critical. It's gonna be a long road back for him."

"Riley's been by. She said Hatfield was also seriously hurt."

"That's right. He probably should be dead, but how do you kill a man who is tougher than wet rawhide? He's a legend around here for a reason. He earned that reputation, and I certainly wouldn't bet against him."

Max agreed with that assessment.

The sheriff walked toward the door then paused.

"The FBI's sending a team. Don't disappear. They'll want to talk to you too."

"I'll be around if you need me."

"You staying at the Crossroads?"

"I want to say no, but the alternative is camping and I won't be doing that for a long time."

"Don't blame you. Got a cell phone number?"

With the paper still tucked under his arm, he put the hat on his head, and left. Max listened to his boots click down the hallway, then let out a slow breath. He looked at his cold breakfast, then out the window where clouds were starting to gather. Somewhere out in those mountains, a killer was still free.

The Jell-O had completely lost containment and was spread across the tray.

———

After talking with the sheriff, the doctor's exam felt perfunctory. Just checking boxes. Blood pressure, heart rate, reflexes. Doc Schaeffer, a tall man who stooped as if perpetually avoiding low doorways, said, "Take it easy for a few weeks. Light activity only. Those ribs need time." He wrote a script for a painkiller and told Max the pharmacy downstairs could fill it.

Max found his own clothes in the bedside drawer—jeans, a light cotton T-shirt, fresh socks and underwear. Riley must have brought them. He carried them into the small bathroom and caught his reflection in the mirror. His face was a roadmap of fresh bruises layered over fading ones. Purple and green watercolors bleeding into yellow edges. The hunter's fingers had left distinct marks on his throat. His chest was worse—a mess of dark bruising from the precise, devastating strikes the hunter had landed. His knuckles were swollen and split from hammering against tactical gear, each strike doing more damage to himself than his opponent. Even pulling the T-shirt over his head took effort, his fingers stiff and clumsy. New scars to add to his collection.

Ethan's room was three doors down. Max paused in the doorway. The lights were low, monitors casting a pale glow across the institutional beige walls. Ethan slept, his face still bruised but peaceful. Riley sat in the chair beside him, her nose splinted and the skin around her eyes mottled in fading purples and yellows. Max smiled when he noticed the cast iron pan on the table next to the bed. She looked up and raised a finger to her lips, then quietly joined Max in the hallway.

"Heard you're getting sprung," she said, easing the door closed behind her.

"Free to flee the hospital food, but not the immediate area. Sheriff said the FBI's coming to town like you predicted."

"Already here. They've got multiple teams up at the caves."

"Good." Max remembered the shrouded figures in their stone alcoves, each one somebody's missing person. "He needs to answer for what he did."

"Word is they're finding things. A lot of things. Physical evidence this time, not just forest legends."

They stood in silence for a moment. Max hoped she was right, but the hunter had evaded capture for years. He was still out there, maybe watching, maybe planning. If they were lucky, maybe bleeding out in a cave somewhere. But Max doubted he'd go quietly.

"Need a ride?" Riley finally asked.

"If you're offering."

"Sarah's back at the motel, but Hatfield's upstairs," she said. "Want to check in?"

The ICU was brighter, more sterile. A nurse at the station started to wave them off until recognition flickered across her face. "Five minutes," she said.

They stood at the observation window. Even through the glass they could hear the hum of the machinery keeping Hatfield alive. Much more than Ethan or Max's rooms downstairs. Tubes and wires disappeared beneath white bandages. Patty sat beside the bed, her hand resting on his arm between the IV lines. Max watched for a moment, then turned away. He hoped Hatfield was stubborn enough to pull through. There had been enough death already.

———

After filling Max's prescription, Riley drove him back to the Crossroads. The lot was filled almost to capacity. The same thing with the Sunrise across the street.

"Place looks busy."

Riley grimaced. "Press. These are the lucky ones who grabbed rooms close by. I heard there are even more staying over in Cumberland. I imagine it's going to get worse as more details come out."

"He must be happy."

"I'm not sure," Riley replied. "All the guests just interrupt his reading."

Riley pulled into one of the few empty spots. Max spotted his SUV a few spots over. "I moved your car back over here when I was looking for clean clothes to bring you. We got the same rooms."

"Thanks."

They climbed out, Max very slowly, and she handed him a room key. "Search teams cleaned up base camp yesterday. Brought everything down. I put all the gear in Ethan's room —figured he'd be stuck in the hospital the longest." She used another key to open Ethan's door.

The packs were heaped in the corner of the room like forgotten casualties. Mud had dried in crusty patches on the fabric. The straps were frayed and stained. They smelled of wet earth, smoke, and something deeper—that penetrating scent of the caves that seemed to cling to everything.

She pointed to a plastic bag among the packs. "Your clothes from that night are in there, though I'm not sure anything is salvageable."

Back in his room, he took two painkillers the size of horse tranquilizers and carefully climbed in the shower. It felt like salvation. Like being baptized into a new life. Max stood under the spray until his skin turned pink, watching dirt and dried blood swirl down the drain. The water couldn't wash away the memories of those caves, of the hunter emerging from shadows like a nightmare made into flesh. But maybe that was okay. He'd add those ghosts to the others that kept him company on sleepless nights.

When the water ran cold, he finally stepped out. He could feel the painkillers softening the edges of the world. He dried off, carefully pulled on a clean T-shirt and shorts, and collapsed onto the bed. The mattress that had felt lumpy and uncomfortable his first night now seemed to cradle every aching muscle. He'd never felt anything so soft in his life.

CHAPTER SIXTY-ONE

A sharp knock jolted Max from sleep. His body protested every movement as he tried to sit up. His ribs screamed. His neck felt welded in place. Even his eyelids hurt. The knocking came again—three loud, evenly spaced raps that he recognized from countless encounters with law enforcement. It must be a course at the academy. How to knock. He guessed it was the FBI at his door.

"Coming," he called out, his voice rough with sleep. He rubbed at his eyes and shuffled to the door. The cheap motel carpet scratched against his bare feet. Without the hospital's industrial-strength painkillers flowing through his veins, each step awakened new layers of stiffness and pain. The prescription pills they gave him muted the worst of it but left enough to remind him he was alive. And that surviving wasn't the same as being whole.

It wasn't the FBI. Sheriff Whitaker stood in the doorway, filling the frame with his broad shoulders. His face showed the stubble of a long day. Behind him, crickets chirped in the darkness.

Max squinted and held up a hand against the glare from

the diner's security lights blazing across the street. Even that small movement made his shoulders ache. He turned away from the brightness and retreated into the dim sanctuary of his room. The sheriff took off his hat as he followed and closed the door.

"What time is it?" Max asked.

"Just past eight."

"PM?" Max ran a hand through his hair. He'd slept nearly ten hours and felt like he could go ten more.

"Yes."

Max eased himself back onto the bed, each movement a careful negotiation with his injuries, while Whitaker took the room's sole chair. The sheriff slumped into it, his crisp uniform now wrinkled and his shoulders sagging, as if the weight of the day had slowly deflated him.

"Making sure I didn't skip town?" Max asked.

"If I thought you would run, I wouldn't have let them discharge you." Whitaker pulled out his notepad. "Got some information about your hermit. Name's Daniel Reeves. You were right about the photo—it's his sister, Katherine."

"You found him?"

"It took a little time. He hadn't returned to the main house. But the town registrar had a fishing cabin as part of the original parcel, a few miles from the main property on Lake Hamilton. A couple of deputies found him there this afternoon." The sheriff flipped a page. "Reeves says a man in full camo and a mask attacked him at his house about a week ago. Matches your description of the hunter. Would've been worse, but his dogs intervened. Knocked the attacker's gun away. Reeves took a knife wound, one of the dogs got cut up too, but they'll both recover."

"That explains the blood we found in the kitchen," Max said. "What else did you find out?"

"Bill Tanner—the former sheriff—remembers the Reeves

family. They were fairly prominent around here until both parents died in the late '90s. Katherine disappeared in '05 while hiking. Daniel's been obsessed with finding her ever since."

"How did the parents die?"

"Nothing suspicious. Pancreatic cancer for him and an aneurysm six weeks later for her."

"That's some shitty luck for the kids."

"Folks around here have a saying: When trouble comes, it brings the whole family. The Reeves kids found that out the hard way."

"And Daniel Reeves is the one who reached out to Jake?"

"Yes, he confirmed they met online in a chat room that Reeves runs. It appears they bonded over the shared loss of their missing siblings."

"Why didn't he go with Jake?"

"He was diagnosed with multiple sclerosis about 10 years ago. He can't handle the physical demands of searching anymore. That's why he reached out to Jake Cotter online. He could feel his time running out. Though even reaching out wasn't easy for him."

"What do you mean?"

"Severe anxiety disorder. Barely leaves his little compound these days. He has most things delivered and dropped off at the end of his road. Says the MS medication makes the anxiety worse sometimes." Whitaker leaned forward. "But he wanted answers about Katherine more than he feared talking to strangers. Even if it was just online."

"Did he know about the caves? About what was happening up there?"

"Says he didn't. He never made it up there himself. Just knew there were stories about Grave's End. Found some old survey maps that suggested its location and the *potential* for a cave system in the area. He said based on the missing persons reports and his own research, it was the most likely spot that hadn't been thoroughly searched. That's what he shared with Jake." Whitaker stood. "FBI's going to want to verify his story, of course. But initial evidence supports his account."

"So the hunter finds out about Reeves and his investigation and pays him a visit with the goal of taking him out?"

"That's the theory. If you hadn't told us about him, no one probably would have found him for a long time."

"How did he find out about Reeves? It sounds like Reeves had been searching for a long time. Why attack him now?"

The sheriff shook his head. "All questions I'd like to know the answers to as well. I think Reeves staying mostly online and out of town might have contributed to it. But eventually word leaked out. Maybe it was all getting a little too close for comfort. Maybe the hunter felt like he had to act."

They each considered that. Max felt like he was still missing a piece, but his sluggish mind couldn't connect the dots.

"And Katherine?" he asked instead.

"We're still processing the remains from the caves. It'll take time to make identifications. DNA testing. But given the timeframe..." The sheriff let the sentence hang.

Max nodded. Another ghost to add to the forest's collection.

"I appreciate the update," Max said.

"You pointed us in the right direction, so I thought you'd like to know."

"I want to know when you find him."

"All right. The Feds are sending in everything short of the Marines. FBI's got their forensics team crawling through those caves with tweezers. Forest Service has rangers on every trail. He won't be able to disappear again."

Max studied the sheriff's face, looking for conviction behind the confidence. He'd seen what the hunter was capable of, seen the years of preparation in those caves. Someone that methodical would have planned for this too. Have escape routes, supplies cached away.

"Get some rest," Whitaker said, moving toward the door. He paused, hand on the doorknob, then asked, as if reading Max's thoughts, "You don't think we'll find him, do you?"

"Hope I'm wrong, but a man like that...he plans for everything. Even failure."

Whitaker nodded slowly as if the same thoughts had occurred to him as well. "FBI will probably want to talk tomorrow."

"I'll be here," Max replied. "Not sure I could move if I wanted to."

After the sheriff left, Max lay back down on the bed. His body begged for more sleep, but his mind churned with the new information.

———

Max lay in the darkness and stared at the water-stained ceiling. His body still ached for more sleep, but his mind raced with questions about Daniel Reeves, his sister and what her last few hours must have been like. He gave up after twenty minutes of tossing and turning, each twitch a reminder of his injuries that set his mind racing off in a new direction.

He tried another shower, but the weak stream did little to ease his stiffness. He dried off and found the orange bottle from the hospital's pharmacy. The label warned against operating heavy machinery. That wasn't in his plans. He swallowed two pills with tap water, hoping they packed more punch than the Crossroads' water pressure.

His stomach growled. The bottle had also advised to take with food. That was a plan he could accommodate. Through the window, he could see the Sunrise's neon sign still glowing. Half the lot was now empty, unlike earlier in the day. The security light showed six or seven mostly identical mid-sized sedans that screamed 'rental car.' He imagined the missing journalists had discovered the Crooked Nail's stronger offerings up the street.

He slowly and carefully trekked the short distance across the street. The bell jangled as he pushed open the diner's door. Patty stood behind the counter, refilling sugar dispensers. She glanced up as he dipped a finger in the payphone's change dispenser. Still empty.

"You're supposed to be resting," she said.

"I did. Ten hours' worth." He eased onto a stool, his ribs protesting. "Didn't expect to see you here."

"No change with Clint." Her voice was flat, and her hands kept moving, methodically filling each dispenser. "Not sure if that's good or bad. He's not getting better, but he's not getting worse either."

"Still fighting."

"Always." She filled another sugar container. "I can't stand being at home alone. If I'm not at the hospital, I'm here. We should be closed, but I don't know what else to do. At least with all these reporters around, business is good. Won't have to worry about making rent this month."

"Speaking of business, I'm starving. Burger with an extra patty, extra cheese, extra fries. And a large chocolate shake."

The ghost of a smile crossed her face. "You sure you can handle all that?"

"Watch me."

Patty relayed the order then moved off to make her rounds, coffeepot in hand. Max looked around at the scattered patrons who filled nearly every booth and half the counter stools. Two men in rumpled suits huddled over laptops at one booth, while a woman in the corner scribbled in a notebook between bites of pie. Near the window, a cluster of young reporters pecked at their phones, probably filing updates with their editors. Or updating social media. What exactly did a reporter do these days? A photographer dozed in a booth, his camera bag beside him, while his colleague studied a map of the Monongahela spread across the table.

He wondered what they'd make of it all. Would they capture the absolute darkness of those caves, the musty smell of decay that clung to everything? Could they convey the terror of being hunted through the woods, or would it just become another sensational headline: Multiple Bodies Found in National Forest or Serial Killer's Cave of Horrors. The thought of seeing the entire ordeal reduced to lurid clickbait made his stomach turn.

Tomorrow's papers or newscasts would probably lead with Vance Cotter's name. The missing heir of a wealthy Boston family always made for a good lede. The other victims might get a paragraph each, their lives and deaths condensed to a few lines of text. The real story—the courage of a sister searching for her sibling, a man's desperate quest to find his brother, the years long efforts of Reeves, the sacrifice of a man like Holcomb—would get lost in the shuffle.

When Patty returned, she put the shake in front him and Max asked, "How long have you and Clint been together?"

"Twenty years, give or take." She started wiping down the counter. "We never made it official. Neither of us are church-going folks. Met him right after his divorce. He came in every morning for breakfast. Always ordered the same thing—two eggs over easy, wheat toast, coffee black. Took me three months to get him to try the hash browns. Six months to get him to smile." She paused in her cleaning. "A year to get him to ask me out."

"Worth the wait?"

"Most days." She looked up as the cook rang the bell. "There's your heart attack on a plate."

The burger was perfectly greasy, the cheese melted and dripping. His concerns about the current ethics of journalism did not dull his appetite. Max ate until his stomach felt tight and uncomfortable. It was glorious. The shake was sweet, cold, and thick enough to bend the straw. He found himself thinking that grease, salt, and sugar would make a far better protein bar flavor than the sawdust-and-peanut-butter combinations he'd endured in the woods.

Patty cleared his plate. "Guess you were hungry."

"Hospital food leaves something to be desired."

"That's putting it kindly." She started to say something else, but the bell above the door jangled. A man and woman entered, both carrying camera bags and looking travel-worn, their press badges dangling from lanyards around their necks.

Max stood carefully. "I hope Hatfield pulls through."

"Me too." She gave him a tired smile. "Get some more rest, Max. You look like yesterday's meatloaf."

He walked back across the street to his room. Behind him, the diner's lights cast long shadows across the parking lot. Beyond the diner were the dark, jagged teeth of the Alleghenies. Somewhere in those mountains, a killer still roamed free. Max wondered if he was watching the town fill with strangers, watching them dig through his secrets. Watching and planning his next move.

CHAPTER SIXTY-TWO

Max lay in bed and stared at the ceiling's peeling paint that curled down like withered fingers, too wired to sleep despite his exhaustion. The painkillers should have knocked him out, but his mind raced. Something nagged at the edges of his thoughts, just out of reach. He'd spent too many years trusting those instincts to ignore them now.

He grabbed the remote and flipped through the channels. Nothing but talking heads speculating about the cave discoveries, reality TV shows, and a baseball game he didn't care about. He picked up his dog-eared Lehane novel, but the words blurred on the page.

The silence pressed in around him, broken only by the hum of the ancient air conditioner. If he couldn't sleep, he could at least be productive. He pushed himself up with a groan, his ribs protesting. He'd broken them before and he knew it would be at least a few weeks before the involuntary groans stopped.

Max shuffled down to Riley's room and knocked softly. It was late, but still before eleven. No answer. He tried again, a little louder. Still nothing. He looked around the parking lot but didn't spot her car. She was probably at the hospital with Ethan, or maybe the sisters had made the drive to check on Jake.

He needed to do something. Anything. When his thoughts got tangled like this, he organized. Cleaned. Put other things in order until his mind followed suit. Back in Southie, his aunt used to say he was the only teenager who actually liked folding laundry.

He thought about the hunter. His cave setup, his supplies, everything arranged with military precision. Max pushed the thought away. Being organized didn't make him like that monster. Did it?

He made his way to Ethan's room. The lock was cheap, like everything else at the Crossroads. Max had it open in seconds using his room key and a pen. The packs from their expedition sat in a heap by the wall, caked in mud and smelling of wet fabric, mud, and body odor.

The motel's vending machine was perpetually broken, but there had to be a laundry room somewhere. Jeb would be too cheap to contract out the linen service. He found the maid's supply room at the end of the hall. Another cheap lock. Bingo. Inside, a pair of old industrial washers and dryers from the Nixon administration lined one wall, alongside shelves of cleaning supplies, stacked towels and bedsheets.

Max dragged the packs inside and began sorting through them. His aunt's voice echoed in his head: Empty every pocket, Max. You never know what stories they hold. He smiled at the memory as he emptied compartments and pouches.

The first load churned in the washer as he prepped the second. His fingers brushed something in a side pocket of one of the backpacks—a button and cigarette butt. He recalled Sarah telling the group she'd found them in the caves.

He studied them again under the harsh fluorescent light. The button's metalwork was intricate, higher end than your average Walmart garment. He set them aside to give to Whitaker or the FBI in the morning.

He switched loads, the familiar routine soothing his restless mind. The dryer's rhythm became a meditation as he organized the remaining packs. Everything in its place. Everything orderly.

He pulled clothes from the last pack, letting them fall into a pile. His hands moved automatically until something made him pause. He picked up the last item he'd dropped in the pile. A jacket. What had caught his attention?

Max held it up and ran his fingers over the material. Quality outdoor gear, worn but well maintained. The fabric was a dark olive green, almost black in the overhead light, with reinforced shoulders where a pack would rest. The zipper had been replaced, a heavier gauge than the original. A few small tears had been meticulously repaired, the stitching neat and even.

Then he saw it.

A missing button, on a pocket, low, off the left hip.

Torn away recently judging by the loose threads.

Maybe not even noticed yet.

Pieces and half-formed ideas that had been floating just beyond his grasp began to snap into place.

No. No. No. No.

The dryer buzzed, making him jump. Down the hall, a door slammed.

He knew who the hunter was.

For a moment, Max stood frozen in the laundry room, the jacket clutched in his hands. The fluorescent lights buzzed overhead, too bright, too harsh. He needed to tell someone. Now. He needed to be sure.

His fingers trembled as he gathered the clean clothes and shoved them back into their respective packs. Sweat beaded along his hairline despite the room's chill. The jacket with the missing button he folded carefully, separately. Evidence. He hefted the stack of packs—heavier now with dampness—and made three quick trips to ferry them back to his room, his eyes scanning the empty hallway with each pass.

He laid the jacket across the desk chair, grabbed his phone and key card, then headed for Riley's room again. Knocked. No answer. Again. He heard no movement behind the door. Still not back.

Max stepped away from the door and stood in the parking lot, the jacket still clutched under his arm. His breath fogged in the cooling air as he stared up at the mountains. Something was there, just at the edge of his understanding, like a word caught on the tip of his tongue.

The Sunrise's windows glowed across the street. A few patrons lingered inside despite the late hour. As one left, a motion sensor clicked and a bright-white light flooded the parking lot. Max held a hand up against the light. He tracked the man as he walked to his car and passed beneath the security camera mounted near the light.

Its small red LED blinked steadily in the darkness.

Max pulled out his phone and dialed.

"Bit late to schedule a haircut," Lawrence said.

"I need your help," Max said and then explained what he wanted.

After he hung up, he went back to his room and logged onto the shaky Wi-Fi with his phone. Eight dollars later, he had a 30-day subscription to the *Cumberland Times-Herald* and all its archives.

Soon Max was scrolling through decades of local history.

He started with the most recent articles and worked backward. Two hours later, his eyes burned from the screen's glow, but the picture was becoming clearer. The how and when were taking shape. He didn't want to contemplate the why.

The walk to the office seemed longer than usual, his ribs barking with each step. Jeb glanced up briefly from his Civil War tome as Max entered.

"Do you ever sleep?" Max asked. "Or did the Confederacy hire you as their night watchman?"

Jeb's mouth twitched, almost a smile. "Sleep's for folks without history to protect."

Max nodded toward the ancient desktop computer in the corner. "I need to print some articles. Printer still work?"

"Dollar a page."

"Highway robbery. How about I trade you some fresh gossip about what they found in those caves instead?"

Jeb's eyes flickered with interest. He set his book down. "Deal."

Max pulled up the browser and logged into his email account. He'd forwarded himself the links he needed. The printer wheezed to life. As pages emerged, Max leaned against the counter and fed Jeb carefully selected details, holding back the most important parts. The clerk's eyes grew wider with each revelation.

"Jesus," Jeb whispered when Max finished, his typically impassive face now animated. "And they're sure it was all the same guy?"

"That's what they're thinking," Max said, gathering the warm pages and tapping them into a neat stack. He tucked the pages under his arm. "Thanks for the printer."

Back in his room, Max spread the articles across the bed. His phone buzzed.

"You were right," Lawrence said. "Eddie found the order. We have the serial numbers. They're sequential."

"Thanks." Max disconnected.

More pieces falling into place.

———

When he opened his eyes again, sunlight streamed through the gap in the curtains. He'd fallen asleep surrounded by newspaper clippings. For once, no dreams had haunted his rest. Even his ghosts had let him rest.

He dressed carefully, mindful of his ribs, then found Whitaker's card on the nightstand.

He dialed the sheriff's number. "We need to talk."

CHAPTER SIXTY-THREE

Max shifted his weight on the concrete bench, trying to find a position that didn't make his ribs scream. From his spot near the hospital's main entrance, he had a clear view of everyone coming and going. The automatic doors whooshed open and closed, each blast of cold air carrying the sharp bite of antiseptic. He'd taken two pills an hour ago, but they barely touched the edges of his pain. The rope burns across his palms still felt raw from hauling Holcomb's deadweight up the waterfall, and his throat still bore the dark imprint of the hunter's fingers. Fresh bruises bloomed beneath his clothes like poisonous flowers.

He caught his reflection in the glass doors. He looked like he'd gone ten rounds with a cement mixer and lost badly on points.

The distinctive transmission whine of an old car caught his attention and made him smile. The silver Camry appeared at the lot entrance, Sarah visible in the passenger seat as Riley navigated around a delivery van.

Max watched as Riley pulled the Camry into an empty

spot near the entrance. Sarah shifted gingerly in the passenger seat to get out, her movements careful and measured. She wore a walking boot and boosted herself out of the car with crutches. As they approached where he waited by the hospital doors, he could see the toll of the past few days still etched deep on their faces. He was sure he looked much the same.

"How's Jake?" Max asked.

"Better," Sarah said. Her face showed exhaustion but her eyes were brighter. "He woke up for a few minutes. Squeezed my hand."

"Doctor says the swelling in his brain is going down," Riley added. "Long road ahead, but he's fighting."

"Why did you want us to meet you here?" Sarah asked.

"Let's check on Ethan first."

———

They entered the hospital's main lobby. Max had walked these halls enough times in the past few days that the sharp smells of solvent and antiseptic barely registered. They passed the gift shop, its shelves stocked with wilting flowers and sad-looking teddy bears, and headed for the elevators. The same tired-looking volunteer manned the information desk. She glanced up then back down at the crossword puzzle spread out before her.

The third floor was quiet at this hour. Their footsteps echoed off the waxed linoleum. Max had memorized the route—past the nurses' station where Andrea would be starting her shift, around the corner where the ice machine hummed constantly and the fridge was full of orange Jell-O, then down to the cluster of rooms reserved for less critical patients.

They found Ethan's room easily. The lights were dimmed

and monitors beeped softly. He slept, one hand curled around the handle of the cast iron skillet that rested beside him on the bed.

Max raised an eyebrow.

"He won't let them take it," Riley whispered, her voice a mix of concern and understanding. "The doctors think it's a trauma response. Said as long as it keeps him calm, they're not going to fight him on it."

Max said nothing, just nodded. Some survival mechanisms didn't need explaining.

"He looks better today," Riley continued. "On the outside at least."

"The nightmares might take longer," Max said. "Trust me on that one."

"I know. I'll help him. Or get him the help he needs." Riley's voice softened. "I know how tough it can be to go it alone..." She trailed off.

"Good. He'll probably need it, though he ended up being tougher than any of us expected."

"Soft and gooey outside, hard as a rock on the inside." Riley smiled slightly. "Like one of those fancy chocolate truffles."

"You never can tell about people," Max said. "Sometimes they surprise even themselves."

———

They took the elevator one floor up to the ICU. The antiseptic smell grew stronger as they stepped off the elevator. Or maybe that was Max's imagination. Everything felt more sterile up here, more serious. Wide corridors designed to accommodate rushing medical teams. Nurses moved with purposeful urgency. Even the lighting seemed harsher, as if shadows weren't permitted to linger.

A security guard flanked the nurses' station near the elevator bank. He waved the three of them through—their faces had become familiar over the past few days. A sign on the wall reminded visitors to use hand sanitizer and limit their stays to fifteen minutes.

They made their way to Hatfield's room at the end of the hall, its sliding glass door partially open. Various machines crowded around the bed, their screens displaying vital signs in glowing digits and jagged lines. The chair beside his bed sat empty, but moments later Patty entered carrying a steaming cup of coffee. She stopped short when she saw them.

"What are you doing here?" She moved between them and the bed and sat in the lone chair.

Max's phone chimed. He checked it quickly, then returned it to his pocket. "You said you'd been together for twenty years, right Patty?"

"That's right."

"But you've known Hatfield a lot longer?"

She hesitated. "Sure, I guess. We both grew up here."

"Long-time locals, right?"

"Sure."

"You and your sister and Hatfield."

Her face went blank. "What does my sister have to do with it?"

"Where is your sister now?"

Patty's finger jabbed the nurse call button. "I think I'd like you to leave."

"When Riley and Ethan first told me about Jake and Sarah and Vance, they mentioned other missing people. Riley found seven, but she only looked at recent cases. She didn't look back 40 years. To your senior prom night. That was quite the local mystery."

"I don't know why you think Laura's disappearance has anything to do with this."

"I'll tell you. With serial killers, the first kill matters most. At least that's what I've been told by a lifetime of movies and books. Maybe that's bullshit. But there's probably a kernel of truth to it. I don't know exactly what happened. Maybe it was an accident. Or an argument that got out of hand. But I think you killed her and got your friend Clint to help you cover it up. Were you using the caves then, or is she buried somewhere else?"

The warmth had drained from her voice. "Get out."

Max ignored her and kept talking. "Maybe that would have been it. You got away with it, after all. But then a strange thing happened, didn't it? You realized you liked it. You wanted to do it again."

"You have no proof. These are all lies, just like back then." She hammered the call button.

"You're right, I have no proof about your sister. Just hunches and guesses. But I *do* have proof about what you and Hatfield did to those people in the caves. You make quite the team."

Max glanced over at the bed. Hatfield's eyes had opened, fixed on Max.

"What are you talking about?" Patty's voice rose almost to a shrill scream. "We did nothing wrong. Clint almost died out there with you."

"He almost died, but he wasn't like us. He was hunting us. With your help."

"STOP SAYING THAT."

"What was your job? Scout potential victims as they passed through the diner? Pass word on to your partner? I wondered how the hunter could be in two places. The timing was almost impossible for one person. But two people could sabotage our camp, stalk around it, make us think we were going crazy. Two people could re-supply each other. Still, you had to keep showing your face in town. Must have been exhausting, all that back and forth. Getting Hatfield away from the bottom of that cliff must have been close. Love gives you strength, I guess. Love and madness."

Max stepped to the opposite side of the bed. Hatfield's eyes followed. Max pressed down on a bandaged shoulder. Hatfield was too drugged to react much.

"What are you doing? Get away from him!"

Max disconnected the IV line. An alarm started beeping but no nurses appeared in the doorway. "I noticed your security cameras at the diner. Insurance purposes, right? Hatfield seems thorough—if he ordered cameras, he'd want his money's worth. Probably bought a case. The diner needed a couple, but he had ideas for the rest. Did you know when you order a case, or in bulk, you often get sequential serial numbers? The FBI might find that interesting."

Hatfield moaned as the pain began seeping through. Max pressed harder, thinking of the bodies in that crypt. Thinking of the darkness and pain they would have been in at the end. He dug his fingers in a little harder. Hatfield's eyes rolled and he let out a moan around the breathing tube.

"Stop it! Just stop. Leave him alone."

"Why? Did you two stop when people begged? Or did that make it more fun?"

"Stop saying that. We had nothing to do with any of it."

Max let go and pulled out the plastic bag from his jacket pocket. "The FBI might be interested in these, as well. Maybe not the button—a good lawyer might be able to explain that away or muddy the water enough for reasonable doubt. But Hatfield's DNA on the cigarette butt? Juries love DNA now. We know Hatfield loved his chewing tobacco. Maybe he liked a more direct hit when he had someone in the caves." He saw a look flash across her face. "Or maybe you did."

Her face closed down and she said nothing.

Sheriff Whitaker entered, a nurse scowling and crowding in behind him. Max stepped back as she reattached the IV and fussed with the machines.

"Sheriff, thank God. Get this maniac away from me."

"My pleasure, Patty." He stepped forward and locked the cuffs around her wrists. Max handed him the bag with the cigarette and the button as he led her out of the room.

CHAPTER SIXTY-FOUR

The sun had almost set by the time Max returned to the Crossroads. His head throbbed from hours of fluorescent lights and repetitive questions, first from the sheriff then an endless rotation of FBI agents. The paper coffee cups had piled up as he told the story again and again, his voice eventually growing hoarse. He felt wrung out, mentally and physically. Ultimately, he'd provided contact information along with signed statements and been cleared to leave town. And yet here he was, paying for another night.

His body felt like it had aged decades in the past week. The painkillers had worn off hours ago, leaving his ribs screaming at every movement. The thought of the long drive back to Vermont made him wince. One more night in Grimswood wouldn't kill him. Probably.

Riley sat in one of the motel's cheap plastic chairs she'd dragged out onto the walkway in front of her room. The room's door was propped open. Max walked over and pulled the second chair outside, lowering himself carefully into it. Across the street, the Sunrise Cafe's windows glowed with harsh portable work lights. FBI techs in white coveralls moved methodically through the interior, photographing and cataloging.

"Been at it for hours," Riley said in greeting as she tucked the silver streak of hair behind her ear.

Max watched them work for a few minutes. "Finding anything?"

"Hard to tell from here. But they keep bringing out boxes."

A cool breeze carried the smell of fresh rain and pine from the mountains. Storm clouds gathered over the Alleghenies, their dark masses swallowing the last light of day. Max had grown familiar with this sight during his stay in Grimswood—the way weather rolled in fast and mean, like the mountains themselves were spitting out storms.

"Want to grab a drink at the Nail?" Riley asked.

"Better not. Remember what happened last time?"

"Yeah. We kicked some ass. It was sort of fun."

"I'm in no shape to kick ass right now."

"Why do you think those guys jumped us anyway?"

Max looked down the road toward the town's watering hole. "I think it was Hatfield or Patty," he eventually said. "Trying everything they could to keep us away from those woods. They tried a similar scare tactic with Daniel Reeves, our hermit too. Keep out and keep away from Grave's End."

"Didn't work."

"No, it didn't."

They watched another agent emerge from the diner carrying a white cardboard evidence box.

"What about Jamie though?" Riley asked. "Why include him in the search party?"

"Been thinking about that. Hatfield was playing a long game," Max said, his voice low. "Jamie worked those guided tours with him for years. I'm betting he noticed things—patterns, inconsistencies."

Max leaned forward. "When we were in The Gardens, Jamie told me 'he lied.' Just that. At the time, I didn't know who he was talking about, it seemed meaningless, maybe random after the head injury, but now..."

He shook his head. "Jamie was there on those search-and-rescue missions. Maybe he spotted something that didn't add up, or collected tiny discrepancies over time. The kind most people would miss."

"And I'd bet everything that Hatfield sensed those suspicions. A predator like that—they develop a sixth sense for threats to their survival." Max's eyes hardened. "Jamie was never supposed to make it out of those woods alive either."

"Two problems, one solution?"

"Something like that."

Riley shook her head. "I keep thinking about all those people at her counter. The way she'd remember their coffee orders, ask about their kids. She served me pie the day after we got back from those caves. Asked how Sarah was doing like she actually cared."

"It's impossible to understand people like that," Max said. "Normal people can't comprehend it because we're still operating with normal rules and normal emotions. But they're beyond that. Everything's twisted—every interaction, every relationship. That pie, that concern? Just another performance." He watched another FBI agent exit the diner. "Patty probably started with her sister—maybe an accident, maybe not. But nothing happened. No one found out. And she discovered something about herself. Maybe she liked it. Maybe she was even good at it. Hatfield might have even started helping her out of love, covering up her messes. My advice? Put it aside. Try not to think about it. Leave it to the pointy heads at the FBI or the freaks in internet chat rooms."

"You think we'll ever know how many they killed? How many people suffered up there?" Riley asked quietly.

"I don't know. Maybe. I'm sure they're going to push them hard. West Virginia doesn't have the death penalty, just life in prison, but with the crimes occurring at least partially on national park lands some of the charges could potentially be prosecuted federally, where the death penalty does still exist. Maybe they can use that to get at the truth and get more families answers."

They were quiet for a moment. Max could just hear the faint squeak of the Nail's sign in the wind.

"Even if Holcomb had gotten back alive, it would have taken a hell of story to explain away all that death," Riley finally said.

"They'd done it before. They'd been doing it for so long maybe they felt almost invincible."

"They weren't."

"No one is."

Lightning split the sky, followed immediately by a crack of thunder that rattled the motel's windows. The forensics team scrambled to protect their evidence from the coming deluge, their white coveralls ghostly in the quickening dark.

"What's next for you?" Max asked.

"Back to Boston for a bit. Sarah needs help with her physical therapy, and Jake's got a long recovery ahead. After that..." Riley shrugged. "Thinking about reopening the dojo. Combat training feels more relevant than ever."

"And Ethan?"

"He's moving back to Philly, closer to his sister's grave. Says he needs time to process everything. But we'll stay in touch." She smiled faintly.

"Sometimes the people who go through hell with you end up being the only ones who really understand."

"You leaving now?" Riley asked.

"Yeah, but in the morning. Need some sleep first."

"That crappy bed never felt softer, huh?"

"Funny what a few days in the woods with a couple of psychopaths will do to your perspective."

Max pushed himself up from the chair, his muscles protesting. His phone buzzed in his pocket—another missed call from Vic. That made six today. He'd talk to her soon enough, then tell her everything tomorrow in person. Well, maybe not everything.

He took a few steps toward his room before Riley called after him. Maybe she saw something in the look on his face.

"Hey. Make sure you deliver that message when you get back to Vermont."

"I plan on it." He thought of Vic waiting at the Cliffside, probably repainting another room to keep busy. The image pulled at something in his chest.

Max unlocked his door as the rain began to fall in earnest. Behind him, Riley remained in her chair, face turned up to the darkening sky. He wondered if she was thinking about Sarah and Jake, about Vance, about all the ghosts they'd stirred up in those mountains. Or maybe she was just letting the rain wash it all away.

He had his own ghosts to face. But for the first time in a long while, he was looking forward to going home.

9 798990 787674